## "DEAR GOD I ROWENA, YO PASSIONS IN

He touched his mouth to moving slightly in a soft kiss. Her skin burned against his as she felt the strength of his chest against her breasts, felt his hard thighs touching hers. In dizzying response to these sensations, she forgot about walls and keeps, halls and servants. Instead, she caught her breath when his kiss deepened, then met his hunger with a very real need of her own. His hand slipped inside the remnants of her gown and caressed her breast. He kissed her cheek, her neck, the base of her throat.

There was a tap at the door. "My lord," a servant called out, "we cannot find your lady. Shall we begin a search?"

He straightened. She stared up at him. Slowly, slowly, he smiled, his look fierce with desire. "Never mind," he said, his gaze trapping hers as he eased the torn gown off her shoulder. The garment fell into a pile around her ankles. She wore nothing beneath it. He drew a quick breath. "I have found her."

# WINTER'S HEAT

by

Denise Domning

A TOPAZ BOOK

TOPAZ
Published by the Penguin Group
Penguin Books USA Inc., 375 Hudson Street,
New York, New York 10014, U.S.A.
Penguin Books Ltd, 27 Wrights Lane,
London W8 5TZ, England
Penguin Books Australia Ltd, Ringwood,
Victoria, Australia
Penguin Books Canada Ltd, 10 Alcorn Avenue,
Toronto, Ontario, Canada M4V 3B2
Penguin Books (N.Z.) Ltd, 182–190 Wairau Road,
Auckland 10, New Zealand

Penguin Books Ltd, Registered Offices:
Harmondsworth, Middlesex, England

First published by Topaz an imprint of Dutton Signet,
a division of Penguin Books USA Inc.

First Printing, February, 1994
10  9  8  7  6  5  4  3  2  1

 REGISTERED TRADEMARK—MARCA REGISTRADA

Printed in the United States of America

This book would never have reached print without help, and now is my chance to give credit where it is due. First, I must humbly thank Joan Domning, my mother, for standing over me and pounding writing basics into my brain. To Larena, Sandy, Barbara, and Lisa of my first critique group, and Charla, Dana, Carol, Marguerite, Debanie of my second group: as much as I hated it, you were right. And, finally but most importantly, to my husband, Ed. Without you I might never have known what true love is.

# Prologue

THE convent's high stone walls, walls stained pink by dawn's rosy glow, echoed with the plainsong of the nuns. These simple harmonies floated up into the frigid February air to twine like sweet smoke around all it touched. It soothed and calmed the armed men and war-horses waiting in the courtyard, making the sudden scream all the more startling.

"Nay, you cannot!" the woman shrieked. "Help me, come help your abbess."

As the church doors fell open, the horses danced nervously making their masters curse and struggle for control. Shocked nuns and muttering servants seethed into the courtyard only to freeze in terror of an attack.

A mailed knight pushed through their ranks, dragging with him a small, habit-clad woman who kicked and clawed against his unbreakable hold. Their lady abbess came chasing after him. "You cannot do this to her. Do not take her from me. Not now. I beg you."

Undaunted, the knight dragged his prisoner toward his waiting men, ignoring the older woman's pleas. The convent dwellers shuffled uneasily into a semi-circle behind their lady. The man's captive fought on despite the hopelessness of her position, her eyes wide and her face ashen with fear. "You must stop him, my lady," she begged at last. "Do something."

At that, the knight hit her. She dropped limp into his arms, and he turned back to the abbess. "Have my daughter's belongings sent to me at Benfield before this day is through. I'll not wait for them."

"What can I do?" Tears stained the churchwoman's cheeks. "Someone help me," she urged of those who stood behind her.

Several serving men dared a half step forward, but they halted when the man put his hand to his sword hilt. This was a convent, not a keep. There was no one here to challenge a battle-ready warrior.

The girl moaned when he handed her up to one of his mounted men. She kicked weakly at him, but he ignored her. "You'll pay with your life if you release her," he warned his man. A moment later he mounted his own steed.

The abbess sank to her knees in the frigid mud. "May God go with you, my little Wren. Do not let them defeat you. Never forget—" Whatever else she said was lost as the man set spurs to his steed and called forward those who followed him. Their horses' huge hooves dug deeply into the ground, leaving the earth torn and broken behind them.

# Chapter One

ROWENA of Benfield stared straight ahead. Beneath soft black brows, her wide-set blue eyes were fixed and unblinking. Neither the irregular jolting of the trotting horse nor the rider's cruel grip disturbed her. A biting wind teased out ebony strands from under her white wimple and stabbed through the thick gray wool of her habit. It stung her cheeks and the short, straight line of her nose until her pale skin burned and reddened.

Her father had taken her mantle so she'd be too cold to escape and, now, she was frozen through and through. Deep beneath her icy calm she battled to control her anguish. He'd taken more than her mantle; he'd torn from her all her life's hopes and dreams.

Although the manor house at Benfield was only ten short miles from the abbey, a lifetime separated them. It was the difference between the wealthy, ordered serenity of the convent and the harsh poverty of her birthplace.

The troop raced past the village's cottages, huts, and hovels, scattering peasants, chickens, and geese. The ancient gate in the tottering circle of the keep's defensive wall stood open in slatternly invitation. They entered at a brisk trot, their horses coming to a welcome halt before the stables.

The manor house was no more than a simple wooden building grayed with age and disrepair attached to a squat, stone tower stained with moss. Hall, byres, barns, the stable, even the dovecote, all suffered the same moldly thatch for roofing. Neglect lay as heavily in the air as did the smell of latrines left too long uncleaned. In the yard, servants and peasants worked in an uneasy cooperation. They did not use the French language of their Norman masters, rather they spoke their own guttural English as they hastily prepared for the wedding of Lord Benfield's daughter.

Her wedding. Rowena glanced up at the windswept and icy blue sky. A solitary, hunting hawk floated high above her. She could not even summon up envy for the creature's freedom. Beyond help, beyond hope, she was.

Her father dismounted and dragged her off her perch, his hand clamped hard upon her arm. His steel-sewn gauntlet ripped into her sleeve. With a jerk, he pulled her through the doorway and into the hall.

Beyond hope she might be, but there was no man who'd make her go like a lamb to the slaughter. She pried at his fingers and struggled against him as her shoes slid in the fresh rushes that covered the hard earthen floor. As he forced her past linen-covered tables set around the great open hearth, she grabbed at benches, baskets, cups, anything to slow their passage. The dogs yipped and snarled, eager to join the fight and servants scattered to find hiding spots from where they could better watch. But he inevitably wrestled her through the long, narrow room toward the back wall.

"Stop," she finally cried out, breaking the silence between them. "No farther, not until I know why."

Lord Benfield whirled on his daughter. "Watch your tongue, girl," he growled, "or you'll feel my fist again."

Unthinkingly, she put a hand to her face and stroked the already purpling bruise at her slender jawline. Her eyes narrowed. In a hard voice, she asked, nay, commanded, "Why?"

"Why, why," he mocked. "Is it not enough that I got for you a husband who is a powerful lord with rich holdings? He cares little that you are overage, only that you can yet bear children."

"How pleasant," she snapped back. "Does he know I have no dowry or have you not yet told him this inescapable truth?"

"Girl, you have dowry enough for any man. 'Tis you who've inherited all your maternal grandfather held."

"All? Me?" she said in shocked surprise. "But, what of Philippa?"

"Philippa?" Her father's laugh was odd and high-pitched. "Her husband can keep what she took with her when they married. To you goes all else, everything I have received through your mother."

Her eyes narrowed. "If my mother had an inheritance, she would see that I got nothing and her favorite received it all. How can you give me what is hers?"

"Your mother cannot inherit; her father's will forbids her from ever holding a furlong of what was his." He paused, seeming to savor the thought of his wife so humbled.

"There is more," she said, eyes hard and voice the whip crack of command. "Tell me. Why are these holdings not divided with my sister? And why can I not have what is mine to buy me my position at the abbey? Why must I marry?"

"Do not use that tone with me, girl." Her father once again lifted his fist.

Rowena only waved away his words. "Oh, be done with your threats and your pomposity. I am no child to frighten, but a woman of one and twenty. If you batter me into senselessness, you cannot hurt me any more than you have already done."

"How do you dare?" he gasped.

Rowena cut him off before he could continue. "I dare because I am already dead. Aye, Father, this marriage of yours will kill me as surely as the summer's heat withers a spring blossom. Now," she continued, her words clipped and cold, "you will tell me why I am suddenly your only heir."

"And to think that I pitied you," Lord Benfield ground out.

"Pitied me?" She choked on a soundless sob. "If this is your pity, God have mercy on my soul. Father, how well will your pride withstand the blow when my new husband curses you for what you've done to him?"

"How so? What is this awful defect?" he sneered. "Before me stands a maid who, even though she is dressed in an ill-fitting, coarse habit, is both comely and shapely enough to turn a man's head. Where is your defect?"

"Here, Father," she returned, touching a slender finger to her temple. "Here. Because Philippa was your eldest, I dared not dream of marriage. Is it not still true today, in the Year of Our Lord 1194, that a second daughter is convent bound?

"But I was not defeated. And, Sweet God in heaven, how I worked. I learned to read and write and tally up a column of figures in a moment's time, knowing that if the convent would be my life I would be more than a simple nun. Pride is my sin, for I coveted the power the Church could give me. 'Twas to this end I humbled myself and bit my tongue when the nuns taunted me because you would not allow me to take my vows. I bid my time patiently, because I knew—" She swallowed hard, then lost all pretense of calm. "Now," she screamed, "you tear from me everything I desire and tell me it is for pity's sake! I say you lie. Why are you doing this? I will know why."

"Oh, spare me your venom." Her father smiled a hard smile. "What foul words you spew will not stop this wedding."

Rage exploded free of her control. "Damn you!" She swung a vicious foot at his shin. Her shoe rebounded from his mail-clad leg. "Kill me, kill me now and have done with it. Better that I die than wed and bed any man. It is better to be dead than be your heir. Damn you, damn you to hell," she raged, and grabbed his mantle at the throat as if she could force him into honesty. "Tell me why."

Her father easily plucked her hand away, then held her at arm's length from him. "Because," he said, then repeated in a sudden, strained voice, "because, Philippa is your mother's bastard. Ha—" he threw his head back and laughed. "At last, I've said it. The truth wins out. The old man's dead, and there's no reason for secrecy any longer." His grin was cold and cruel. "Philippa's no spawn of mine, and I did not accept her when I married your mother. She cannot inherit. You," he said, with chilling emphasis, "are my only legitimate child."

He turned on his heel and dragged Rowena to the back of the hall. There at that wall was a door, the only one within this manor house that sported a lock, his own bedchamber. He tossed her inside as if she were no more to him than a sheaf of wheat and slammed the door. The key scraped at the lock, which gave a rusty groan.

Stunned, Rowena lay amid the dry and dusty rushes for a moment, then came slowly to her feet. In disbelief, she threw herself against the heavy door, but she achieved only spent rage and bruised fists. It was in hopeless calm that she finally sank to the floor and indulged herself in an ocean of pain.

She stirred. Had it been hours or minutes since she'd arrived? From outside came the thunder of hooves, the jangling of harnesses, and hoarse cries of men. The noise pried her steadily from her pain-dazed state into alertness. Someone had arrived, no doubt her husband. Her eyes stung, but she refused to cry. All the tears she shed would no more free her than they would stop her wedding. A shattering sigh shook her to the core.

"Enough," she demanded of herself. Pity was only self-indulgent. It depleted energy without resolving the issue. How long had it been since she'd last given way to it? Too long ago to even remember.

In the wall was a narrow window covered by a simple wooden shutter. Rowena threw back the plain panel to reveal a thin slice of sky and let day's light tumble past her to chase heavy shadows from the dusty corners. Although the air was still light, she guessed it was a good three hours past midday.

So, it was hours that she'd been locked in here without so much as a cup of ale or a bite of bread. She breathed deeply. This February had been a harsh one, and the still freezing air cooled her hot face and eased the ache in her lungs.

She turned away to stare once more around this room. The poverty of Benfield had not stopped out-

side this thick door. The master's private chamber
was barely more than a storeroom with a hearth set
in the corner. Neither straw matting nor an embroidered wall hanging was in evidence to keep the winter's chill from seeping in. A single trunk squatted
beside a solitary chair. The only sign that it was not
a nun's cell was the huge bed, which dominated the
room. Thick, spiraling posts jutted up from each of
its four corners to support a wooden canopy draped
with heavy bed curtains. Drawn back to each corner
of the bed, these curtains revealed the soft mat-
tresses and thick blankets that filled its dark, cavernous interior.

The lock groaned. She whirled to face the door
as a woman carrying a basket entered. No taller
than she, her visitor's tawny hair was bound in a
thick braid and concealed by a wimple of homespun. Simple garments of green and gray clung
close to a girlishly slim silhouette. Her features were
beautiful, but bitterness deeply etched the set of her
mouth, and her green eyes were dull and lifeless. It
was a moment before recognition occurred, then
Rowena gasped. Her mother.

All at once she was five again. She crouched,
tangle-haired and frightened lest she be seen and
sent away, before the door to this very room. Inside
sat her mother. And Philippa.

Philippa, the golden-haired child, petted and
cherished. In her recollection, her sister wore a
clean and pretty gown and sang to their mother a
playful, happy tune. Every so often her mother's
sweet voice rose to intertwine with her sister's, and
in that moment, the child Rowena knew what
sounds angels made in heaven.

How many times had she streaked, barefoot and
unkempt, from this hall while her sister and mother

loved each other? Memory after hurtful memory tumbled through her, one upon the other. *Enough,* she cried to herself. She turned and slammed the shutter closed. The room plunged into dimness.

"Why did you do that?" The Lady Edith of Benfield's voice was toneless and flat, the voice of an old woman, not one in the midst of her third decade of life. She pulled the door shut behind her, then moved gracefully to the hearth and brought a fire to life upon it. The room brightened only slightly.

Rowena's hands clenched at the pain in her heart. "Have you nothing to say to me? No greeting? Not even a 'How do you fare'?"

"What would you like me to say? We both are well aware, as is every other soul in this keep, of how you feel."

Her mother turned and brushed cobwebs from the chair at the wall, then seated herself. "I am to supervise the maids as they prepare you for your wedding. There is not time for a bath, but I have ordered a basin of hot water so you may wash." From the basket she carried, she took a piece of needlework and picked an imaginary speck of lint from its surface. She calmly pushed her needle through the linen stretched within the wooden frame.

Rowena's rage outstripped her pain as her mother's needle flew. "I have suddenly remembered what I must have worked so hard to forget. I have not even the smallest place in your heart. Please forgive me, but it has been fourteen years."

"Leave me be, Rowena." The words were short and clipped.

"Leave you be? I would like nothing so much as that, but I seem to be trapped here. Be gone with you." Sarcasm lay thick and heavy in her tone.

Her mother shot her a sharp glance. "And I thought the nuns would have taught you to curb your headstrong ways and sharp tongue. Lord Graistan has just arrived, and your father has some last-minute details to discuss with him. I am here because I was sent here."

"Thank the heavens," Rowena snapped. "For a moment I was worried lest you actually meant to spend time with me."

"You rage like a spoiled child." Lady Benfield took another stitch.

"Oh, that I most certainly am not. Anything but that could be proved by the shameful way I am being married." She ticked the items off on her fingers as she spoke. "Without warning, I am dragged from the life I love, held prisoner in my birthplace, and forced into marriage against my will. Do I guess wrongly in thinking that no lord, other than my father and my new husband will break bread at my wedding feast? Nor, if I am right, will any noblewoman save my mother witness my bedding. Could it be that the village priest will be the one who condones this horrid deed?" She stared at her mother who looked away. "I see I have guessed correctly. But, then, I have always known I was not the favorite."

"Are you quite finished?" Edith raised a single, tawny eyebrow.

"You must be lifeless to the core. Tell me, madam, is there not even a single grain of love within you for your youngest child?"

The woman coolly considered her daughter for a long moment. But, when she turned back to her needlework, Rowena saw that her fingers trembled so badly she could not catch the needle. "You are not my child," she said at last, her voice breaking, "you are your father's spawn. The two of you are as alike in temperament as you are in appearance. Now, you, too, would demand from me what is not yours to demand."

Rowena waved her words away with an impatient hand. "Call it simple curiosity, then, Mother. You spurned me. I will know why."

"You will," she hissed and hurled her handwork at the wall. The wooden frame shattered and fell to the barren floor. A ruthless kick sent linen and wood clattering across the room to rest, splintered and tangled, against the room's single chest. "You will," she repeated with an angry gasp. "Today, you and your sire are the victors. Think you'll someday sweep into this place and hear 'my lady, my lady' from my lips? Place no wagers on it, for I'll yet make a pauper of you. You'll have no groat of what should be mine and Philippa's after me."

"What great hurt could I have possibly done to you before my seventh year to make you despise me so?" Rowena sank into the chair her mother had vacated and cradled her head in her hands. Her parents, locked in a selfish war of hate, had made her their weapon of choice. "Why vent your spleen on me and not Philippa if she is bastard as he says?" Her voice was steady, but within her grew a cold emptiness.

Her mother narrowly eyed her. "If he thinks the world will believe his claim now, after so many years have passed, he is mistaken. I will name his words vicious lies. Aye, I will call your whole marriage contract a lie, fabricated by your father to deny me the chance to regain for Philippa any of the wealth my father stole from me. My father," she went on, her face evilly twisting, "may his soul rot in hell, who saw me wed to the Oaf of Benfield to humble me after my mother's death. Me," she laughed, still incredulous despite the years, "for whom no less than an earl had once been considered. But he never dreamed he'd outlive all his sons and see his daughter's children be his only heir.

"Now, your father foully names my beloved daughter a bastard to leave her with only the paltry fields she took with her when she wed.

"How your father loves you," she said with a crooked grin. "He wanted a powerful husband for you, one who could keep these stolen lands from their rightful owners. It mattered naught to him what sort of man he was. I will give you warning now, Rowena. He is a hard, cold man who seeks only wealth from his marriage to you. Try and cross him as you did your father this morn, and he'll snap you between his hands like a dry twig."

Rowena sagged. Her strength, far overstretched by the events of the day, gave way. She hid her eyes as the words slipped from her in a whisper. "Help me, Sweet Mary Mother of God, I am afraid, I am greatly afraid."

"You?" Edith asked with a sneer. "You, the haughty, commanding woman who so recently dared her father to beat her to death, are afraid?"

Rowena shrugged. The movement of her shoulders conveyed both insolence and vulnerability at once. "Life has taught me bitter lessons, madam. I am, as you have said, commanding. I am also prideful and solitary by nature. The priest at the convent admonished me to adopt gentleness and meekness in my manner." She drew a shaky breath. "I swear by the Virgin, I tried, I truly did. I cannot change. It is not in my nature to be less than I am. Now tell me, Mother, how well will my husband like me?"

Her mother smiled in grim satisfaction. "Poor

rich heiress. He will not like you at all, but, then, you have been purchased for your lands and your womb. No matter whether you bear him sons or no, I do not imagine you will live long after Philippa receives the rights to my inheritance, and you are poor once again. He's killed two wives before you, you know."

She twitched the soft material of her skirt away from her feet, then went to the window and opened the shutter. Light once more filled the room. Edith stared out at the sky for a long moment before speaking once again. "God curses women who dare to dream of love or who hope for respect. Arrogant brat, you thought you would fly free of all this with your convent-inspired ambitions? Well, welcome to earth with the rest of us sinners." There was a tap at the door. "Come," she called out.

Several maids entered bearing a ewer of water and arm loads of clothing. When her mother turned away from the window, her hate was once again well hidden behind a bitter mask. "Stand up, daughter. You must be dressed now."

It was pointless to resist, so Rowena did as she was bid. All too soon the maids had washed away the signs of her travels and her hurts. She donned a fine linen chemise, then an undergown of deep blue. Its high neckline had been stiffened by heavy embroidery done with silver thread, no doubt her mother's handiwork. This design was repeated in unheard of luxury about the wrists of the undergown's close-fitted sleeves. Her overgown was sleeveless and made from samite in a shimmering rose red. The same, silvery pattern of embroidery trimmed its shortened hemline. All this finery was caught at her waist with a silk belt sewn and studded in silver. The crowning touch was a fine, silver-

and-pearl band, which capped her free-flowing black hair.

She smoothed the luxurious materials of her clothing over the full lines of her body, then touched the rich band. "A fortune wasted on an unwilling bride," she murmured.

Edith sneered. "My husband seeks to buy Lord Graistan's respect. You have been clothed to the limit of my father's tightly held purse and in the highest fashion as a part of your dowry."

"To what end?" Rowena's laugh was harsh. "Neither I nor my appearance is of any importance to this husband of mine." She lifted a rich, fur-lined mantle, threw it over her shoulders and fastened the clasp. The dark cloak nearly extinguished the brightness of her bridal costume in its heavy folds. "I am ready."

Her mother threw open the door and stood aside. Rowena swept past her into the hall. There were no ties to bind her to the past. All that remained was the future.

# Chapter Two

ROWENA'S step did not falter as she left the bedchamber, but she paused as she drew nearer to the center of the hall. The two men who stood in the circle of firelight at the huge hearth were deeply immersed in argument. Any information she might garner before being noticed might likely prove beneficial. As her mother started past, Rowena caught her arm. With a silent motion she asked for a few moments to eavesdrop. Edith shot her daughter a hard look, then shrugged in acquiescence.

It was not unusual for a long, narrow room such as this to ring with the noise of its many occupants. But, for now, the castle folk were maintaining a discreet silence so they might better hear the quarrel without appearing to do so. She strained to see the noblemen.

Dressed in a garish costume of red and blue and bejeweled in the newly inherited wealth, her father paced angrily before the fire. Only when he whirled away did she clearly see the other man who must be Lord Graistan, her husband-to-be. He stood a full head taller than her father, which meant he would tower over her.

When he tilted his head slightly, she saw his jawline was clean shaven against the fashion set by

King Richard, called the Lionheart. Thick, burnished chestnut hair curled lightly over the collar of his mantle. When he lifted a hand, firelight caught in the gemstone of his only ring. In his simple tawny brown tunic beneath a sturdy, plain mantle, he hardly looked the part of a bridegroom.

To others it might appear that Lord Graistan stood casually before the hearth, but she recognized full well the pride that infected the set of his shoulders and the arrogance in the line of his jaw. Carefully, cautiously, she slipped forward to hear what they were saying.

Just then Lord Benfield stopped in his strutting anger and threw his arms wide in frustration. "Why do you now play the reluctant bridegroom? I must hear from others that you plan to delay the wedding, and I am forced to summon you here to confront you. I thought you agreed to wed my daughter." His words echoed through the quiet hall.

Rowena cringed. Surely, the servants found this wholly reluctant bridal couple more diverting entertainment than any musician, mummer, or juggler.

When the trembling echoes died away, Lord Benfield continued in a somewhat quieter voice. "It was my belief you found our terms satisfactory. Have I not already given your churchman cousin our contract and all the rest you desired him to hold for you? Why then must I force your hand to conclude this deed only to have you seek for some other excuse by which to withdraw?"

"How reluctant can I be, Benfield?" Lord Graistan said, his voice deep and his words unhurried. "I am here. I simply thought you might wish to arrange a more elaborate affair for the wedding of your daughter and heir."

"You simply thought!" her father mocked. "This

is nothing more than a ploy to prevent this marriage until Lent is upon us and no marriages might be made."

"I would hardly call Prince John's attempt to steal his brother's throne a ploy. Nor did I ask to be called to arms to serve my king."

Rowena raised her brows in grudging admiration for his clever phrasing, but her father was not dissuaded. "You twist my words against me," he protested. " 'Tis you who would use a siege which might last for months to escape an obligation that could be dealt with in a day and night's time. You knew I wished this deed completed swiftly. If you had intended in good faith to wed my daughter, you'd have paid the scutage instead of going yourself."

"Too many men these days seek to shirk their knightly duties that way." The words were a naked rebuke. "Besides, where's the hurry? Our contract will stand. Let us celebrate a betrothal this day and a wedding this summer when the weather is pleasant and I am released from service. My cousin will officiate, and your new vassals as well as mine will attend. Although my men have all approved our contract, they will feel slighted if I wed in seeming secrecy."

"Betrothal is not enough." Her father clenched his fists in impotent rage. "What will happen to her if you spill your life's blood on the field of Nottingham? I must needs begin again the search for a husband to wed her."

"Your concern for me is touching," the tall man returned dryly, "if somewhat misplaced. The taking of Nottingham will most likely be a tiresome and dirty affair, but not particularly dangerous. Besides, in my family it is not the men who die young." The honest bitterness that stained his words told Rowena he had mourned the wives he'd lost and made lies of her mother's words about murder.

"I want her wedded and bedded now," her father demanded. Then he shut his eyes and took a long, deep breath. His words were calmer when he spoke again. "Perhaps you do not intend to fall at Nottingham, but I have not the arrogance to defy death. I cannot afford to leave her unmarried when her claim to these lands will be contested by her sister's husband. I came to you because I was told you would be a strong and just protector. Have I found one?"

"You have, but what if I insist upon betrothal?" Lord Graistan shrugged as if he, himself, did not expect his request to be taken seriously.

Benfield stared at him. "I would consider our contract void. She must be married as quickly as possible. Will you allow her dowry to slip so easily from your fingers?"

Lord Graistan nodded slowly. He had expected no other response. "So, where is this prize of yours?"

At his words, Edith stepped forward. Her movement caught her husband's eye, drawing his attention to his daughter. "Here she is now. Rowena!" He beckoned imperiously.

She crossed the room to them and dropped into a deep curtsy before Lord Graistan. As she straightened, she looked boldly up at him. His eyes were gray and as hard and cold as the stones that made up the keep walls. The harsh angles and planes of his face gave his features a bitter cast. Not even the tendrils of dark hair that lay lightly against his cheekbones lent him any softness. He could easily snap her in two, she thought, once again revising her mother's terrible claim.

He studied her intently in callous appraisal from

the pearls in her hair to the toes of her plain shoes. There was an expression of slight surprise on his face when he once again met her gaze. "You jest," he finally said, his eyes never leaving hers. "She does resemble you, Benfield, but this cannot be your daughter."

Her father's anxious gaze darted between them as he stuttered in nervous agitation. "What! Now you would accuse me of attempting to pass another off as my daughter? What nonsense is this, Graistan? Rowena"—he jerked angrily on her arm—"stare not upon your betters. If you seek to destroy with your rudeness what has been so carefully planned, I swear I will see you flayed alive."

She shot her father a scathing glance, but bowed to the possibilities in his words and studied the rushes that lay deep on the floor.

"Nay, Benfield," Lord Graistan snapped. "You spoke volumes of her convent-guarded virtue, but not once did you mention her appearance."

"What has her appearance to do with the marriage contract?" her father spat out. "Had you spoken of your desire to see her, I would have arranged it."

"I thought you had confined your daughter to a convent because she was an ill-favored wench. At her age what should I have expected?"

Rowena smiled even as her father laughed. "Are you saying you wish my daughter were ugly?"

She could not resist peering up at him from her meek pose. Lord Graistan's face was clouded in irritation until he caught her amused glance. He trapped her gaze with his, and his finely arched eyebrows slowly rose. Seemingly against his will, a smile steadily bent his lips. In that moment he changed.

Gone was the dour, glowering lord. In his place stood an attractive man with a warm and charming smile who made no attempt to hide his amusement even though it was directed at himself. "Do not ask me to explain," he said, his words touched with laughter, "for I will not."

She was not prepared for this. Here was a powerful, complex lord in the prime of his life while she was an overeducated, overaged woman with no experience at all with men. What sort of marriage could this be?

"What is this?" He crooked a finger beneath her chin and slightly tilted her head. "She is bruised, Benfield."

Her father only grunted. "She misunderstood something I told her this morn."

"I see" was all Lord Graistan said. After a quiet moment, he continued. "It appears there are no further impediments here. May I escort you to the chapel, my lady?" He inclined his head in invitation as he offered Rowena his hand.

"As you command, my lord." She took his hand, although she was reluctant to do so.

He quickly lead her between the long trestle tables, expertly dodging the servants who were placing additional torches along the wall. Once past the hall door, they carefully picked their way across the bailey until they reached the keep's gate. Here they stopped, no more than a dozen steps from the walls and the village church, which would serve noble as well as peasant this day.

"Now it is your father who delays us," he said. She looked past his shoulder at the hall. Her parents had yet to emerge from the door. The barest hint of mockery touched his tone as he spoke on, "Tell me, my lady, surely you must pine for a more elaborate ceremony. All this haste seems unnatural to me."

Rowena felt no need to be truthful. "It matters naught to me, my lord." The chill breeze caught at her mantle until the rich garment billowed out behind her. With trembling hands, she pulled it more tightly around her. Why did the cold not seem to affect him? She shivered again.

He stepped nearer until the greater build of his body shielded her from the wind. "Then, you are most unusual among women if the poverty of this affair does not concern you. Or perhaps"—he took her hand again, his fingers intertwining with hers—"it is only that you do not find me to your liking."

Rowena glanced sharply at him. "You are teasing me, my lord. I have seen you for only a few moments and spoken to you even less. How could you expect me to know whether I found you to my liking or no?" Asperity honed her words to a fine edge.

Lord Graistan's smile did not touch the guarded expression in his gray eyes. "I am gratified to know you have yet to judge me, my lady. I am very vain and could not easily tolerate a harsh verdict. Do you suppose the servants are disappointed we do not act the part of lovers?"

She started in surprise at this nonsequitur. "Lovers? We are barely acquainted. The servants know that." Did he think she was a fool?

"Oh, but even the barest hint of affection would please the crowd." He gestured to the serving folk and peasantry, who watched them from a respectful distance.

She eyed him narrowly. "My life is no man's entertainment." He was toying with her, the way a cat plays with a mouse before devouring it. His faintly mocking smile was proof of that.

There was a moment's silence between them, then she could resist her question no longer. "Might I ask you something?" When he inclined his head, she continued. "It does not concern you that I am an unwilling wife?"

This made him laugh out loud. It was a deep, rich sound of amusement. Then, still grinning widely, he said, "My sweet, all wives are unwilling. That is the nature of wives. Come, it is time." Her parents came to join them and, much too quickly, she stood with him before the doorway of the tiny village church.

The priest nervously cleared his throat. This was an awesome moment for one so humble as he. Noble marriages were always celebrated at the abbey. He was just a peasant's son who knew more of flocks and fields than Latin rites. Before him now stood both his present lord and one even greater who would someday hold this manor. He turned to the bride and asked if she entered willingly into holy matrimony.

"Of course she does," Lord Benfield growled out. "Get to the meat of it."

He once again cleared his throat. His hands trembled in growing nervousness as he asked, "Be there any obstacles to this wedding? You are not relatives?"

"Fool!" his lord yelled at him, "get to the recitation of property and the vows."

The priest jumped, nearly colliding with the bride, then straightened his stained and darned surplice. Once again he cleared his throat. "My lord, you have not given me a l-list to recite," he stuttered.

"God's teeth," Lord Benfield cursed. "I will do it."

Rowena listened carefully to her father as he chanted out the lands that made up her value.

"The keep at Provsy and its village and the right

to the church therein. Four furlongs of arable land and the woods at Oxbow—"

Rowena was astounded. She had not known her mother's family was so wealthy. When he was finished, her husband began the recitation of what would be hers throughout their marriage.

"I, Rannulf FitzHenry, Lord of Graistan, Ashby, Blacklea, and Upwood, give to my wife as her dower the manor of Upwood with its three ovens, two mills, and dovecot. Four hides of arable as demesne will see to her needs as well as the right to customary collection of all fines, fees, and merchet therein. This will she hold until her death." Then, he paused. "Only if she agrees as a condition of this marriage to hold in trust for my natural son, Jordan, the manor, and all customary lands attached to it, at Blacklea. Unless she so swears, this marriage will go no further."

The only sounds were a low moan from her father and the wind whistling through the open church door. Startled, she stared at her husband. Here, her mother had not lied, he cherished his natural son.

"We never spoke of this," her father shouted when he finally found his voice, "I will have none of it!"

A deep sense of irony twisted in her stomach. This was the culmination of a fine business proposition, held in the best manner of business dealing. It only remained to be seen who had cheated whom. But, if she refused this man, her father would swiftly find another to take his place.

Lord Graistan's fingers tightened ever so slightly on hers. She looked up. He waited, his eyes cold and gray, but there was something almost hopeful in the way he held his head. A subtle warmth flowed through her, and she smiled a very small smile. The corners of his mouth quirked upward and his eyes softened.

"I swear." Rowena's calm, firm voice overrode her father's complaints. "I do vow that the manor at Blacklea"—she paused, looking for confirmation in her husband's eyes—"be held in trust for my lord's natural son. I accept the conditions of this marriage as true and binding. I, Rowena of Benfield, take thee as my husband."

"And, I, Rannulf FitzHenry of Graistan, take thee as my wife. I present to you this token of our pledge," he said, not waiting for the priest to ask him. He produced from the small leather purse that hung at his belt a silver ring, tarnished with age and deeply etched with whimsical tracery. It was set with a large stone, a milky lavender at one end that deepened into royal purple at the other. He handed it to the priest, who quickly blessed the ring and handed it back to him.

Then, he placed it successively upon the first three fingers of her right hand, to bless the pledge, then on the middle finger of her left hand. "Accept it in remembrance of your words this day."

"Stop," Lord Benfield cried out to the priest. "There will be no marriage this day."

Both bride and groom turned to look at him. Suddenly, a wall of surly men rose up just below the church steps. Although unarmed, they were daunting enough to stop a single nobleman. Her father sputtered in helpless rage.

"What is your complaint over a single, insignificant manor entrusted to my son?" Lord Graistan's fingers entwined with his wife's, and he pulled her slightly behind him. "Now, why do we not say mass and repair to the hall to restore our good humor with the feast?"

With that, he took a handful of coins from his purse and tossed them into the crowd. As the servants and peasants scrambled to grab what they could, he spun on his heel and led his wife into the church. Their walk up the aisle stirred up an airy cloud of dust. The priest had been hard at his plowing and had not seen to sweeping out the nave.

"Aye, let us do so, and quickly," Lord Benfield growled, "for I am badly in need of drink to wash away the foul taste of these dealings. I am glad I have only one daughter to marry." He stalked past Lord Graistan's men and followed his new son into the church.

Unnerved by the happenings, the priest stumbled through the service, then bid the couple to seal the deed. Rowena turned her face up to accept the brief, ceremonial kiss expected in rites such as these. She was hardly prepared for the shock of her husband's warm mouth touching hers. His lips were soft and lingered against hers in the most disturbing way. She gasped softly and drew quickly away. He frowned at her as if she'd done something amiss. After a moment's hesitation, they both stood, then left the church.

The servants and peasants alike followed them back into the hall, laughing and shouting in high anticipation as they streamed in to join the feasting. Quickly, the dogs were chained into a far corner for the duration of the meal. Beneath each table now sat an alms basket for collection of food scraps for the poor. Additional torches were set into sconces along the wall and brightened the normally dim room into an almost festive glow.

Her husband led her to the high table at the top of the room. For this evening, they would have the seats of honor set with carved wine cups. While there were no special chairs, they found their places on the bench above the tall salt cellar. Like the servants, their plates were a thick slice of day-old bread to receive and absorb the soups and stews that would be served. But they had three, one for each course, while the commoners had only one.

Through the hall door came a man bearing a large basket. Wafting along with him was the yeasty smell of his fresh-baked wares while the scent of meat roasting in the cooking shed followed on his heels. Others moved around the tables filling cups with wine for nobles, and ale and beer for the rest.

At a lower table a musician tuned his instrument while he awaited his meal. The discordant and melancholy harmony wove itself into the newborn gaiety in the hall. Rowena winced.

For all of what remained of her life, she would preside over a hall similar to this one. Each day she would give the same orders to her maids and hear from them the same reports. If she was fortunate and her husband allowed, she might attend a fair or market in a nearby city or town from time to time. But mostly likely her home would become her prison. Such was the fate of one who would have been, could have been, a powerful and influential churchwoman.

From the moment they shared the water in the hand basin at the onset of the meal, she could not escape her new lord's courtly attentions. Too sensitive to the mockery beneath his manner to be flattered, she wondered if his attitude was naught but a ruse to forestall any personal inquiry she might make.

As the none-too-lavish meal ended, the jugglers moved away from the open space left in the center of the room and the musicans took their places.

Although they were louder than they were competent, their raucous and gay tunes helped her wean her thoughts away from the man next to her. Later, she lost herself completely in the playacting of the mummers who followed the musicians.

"Do you never speak unless spoken to?" Lord Graistan's quiet words were barely audible over the noise in the hall.

She glanced sidelong at him. Whatever slight peace she had enjoyed since the meal's end dissipated. "I admit to no knowledge of what is expected of wives. Nonetheless, I had always been under the impression that men prefer silent women."

"You seek only to please me? My lady, you flatter me."

She sipped her wine while carefully formulating her answer. "I would not have taken you as a man so easily flattered," she said slowly.

Lord Graistan raised a cautious eyebrow. "So, you have now had the time to better judge me, have you? And how, now, do you feel about our marriage?"

Rowena sighed and set her cup down. What on earth did he expect her to say? "You must content yourself in knowing I have only some impressions. Please take no disrespect, but, if you find me wary, it is because I am cautious by nature."

"Wary of me? There are those who would laugh at that." He suddenly seemed to withdraw once again into himself, and he turned away.

She let her attention return to the actors and was startled when a moment later he said, his lips very near her ear, "I assure you, you are not what I expected. You are an attractive woman."

When she turned to look at him, his eyes were soft as he watched her. "I was not taught to think of myself in that way," she murmured.

His arm encircled her waist, and he pulled her nearer to him on their bench. Before she could protest, his lips touched hers. She gasped lightly at the shock of flesh on flesh. His mouth moved just a bit, but it was enough to send a deep tremor down her spine. Her breath caught.

In an oddly intimate caress, his hand slid up her arm along the closely fitted sleeve of her undergown. Within her soul a flame burst into being, awakening life where before there had been nothing. He plied her lips with light, taunting kisses, his fingers drawing small circles in the bend of her elbow. Tiny shivers tingled up her arm. When he finally eased back, his mouth brushed her ear. "Did I not tell you they wished us to behave as lovers do?" he whispered.

"What?" Her mouth barely moved as she spoke. In the blazing warmth his touch had awakened, Rowena could find no sense in his question.

"Listen." He kissed her earlobe, then released her from his embrace. The hall rocked with cheers. Even the mummmers were amused. They began an obscene pantomime of the night's expected conclusion.

Rowena's eyes narrowed, her face an icy mask of disdain. "It amuses you to humiliate me. Have you finished or might I expect to fall into other traps before this evening is done? Ah, but then"—she smiled coldly—"it would ruin your pleasure if you were to warn me."

"Humiliate?" Her husband's face was devoid of expression. "Not humiliate. I cannot help that I am tempted beyond propriety by your loveliness."

She only stared coldly at him. "Such a glib tongue for one who earlier had done all that was possible to avoid this wedding. I daresay it is I who should now be flattered. Should I believe that you have suddenly discovered that I am your one, true love?" She shot him a mocking smile. "Unfortunately, your words have not even the flavor of truth to them."

"Ah, your tongue has cut me to the quick," Lord Graistan said with a smile, not in the least wounded.

"Aye, my tongue can be sharp. You would have known this had you more closely examined this piece of merchandise before you purchased it, my lord." She kept the same mocking tone.

"Wife, you set yourself before me like a keep with its defenses up and its gate barred. I am dared to lay siege to you. Have a care. You are too innocent in the ways of this warfare. I will reduce your walls to rubble." He was still laughing at her.

Rowena frowned. She started to speak, but he pressed a gentle finger to her lips and smiled a lazy, confident smile, then spoke. "Winter nights are long and cold." He ran his fingers down her arm. "I will welcome you with open arms to my bed." He beckoned a nearby servant. "Inform my Lord Benfield"— he paused to watch his father-in-law spew drunken curses at a servant too slow refilling his cup—"nay, my Lady Benfield that her daughter is ready to retire." Then he turned back to his wife. "I think I should now closely, very closely, examine the goods I have purchased this day."

# Chapter Three

*R*OWENA rose without argument and stared haughtily down at her husband. "How true. This day has dragged on long enough. Besides, I am mortally tired." He only smiled, not fooled by her bravado.

She turned on her heel and followed her mother into the bedchamber that had so recently been her prison. When the door shut behind her, her eyes closed and she swallowed. There was no escape for her.

Being convent raised had not sheltered her from the realities of this earthly plane. Although virgin she was, she knew well enough what was expected of her. Could she freely allow her husband to use her as she knew she must? And, what of him? Would he make her his victim and abuse her? Some of the nuns who had once been wives told such tales. She choked on her fear. Behind her closed lids, she conjured up an image of herself raped and bruised on her marriage bed. When she at last opened her eyes, the room held new meanings in its homely furnishings.

The flickering night candle near the door gave it all a sinister bend. The trunk squatting at the wall seemed to shift out into the room while the chair beside it crept more deeply into shadow. The bed

was by far the worst. Its thick spiraling posts cast
evil forms onto the wall behind it, and its dark,
cavernous interior seemed no more than a malevo-
lent craw. Once again, she shut her eyes.

Her mother had seen her look. "It was my mother's bed," she said, her voice oddly wistful. "It is all
I had left of her, but it is mine no longer. Your
father has given it to Lord Graistan as part of your
dowry."

Rowena sagged. If only she might once again have
the simple, straw-filled pallet that had served her so
well in the convent. It, at least, had never appeared
as though it might devour her. "I do not want it,"
she said, fear sharpening her voice. "You keep it."

Her mother shot her a hard glance. "Do me no
favors. I do not need your pity." She turned away
to the hearth as her maids entered the room and
set briskly to their work. Precious candles were
placed in ornate metal branches, and the fire fed
until the room glowed with gentle light. They
stripped the bride of her wedding finery until she
stood unclothed, her hair combed smooth once
again. When all was done, she was wrapped in a
soft, wool robe to ward off the chill.

They had only barely finished when a heavy knock
broke the tense stillness in the room. Rowena
clutched fearfully at her single garment's neck.
Edith glanced in irritation toward the closed door.
"Is he so eager for you? He barely allows us time
to make you ready."

The priest opened the door and her father stumbled in, leaning heavily on his son-in-law's arm.
Benfield swayed noticeably and glanced, bleary-
eyed, about the room until he saw his daughter.
"Impertinent twit," he mumbled. "Didst swear she'd
rather die than bed a man. Well, she'll see her

comeuppance this night." With those words, he lurched to the side and fell against the wall. He slid gracelessly to the ground, emitted a deep belch, then snored.

Lord Graistan's expression remained impassive as he watched her father's exit from the conscious world. Then he gave a short laugh and handed his cloak to a maid. "Did she?" he murmured. His low, suggestive tone teased an amused response from the serving women. He turned to the priest. "When you've finished blessing the bed for us, Father, will you stay to help them take their lord out of here?"

With one pull he removed his gown. A moment later and his boots were off, then his shirt, until he was clad only from waist to toe in his stocking-like chausses. Rowena stole a swift glance.

The fire's light made his bared skin gleam ruddy. His was a work-hardened frame that radiated power in it every solid curve and angular plane. Several livid scars cut across his chest and served as proof that he kept his livelihood by his sword. Dark hair trailed down his chest to disappear beneath the drawstring waist of his chausses.

He chuckled, and she knew he'd caught her glance. Rowena drew a quick breath and turned away, but it was too late. "Have patience, wife," he teased. "This poor maid must work the knots from my cross-garters before I can remove my chausses." The kneeling woman tittered as she unwound the strips of fabric that crisscrossed his legs from ankle to knee and kept his stockings from sagging.

Until this night, Rowena had never had a complaint with the custom of bedding the bride and groom. It was sensible, even practical. How better to make certain, prior to the consummation of the marriage and in front of as many witnesses as possible, that there was no hidden physical defect in either party? Now, as a maid pulled at the sleeves of her robe, the sour taste of reality filled her mouth.

As she herself had said, she was purchased goods to be examined for blemishes before the final transfer from seller to buyer. Nude and vulnerable, she turned to reveal herself to her husband. It was her shame, not the cold air, that made her skin prickle.

Lord Graistan stopped undressing, his chausses dangling from his fingers. For a short, silent moment, it was as though there was no one save the two of them in the room. His gaze lingered on her body, touching her full breasts, slim waist, and gently curving hips.

She looked at this lord who now owned her. Long legs, narrow hips, broad chest, strong arms, arrogant man. If he chose to take her against her will, she would be powerless to stop him. Rowena Benfield, once sure she would be owned by no man, intensely felt her loss of freedom. She glanced up at him. He met her gaze and took a half step forward. His movement broke the spell woven around her.

"Well, my lord," she asked acidly, "am I worth the price?" Even her mother gasped at the harshness of the question.

"I am pleased so far," her husband answered, his voice soft and deep, "but the night is still young, and there is a test or two remaining 'ere it's over."

Those women still gathered behind her chuckled and loudly whispered their bawdy comments. He laughed, and Edith stepped closer to her daughter. Rowena shifted away in startled surprise at her mother's seemingly protective movement.

"May she retire now, my lord?" her mother asked.

He glanced at her, then turned his attention back

to his wife. "But, she has not yet answered. Do you find a flaw?" His tone was intimate.

How could he be so casual about this? "Nay," she snapped, then immediately retreated to the great bed and slid between the cold sheets. The maids laughed at her cowardice, but her husband silenced them. "Have mercy on us," he pleaded mockingly. "A body could freeze solid in here in just moments. Now, would that not be a sorry waste of flesh?" The women chortled.

He tapped his father-in-law with a bare foot as the priest dragged the nobleman out the door. "Do not worry overmuch, Father; I doubt he will notice his humble departure." He crossed his arms against the chill and waited patiently for them to do as he had bid. After they had filed out, he quietly shut the door behind them.

Rowena had heaped the many, soft blankets about her, but she was still cold. In wary fascination, she watched her husband snuff out all but the night candle until the air reeked of burned wick and deep shadows again whispered in the corners. The night candle flickered, and the embers on the hearth spat and hissed. A moment more and he was at their bedside.

She lay tensely back against the bolsters and waited. The mattress dipped beneath his weight. Her teeth clenched. Linen rustled impatiently against linen as he arranged the pillows to suit him. Still, she waited.

Each passing moment died a long and agonized death. Only the low moan of the rising wind broke the silence in the room. Why did he hesitate? She wanted it over and done with, now.

As minutes ticked away, she again recalled his conversation with her father. Perhaps her new husband still wished to be free of this contract. If he did not consummate their marriage, there would be no expensive petition to the pope; only an application for dissolution to his churchman cousin. But, then, he'd lose her dowry.

The clean sheets fairly crackled as she shifted slightly to look at him. He'd left the bed curtains open and lay covered to the waist by the blankets. His fingers were laced behind his head and his eyes, shut. She could not imagine a more relaxed pose. Golden firelight gleamed against his exposed skin and shadows traced the masculine swell of his chest.

She studied the generous sweep of his forehead, the narrow line of his nose and well-molded lips. Not a truly handsome man, she thought, but not unattractive, especially when he smiled. As she watched, fine lines of amusement began to play at the corners of his closed eyes.

"Do you like what you see?" Slowly, his eyes opened. The taunting warmth of his words was reflected in his soft gray gaze.

She immediately looked away as her cheeks burned in embarrassment. He made her feel like a child caught where it should not be. Hard words hid her chagrin, "It hardly matters, does it, my lord?" Instantly, she wished she'd not spoken. What a stupid girl! What if her words incited him to cruelty?

Her husband only laughed. "It matters, if only to my vanity. My given name is Rannulf. I prefer that form of address from those who know me well." His words implied that she would soon know him very well. So, he'd had no intention of leaving her virgin. Once again he had toyed with her and won.

"As you like, my lord." She eased back down against the mattress.

"Rannulf," he prompted.

"Rannulf," she answered uneasily.

"So, my lady wife," he said, then sighed, "we are to make a marriage tonight. What say you we begin this task of ours now?"

She steeled herself for his touch. At least the deep shadows made the fulfillment of this duty easier. She lay tensely beside him and waited.

He rolled to his side, his eyes now a pale gleam in the night. When he brushed a strand of hair from her face his touch was gentle. "If you will try to be less fearful, I would make this as painless for you as possible. Of course, this is assuming you are yet virgin."

Rowena sat bolt upright with a gasp of outrage. "What! Now you presume too much. Please recall that I have lived fourteen years in a convent."

He only laughed quietly. "What have convents to do with virginity?"

"Be assured that what I held precious for the Lord God, I now surrender to you," she sarcastically spat out, and clenched her fist into the bedclothes.

"Stay angry, wife Rowena, I like you better this way. Consummation of marriage is not as horrible as you might think."

"You questioned my honor apurpose?" she cried out. When she would have said more, his mouth took hers. Outrage made her try to pull away from his touch, but his heated kiss consumed her anger and confused her senses. She could not resist when he urged her down against the mattress.

Trapped in a web of sudden and overwhelming sensation, she closed her eyes and sighed. His was an unexpectedly clean scent. She savored the taste of his mouth on hers. Against her arm she could feel the hard curve of his shoulder, yet his skin was soft where it touched hers.

Something stirred within her, warm and deep and hidden. He pressed a kiss just below her ear. It stirred again. She caught her breath. His fingers stroked her palm.

Again, he pressed his lips to her throat, this time slightly lower, then he set another kiss lower still. The stirring within her grew into a faint tenseness. She sighed and the tenseness eased. Her fingers twined with his, and her other hand found its way to the nape of his neck. Gently, she combed her fingers through his hair and shivered at its silkiness. Trapped in her own need to feel, she trailed her fingertips down his nape to his shoulders and back again.

He groaned low in his throat. Startled back to her senses, she snatched her hand away and burned with shame. How could she have been so forward? She tried to pull away, but he caught her in his arms. Without a word, he once again took her mouth with his. She lay still and cold beneath him in her shame.

"Do not run away," he whispered, but his words were laced with laughter.

"How could I? You are holding me," she whispered in return, her arms still held tightly at her sides.

"And would you run if I did not hold you? I think not," he breathed into her ear. Rowena shivered. "I think"—he paused to kiss her throat—"you will do as pleases both of us, not just me."

"You mock me." With great determination, she pressed her hands into the sheets and stayed perfectly still, even as his caresses seemed to dissolve her spine.

He paused and braced himself up on his elbow. "I promise I will tease you no more, at least not with words." His hands slipped up from her waist to cradle her breasts.

Rowena gasped and twisted. Outrage fused with pleasure in an unholy union as he lowered his mouth to kiss a line between his hands. The sensations he awoke were unbearable, yet she did not want them to cease. She tried to pull away, to escape the enormity of what she was feeling. Too late. She was pinned to the mattress between his arms.

All rational thought fled in the face of her primal need to feel. She knew the heat of his mouth against her breast and reveled in the roughness of his callused palm as he stroked her stomach. When his hand slid lower to touch her nether lips, she trembled beneath him.

Her hands found and caressed the hard line of his shoulders. His teasing fingers made her cry out and try to twist away while, in truth, she wanted to do no such thing. Her lips found his throat as he lowered himself to lay full length atop her, his legs between hers. His hoarse and whispered words were unintelligible as she kissed his neck. She spread her legs further to better accommodate his weight upon her. The heat between her thighs fairly scorched her.

Pain, tearing pain. Rowena cried out and arched beneath him as her virgin blood flowed. Her fingers dug deep into his back, and she bit her lip to still her cries. The fullness within her was both foreign and welcome in one incredible instant.

Her husband lay still atop her. With gentle fingers, he combed her hair and stroked her cheek. "Forgive me." His words were oddly breathless. "Have patience, your pain will pass in a moment."

Rowena's eyes stayed half-closed. A moment slipped by. Slowly, the burning ache eased. She fought the urge to shift. It was not her husband's greater weight that made her wish to move. Instead, it seemed to be the very sensation of his skin touching hers.

He had twined his legs between hers until her calves lay across his. When had he done so? His hands sought out and stroked her cheeks with his fingertips. Then, his fingers found their way down either side of her neck in a feathery caress. She shivered and gasped as a tiny spark of heat seemed to explode within her.

He took her sound to be an invitation and touched her mouth with his. Slowly, his soft, teasing kisses gave way to a passionate taking of her mouth. A new intense sense of fullness awoke within her, banishing all remembrance of her pain. Within her lay some hidden destiny her body urged her to fulfill, but, try as she might, she could not imagine what it was. She shifted uneasily beneath him, not knowing why she did so. As she moved, so did he. She gasped, but not with pain.

"I promise this will not always hurt you so," Rannulf breathed into her ear between kisses. He moved again, then again.

A subtle pleasure pulsed within her that quickly tumbled into a greater need. Rowena shifted to accommodate his thrusts, finding yet greater pleasure as she did so. He buried his head against her neck, his breathing ragged and quick, and she embraced him in mute acceptance of her womanhood. But, when his movements quickened, then ceased, she nearly cried out in complaint. There was something more; something she could not identify. What more could there be between a man and a woman?

For a long moment he lay atop her gasping in his exertion. Then, he eased slightly to one side. His eyes were heavy lidded with his ebbing passion while the smile that bent his mouth was warm and untroubled. Slowly, Rowena smiled in return.

He kissed her cheek, then the tip of her nose. When, at last, his mouth met hers, her lips clung to his as she enjoyed the taste of him, the warmth of his lips, and the glorious feeling of his mouth moving against hers.

Then, he drew away, his expression slowly clouding. As she watched his smiling warmth dimmed to stark confusion, then into a harsh coldness. He eased further from her in the bed, as if he truly feared to touch her. "Best you sleep well this night. We travel to Graistan on the morrow. I must be on about my business." He sat up and impatiently tugged the bed curtains closed around them. When he lay down, it was with his back to his wife.

"Tomorrow?" The word spilled bitterly from her lips, but it was not the morrow's leave-taking that bothered her. His sudden coldness deeply stabbed her, destroying all the warmth and pleasure they had just shared. What had she done to make him stare at her so?

He raised up on one elbow to look over his shoulder at her. The dour lord was back. "My men and vassals await my arrival at Nottingham. Be content that Graistan is not so far and the short trip will not trouble you much." He settled into the mattress and drew the bedclothes over him.

Rowena shuddered. She stared at his back, but soon his breathing was deep and even. Slowly, she eased across the bed into the corner farthest from him. There, hidden in the deepest shadows of the bed, she struggled to straighten her painful thoughts.

Reason and order had fled, serenity was shattered. In their place sat the memory of their lovemaking and his cruel rejection.

She had known that she would be no more to him than an instrument, a harp to be set aside when the song was finished. What she had not known was how painful that setting aside would be. Leaning her head against a bedpost, she swallowed her pain and felt the coldness within her grow colder yet. At long last, she settled deep beneath the bedclothes and as far from him as possible. It was a long while before she slept.

Rannulf lay still and forced his breathing into an even, relaxed pace. His new wife lay at the far side of the bed. Cruelty did not come easily to him as it did some men. Yet, he reminded himself of how necessary it was.

If only she had been the ugly, docile girl he'd expected, then he could have been kind and still have felt nothing toward her. Instead, she was a fiery, passionate, and beautiful woman. His lips moved in a silent curse. He was married again, this time trapped into it by his own avarice.

When his cousin, Oswald, who served Benfield's new overlord, the Bishop of Hereford, had sent her father to him with this contract, his first impulse had been to refuse. After all, he had his heirs in his half brother, Gilliam, and his natural son, Jordon. But when the man had explained the extent of his daughter's estate, he'd been stunned. He could not let the opportunity slip away, especially when it lay so close to his own heart, Graistan.

Rannulf listened. There was no sound but the wind. He peered over his shoulder at her. She was curled onto her side, her back to him. When he was sure she slept, he rolled toward her. Even now he ached to reach out and draw her near, to feel the softness of her skin against his, the silkiness of her hair twining around his arms. He remembered the sweet taste of her and shuddered.

She had wanted him. Even in her innocence, she'd shown him that. He'd touched her and a flame of raw desire burst into life in her eyes. No other man had ever awakened her passions; she had not even known herself capable of such feeling. God, he wanted no more than to lay abed with this woman and teach her more of pleasure. He ached to kiss her once again into awareness of her womanhood.

But he would not be staying at Graistan with her. Aye, he had awakened these passions of hers, now who would she find to satisfy them while he was gone? He balled his fists against such thoughts, successfully burying them where they belonged, back in the darkest corner of his mind. Yet, despite his efforts he could not escape his sense of impending heartbreak.

His life was cursed. Once, long ago, when he'd been younger, less jaded, he'd dreamed of a marriage such as his father had known with his second wife, Ermina. Theirs had been a true love, filled with great passion and caring. But, if his own first marriage had been dull and fruitless, his second had been a catastrophe that had nearly torn his family asunder. Rannulf had sworn then not to marry again.

Here was what came of greed. Beside him lay a woman who would no doubt destroy his life even more thoroughly than his last wife had. And him with it. He sighed. It would be best if he never came to care for her. If she grew to hate him for it, so be it. Better her hate than his pain.

He resettled the bedclothes up over his shoulders and waited for sleep to overtake him. The wait was dark and empty, and his wife cried out in her dreams. It was a struggle not to take her in his arms to comfort her. At long last he drifted off and had no dreams of his own.

It was the relentless drumming of sleet against the shutter that awakened Rannulf. And his wife as well, for she sighed heavily and rolled to her side. Outside, the wind howled and sent fingers of icy air probing into every corner. She shivered as a draft fluttered in the bed curtains. He stirred a little to let her know he, too, was awake.

He studied the tumble of her thick black hair against her pale skin. The contrast was as startling as she was. Without effort, he recalled the full lushness of her body and her instinctive response to his lovemaking. Before he could stop himself, he reached out and caressed the gentle curve of her back where it narrowed into her waist.

She gasped and rolled out of his arm's reach. "I thought you still slept," she said ungraciously.

"How can a man expect to find any rest when his wife constantly moves about all night? He kept his tone light. "Your dreams were not pleasant."

"I cannot recall, my lord." She lied. He knew it.

"How quickly you have forgotten my name." Why did he press it if he wanted her to remain distant?

She only shrugged. His cruelty had done what he'd wanted. It would be a long while before she would again allow herself to be vulnerable to him. But what he'd done to her gouged him as well. "Damn," he muttered.

She turned away and opened the bed curtains.

Watery gray light pushed past her but made only a small dent in the darkness within the bed. Even after she'd gathered the bedclothes about her, she still shivered.

"Our ride today is going to be less than pleasant." Rannulf's voice was flat with a disappointment he tried not to feel.

She glanced at him from over her shoulder. "You still mean to go? It is freezing outside. The roads will be barely passable."

"I know that well enough without you telling me," he said sourly. No doubt it was the Lord God's punishment for what he'd done to his wife. "I am honor bound to go to Nottingham and join with those men loyal to King Richard who now besiege that filthy keep. But, first, I must get you to Graistan." He eased from the bed and gathered his clothing. With an angry sigh, he shoved first one leg then the other into his chausses and jerked at the waist cord.

His wife rubbed her face with weary hands. "And what will your servants think when you leave me with hardly more than a 'fare thee well'?" She wrapped a blanket about her and, to his surprise, slipped from the bed to tie his cross-garters for him.

Rannulf stared down at her as she deftly wrapped the cords about his calves and knotted them in place. No begging or pleading that he should not leave her. No tears or pretty rages here. He'd been more effective than he'd dreamed. All she would now care for was the power and comfort Graistan keep could lend her. For some reason this angered rather than soothed him. "Graistan has been too long without a proper housewife to see to its corners and bins. If you are capable of managing them, my servants will easily accept you. But, if you meddle where you have no experience, they will rightly snub you. Remember this, if you overstep your bounds, do not come crying to me, for I will not help you."

"My dear lord husband," she snapped in exasperation, still kneeling at his feet as she peered up at him, "let me assure you that I have not yet needed to 'come crying' to anyone for help in managing servants." With her small, wifely deed completed, she retreated to the bed and out of his reach. "Take care of your duties, and I will take care of mine."

His shirt went on with an angry jerk. Rannulf could not restrain a return thrust. "Ah, I see it clearly now. You will run the distance, but you will take not one step farther. You will be a dutiful wife to me." He made duty sound like a curse rather than the rightful aim of every woman.

She smiled a hard, calculating smile. Her eyes, eyes so blue they were nearly purple, should have been warm with longing for him. Instead, they shot daggers at him. " 'Tis true. There is little else I can bring into this contract of ours save my devotion to duty."

Rannulf yanked his robe over his head and wrenched his belt tight about his waist. A muscle tensed in his cheek as he fought his anger at her masterful control. Finally, he spoke. "Remember only this, Rowena, duty does not warm the heart."

Her eyes flew wide in disbelief at his warning. "In response, I would say that bitterness cannot be the friendliest of companions."

For a single, astonished instant, he stared at her. She had pierced his heart with her words, destroyed his barricades, and stormed his defenses. Rage came swiftly on the heels of surprise. "I am a tolerant man, some have said overtolerant, but you push me to my limit."

Instead of meek submission, she shot him a hard

smile. He'd never met a woman so bold. "What little bird gave you to understand that you might say what you please to me without offering me the same courtesy in return?"

"You dare too much," he muttered, his words harsh and dangerous as anger rapidly seethed beyond his capacity to control it. "Is it your wish to goad me into violence?"

"No, my lord. Perhaps I do dare much, but then, I have nothing to lose. In just one day's time all I've been taught to hold dear has been taken from me. Now I am asked to accept, without comment or complaint, a life that is wholly foreign to me. I know nothing of being a wife, but I have learned much about the running and maintenance of an estate. It may be you will find my manner too straightforward for your tastes, but, my lord, it is just that—my manner. Would that I die before I give up that part of me."

Outside, the wind howled and sleet spattered the shutter. Unexpectedly, Rannulf felt the stirrings of respect amid the bitter dregs of his disappointment. Perhaps if he had never married Isotte, things could have been different for them. His shoulders drooped under the burden of his pain. It was too late for that. "I will not argue with you." There was nothing but dullness left in his heart. He turned his back on her and shoved his feet into his boots. "Graistan keep will be at your disposal, even if its lord is not. Be ready to leave within the hour."

"As you wish, my lord," she said quietly, almost meekly. He spun on his heel and jerked open the door. A maid nearly fell into the room. The hapless woman cried out in surprise as she dodged him, but he did not pause in his haste to be away from his wife.

Rowena listened until she was sure her husband was beyond earshot. Then, she dropped her blanket and reached for her robe. Had she meant to goad him into violence? Was it disappointment she'd felt when he hadn't struck her as she had expected? It was as if she'd wanted to see his passion, any passion be it even hate, rather than the dullness he showed toward her.

"My lady," the maid cried out, "do not rise yet. The sheets! I must call your mother to witness."

"Sweet Mary, there can be no doubt of my purity, whether I remain upon the bed or not. Bring me water for washing and fresh, warm clothing. I am not wont to wear my wedding garb again this day." She paused to add beneath her breath, "or ever." Then, she continued more loudly. "There is much to be done. Inform the Lady Edith my husband desires to leave within the hour."

"What?!" the maid squeaked.

Rowena yanked on her bed robe and cinched the belt tight. "I've got no time to waste, woman. Move!"

The poor woman leapt to do her bidding, not even bothering to close the door behind her. Rowena almost smiled as she shut the door. At least she had clarified the terms of their marriage.

Rowena huddled more deeply into her cloak, cold beyond complaint. Even protected by thick, leather gloves, her hands had lost all feeling. Her hair, though covered by her wimple and a fur-lined hood, was damp with the icy rain.

Her husband pulled the bay he rode into line with her little mare. She glanced up at him. Where his cloak and surcoat did not cover it, his chain mail gleamed with the moisture it collected. "How much farther, my lord?" Her voice was hoarse.

"Too far," he snapped.

The continuing drizzle had turned the road into naught but thick and frigid mud, it being not quite cold enough to completely freeze. Burdened as they were with the ox-drawn carts, their progress had been at a snail's pace. After a moment's angry silence, he called back to his master-at-arms who rode a short distance behind them. "Can we move them no faster?" He stared in disgust at the peasants and their beasts of burden.

In those carts was her new wardrobe along with the massive bed that had once been her mother's. Her father had actually threatened to throw everything from the top of Benfield's wall if they did not take it with them. Although her husband had protested vehemently stating his need for haste, he could not afford to refuse; the bed was too rich an item to risk. He had agreed.

She turned slightly on her saddle to consider Temric, her husband's man. His expression remained stonily impassive beneath the hood of his plain, woolen cloak. The taciturn man wore armor of the plainest sort with no sign of decoration. Bearded and of medium height, his even features spoke of common ancestry. But, although he could certainly be no knight, Lord Graistan treated him as if he were, even giving him command of his true knights, men of noble birth.

Briefly and without the slightest change of expression, Temric's brown eyes met hers. "My lord, if we push any harder the thing will mire in the mud at every turn of the wheels rather than every third turn."

"God's blood!" Rannulf managed to make the low-voiced utterance sound like a scream.

Temric straightened slightly as what might have

been impatience flashed across his face. "Have you not yet tired of souring your stomach? And if you have not, I beg you to spare the rest of us."

Rowena caught her breath. Surely, her lord would cut the man down for daring so much. She would have never have tolerated such impertinence from one of lesser rank. To her astonishment, her husband only groaned. "Has there ever been such an ill-fated venture?"

"I agree," she snapped, "that our wedding was not what I desired, but do not curse God and call it ill-fated."

"A poor choice of words," he said by way of apology. "Temric, I can afford no more time lost. Do I remember that nearby here lies a small hamlet? Let us pay some husbandman to keep the carts and be on our way. Have Gilliam send someone to fetch it later."

"Should you push your lady so hard?" Once again, the commoner dared to criticize his lord. Were all the servants at Graistan accustomed to such freedoms? She frowned. If this was so, the advent of her rule would bring them all rudely back to earth.

"I have no choice," her husband responded. "Unless"—here he paused in thought—"unless . . . it is not the best of options, but it will work.

"If we could locate a dwelling there that is a suitable place for my lady, you and four men could house the carts for the night. Early on the morrow the roads will still be frozen, and it will be easier for you to finish the journey to Graistan. Aye," he continued, a new enthusiasm infecting his voice, "then, I will be free to continue on to Nottingham. Even better, this will give you the chance to escort from Graistan those supplies this impromptu wedding prevented me from obtaining." Rannulf eased back into his saddle, obviously pleased with his plan.

It was equally obvious to Rowena that a suitable dwelling would be found, be it house or shed. "And what of me," she asked. "Am I to introduce myself to your servants without their master at my side to confirm my rights as their lady? How will they even know me?"

His glance was disinterested. "The needs of my king must come before those of my wife. My half brother, Gilliam, who is my steward and holds Graistan during my absence, will stand in my stead." He gave it no further consideration; his difficulties had been solved. With that, he urged his horse forward.

"You have all my gratitude," she bit out beneath her breath. Temric glanced impassively from one to the other, then repeated in the English language his lord's commands. The troop turned off onto the narrow lane.

Fuming silently to herself, she followed him as their party made its way along the track. She cursed this arrogant husband of hers as well as her father. Never had a man done her a favor, nor did she foresee any such an occurrence in the near future.

She heard the place well before they arrived. In the utter stillness of the winter woods, the gentle lowing of cattle and the bleat of sheep echoed eerily through barren branches. It was not much, only a knot of tiny buildings around which stood a helter-skelter wall of tree limbs woven with branches. Smoke drifting from the rooftops was absorbed into the heavy, leaden sky.

At Temric's call a man appeared from the nearest cottage. Although he bowed and scraped before them, his eyes were narrowed and suspicious until he understood what was required and that coins would be offered. After a few minutes of fervent bargaining, during which the man displayed a greedy smile, Temric turned to Lord Graistan.

"He says they will house the carts, and the men can use the shed"—he pointed to a lean-to—"while your lady may have the use of his home."

Rannulf interrupted, "At what price?"

"Do you not think it wise to ask me if I intend to stay in this place before you open your purse and waste precious coins?" she asked sharply. "How far are we now from Graistan?"

Her husband shot her a calculating look. "Perhaps four hours if you travel without the cart."

"Then I intend to be on my way." She resettled her gloves between her fingers and straightened her wimple. "If you will not see to my needs, I shall have to attend to them myself. Besides, I have had the opportunity to visit places such as this. At night the beasts of the fields share these quarters with their masters. The warmth might be welcome in winter, but the stench is enough to make breathing impossible. Temric, do you ride with me?" For the briefest instant, Rowena would have sworn that she had astonished the man, but, if she had, his face immediately fell into his usual closed expression.

Rannulf turned angrily toward her. "Do you think to shame me in front of my own men? If so, then you have sadly misjudged them and their loyalty to me. Spare me your venom and your claws."

"My dear lord husband," she snapped, "I refuse to stay in a filthy hovel when in hours' time I could be where I can bathe, eat, sleep, and breathe in comfort."

For a moment, it appeared that he had more to say, then his mouth shut into a hard and narrow line. "As you wish." He turned to his master-at-arms. "If my lady wishes to ride, let her ride."

"As you say, my lord, but let the lady know that there is no place to stop between here and Graistan more suitable than this for one such as herself. Also, let her know that the ride is not an easy one."

She smiled archly. Convent life, if lived true to the principles of the Roman Church, taught inner strength and stamina. Oh, there were those to whom a nunnery offered softness and shelter, but she had not been one of that ilk. "You may tell your master-at-arms that he will have no burden on his hands."

Temric nodded curtly, no longer giving service to the customary protocol and now speaking directly to his lady. "Then, give me a moment, my lady, to see to the carts. My lord, it appears that it will cost you only two pence to store the carts and feed the oxen and their drivers. For another two pence, he and his sons will assist in bringing them to Graistan on the morrow if we leave men to guard them on their way."

"Then, let it be so." Rannulf nodded.

Temric dug the coins from the purse he wore at his waist and tossed it to the man, then unfastened the purse and threw it to his lord. At his command, four men sent their horses through the gate. The peasant called his sons from the hut to help the drivers guide the oxen and carts into the compound.

Rannulf stuffed the leather pouch into his glove's cuff. "Gilliam knows what I need and, by all rights, it should be ready and awaiting your arrival. Take your ease for a day if you wish. There will be supplies enough with Ashby's company to see to all our men." He laughed, and Temric nearly smiled as they shared some private jest, then her husband turned to her.

"Tell Gilliam that I said you are to do as you wish with the servants and that they are to obey you as they would me. No, do not say that." He held up a hand and briefly closed his eyes. "Say to him that you are to be obeyed in all things as his mother would have been obeyed. Temric"—he glanced around—"bear witness to any who question that I have said so."

For a moment, there was silence between them while he stared off into the forest. When he turned back to her, he shrugged and said, "Your lands are too well matched with mine, I could not allow them to slip into another's hands. You will not be alone at Graistan. Gilliam will see to it that you are well treated."

Was this an apology? It was better to assume it was. She cleared her throat, then finally said, "May the Lord God keep you safe in your endeavors." It sounded like the wifely thing to say.

"And you, yours," he returned. But, he offered no gesture of farewell, only sent his bay crashing across the frost-crusted field. He and the men who followed disappeared quickly into the tangled branches and dead bracken until nothing but silence once again surrounded those who stayed behind.

# Chapter Four

*T*EMRIC set a brutal pace, but Rowena's presence slowed them not one whit—although she well knew he'd expected it. Still, pride in her achievement did not thaw frozen fingers and toes or make the misery pass more quickly. It was only when day had fallen into an icy, blue twilight that this wide, well-traveled road led them to Graistan, her new home.

Set atop a sharp lift of land guarded by a river's bend was a tall stone keep. Surrounding the great square tower was a massive wall with defensive towers at its every turn. Proof of her husband's might and prominence lay not only in this powerful keep, but also by the town below the castle. This fledgling enterprise nestled safely between castle and its own walls. Rowena's heart soared at the sight. Where there was trade, there was wealth.

They thundered past outlying farmland, meadows, and orchards, then through the town's gate. Here, their pace slowed along the narrow lanes that twisted and curved at will and with no apparent reason. With night now closing in, only a solitary few remained out and about. The eerie wail of yowling cats shattered the chilled quiet. She glanced upward, searching for the source.

The tall houses were framed in dark, thick tim-

bers. Some were freestanding while others were
crammed, cheek to jowl, against their neighbors. Although twilight had grayed their colors, each house
bore painted wood trim, some carved into fanciful
designs. Merchants' homes were easily identified by
the emblems that hung over their doors. Each pro-
claimed the nature of their owner's business, be that
carpenter, potter, or wine seller. Butchers, tanners,
and fishmongers were easily identified by their reek-
ing odors, as were the bakers, cookshops, and chan-
dlers with their sweeter smells.

As they turned a sharp corner, Rowena caught
her breath. There, nestled in a corner was a gold-
smith's shop. Wealth, indeed.

Excitement pushed aside exhaustion. She spurred
her mare through the armed entrance of Graistan
keep, then past the byres, barns, sheds, and stables
of the outer bailey. They did not hold her interest.
What she wanted lay within the close, inner walls.
To become lady of this hall and town would challenge all she ever learned, a challenge she gladly
accepted.

Once past the inner gate, Temric's piercing whistle brought a tumble of grooms from the stables.
Serving boys, heralded by a pack of yelping, snarling
dogs, flew down the stairs from the hall door into
the courtyard.

A blond giant of a man, taller even than her husband yet barely older than she, pushed his way past
the dogs and boys toward them. Worry creased his
brow and touched his guileless blue eyes. "Temric,
where is Rannulf," he called out, his voice, deep
beyond his youth, reverberating against the overshadowing walls.

Rowena peered up from beneath her concealing
hood at him. Where her husband's features were all

sharp angles and deep plains of life's experience, his face seemed boyish in its softness. Only the fine embroidery that trimmed the neckline of his bright red tunic and the richly decorated leather of his belt indicated he might be Lord Rannulf's kin.

Temric dismounted, kicking away the dogs as he did so. "Gone on to Notthingham. Sir Gilliam, come give your new lady your hand."

"New lady?" the boy blurted out in surprise before he caught himself. "But, I thought—"

She bit her cheek to keep from smiling at his consternation as his fair skin colored. My, how quickly the potential loss of her dowry had turned a reluctant bridegroom into a husband. This Gilliam ran a distracted hand through his curly mop of golden hair and yanked at his tunic to hide his discomfort as he came to stand by her side. He was so tall, she nearly looked him eye to eye from her perch atop her mount.

"Sir Gilliam, I was Rowena of Benfield until yesterday." She had to introduce herself since her husband was absent and there was no one of rank to do it. "You are my husband's brother?"

Tongue-tied in his embarrassment, he nodded and lifted her from the saddle to set her on her feet in the frozen mire. The sudden pinprick sensations in her legs made her grit her teeth against a yelp of pain. Not for the first time, pride had driven her where common sense had well known she should not go. She tried to take a step and faltered. Only Sir Gilliam's powerful arm kept her from falling face first into the mud.

She grimaced and glanced up at Temric. "Such is the price of my arrogance," she said to him. "From now on I shall remember to be more humble when you state that the ride is to be a hard one."

The commoner made a noise that could have been either a cough or a laugh. His brown eyes mellowed to nearly golden as his face softened, and he smiled at her. "Welcome to Graistan, my lady." Even as she blinked in surprise at his sudden friendliness, his features hardened once again into his usual flat expression.

He turned to his lord's brother, "Are the supply wains loaded and ready to go?" The young knight gaped at him as she glanced between them. "Well," he growled, "have you or have you not got the wains?"

His demeanor and harsh words left no doubt that he accorded this young nobleman only meager deference. So, it had been either her husband's whim or his liking for his brother and not this knight's skills that made him Graistan's steward. In that case, it was doubtful Gilliam would be of any help to her in making Graistan's servants hers. She would do better to carve out her own niche.

"Nay," the tall man managed at last. "Henry and his men left here with them yestereven, thinking to meet Rannulf along the road from Benfield. He took the wagons with him."

Temric grunted. "Then, he'll not meet him 'til Nottingham. I'd best be gone at first light to see if I can catch him." He took a step away, then turned back. "Your lord sent you a message. He says that the servants are to respect their new lady's wishes as they would have your lady mother's. My lady"—he directed a brief bow in her direction—"I wish you well in your new tasks. I have no doubt that Graistan is once more in good and capable hands." With a final, short bow, he spun on his heel and started toward the hall stairs.

Strange man, strange day. She shook her head,

then looked up at her brother by marriage. He stared openmouthed at the soldier's receding back. She finally asked, "Is something amiss?"

"Nay, no, not at all," he stuttered, "no, it is just that—that is, Temric is not—ah,—not one for so many words." He stopped, cleared his throat, and started again. "Come inside, my lady. Take care on these stairs, the steps are slick with ice. Allow me to apologize for what is sure to be a threadbare welcome," he said, with a nervous laugh. "We did not expect you."

"I fully understand." She was grateful for his rock-hard arm, since her legs still wobbled from the long ride. Together, they climbed the stairs, passed the iron-banded outer doors to the armed entry room beyond them. No salt on the steps, no straw applied to the mud in the courtyard. And she could smell the garderobes. Aye, Graistan had desperate need of her skills.

At the top of the stairs stood the porter, his hand possessively against the hall door. When they turned toward him, he bowed in greeting, then opened his door wider to admit them. The dogs followed them in and dispersed happily around the room.

Her new brother led her beyond the tall portal and past the screens that limited the great room's necessary draft. Here, he stopped. "Shall I introduce you?"

"Give me a moment to look," she replied, removing her gloves and working at her cloak's leather ties. The hall was as square as the tower itself, but was divided in twain by a row of pillars. These massive stone arches supported a second floor that reached only halfway across the great room. On the open side, torches burned in sconces beneath the enormous cross beams and two hearths, equidistant from each other, spewed their merry warmth and light into the room. Colorfully painted linen panels hung on the thick stone walls functioning as both decoration and a barrier against the cold.

Yet, the hearths were choked with ashes and the once gaily painted beams were black with soot. The tables, which should have been stored after the evening meal, still stood around the room, their cloths ragged and stained. Beneath her feet the rushes had been beaten into dust. All this despite the fact that more servants congregated in this hall than the abbey had supported, even when she included the serfs from the outlying hamlets.

She pursed her lips in consideration. How long would she have before her husband's return? A warm kernel of determination awoke within her. Come crying to him for help, indeed. She would restore this hall to its former glory and right quickly, too. To do so, she would need these servants as her own this very night. That was not so difficult. It had been the abbess's first lesson: "To take command, one must first create the illusion that command is already yours." All that waited now was the opportunity.

It was on the strength of her pride alone that she shook off her physical woes even as she shook herself free of her sodden cloak. She glanced up at the nobleman waiting patiently at her side. "Now, Sir Gilliam," she said, imperiously drawing herself up to the limit of her slight height.

"Come all ye folk to greet our new Lady Graistan." He had no need to shout, his deep voice thundered about the hall. He stepped away to bow before her. "Please enter this hall, my lady," he said. "As my brother's steward, I bid you well come to Graistan keep. Enter and take your ease within these walls."

Most of the servants knelt or bowed, but a few stood in studied nonchalance, refusing to acknowledge her. She stared pointedly at them. Beneath her cool gaze, all but one bent their knees in halfhearted greeting. Her eyes narrowed. That one was a stout man with a polished bare pate and a pompous carriage.

He met her gaze with a raised and scornful eyebrow. His fine, woolen tunic and studded belt shouted to all who viewed him of his high rank. A servant of rank this was, but a servant nonetheless. In his arrogance he had obviously forgotten this. She almost smiled. The Lord God had given her the opportunity; he would do most nicely as her first example.

"Your welcome is heartily appreciated," she called, raising her voice to be clearly heard, then crooked her finger at her chosen victim. "You there, come and take my cloak," she said.

Gilliam, startled by her unexpected command, turned to look. "That's our wardrober, Hugo," he blurted out, aghast that she would require the man who ruled Graistan's treasury to do such a menial chore.

"Thank you, Sir Gilliam," she said, accepting his information with a gracious nod, but ignored his unspoken plea to let the man alone. "Wardrober, my cloak must be cleaned before the morrow as I have a need for it then."

Hugo sneered down his narrow nose at her. "I am no woman to do your bidding. Find a laundress. I answer solely to Lord Rannulf. Cocking a shoulder and thrusting out his chest, he crossed his arms and shoved his hands into his wide, fur-trimmed sleeves.

"Do you now?" she smoothly replied. At the periphery of her vision she caught the lower servants' laughter. So, he was not well liked, all the better for her. "Upon my marriage to Lord Graistan, I became flesh of his flesh and bone of his bone. His servants, from the lowest stable lad to yourself, became mine at that moment. My lord husband has commanded me to do as I see fit in this keep. And I deem it fitting you should care for this cloak."

The man only sneered. "And if I refuse?"

"Then I will see to it that you have an inch or two of skin torn from your back this night." She uttered her words with such complete calm that it was a moment before it registered with those who heard her. Some of the folk tittered nervously; others, including Sir Gilliam, gasped.

"If need be," she said, softly, "I will do it myself." Her cloak hung from her outstretched hand.

Hugo tensed. For a moment as their gazes locked, it seemed he would refuse, but his courage was brief. She knew, and he became convinced, her threat was no bluff. Pomposity warred with humiliation as he grabbed the garment and stalked out of the hall.

Quiet laughter followed his departure. For the moment his arrogance was gone, but she knew better than to believe it would not be back. She held her hand up for silence. "Know you all," she called out, straining her aching throat, "that this is my way. While I will rarely ask you to perform duties not within the scope of your day-to-day tasks, I value highly and richly reward loyal service performed in a prompt and capable manner. Incompetent service or disrespectful behavior will bring swift punishment.

"Now, some have said that my punishments are

harsh, but no one has ever said that they were not justly due to those who received them. Woe to the one who must be told twice what is expected of him." She looked from face to face. "On this night, I expect only that someone prepare my lord's bed-chamber for me."

There was a bare second between her words and a flurry of action. The air was peppered with a number of "Yes, my lady's." Men and women hurried away either to do her bidding or to put a safe distance between themselves and her.

Well, it was a beginning. The servants were startled enough to obey for now. When their fright wore off, they would be accustomed to her. Pleased with what she'd accomplished, she looked up at Sir Gilliam.

He watched her with an expression of such horror that she frowned in puzzlement. "I did not take your bed, did I? I simply assumed that I would occupy my lord's bedchamber."

"Nay. Would you have?" His voice was strained and his blue eyes were now a hard gray.

"I beg your pardon?"

"Taken a whip to Hugo?"

She shrugged. "I have come here without my lord to force them into obedience to me. If I am to be lady in more than title alone, I dare not tolerate arrogance from anyone, no matter his rank. Yes, I would have taken a whip to him in full view of every other soul in this keep. What's more, every one of them would have respected me for it. His greeting was insolent and his behavior intolerable."

The young man started to respond, then glanced up at the balcony that fronted the overhanging second story. By now, judging from the number of female servants who had raced up the narrow stairs leading to this balcony, Rowena had guessed this was where the women's quarters and the master's bedchamber would lie.

There appeared along the balcony a woman attired in so rich a blue gown that it named her noble despite the absence of an overgown. Hair the color of the harvest moon was caught in a single plait and pulled over her shoulder. It was uncovered as though she'd been suddenly called away from preparing to retire.

"Gilliam, dearest boy, why did you not send for me when our guest arrived?" she chided, her voice as sultry as the lush curves displayed by her carefully fitted gown. "Ah, a woman. How exciting." As she descended, she lifted her gown ever so slightly to reveal soft leather shoes and delicate ankles. The dainty silver circles about her wrists jingled merrily when she moved.

The closer she came, the further Sir Gilliam's features disappeared beneath a mask of bitterness. Rowena lifted a brow in surprise. Now, she saw his resemblance to his brother; at least the hardness was not aimed at her. She turned to greet the woman only to stop short in surprise.

Eyes so pale they were nearly colorless met her gaze. They were made all the more startling by thick, dark lashes. Delicate color tinted her finely featured oval face and warmed her perfectly shaped lips. This woman was beauty personified.

But, as Rowena looked closer, she saw that fine lines touched the corners of her eyes and mouth. The youthful blush and the darkened eyelashes had been made so by some unnatural method she could not fathom. This woman was older than the score or so she had first appeared.

"Oh, it has been so long since I've had any visitors

of rank here. Gilliam, you must introduce us." Her voice was light and sweet as she lay a long-fingered hand on his arm.

The young knight jerked away from her touch as his face twisted into a black and mocking grin. "With pleasure. Lady Maeve"—he turned the honorific into a curse—"meet my brother's new wife." With that, he strode rudely away.

His announcement had been meant to shock, but this lady only smiled prettily at the noblewoman before her. "Good heavens, I thought the ceremony had been delayed. Could you possibly be the ancient nun with a warty nose and hairy chin that my brother was sworn to wed? But, you are neither ancient nor ugly, although I do see the touch of the convent in your face."

"I am Rowena, Lady Graistan," she responded stiffly. What did she mean she saw the convent in her face?

"Oh, now I've gone and set you all aprickle with my careless tongue. You must forgive me. Sometimes I am such a featherhead." Her husky laugh somehow made a falsehood of her words.

"My husband spoke of his brother, Sir Gilliam, but—"

A sigh of fond irritation interrupted her. "How like that creature to forget who butters his bread for him. But, he is a man, and you know how men are." Lady Maeve's airy wave stopped mid-gesture. "Ah, but you do not know, do you? You were to take your vows. Poor child, torn from your calling. How fortunate for you to have an experienced wife to teach you in the ways of this worldly vale." Kind words cloaked the challenge.

Lady Graistan's face was a mask of polite interest. Did this woman think to continue ruling the hall

against her new lady's right? If so, she had sadly
misjudged Graistan's folk, for in one night and by
one deed they were nearly Rowena's. Perhaps she
was just testing the newcomer's mettle. "My
thanks," she responded blandly, then could not resist an answering jibe. "But, from what I see here,
we shall both be scrubbing walls for weeks to
come."

As Maeve drew a surprised breath, Rowena
turned toward the female servant who had been
doing her best to catch her lady's eye. The maid
bobbed a quick curtsy. "My lady, Ilsa has sent me
to fetch you if you are ready to retire. Your chamber
is prepared. Shall I lead you there?"

"If you please," she replied in open relief. "Pardon
me, Lady Maeve, but I am tired to death. Perhaps
we can become better acquainted in the morning.
Let me bid you a good night."

"Oh, but I will come with you to the woman's
quarters. Here, let us go together." She reached out
to take her lady's arm, but Rowena quickly stepped
away.

"You mistake me. I am using my lord's chamber."

Only the hardness of this woman's eyes reflected
her growing irritation. "Please, sweetling, be careful
not to trespass here and step wrongly with your husband this early in your marriage. Rannulf does not
share his bedchamber; not even with his wife. Why,
even my sister, whom he loved as life itself, always
kept her place in the women's quarters."

Sister? So, this was not her husband's blood kin.
That shed a whole new light on the matter. "Be that
as it may, if my husband wishes me to sleep in the
women's quarters, he will tell me so. Now, I really
must bid you good evening." She turned and with-

out a single backward look followed the maid up
the stairs and along the passageway.

The serving woman threw open a door and
pointed through a tiny antechamber to the illumi-
nated room beyond it. "Through there, my lady. Old
Ilsa will be right along with your tray."

As Rowena started through the small room, her
stomach fell in disappointment. So rich a keep had
suggested an equally rich solar. Could this tiny
closet be it? Four steps took her into the lighted
chamber where she stopped short and gasped.

Several large chests sat in the far corner. Bossed
with shining metal bands, they were painted deep
green with wooden trim stained red and carved like
twining vines. Near them stood two well-cushioned
chairs, painted the same green color, and a small
table set with a single, flickering candle in a silver
holder. Only the bed seemed lacking, as it was neither large nor fine.

Even though the small fire on the hearth had only
recently been coaxed to life, the room was not cold.
She quickly saw why. Neither stick nor stone of the
walls showed, so completely were they covered with
hangings. The glorious reds and blues of these embroidered panels glowed in the firelight. While she
was no needlewoman, she recognized fine work
when she saw it. She started forward to examine
one piece more closely and nearly tripped.

Her muddy boot sank deep into a thick, brilliant
material patterned in an alien design. She stepped
off and frowned. Surely, so beautiful a thing was
not meant for such a degraded use. Some servant
had erred. Tiptoeing along the wall to avoid it, she
gingerly seated herself in one of the chairs. Every
muscle ached, strained as they were from her long

ride. It hurt even to bend over and pull off her boots and stockings.

Her toes bared, she glanced quickly at the door, sank her feet into the material on the floor, and smiled. It was as thick and soft as it was lovely. Fully enjoying the sensations, she unwound her heavy, woolen wimple and hung it over the back of her chair, then loosened her braid. With the comb from her purse, she smoothed away all the tangles.

When she looked up again there was a tiny, wizened woman staring curiously at her from the doorway, a tray of breads and cheeses in her hands. "Good even, my lady," she said in a brittle, old voice, then bowed with the stiffness of one whose bones had seen too many winters. "I am Ilsa. I would be most pleased to serve you if you've brought no maid of your own. I hope you will forgive Graistan its poor welcome." Words tumbled from her lips in rapid succession and whistled through toothless gaps in her gums as she stepped spryly into the room.

Her lady's upraised hand stopped her. "Is this thing meant to be walked on?" she asked, pointing to the floor.

"Oh, aye." The maid pulled the sodden wimple from the back of the chair and sharply snapped it into the air. Water droplets spattered into the hissing fire. "Infidel, it is," she said, hanging the headcloth on a peg by the door, "brought back from the Holy Lands. Lord Henry, that would be your lord's father, said such things were commonplace there."

Rowena concealed her yawn behind her hands. "I say give me a simple straw mat that I can walk on after I've been in the garden."

The old woman's laugh was a chicken's cackle. "Temric spoke rightly," she said cryptically as she turned down the bedclothes. "Will you eat this night?"

"I want nothing more than to crawl into yon bed and sleep for days." Another wide yawn interrupted her. She rubbed her face with her hands. "But, I must be up before dawn and I must bathe. The water will need to be very warm, for I am going to be very sore." She rose stiffly to her feet.

"Here, let me assist you." The maid was at her side in an instant, her thick fingers deftly loosening the overgown's lacing. Freed of both gowns and her chemise, Rowena staggered gratefully across the room and climbed into bed.

"Oh, my poor dear, these things are wet through and through," the old woman clucked in concern. "And what is this Temric tells me? You've nothing else until your cart arrives on the morrow? Well, these will just have to be cleaned tonight, then."

Suddenly, but only for a brief moment, Rowena wished she'd waited for the cart. A fine lady needed fine clothing. All she had was this worn, chestnut-colored traveling gown she'd borrowed from Ben-field. "Ilsa, I handed my cloak to the wardrober in the hall."

"Aye, so I and every other soul in the hall knows." She snorted in laughter. "You could not have chosen better than to hand it to that ass."

"Arrogance he does not lack," she said wryly, pulling the blankets up over her. "However, I must be certain that the chore I gave him is rightly done. It is truly a fine garment and will cover these things until my own gowns arrive."

The maid cocked her head and raised an eyebrow, looking for all the world like a bird considering a worm. "In this hall, one can be made to pay a price for usurping one's rank."

That shook the cobwebs from Rowena's head. She looked up, her gaze sharp and hard. "Ilsa, you cannot be punished for doing as I command by any save myself. Nor can anyone else."

The answering smile was wide with approval. "Then, I shall bid you good night, lady. The chamber pot is there, behind the bed curtain"—she pointed to the wall at the opposite side of the bed—"and if you have need of anything this night, call out. I will lay my pallet in the antechamber."

"Are the women's quarters so far?"

"A world away, my lady." She hurried out with her lady's gowns, closing the door behind her.

Rowena lay in the bed, savoring the soft mattress. Slowly her frozen limbs began to warm and relax. Her eyes closed, and she breathed deeply. There was something familiar about this bed, but she could not put her finger on what it was. Then, just as she drifted into sleep, she realized that the bedclothes smelled ever so faintly of her husband.

# Chapter Five

AT dawn, just as requested, Ilsa awakened her mistress and Rowena eased her sore muscles in a warm bath. When she at last toweled herself dry with a rough linen cloth, her clothes, cleaned and dry, lay across her newly made bed. She lifted her cloak to examine it. "Hugo?" she asked.

"There's a laundress with a bruised eye this morning" was the old woman's response.

"I see." She dressed with her usual care, but her new maid had a way of tightening the overgown's laces that made the old thing cling to her every curve. Afterward, she nervously submitted while her hair was combed and plaited. It was odd to have someone do this most intimate chore. When the last ebony strand was confined, a fine cloth was draped around her head and face. A thin gold band studded with gleaming blue stones held the wimple in place.

"There," Ilsa said with a satisfied breath. "'Tis good that I locked away some of my Ermina's belongings up here. When our fine Master Hugo gets his sticky fingers on things, they go into his chests and rarely come back out. Oh, see how the stones complement the color of your eyes."

Rowena could not recall the exact color of her eyes. The last time she'd given any thought to her image, she'd been a scrawny woman-child with eyes too big for her face and wild black hair that ever threatened to escape her demure wimple. But, as she took the polished metal mirror the old woman offered, she raised a finger to touch in disbelief this reflection.

Eyes of deep blue stared back at her from beneath thick, dark lashes. The sheer wimple and rich band made her ebony hair glow with hidden lights. Her smooth, pale skin brightened with a dismayed blush when she realized her vanity. "How quickly a dowdy nun can be corrupted," she murmured, handing back the mirror. "Best you take this thing before I begin to believe what I see."

She stood and brushed away her unease as she smoothed her gown. "Ilsa, I want to meet the ranking servants these next days. Must I use my bedchamber or the hall? Is there no solar?"

"There is a solar, lady, but it has been locked since Lady Isotte's death some five years ago."

Only Rowena's clasped hands gave away her rush of excitement. Surely the solar would match this room in luxury. Although she ached to see it now, it would have to wait until after mass. "Good. Our first chore after we break our fast shall be to open that room. We have not yet missed mass, have we?" She threw her cloak over her shoulders, then belted it until only a bit of her borrowed gown showed.

"You will attend mass, my lady?"

She stared at her maid from over her shoulder, astounded at the other's surprise. "But, of course." Everywhere, everyone attended mass each morning, did they not?

"Of course, my lady, of course." Ilsa's wrinkled cheeks creased in a contented smile as she preceded her mistress out of the room.

Access to the chapel lay directly off the hall. Accustomed to the larger abbey church, this small nave seemed narrower still because of the thick supporting pillars. Nor did it appear that the servants were required to attend, as only a few older folk stood waiting for the service to start. Well, that would change. As of the morrow, everyone would be present for the good of their souls.

Still, all was not poverty and disuse. Expensive candles in gilded branches revealed delicate carvings in the stonework. Dawn's light shone through the narrow window behind the altar and caught in the golden embroidery of a fine altar cloth. There was a strong similarity between this handiwork and the hangings in her bedchamber.

The castle's chaplain was stone-deaf with the fragile, bent look of the very old, yet he warmly greeted his new lady before moving to the altar. In a voice deep beyond his withered body and beautiful beyond his plain face, the old man sang out the service. She lost herself in the power and majesty of this familiar ritual. The soaring Latin phrases lent her their strength as they lifted her spirits. Once again, she felt connected and whole. As the last note died away into shivering silence, she knelt a moment longer, unwilling to give up her precious serenity. When she finally stood, she was at peace with the Lord God and ready for this day.

The few steps from chapel door to hall brought her soundly back to earth. The dirt and darkness was worse than she remembered. Narrow, defensive windows cast their hopeless slivers of light into the smoky dimness. Neither the smoldering torches nor the roaring blazes on the twin hearths could alleviate the skulking shadows. She stared in disgust at the dogs rooting through the rushes for scraps they most surely would find.

Breaking the fast at Graistan seemed a casual affair. Although the nuns at the abbey fasted through the morning meal, their servants had dined on warm vegetable potage, fresh breads, and both hard and curded cheeses. Here, there was only one table other than the lord's, and it was set with two small wheels of cheese and hard rolls. Nothing warm was offered nor would anyone be tempted to tarry when no place to sit was available.

Rowena frowned. Productivity was better gained with honey than vinegar. It was patently obvious that vinegar had not worked at all in this hall.

The Lady Maeve was already at the high table. Her rich mantle lay open to display a gown of rose red beneath an overgown of the palest blue trimmed in vair. Brilliant gems glittered at the woman's throat and wrists. Rowena grimaced in dismay, not wanting to waste time in polite conversation when there was so much to be done. But, there was no help for it. She crossed the room and chose a bench near, but not too near, the noblewoman.

"Good morrow, dear Rowena," Lady Maeve purred in greeting, using her lady's Christian name in unwarranted familiarity. "How well you look this morning. Last night your face was so pinched and pale, I felt sure you would fall ill. Where did you get that band? You must give me your jeweler's name. It is so lovely, but your costume hardly does it justice."

She leaned forward and added in a low voice, "Do not tell me you've nothing else to wear but that old thing. Nuns are not the ones to stress the importance of attire, so perhaps you do not know. Your position as lady here requires a finer dress than that."

"My thanks for your concern," Rowena replied with a smile as she used her eating knife to cut herself cheese and bread. After a single bite, she pushed it away. The cheese was salty and tough, and the bread tasted sour. She carefully tasted her watered wine. Vinegar. She set it aside. "Did I mishear you when you said your sister was wife to my husband?"

"Oh, how clever you are to remember that from last night," the woman replied ingenuously. "Aye, Isotte, God rest her soul, was wife to Rannulf. When my husband died nigh on two years ago, my stepchildren threw me from my only home and paid me only a pittance for my dower properties. I had no one to turn to save Rannulf. His undying love for Isotte led him to open his home to me. I have tried to repay him by acting as his housekeeper, but as you have shown me, I have done poorly at it." Her face was the picture of dismay as she glanced around. "It is such a large home, and there is so much to keep straight."

"Perhaps, if you had lifted a finger," Sir Gilliam growled, startling both women, "but that would have been too much for you. Good morrow, my lady," he said to Rowena as he seated himself at the far end of the table. He wore a rough, mud-stained tunic and heavy boots. His complexion was reddened, as though he'd already been outside for hours. "Your carts have arrived."

"Good news," she said with a smile, then decided not to hesitate. "Do you know of any reason I should not unlock the solar for my own use?"

Maeve's gasp was audible. "Surely Rannulf did not give you that freedom. Why, he never allowed me—" she stopped abruptly.

The young knight grinned malevolently at her, then he turned to his lady. "Since the room was built for my mother and Rannulf said you were to be treated as she was, you must open it. No doubt it is locked to keep those who should not use it from doing so." He shot a black look across the table at the fair-haired woman, but she only smiled sweetly in return. "Haven't you somewhere else to be?" he snapped.

"Not yet, sweetling," she replied, then with a studied, languid motion she stretched, displaying her lush curves beneath the tightly fitted gown. He grunted and looked away.

"Has Temric departed yet?" Rowena asked, glancing between the two of them.

He cut himself a slab of cheese and stuffed it in his mouth. "At daybreak," he replied, spewing crumbs across the table. He followed the cheese with an entire slice of bread and washed it down by drinking directly from a nearby pitcher. "Did you wish to send a message with him for my brother?" he asked, wiping his mouth on the back of his hand.

"Not particularly," she murmured, shocked at his boorish behavior. Lord Rannulf had used his manners to goad her, but at least he'd had them to use.

"Pig," Lady Maeve said mildly, although her eyes gleamed with a dangerous light. "Lack of manners will not drive me from this table. You will sorely rue the day you go too far."

He ignored her and kept his attention on his lady. "You look rested. I take it my brother's chambers suit you well." This was followed by a sly glance toward the other woman, as if he expected a reaction.

But she simply turned toward the Lady Graistan and added, "Yes, dear, is that bed not deliciously comfortable?"

"How would you know? You've never laid your

skinny backside on it." The angry words carried clearly about the room. His look was pure hatred.

"Are you certain of that or are you only hunting again?" she answered with a silvery laugh. "Best you be careful, I may someday tell you what you want to know. For now, I must go. The girdler in town has finished my new belt." She rose and walked with studied grace toward the stairway.

"Have a care and do not grow tired on your journey," Sir Gilliam called after her. "We would not want you to have to search out an empty bed so far from home."

Her beautiful features twisted in rage as she whirled to face him. Instantly, patience replaced the anger. "Oh, silly boy," she chided him, "you are such a tease." Her gay laughter followed her from the hall. As she disappeared up the stairs, the young knight sprang to his feet and strode angrily from the room without a word or glance at his new lady.

Rowena stared after them for a moment, then drew a deep breath. "Well," she said to herself, "welcome to Graistan keep." With that, she stood and glanced around the room for a place to start.

"You," she called to a young boy sweeping half-heartedly at the ashes in the hearth. The boy squeaked and cowered in fright behind his broom. "Call together the scullery lads." The boy did not move until she clapped her hands and said, softly, "Now." He instantly leapt to his task.

"You," she motioned to a woman, "see that the boys clean these tables." Then, fearing the meaning of the word *clean* would be misunderstood, she amended her command. "I mean scrubbed until they are naught but smooth wood. The rest of you, remove these filthy rushes and burn them. But, before you lay others, this floor is to be washed, twice. Is there a pantler?"

"Here, my lady," a man stepped forward.

"The bread tastes sour. Your flour is bad."

"But, my lady"—the man practically groveled—"that is all we have. I can do no better."

Rowena rolled her eyes. "I was not accusing, so do not waste my time with excuses. For now I want you to look to the stairs outside yon door. If there is ice on them, sprinkle them with salt. And you"—she pointed to another man—"tell the stable master that I want straw spread throughout the courtyard before this hour closes. Ilsa"—she gestured to her maid who waited nearby for her—"gather the women you need and meet me in my chambers." She turned and ascended the staircase, satisfied by the swift reactions to her commands.

The women presented themselves to her in the passageway, then she looked to Ilsa. "And the solar is—?" She raised her hands in question.

"This way, my lady." The old woman entered her master's bedchamber and crossed to the hearth wall. There she lifted a heavily embroidered panel to reveal a door. "When I first came here with my Ermina, she was Lord Gilliam's mother, there was no door here. It was all one room with the women's quarters."

The cloth slipped from her hands, burying the woman in its dusty folds. She pushed back the hanging again then threw her meager weight at the door. It didn't move. "In those days they used only curtains to separate the sleeping area from the solar and solar from the women's quarters. Lord Henry built these walls to make Ermina her own, private chamber."

"Is there no other way in?"

"There is, but it has been locked from the inside."

Rowena stepped forward and yanked the hanging from the wall, raising a cloud of dust. Her hands were now streaked with dirt. Perhaps she would be glad she wore nothing finer before the day was done.

Ilsa looked down at the dust pile then back at her lady. "You will have quite a task with this keep."

"So I've noticed, but I am equal to it." She brushed off her hands and tried the latch. "It's not locked, only caught. Push with me." They threw themselves against the door. With a splintering creak, it swung open. Rowena stepped within and gasped in pleasure.

Although the air was cold and musty, dust motes danced along a row of windows where the newborn day pried through the shutters. She stepped quickly to the wall and threw back the wooden panels, then turned a slow studious circle to memorize every detail while hardly daring to believe what she saw.

The jeweled tints on the walls glowed to life in this little bit of winter-weakened light. From the pleasant herringbone pattern in the stonework above the hearth to the small chairs pushed to one side, this was a room meant to please a beloved wife not confine a woman. A quick brush of her hand through the layer of dust and cobwebs on the wall revealed an elaborate crisscross pattern painted in reds and greens on the plastered wall. From each cross a bluebird darted upward, as if startled.

"It is so beautiful," she finally breathed. "Why should a room such as this be neglected? Such a treasure should not be so abused."

Ilsa shrugged. "Lord Rannulf's second wife, Lady Isotte, said the windows let in evil humors so she sickened each time she entered. Methinks the sickness was within herself." This was a quiet underbreath. "So, it had little use during her short reign here. After her death, Lord Rannulf left only my lady's things in the room and ordered it locked." The old woman crossed the room to open the far door, then smiled at a serving woman's startled gaze. "Here are the woman's quarters."

Rowena opened the door opposite the windows. Maeve stopped short in the passageway with a cry of feigned surprise. "Oh, my," she gasped, "you startled me." She stepped inside and peered curiously around. All the serving women, including Ilsa, backed away from her, but she did not seem to notice.

The Lady Graistan ignored the noblewoman as she addressed her maids. "I want to use this room yet today, so your cleaning must be both thorough and swift. Take care you do not leave even a single strand of spider silk for me to find. Move the long table over there and set these two chairs before the hearth." She pointed at the moth-chewed cushions lying on their seats. "Can you replace those?"

"We will find you something," said Ilsa, already brushing dust from the table. "And you will have the room before midday."

"So be it," her lady said with satisfaction. "Oh, waiting in the carts below is a bed. I want it set up in my chamber since it is the finer piece. Store that one." She pointed to her husband's bed.

"But that was Rannulf's mother's." Maeve's silky voice brought all attention back to her. "Why, how often he has shared with me the story of that bed." She looked through the door into the chamber beyond it. "I have often admired its beauty."

Rowena stared hard at the woman with her painted face. It would hardly surprise her to learn her husband had slept with the sultry bitch despite the threat of incest. But, if the creature thought that gave her some claim here, she was greatly mistaken. "Since you have admired the bed, perhaps we could give it to you so you may have the use of it."

The serving women tittered their amusement, but the comment did not give Lady Maeve even an instant's pause. "Why thank you for offering, sister, but there is hardly room for it in the women's quarters."

"Well, then, it must be stored. Oh, and by the by, does your offer of assistance still stand? There is so much to do this day." She waited, knowing full well what the answer would be.

"How I would like to," the noblewoman replied with a sigh that was meant to convey consternation, "But I did promise the girdler I would be at his shop this morn. Perhaps when I return?" She let the question hang in the air while she nodded her farewell and left the room.

Rowena's laugh was short and hard, then she turned to the women. "Now, since you know what you must achieve, I am off to the kitchen to see what I can do with the food in this place." She retreated to her bedchamber and removed her cloak. Practicality won over image; it was going to be a long, dirty day and was much better faced in something she did not mind ruining. As she made her way slowly from her bedchamber to the hall, she cataloged in her mind the chores to be done and who would do them. How odd that the removal of a single bed could make her feel as if this place was home.

Hours later found her at the foot of the steep, twisting stairs in the keep's northwest corner. Far above her on the tower's third floor lay a tiny wall chamber and her destination. She hesitated.

It made no sense. If Rannulf so prized his bastard son, why did he keep the poor child trapped in this room away from hearth and kitchen? Well, no longer. A man-child, even an illegitimate one, was the promise of the future and needed to be carefully guarded.

She glanced down at herself and wiped dirt-streaked hands on her skirt. The filth of Graistan was horrendous, and it seemed as if most of it now coated her. After the noon meal, she'd donned a servant's rough overgown to protect her clothes. She could hardly wait to be out of them and soaking in a tub of warm water. Well, as soon as this chore was finished, so was her day.

With a tired sigh, she started climbing. Her mind wandered to tomorrow's chores as she began organizing them by their importance. The darkness in the stairwell was almost complete except where the orange sunset exploded through the two west facing arrow slits. She heard nothing until he flew into her.

For one breathless moment, she teetered backward. Smooth stone wall offered no handhold for her clawing fingers. With a desperate lurch, she regained her balance. Heart pounding, she leaned against the wall, her fingers shaking with the knowledge of how close she came to falling.

"I did not see you," whispered her assailant as his small hand touched hers. "Did I hurt you?"

She breathed deep to steady her nerves. "Nay, by the grace of the Lord God. What of you?"

"Nay."

"Has no one ever told you not to run on these

stairs? We could both have been killed." Her voice was harsh with fear.

His trembled briefly. "I am sorry," then, as if suddenly remembering, he continued more strongly, "and you may not speak so to me. Alais says all the maidservants must speak to me with respect. You have not been respectful."

How old had they said he was? Five? Surely no more than that. Rowena snorted in indignation. "I do not need to be respectful to little lordlings who endanger my life. I should take you over my knee and show you how much I respect you with the palm of my hand. Come, better that I return you to your Alais and tell her what you've done."

The tremble was back. "No, please, I am sorry I was mean. Do not take me back. I am running away."

She stared hard into the dark, trying to better see his features. "Running away? But, where to and why?"

"To the kitchen. I am so hungry, but Alias says we cannot have anything to eat until after nightfall when the new lady will be abed." The boy gave a small sob. "Why did my papa have to get a wife? Now Alais says we must hide from the dragon while my papa is gone."

Her eyebrows shot up in surprise. "Dragon?"

"That is what Alais calls the new lady because she will send me away to be a beggar if she finds me."

"A beggar? Nay, you are mistaken." Had she unknowingly said something that had been taken as a threat toward the boy?

There was a long pause. "Do you think so?"

"Oh, of that I am quite certain. You will never be a beggar. Someday, you will be the lord of Blacklea."

"But," he said, the tremble gone again from his voice, "Alais said."

"Alais is wrong," she retorted.

"Jordan," called a woman from above them. Her voice was at once angry and worried. "Jordan!" Slow, plodding footsteps followed.

"Oh, no," Jordan whispered, grabbing her hand. "Do not let her take me back there. I hate that room. I want my own bed. My papa will reward you if you take care of me," he generously offered. Eager fingers tightened around her palm.

"I can help you more than you think, but only if you do not act like a coward and run away."

"I do not want to be a coward," he said, "I want to eat."

Rowena laughed out loud. "Jordan is here," she called upward. "We are coming up."

The footsteps stopped. "Who is there?" The woman's voice was harsh and accusing.

"Only a dragon," she replied. There was a loud gasp, the footsteps hurried back up the stairs. She clasped the boy's hand in hers. "Come with me."

They climbed a few stairs before Jordan spoke. "Why did you tell Alais you were a dragon?"

She paused beneath the second arrow loop. The dusky glow of the setting sun burnished the boy's hair with the same auburn lights she'd seen in his father's. Still holding his hand, she studied him, then shook her head in wonder.

Jordan was his father's very image. His eyes were the same, clear gray; his mouth had the same bend. No wonder Lord Rannulf had claimed him as his own; he could not deny him.

"Why," he demanded, then his eyes narrowed. "I have not seen you before. Are you a servant to the new lady?"

"Worse," Rowena said with a smile. "I am the new lady herself."

His eyes widened, then he smiled as if they were sharing a jest. She caught her breath. It was her husband grinning at her irate protests of innocence. "You like lads, I can tell. You will help me with Alais." He tugged at her hand as he hurried them up the stairs.

A few more turns and they entered a small chamber. The room was cold and damp, cut as it was from the very thickness of the walls. Two straw mats lay on the floor with only a few, thin blankets to make them into beds. A small horse carved from wood lay on its side in one corner, while scattered in another were tiny, wooden men from a chess set. And then there was Alais.

She was seated on a stool, her massive thighs pouring over the edges. Fine, light hair straggled from beneath her stained and untidy wimple. The plain gown she wore was patched and stained. This slovenly creature was hardly the sort Rowena would have expected as a nobleman's nurse.

"Look, Alais," Jordan called, "I have found the new lady, and you were wrong. She likes lads. Now we can go back down; we can eat." His enthusiasm made him jump. "Tell her we can eat," he said to his stepmother.

"I cannot tell her anything until you have properly introduced me to your nurse, Jordan," she chided gently. "You must ask me my name, then you must tell it to your nurse so that she may know it. Someday, you will be a knight, and a knight is always careful to observe proprieties, even where servants are concerned."

The woman frowned at this, her beefy arms

crossed over her pendulous breasts. It was obvious she did not consider herself a servant.

"I am Jordan FitzRannulf," he replied with a half attempted bow toward the newcomer. "What is your name?"

She was pleased to see someone had tried to teach him manners. "I am the Lady Rowena of Graistan and your new stepmother. It is very nice to have you in my family. Now, you must introduce me to Alais," she prompted.

Jordan nodded, then tightened his mouth in concentration. "Alais, I have brought the Lady Rennena—Ronnena." He whirled back to his stepmother and whispered, "What is it?"

She laughed. "It is an English name, and some find it hard to say. Those whose tongues will not do it often call me 'Wren.' So may you, if you like."

He sighed in relief. "Alais, here is the Lady Wren. Now, we can go eat." He grabbed at his nurse's hand, as if he by his tiny size could lift the huge woman.

"Alais," Rowena said, all the warmth gone from her voice, "immediately return Jordan's belongings to the women's quarters. Come, lad, I will find you something to eat." She held out a hand to the boy. "Your nurse has work to occupy her just now."

The heavy woman leapt up with surprising quickness from her stool. "Be gone with you," she cried out, snatching at the boy and missing. "He is in my charge until Lord Rannulf returns. Do not interfere. The Lady Maeve has told me of your ilk and vowed to help me protect him from you."

Rowena's eyes narrowed. "Is this your protection I see here? Hardly protection; instead, I say you have threatened this boy's well-being. I find you incompetent in your position and hereby relieve you of it. Run to Lady Maeve, if you wish, but she'll be no help to you. Now, go find your living elsewhere."

Alais screeched out her denial, tears bursting from her eyes. "Do not take my baby from me," she sobbed. "Nay, you cannot force me to leave him. He needs me!"

Jordan stared between the two of them. "Alais must leave?" he asked quietly.

His stepmother nodded. "She was far too careless with you."

"But, who will care for me while Papa is gone?" His eyes were wide with fear.

"I will," she replied firmly. "Do you know Ilsa, my maid?" When he nodded she continued, "She will help."

"But, what if I need to see Alais?" There were tears filling his eyes now.

"Do you need her?" Rowena asked with a sigh.

"Oh, aye, she is my Alais," the boy replied.

The Lady Graistan turned to the massive woman. "For his sake, you stay. However, from this day forward anything you do with him will be by my command. Disobey, and you will go."

"Thank you, my lady," she sniveled. "Thank you."

"Alais will stay with you because you love her." She held out her hand, and Jordan took it without hesitation. The warmth of his fingers in hers made her smile. "Now, boy, shall we find you something to eat?"

"To eat, to eat, to eat," he sang happily as he bounced alongside her out the door and down the stairs.

It was well past Compline when Rowena finally crawled beneath the bedclothes. While Graistan had yet to offer up its secrets, she already knew something was very wrong here. True, not so long ago,

every castle, abbey, and town had been stripped
virtually bare to ransom England's King Richard
from the German emperor. That still couldn't explain why this keep lacked enough in store to withstand even the briefest siege. And, what little was
there was of the poorest quality. For now she would
buy what she needed from local merchants with a
promise to pay when Lord Rannulf returned. That
would give her the time to learn more about Graistan's resources before she reviewed the accounts
kept by Hugo Wardrober.

With a yawn, she slipped down beneath the bedclothes. A smile quirked at her lips as she touched
her bedpost. How odd that two days ago she had
despised this bed. Now, it marked this room as hers,
shared with no other, just as the rest of Graistan
would be hers after she was finished. She would
put her mark on it all. She dropped quickly into a
contented slumber.

# Chapter Six

RANNULF sighed and paused in checking the links of his mail hauberk. He'd not had a squire with him in two years and had become accustomed to doing this chore for himself. Outside his tent door a steady drizzle fell as it had for the past two days. The rain had temporarily stilled the terrible noise of the siege engines and sent men to gather quietly around their fires or in their tents. For the time being the world was once again a peaceful place filled with the contentment of a newly awakened spring.

He held his hands above the glowing coals in the brazier's flat pan before returning to his task. Stretching awoke the tiny creatures that had taken up residence on his body. His skin crawled with their movements.

He was tired; tired of his tent, tired of being filthy, and, most of all, tired of pitting men and machines against unyielding walls. The siege had been under way for nearly a month without any success. However, news was that Richard had departed the Low Countries for England. With the king once again in his realm, Nottingham keep would have no choice but surrender.

"My lord, may we enter?" asked Temric from the door.

When he looked up, he all too quickly recognized the mud-bespeckled man behind his master-at-arms. "God's teeth, what now?" An irritated gesture of invitation brought both men into the tent.

With a cockeyed grin and an abbreviated bow, the messenger from Graistan stepped forward and handed his lord the leather wallet he carried. "In that lies a message from Master Hugo and one from your lady. There is also a message to you from Lord Gilliam. He says: 'I hope you are tolerably well but know you cannot be happy without your bathtub. Your lady is doing a fine job, but she raised Hugo's ire when she set me to gathering information from your bailiffs. We have discovered there should be more supplies within Graistan than there presently are, and we cannot yet account for the lack. As to her request of you, I can only say that I find her to be levelheaded and having the greatest care for those things that are yours.' That be all, lord."

Lord Graistan rubbed a hand against his unshaven chin and considered his brother's words. Aye, she was doing a fine job driving his wardrober mad with her changes. "Tell me, Boudewyn, how do you find Graistan keep?"

"All seems well to me, my lord. For myself, food's better than it's been in a long while."

Temric gave a short, harsh laugh. "Then, you'll be less pleased with what you'll find in yon pot, but go eat your fill. I'll call if there's to be a return message."

The messenger gave a jaunty salute and went to join the ring of men sitting about a fire just outside his lord's tent while Rannulf waved his man to a stool at the other side of the brazier. "Stay a moment. I have need of your strength to face yet another of my esteemed wardrober's harangues. Temric, what is she doing to my home?"

His master-at-arms only grinned wolfishly. "Cleaning house, no doubt."

"Cleaning or destroying?" his lord retorted, and opened the leather packet. He chose the folded parchment marked with Hugo's seal and read aloud, " 'Greetings to my most feared lord from your humble servant on this the eleventh day of March, Year of Our Lord eleven hundred ninety four. Your new lady, may the Lord God bless your union, is most adept and conscientious in the direction of the menial servants. I seek to keep you abreast of her doings in the case that you wish to lend your guidance and wisdom in her efforts. You must also know when she extends herself beyond her ability.

" 'Just this day I have learned that over the last week your lady, may the Lord God preserve her, has had Lord Gilliam promise in your name payment to merchants within town for purchases beyond the present means of this keep. These expenditures have been made without my approval or foreknowledge.

" 'I did then beg to explain to her why such purchases could not be made without consultation. Rather than comprehending, she requested that I show her the account book.' "

Rannulf leaned back with a laugh and glanced up. "Can you imagine the look on his face?" he said, then continued reading. " 'It is aberration enough that she reads and writes. Do not allow her to insult the Lord God by letting her meddle with what is a man's work. For a score and ten years I have been your family's faithful servant and you have come to know me as a careful man with your best interest always in my heart and mind. Never have you or your father before you felt it necessary to question my ability to keep the accounts for Graistan.

" 'I most humbly await your decision as regards this matter. Your devoted servant, Hugo, son of Walter, wardrober to Rannulf FitzHenry, Lord Graistan.' "

The same Lord Graistan picked up the other message. The wax was blank as she had neither access to his seal nor the time to have had her own made. He briefly held his knife's blade over the brazier. The warm steel slipped easily beneath the wax. This simple motion rekindled the haunting memory of how their bodies had melded that night.

He flushed with a sudden heat. Like it was yester-even, not over a month ago, he recalled the sweetness of her as she lay beneath him. His fingers curled as though he were once again holding the womanly fullness of her breasts. A tremor shot through him at the memory of her soft touch on his nape. Then, he remembered the deep hurt in her eyes when he had drawn away. His knife slipped from his fingers.

"Rannulf?"

"I am a fool, brother," he said, turning to look at his elder, if bastard, sibling. "I should never have married again."

"So you have said," Temric replied gently, then paused. "She is a good woman."

"You know this by virtue of a single ride with her?" His sarcasm was biting.

"Just as you know it from your ride with her."

He jerked as though struck. "Damn," he whispered. As usual, his brother went straight to the heart of the matter with unerring truth. Silence lay heavily between them for a moment, then he spoke. "Temric, do not leave me, I need you. What is it your mother offers now that I have not offered to you these past years?"

His brother's laugh was rich with irony. "Certainly none of the heartache and work that would come with the lands you keep trying to force on me. And, I'd have barely settled in before you'd be finding me a wife as well. Who knows," he said with a shrug, "perhaps I will find my mother's life is not to my taste and be back begging at your door once again."

"Think on it. Those lands are in Normandy. You could start afresh there, if you wish your past to be unknown to your neighbors."

"No, Rannulf. My response to your offer has not changed in seventeen years. Leave it be."

"I cannot. You are no merchant, you were trained as a knight, just as I was. Our father meant that you should have those lands, just as he meant for Gilliam to have an inheritance."

"You put words in the mouth of a dead man."

"So, he is dead; I am not. Why should you not accept what I offer?"

Angry golden lights exploded to life in his brother's eyes, smothering their usual placid brown color. "If our father wanted me to be more than his unrecognized bastard son, he would have remembered me." He leapt to his feet and stormed out of the tent.

Rannulf stared at the fold of parchment in his hands. As much as he needed Temric, he could no more force his brother into acceptance than he could ease the hurt he'd done to his wife that night. At last, he opened the missive and began to read:

" 'My most feared lord and husband, I, with a heart full of trepidation, do recommend myself to you on this the eleventh day of March in the Year of Our Lord, eleven hundred ninety-four. In this

last month I have been most busily occupied coming
to know Graistan. Your folk have been helpful in all
ways with this task of mine. It is our hope that you
will be pleased to see what has been accomplished
when by the grace of our Dear Lord you return to
us.

" 'Early in my residence here, I didst become
aware of shortages in our foodstuffs. To that end I
have asked Sir Gilliam to purchase from local merchants what is needed.' "

He skimmed her list of purchases and their costs.
The supplies were mundane, the prices average.
What stunned him was that these items were not
presently on hand within the keep.

He frowned. Could Hugo's hysterical letters be
an attempt to hide wrongdoing on his part, not his
usual pompous jealousy? While this seemed impossible in one so loyal, what harm could come from
a new eye on his work? Was his wife capable of
such a task?

He looked back down at her letter. Her script
was small, neatly formed, and without flourish or
embellishment. The purchases were itemized, all
weights and costs were carefully noted. She'd certainly had some schooling in keeping accounts.

" 'When I did question Sir Gilliam with regards
to this situation, I was informed that he had been
your steward only a short time and knew of no reason for shortages. He didst then visit your many
holdings to gain an understanding of their contribu-
tions of this past year so a true accounting could
be made. At the same time he has asked your bailiffs
to speculate on the size of your portion in this coming harvest since the planting has far enough advanced to make such a projection possible.' "

How odd. In Gilliam's message, he'd said she'd

sent him out to gather the information. Her words made it sound as though it had been the boy's idea. Was she being kind or self-effacing?

" 'I do most humbly petition you to allow me access to your treasury to make these accountings. If you doubt my ability, I am capable to the task as my dear lady abbess did ask me to work with her cellaress, and I found in those tasks great satisfaction. We here at Graistan all wish you well in your endeavor and pray that you may return as soon as the Lord God will allow. Your most dutiful servant and wife, Rowena, Lady Graistan.' "

His eyes caught and held on the word *dutiful*. She used the word to mock him, to remind him of how he'd rejected her. His fingers dug into the sheepskin; his stomach churned angrily at her audacity. But she'd written on beneath her signature.

" 'I must recommend Sir Gilliam to you for all his help and assistance regarding my concerns. He has been forthcoming with all that I have needed and most anxious to make certain that those things that belong to you are well tended and secure. Although there has been little threat here to require his strong arm, what challenges he has faced have been swiftly resolved in our favor. Also, your bailiffs send word that his judgments are well received.' "

Rage blazed to life in his heart. Her economical words did not hide the thrust of her meaning. She taunted him by pretending she loved his brother in revenge for his treatment of her on their wedding night. He shoved the letter into the brazier. It exploded into stinking flame.

It took three wineskins and a week's time to wash away the taste of her words. When he had recovered enough to write his response, he wrote to Gilliam and sent Temric with it to be his eyes and ears at Graistan.

By the last week of March the keep and its confines were completely cleaned and refurbished. Even the stables and barns were scrubbed, rethatched, and whitewashed. The storerooms, once barren, had been swept clean and were being refilled with newly purchased foodstuffs.

A rare afternoon sun streamed into the solar, warming the room and bringing the painted birds into vibrant life. Rowena watched the courtyard while she waited for Hugo Wardrober to appear. Chickens scratched and pecked near the stables while a gaggle of geese waddled out the inner gate and toward better pickings in the bailey. With growing irritation, she turned back toward the room. A half an hour had passed since she'd sent for him.

Sir Gilliam and Temric were engrossed in their discussion of the siege of Nottingham. Her brother by marriage sprawled in one of her small chairs, his long legs stretched out before him. His favorite alaunt bitch lay curled at his feet, her tail thumping the floor in the pleasure of being near her master. Her husband's master-at-arms stood stiffly at the hearth, still wearing his hauberk, cloak, and boots as though he did not intend to stay long.

"My lady, did you call for me?" In his finest robe and studded belt, Hugo posed arrogantly at the door to her solar. His features were pulled into an impatient sneer, his bald pate held high, his attitude leaving no doubt that he'd delayed his arrival as long as possible. He glanced around the room and saw Temric. "Ah, so you have received the reply to your request."

"Come within," she said flatly and, without waiting to see whether he did so or not, seated herself opposite the young knight.

The master-at-arms produced a single, folded sheet of parchment. "This message is directed by my lord to his steward—"

"Ha, he does not even address the message to you," the wardrober interrupted.

"Enough." The steel in Sir Gilliam's voice instantly silenced the man.

"However," the soldier then continued, "he suggests that the first portion of the letter, which deals with your requests to him be read in the presence of Hugo Wardrober so no misunderstandings might be had. The second portion is a private message to Sir Gilliam." He handed the sealed parchment to Gilliam, then retreated to stand behind the young man's chair, his expression closed as always.

"Here, you read it." Graistan's illiterate steward handed the missive to her. She had yet to understand why her husband would give a job that demanded education to a man that could neither read nor write. The young knight would be far better employed as the castellan of some small keep.

She took it, smoothed open the parchment, and read: " 'To my brother and steward, Gilliam Fitz-Henry, greetings:' " The large, clear script was easy to follow even though it curved downward along the page. Had he written it or was this a clerk's doing? " 'It is my hope that this message finds you in good health as yours found me. It has come to my attention that my lady has spoken in my name to local merchants in order to purchase supplies for our keep. I am loath to believe as some would have me that you allowed her such excess without need. If you deem these purchases to be sensible, then she is to be indulged.

" 'If my lady wife desires to review the accounts, so be it. To that end, I command my master of the wardrobe to give his lady free access to the accounts.' "

Hugo gasped. "Nay, you have read that to your own advantage." He grabbed the parchment from her fingers and scanned the words. "Nay, my lord, you cannot!" he cried out in protest, as if his lord sat in the room rather than far away to the north of them. Then, realizing the futility of what he did, he shoved the letter back at his lady. "Never," he spat out, fair stuttering over the word, "have either Lord Henry or Lord Rannulf questioned my work. Now, you, a mere woman—"

"Nonetheless, Hugo"—Gilliam's growl interrupted him—"you have heard my brother's command."

Still sputtering in indignation, he glared at them all. "I do this because he commands me to, and I will do it only under certain conditions. Only in my presence may you enter the treasury so I can see you do not mulilate my many years of work. I'll have no ink stains or ragged corners torn away by your clumsiness. Nor will you be allowed to alter any figure or make any notations. The only hand that writes within those books is mine." He turned on his heel and stormed out of the room, muttering the world must surely be coming to an end when a husband let his wife into his accounts.

The young knight laughed at his receding back, the sound short and surprised. "I never knew the man had so much passion. Is there more to the letter?"

"Aye." She opened it further and continued reading. " 'The siege here proceeds as we had expected. Nottingham is as strong a keep as any in England. Machines have come from Leicester and Windsor and men from every reach in realm. Despite this, we still sit and wait, unable to crack the nut and rid it of its poisoned meat.

" 'Our king, may God preserve him, has returned to our shores. It is hoped that he will soon be at Nottingham to bring this action to its rightful end. Both Marlborough and Lancaster have fallen. It is said that the constable of St. Michael's Mount died of fright when he learned his monarch had arrived. Neither Tickhill nor Nottingham are so easily taken.

" 'I hope my marriage has not been too great a burden to you. Please forgive me the surprise of sending such a vixen' "—She stopped, her face red—"Perhaps you would rather read this for yourself." She started to hand it to him.

He waved her off. "Read it? Not I. You know I've got no knack for it; my eyes cross just looking at the thing. Finish the letter, my lady." His eyes were not crossed; instead they gleamed in impish amusement. She cleared her throat.

"Ah—" She hesitated, her eyes scanning over her husband's complaints at being forced into marriage to a shrew. "I cannot quite make out the words, the ink's been blotted," she said, her face still bright red. "He finishes with 'Your brother and lord, Rannulf FitzHenry, Lord Graistan.' "

She laid the parchment on the table and stared hard at Gilliam. His smile told her he didn't believe her. Her gaze shifted to Temric, the bearer of this missive. As always, his features were as if carved from stone.

"And you, Temric, how do you fare?"

"Me, my lady?" Her question sent his eyebrows near to his hairline.

The younger man laughed. "His face will crack if he talks."

He growled something beneath his breath and shot the knight a pointed look. "I am well, my lady, thank you for your concern. You have accomplished a miracle here. The smell from the cooking shed is remarkable on its own. And I cannot recall ever seeing the hall so clean."

Gilliam sat bolt upright. "Amazing! A veritable waterfall of words!"

"Bah," the older man spat out, "your infernal silliness no longer becomes you, boy. I warned Rannulf that making you steward was a waste; that you would never grow up."

"Have I erred?" The knight leapt to his feet, his skin flushing with the reproof. "Has Rannulf seen fit to chastise me? Ask our lady, since you seem to prize her so highly. She knows I did not shirk in the task she set me about. Neither has my sword been idle. There are a dozen thieves who will no longer harass our holdings this year."

The commoner held up his hands in submission. "Enough! My apologies, brother. I spoke out of turn. In all truth, I have no idea what or how well you do here, and I told Rannulf I did not want to know. It is your humor; it always rubs me the wrong way. I apologize both to you and our lady." He bowed toward her, then turned on his heel and strode out of the solar, leaving Rowena gaping after him.

"Did he call you brother?" she asked, unable to believe what she'd heard.

"Aye," Gilliam ground out bitterly, still staring at the door as if he could yet see his elder sibling. "Aye, he's my brother, born to the left side of the blanket." He turned to her, his eyes clouded with pain. "I did not realize how hard it was to come home again. Of the two, I do not know which is worse, Temric with his idea that a single mistake forever damns a man, or Rannulf, who patiently forgives but cannot forget." His voice was harsh and deep with sadness. "Is it not enough for them that I hate myself?"

Before she could say a word, he was gone. She stared after him, then rose. Gilliam's bitch came to her feet and stretched, her narrow tail waving back and forth in lazy invitation. Rowena accepted and scratched the dog's ear until it groaned in appreciation. "I do not find my husband so forgiving," she told the creature. The dog gave her a lolling grin, then padded out to find her master.

# Chapter Seven

ROWENA perched atop the tall stool at Hugo's desk in the treasury. From the slitted window high above her a single shaft of rain-dimmed daylight did little to illuminate the raised table on which she worked. Here, safe within this tiny, narrow room cut from the very walls of the keep, lay the wealth of Graistan. There were trunks filled with cloth and furs, caskets of coins and jewels, as well as the far more valuable agreements between Lord Graistan and his tenants and vassals.

"Four pence for a barrel of eels from Alfred Fishmonger," she murmured softly, squinting in the tallow lamp's meager light as she retallied last year's consumption to verify her findings. Her pen scratched against the parchment scrap she used to figure her amounts. Although she dared not yet sigh and close the book, her task was finally completed.

"I will be back," Hugo announced from his seat on a chest. This was his daily visit to the garderobe.

She muttered her assent, but did not look up until he'd shut the door behind him. Only then did she leap to her feet, pile the parchment leaves into a neat stack, and tie them with their cord. He would be gone at least long enough for her to safeguard these and find Sir Gilliam. Quickly, she hid Graistan's accountings beneath yards of maroon woolen cloth in a chest, locked it shut, and took the key.

His arrogance was unbelievable. More amazing than the missing coin and stolen supplies was the man's thorough documentation of his deeds. Why create a record of his thievery? It made no sense. And, why, when he'd been challenged, did he not expunge the record? Nay, the truth must be he did not believe she had the skill to see what he'd done. In that, he had grossly underestimated her.

She slipped the key onto the ring that hung from her belt, set the cover onto the brazier to douse the flame, then shut and locked the door behind her. Two quick strides and she'd left the pantlery for the hall.

"Will," she called, "find Sir Gilliam and tell him his lady would like a word with him in her solar. He was to be in the stables this afternoon."

"Aye, lady," the servant replied smartly and hurried to his task. She smiled after him, pleased by his prompt obedience. So much had changed since her arrival six weeks ago.

"I heard you call for Gilliam, dear. May I be of help?"

Rowena whirled around to find Maeve sitting near one of the hearths with her needlework in her lap. What in God's name was she doing here? The woman usually rode out all afternoon with her falcon at her wrist.

"You must be finished for the day. Oh, my, what an undertaking this is for you. I am truly amazed at your desire to try your hand at it. So, how do you fare?" She set aside her handiwork and came gracefully to her feet. There was an odd menace in the way she held her body.

Rowena hid her astonishment at the question by

studying her stained fingertips. Then, suddenly, she
knew without question where Graistan's riches had
gone and who had benefited. She cloaked her excitement behind a mask of serenity as she studied
the other woman.

Those odd, colorless eyes revealed nothing; neither did the finely drawn mouth now held in a sweet
smile. The noblewoman lifted a perfectly arched
brow and patted nonexistent stray hairs into place
beneath her indecently sheer wimple. When the
Lady Graistan did not reply, she waved toward
Hugo's domain. "I do not think the wardrober
wishes to leave his room open and unattended.
Should you not wait for his return so he might lock
the door?"

There was no care for Graistan or its wardrober
in these words; rather it was an effort to carefully
guard her own source of wealth. "I've not left it
open," Rowena replied quietly, and waited for the
woman's response.

"You have a key to the treasury?" Maeve's question was harsh and shocked. Then, trying to amend
her error, she said in a lighter voice, "I cannot believe our jealous wardrobe master gave you the key.
That is hardly like him. I do not think even Rannulf
has a key to that room, and I am most certain Gilliam does not."

"I had the locksmith make me one," Rowena said,
fighting to keep the triumph from her voice. "I will
not be locked out of any room in my hall."

Hugo flew up the length of the hall, his dark
robe's wide sleeves flapping around his scrawny
wrists. "You have a key to my room?" he cawed,
looking and sounding for all the world like a giant
crow.

"Aye, that I do," she said, as if it were nothing

remarkable. "I am done for today and have put everything away."

He shoved her aside, his own key already in hand. "You cannot have the key to my room," he protested again. "And, how do I know you have put everything away rightly?" He hied himself through the pantlery, and the treasury's door crashed against the wall as he hurried inside the little room.

She knew when he'd thrown open the casket, where the accounts were usually kept, by his anxious cry and flying footsteps. "You said you'd put all away," he screeched when he again faced her, his hands clutching at the air in panic.

"I have" was her soft reply.

"Then, where are they," he screamed, spittle flying from his lips. He danced on his toes in anxiety.

"They are locked safely away where only I may reach them." She stood calm amidst his storm of protest.

He stared at her, his eyes wide in horror. "I knew it," he cried. "I knew if I trusted you for even a moment's time, you would do something dishonorable, something womanish. If you think to dismiss me, think again. I've watched you over this week. You know nothing about keeping accounts."

"You see what you wish to see, Hugo." She started away.

"Stupid woman," he screamed, and grabbed her sleeve.

She yanked her arm from his grasp as she turned on him, eyes steely blue. "Do you dare to touch me, churl?"

He released her, but did not discontinue his pursuit. "Stupid woman, you think to be rid or me, but I am not so easily displaced. I am the one who sees this keep fed and clothed. Lord Rannulf will soon know what you've done. He will lock you in your solar and put you in your place. I have been here through two lords. I will be here when you are gone."

"Hugo Wardrober," Gilliam's deep, angry voice shook the rafters with its power. "What is this! I cannot believe I find you haranguing your betters."

The man inflated his cheeks in rage. "She has taken my papers and will not give them back. Years I have worked for your family, Lord Gilliam. Never has anyone complained over what I have done until this—this—this woman. You must tell her to give them back." He self-righteously crossed his arms over his thick chest and confidently waited to see his challenger's comeuppance.

"Lady Rowena?" The knight's long legs ate up the distance between the hall door and his lady.

"I have finished what I started," she said.

"And?"

"Is now the best time?" A jerk of her head indicated Maeve's deep interest in their conversation.

"I can think of no better. And?"

"And, four marks are missing." She stated it flatly, quietly. "I must assume that the supplies we were sent but which never appeared in our storerooms have been sold for a profit. He kept no record of that."

The wordrober gasped. His arms fell to his sides, fingers twitching, as he stared in horror at the two nobles. "That is impossible," he rasped out, his voice cracking. "Impossible," he whispered as he visibly drained of color.

"I'm afraid it is very possible indeed," Rowena said. "I believe we should find a secure place for Hugo amid our storerooms where he might remain close at hand until my lord husband returns. We should prepare a second room as well. You see, he has given our wealth to the Lady Maeve."

Maeve gasped in perfectly contrived outrage. "How dare you accuse me," she cried out. "What little I have was given me in pitiful exchange for my dower when I lost my home."

Rowena turned on her. "Do you name your many gowns and pretty baubles nothing? And what of your frequent trips to the merchants in town to buy this and that? Until now, I could not fathom how you came by your riches."

Still the picture of irate innocence, the fair woman set her hands on her hips. "Please tell me how I supposedly got that tight little man to give me anything? After all, your husband had to command him just to open the door for you. I cannot believe you accuse me."

"And, I believed that it was Rannulf buying them for you," Sir Gilliam retorted almost happily. "As to how you would get Hugo to steal for you, I have no doubt you've spread your legs to many a man for no more than a pretty ribbon."

Maeve's face twisted in hate. But, the wardrober's protests overrode whatever she meant to say. "I, with her?" His fingers pulled at his sleeves. "Not possible, nay, not I," he repeated, shaking his head vehemently. "I would never so betray the trust placed in me by the lords of Graistan. I have worked here for years and years, and never has anyone questioned me." His voice gained strength as he continued. "Why do you believe her? She is only a woman. How dare she accuse me of wrongdoing as an excuse for her poor figuring and her desire to rid this hall of another noblewoman."

His lady faced him, her expression supremely secure. "I would gladly hire any clerk you approve to audit your numbers. I have no doubt that he will verify what I have found."

His mouth moved in response, but no sound came forth. Again and again, his lips formed words, but nothing happened. His eyes widened, and he clutched at his chest.

"Gilliam," she cried out, "he is not breathing! Help him." She grabbed at the wardrober, but caught only the corner of his sleeve as he crumpled to the ground.

The young knight knelt at his side and touched his neck. "His heart still beats," he said, lifting the smaller man in his arms as if he weighed no more than Jordan. "I've seen a man die instantly clutching at his chest in just such a manner." He laid him on a bench. Hugo groaned, his eyelids fluttering.

"You," she told a maid, "fetch water and a cloth."

"Nay, wait," the man said, his voice a choked whisper. His face tightened as he grimaced in pain. " 'Tis the priest I need. I'll not die unshriven."

"Call Father," she snapped to anyone listening, then came and knelt beside the bench. "What you mean is you'll not die unconfessed. What good is a tale told to a deaf priest?" Her hard words suggested it would be far better if he confessed to her. Gilliam tried to wave her back, but she ignored him. "The truth. You took it from the treasury and gave it to Maeve."

"Aye," he sighed raggedly, "she has it." He curled up in another spasm of pain. "Oh, Lord in heaven, how I have sinned. In lust I did covet that woman only to become her slave. Now, my life is ruined because of my sins."

"Where is she?" Gilliam cried harshly. Rowena looked around. She'd been right beside them.

"Gone," she whispered with a sinking feeling. They'd lost her.

"At first it was so wonderful," Hugo spoke on, "she made me feel glorious. She was sweet and kind, and I dreamed that we might be wed. I gave her things, beautiful things, gifts of love."

"Tell the guards to find the Lady Maeve. They are to tear the town apart if they must," the young man thundered. "Stay here with him. I will bring her back." He sprang to his feet and loped out of the hall. She took his place, her arms supporting the wardrober on his bench.

"But it was not enough for her. She said it was dribs and drabs and was not she worth more than that?" A single tear trickled out from beneath his closed eyelid. "When I told her I could do no more, she threatened"—his eyes flew open, and he grimaced in pain—"she threatened to tell Lord Rannulf. I have worked here for nigh on thirty years," he told Rowena.

"I know," she said gently, laying her cool hand against his clammy brow. "You are a fine treasurer. Never have I seen so clear a hand or so steady a pen. There is much to be said for the fact that you did not try to hide your crime. It is as if you wished for someone to find you out."

"Perhaps I did." He closed his eyes and coughed out a sob as tears squeezed one after another from the corners of his eyes.

She held his hand until the priest knelt beside him. Then, anxious to give confessor and penitent their privacy, she shooed the servants away.

"We have her, my lady." Two guardsmen approached her with Maeve trapped between them. The noblewoman cursed and fought, her feet kicking out at them even while they tightly held her arms. "She was trying to leave by the postern gate."

"Good. Keep hold of her. You—" she pointed to a man—"go find Lord Gilliam."

"Oh, do, dear, do find him," the woman hissed, suddenly quiet between her captors. "And then what will you do? You cannot force your position with me. Think these servants will do your bidding if I tell them no? I have let you play the role of Lady Graistan," she spat out the honorific, "but you are mistaken if you think you have any real sway here. They fear me; they know the cost of crossing their true lady.

"You there," she called to a woman servant who stood watching the drama play itself out. "Do you remember what happened to you when you refused my order?" The maid gasped and cradled her hand to her bosom. She backed steadily away from the front of the circle, glancing from one nobleman to the other. Maeve's laugh was low and cold. "Oh, your servants remember me well."

"Threaten one of them and you threaten me," Rowena snapped.

"Oh, tra-la, listen to the peahen try to crow. And what could you do to me? Besides, you want your fortune returned," she said lightly, as if she were not trapped between two burly men.

"Bitch." Gilliam strode across the hall, staring in deadly earnest at his sultry sister by marriage. "You'll tell the Lady Rowena what you've done with it."

Two small spots of rage touched her cool, smooth cheeks. "A beardless boy and a nun cannot take from me what I have worked so hard to gain. Do you think for a moment that Rannulf will believe your accusations? Think again. With that commoner in his grave, who will say me yea or nay? It is I who will win this war. Rannulf loves me well, for he dares do nothing less."

Gilliam rocked back as if hit. "You lie."

"Oh, lover, you are jealous," she crooned sweetly.

Rowena made an irritated sound. "You may taunt him all you like, but I believe I know better. As beautiful as you make yourself to be, he did not look your way. Instead, the one you wished for as your lover has kept you locked out of his solar. Could the truth be, he did so to keep you from crawling into his bed? He was wise enough not to put himself in your power by committing incest."

Gilliam laughed in black amusement. "You have met your match, whore."

"You think to goad me, do you, boy? Do not bother, for I know well who I am and what I do. It is you who must have a care where you step, for we are two of a kind."

He blanched. "What do you mean?"

"That's right, lover"—she smiled sweetly—"two of a kind. If I covet my sister's wealthy husband, at least I have done no more than covet as the peahen has so cleverly divined. Can we say the same of you?"

"My lady," the priest whispered into his lady's ear, "it is done."

"He is gone?" she asked, turning toward the priest so he could read her lips.

"Aye, he just slipped away."

"I thank the Lord God you were here for him," she said quietly. "Have the servants help you take him so he might be prepared for burial." She returned her attention to the noblewoman. "And what of her?" she asked Graistan's steward, but the young man stood frozen in place. "Can you make her tell

you where she has hidden it?" she prodded, hoping
to awaken him from his stupor.

"Aye, lover, make me tell. But, if I tell where my
treasure is, I will have to tell our fine lady all else
I know."

"Nay," he cried out in wild desperation, then hid
his face behind his hands. "No, I cannot," he
breathed and fled the room.

Maeve's laugh was wicked. She turned her colorless gaze on her lady. "And, now, Lady Peahen, what
will you do with me?" She straightened to stare con-
descendingly down at the Lady Graistan.

"Vile creature!"

"That may be," she said, as if considering the
merits of the statement. "I have always felt a kinship
to the spider who traps the innocent and unwary in
her sticky threads. Here at Graistan, I found secrets
aplenty to fill my web and satisfy my needs. Do
you think yourself beyond my power? Think again.
Confine me here, and I'll have a servant who knows
the value of my coin open the door. Will you separate my head from my neck, as you are so fond of
threatening? Even dead I can still destroy all you
have built, for no matter how you try to explain to
your lord, he will not believe what I have done. He
dares not, for to do so is to face his past."

Rowena stared at the woman, hearing the ring of
truth in her words. Then, she raised a scornful
brow. "Oh, you make this puzzle so complex only
to lose yourself in your own maze. You are right;
there is little I can do to you here. But you have
admitted to certain sins, and I am duty bound as
your lady to care for your soul. It is time and prayer
that you need.

"Nearby lies a small convent and, if I remember
rightly, their order is silent and most strict in man-

ner. No doubt the abbess will have a quiet cell with a lock on the door where you may spend your time in contemplation while you find your peace with God. It will cost me only a little to compensate her for her trouble. When my lord husband returns, he may do with you as he wishes."

"Nay," Maeve screeched, struggling against her captors. "You stupid twit! You fool! Do this, and I will see you pay dearly for it. No one crosses me." Rage lent her strength, and she nearly tore free of the guards. "You will never get your coins from me."

Lady Graistan only laughed. "Believe me, sister, I will find a way to get their value from you. Bind her and take care how you do it. She is a sly vixen and must not be allowed to escape. I will go with you to pay my respects to the abbess and make certain the cell is appropriate for the Lady Maeve."

"When he finds you've left me rotting in a filthy convent, he will come for me. Then, you must hold dear to your precious solar, for that is all you will hold when I am done with you." The words were uttered like a curse.

The challenge awoke something dark and hard within Rowena. She stepped forward, her hands clenched, her eyes ablaze with the fire of possession. "Your power here is done. What you see now was created by my work and my love. Everything and everyone within this keep is mine. No one, especially not you, will take it from me. This I vow."

Maeve threw back her head and laughed, the sound fraught with evil. "So be it," she cried out as her lady stood watching the men bind her. "If I have to kill you to get it back, I will. You are no different than the servants. You have crossed me; now know my vengeance."

Loud gasps and the murmur of "witch" rippled

through the servants. Their lady heard them and
knew their fear might just do what Maeve threatened. She raised her voice until it carried clearly
about the hall. "Foolish creature, if words are all
you have left to throw at me, you are defeated indeed. Know that from this day on that you have no
power here. Go, find your peace in the convent. In
the name of our Blessed Lady, the Mother of God,
I beseech you to confess your sins and cleanse your
soul." She turned to the men who tightened the
ropes. "Gag her so she can say no more."

Rowena stayed to watch, but against all logic, fear
nagged at her. Why should she believe Maeve's
words? Surely, once he heard the truth, her husband would be glad of what was done this day. Even
if he cared for Maeve as she had claimed, for the
good of his hall and his folk, he would have to keep
her away from Graistan.

# Chapter Eight

*A* soft breeze heavy with the perfume of late spring blossoms set the amethyst silk of Rowena's wimple fluttering against her cheek. She impatiently trapped the ends of her headdress beneath the heavy silver necklace she wore. This simple chain was the perfect complement to her dress, an overgown of silver and lavender silk atop a gray undergown embroidered in amethyst and silver. Magnificence to compensate for her husband's absence.

By tradition the Lord and Lady Graistan led the town's May Day festivities. Unfortunately, Rannulf's last message said he yet waited to be freed from attendance at the royal court. Rather that she were dressed more comfortably and attending these doings at his side. She sighed; she didn't have time for regrets. Today, she would be contracting to buy those supplies her lands did not produce, as well as arranging for the sale of Graistan's surplus wools and wheat before joining the town's council for the midday meal.

As she entered the courtyard from the hall, Gilliam strode out of the stable door, his mail gleaming silver beneath his blue surcoat. "Are you ready to leave?" he called out to her.

"If my maids are ready, so am I," she returned. "Now, do you remember what I have told you?"

He laughed at her tone. "Yes, maman. Twist your chain in your right hand, and I am to dicker for yet a lower price. Twist your chain in your left hand, and the price is right. But why not speak for yourself?"

She snorted in disgust. "Because I am only a wife while you are steward for the great Lord Graistan. Stewards are supposed to chaffer for their lords' goods."

"If I must work the whole day, I will miss all the fun," he grumbled.

"You are such a child." She laughed at him, her amusement taking the sting from her words. She knew well enough how little he liked his stewardship, yet how determined he was to do a fine job to please his brother. "Now, if I could find those lazy maids of mine, we could be on our way."

"We come, my lady," Ilsa shouted in reply from the hall door. She was resplendent in green and gold wool. Her two daughters, dressed in brown and gold, descended the stairs behind her ready to accompany their lady for the day.

Gilliam's blue eyes sparkled with amusement. "Look, an old sow turned into a silk purse."

"Nasty brat," the old woman retorted.

"Oh, be still you two," Rowena sighed in feigned irritation. "Shall we?"

"I am at your convenience, my lady," he said, signaling to the men-at-arms who would escort them, and they entered Graistan's town.

Although dawn had come only an hour ago, the market square was packed with merchants from across the land ready to sell everything from early spring vegetables to splinters from the True Cross. Those who could afford it had set up a makeshift shop decorated with ribbons, flowers, and bright paints. Others simply lay their goods upon a rough blanket for all the world to see. But, poor or rich, every one of them sought customers' attention by shouting out the virtues of their wares.

The aromas of baking onions, brewing ale, and roasting meats mingled in air that bore the more exotic scents of cinnamon and clove. After the weeks of Lenten fasting, the variety of tastes easily tempted passersby into gluttony.

Everywhere, people laughed and shouted. Pipers piped and drummers banged loudly while onlookers kicked up their heels. Beggars mingled with merchants, cutpurses carefully practiced their art, townsfolk dressed in their finest were crushed against the louse-ridden serfs in ragged homespun.

None of this distracted Rowena. Her time was devoted to judging the quality of goods she found. For the most part she was pleased. And, although they were glad to see that Graistan keep was once again buying goods, the merchants found its new steward to be hardheaded in his bargaining.

By noon she was finished, much to Gilliam's relief, and they joined the town council for the feast. The aldermen, made up of the town's wealthiest guildsmen, were accompanied by their wives and children on this shaded dais. Only by a slim margin did Rowena's silk outshine these women's bright samites and rich sarcenets. And not a few of them stared at her gown in obvious envy.

After a meal replete with fine wines and many dishes, there was nothing left for her to do but enjoy the day. Here at the town's center, the better actors performed their plays while the acrobats twisted, tossed, and turned their bodies with amazing agility. Musicians, looking for patrons and silver coins, sang their sweetest below this platform. And, of course, there was the piercing falsetto of the puppeteers who's set their stand exactly at the platform's steps.

Before long, she found herself chatting with the young wife of a master guildsman. Like herself, she was newly married and not from the local area. They passed the time pleasantly discussing the management of household servants as the afternoon slipped away in easy enjoyment.

Rannulf halted before the town walls, his bay dancing slightly with its desire to continue on. "Give me a moment, Roland," he muttered to the creature as he studied his home. Graistan's curtain walls cut a stern gray line through the heart of this town his great-grandfather had fostered. The very sight of the towering keep within them eased his soul like nothing else could. The place was eternity itself.

He smiled. Jordan waited inside for him. Then, his smile faltered. Also within was his new wife. His joy at homecoming soured. A pretty penny he'd cost himself by marrying her. The king had demanded double the fine for wedding without royal consent. His father by marriage would pay the first half, but he'd have to foot the second bit. This atop what he still owed the crown for releasing his forest and chase from the royal control. This Plantagenet was expensive. First, the Crusade, then the ransom paid to the emperor, and now a scutage to finance the reconquest of Richard's French and Norman holdings from Phillip of France. There was not enough money in all England to satisfy its king.

He turned away from his cynical thoughts and raised his hand to the sentry. The town's guardsman called down his greeting, then shouted for those on the streets below to make way for their lord.

Rannulf passed through the gate and into the

warm embrace of his own peaceful and prosperous domain. The streets were crowded with folk. He stared in surprise until he remembered. "Temric, why did you not remind me it was May Day?" he called back to his brother. "We could have arrived last night and joined the festivities."

His brother shrugged. "I did not think of it."

"What do you say we go to the town's cross and see what is what?" At the other's brief grin, Rannulf set his bay to carefully picking its way through the crowd toward the town's center.

All along the lanes folk sent the cry forward until a wide enough path was cleared to let the armed men through the crowd. Those he knew waved and called their greetings. He responded in kind.

As always, the council had raised a platform before the church doors and beneath the shade of two massive chestnut trees. There, in the spot he usually occupied, sat Gilliam. Beside his brother was a woman, resplendent in silver and purple. She was turned away from him, engrossed in conversation with the woman seated just behind her.

What was this? He frowned. Was his brother courting a merchant's daughter without first seeking his approval? But, who stood behind the girl? Why, it was old Ilsa. He'd never before seen his stepmother's servant dressed in anything so fine. Then, he caught his breath in understanding. His wife.

Briefly closing his eyes, he found behind his eyelids the image of her standing before him covered only by the fall of her glossy black hair. Jesus God. He thrust the picture away and opened his eyes.

Now, she looked toward him, a soft smile warming her lips and glowing in her dark blue eyes. Any other woman would have been diminished in so rich a gown, but the brightness of his wife's costume only enhanced her unusual coloring. He studied her, memorizing the gentle curve of her cheek and sweet fullness of her lips. His gaze wandered downward. Although her overgown was not as tightly laced as was the fashion, there was no mistaking the lush roundness of her breasts.

Rannulf swallowed hard. Even though she tried to hide it, within her burned a flame of such wanton passion it could make a man's head spin. He glanced aside, but could not keep his attention away from her. When he looked back, their gazes locked. She stared at him for a long moment, then her smile vanished and her expression stiffened with ... what? Apprehension? Guilt?

His eyes narrowed. Gilliam and she made quite a pair, both young and well matched in their handsomeness. He looked at his brother and struggled with demons he'd long ago thought he'd banished. Then, Gilliam looked up and smiled for the barest instant before his features froze into that familiar challenge.

Rannulf would have said *no*, but the crowd suddenly edged back and waited. Well, if the townsfolk expected that old game ... He gave a brief nod and dismounted as his brother leapt to his feet.

His wife reached out to tug at his brother's surcoat, her action speaking of an easy familiarity between them. Whatever she said was delivered in an urgent tone, her features tight with fear. Gilliam either ignored her or did not hear, for he leapt down from the dais to comically circle his older brother in make-believe wariness.

Rannulf stared at them. Although he knew it was impossible, he could not prevent thoughts of betrayal from awakening. Instantly, he slammed a mental door on them, shocked at himself for even thinking such things. Instead, he concentrated on the game he was about to play. All around him the crowd held its breath. Metal hissed on leather as he and his brother freed their weapons. Then, with a great, ringing clash, steel met steel.

His wife leapt to her feet and cried out. Her words were lost in the cheers of the crowd as they urged their chosen champions on to victory. But, he had no time to discover for whom she feared as his brother easily escaped the trap he'd set for him.

They'd not played this game since before Gilliam's departure for the Holy Lands. Then, his brother's battle plan had been to carelessly throw himself forward, trusting his great strength and larger body weight to carry the day. It had been easy to blindside him and force him into a corner with a feint or two. No longer. The boy'd earned his spurs and learned more than godliness while crusading.

The minutes passed as they met, stroke by stroke. Rannulf's pride grew to match his exhaustion. It was luck, not skill, when he found his opening and knocked away the younger man's blade. "Yield," he demanded, lifting his sword point to his brother's throat.

"You've bested me this time." Gilliam laughed, his clear blue gaze clear and happy.

Rannulf searched his brother's face, looking for something he dared not see, but there was only a carefree boy here. His inner tension eased, and he was shamed by his easlier doubts. "Ah, but you gave me a merry chase," he retorted as he sheathed his sword and pulled off his helmet.

"Welcome home." The young knight gave his elder brother a bear hug that nearly cracked ribs before retrieving his own sword. "During my years abroad, it was this game I missed most of all, old man."

"Not so old yet." He grinned widely. "When you finally best me, I will be old."

"How do you know I do not already let you win?" Gilliam's expression was impish.

Lord Graistan threw back his head and laughed in pure joy. The devil take his problems. He was free of court and obligations. He was home and glad of it, and, most importantly, he had his brother back once again. " 'Tis not you who lets me win, 'twill be I who lets you lose with grace." He turned toward the dais to formally greet his wife.

Rowena drew a deep, ragged breath to calm her rage as her husband neared the platform. It had been a jest! A child's prank! She'd nearly eaten her heart with worry thinking they meant to kill each other while they played a game. Her fingers clenched into the folds of her gown.

"My lord husband." Despite her best effort, her words still bore hard and angry edges.

Her husband's smile died and took with it the life from his eyes. His features fell back into the harsh lines of bitterness she remembered so well from their wedding. "My lady," he replied flatly.

So, he was not yet reconciled to their marriage. Well, that would change once he saw all she'd accomplished on his behalf. For now, he had only to stand beside her here. But, instead of climbing the steps to the dais, he turned and remounted. She stared after him in disbelief. He could not be so cruel. Her humiliation was complete.

"Do you not wish to stay and enjoy the remainder of the day?" his younger brother asked.

"Nay," Lord Graistan replied from atop his

mount. "As you have said, I am an old man. I need
to retire and take my ease after a hard journey."

"Go then, we'll not tarry overlong." A moment
later, her husband had ridden away toward
Graistan.

She choked as anger became hurt. He'd shown
the entire town that he did not hold her in high
regard. High regard! He held no regard for her at
all. She sat frozen in shame while Gilliam received
warm congratulations from the councilmen for his
performance.

When she could finally manage to speak, her
voice was quiet and tense. "Ilsa, I am ready to leave
now."

Her maid turned to her with a wide smile. "Of
course, my lady." She seemed to believe that the
young wife was anxious to join her husband. "Lord
Gilliam, your lady would like to leave now."

As the young knight turned toward them, Rowena
vehemently shook her head. She'd not wanted to
tell him, only to slip away without notice. "Nay, nay,
I did not mean you to come with me," she said,
shortly. "Stay and enjoy. I have a terrible throbbing
in my head and with my lord just arrived, there is
much I must do."

He only shrugged away her protests. "I may return later, but I'll see you safely into Graistan's hall
first."

"As you wish," she replied. She stood and forced
herself to lift her head high. No one would know
that the joy in her life was gone, once again destroyed by her husband.

# Chapter Nine

*R*ANNULF'S irritation blinded him until after he'd passed Graistan's gate house and entered the outer bailey. There was nothing in all her rich dowry that was compensation for having to live with a nasty shrew. He'd wanted to own her lands and had been swayed to agree by her beauty, but he'd forgotten to check her temperament before purchasing. What price in emotional anguish would he pay for his mistake?

They were well within the foreyard before his vision cleared enough that he could look around him. The byres and barns along the walls were somehow changed. As always, geese grazed near the dovecot and ducks swam in the fish pond. He rode through the inner gate into the courtyard and pulled his bay to a sudden stop.

Jesus God! She'd whitewashed the whole damn keep! Whitewash, all over the lower reaches of a place named for its gray stones. What right did she have to do this?

Despite the shock of white walls, he could not help but notice that the courtyard was neatly kept. The stair rail up to the hall had been repaired. Everywhere there were clean walls. For the first time in his recent memory the smell of the stable did not compete with that coming from the kitchen.

"My lord," called the stable master as he herded out his underlings to take the troop's horses, "well come! Well come, indeed. It is good to see you home again."

"Whitewash," was all Rannulf could say.

"Oh, aye." The stable master grinned like a fool. "The lady has made some changes. A good lady she is, too, my lord."

He said nothing, only dismounted and strode up the stairs and into the hall. What he saw at the door stopped him in mid-step. The massive room was almost blinding. Here, too?

Mayhap the paint was not so bad here. The whiteness brought new life to the wall hangings, or had they been cleaned? And, by repainting the sooty ceiling, the roof beams once again showed that they'd been brightly painted. No, they had been repainted, for there had never before been a green one.

He stepped into the room. The pungent scents of marigold and rosemary rose from the rushes at his feet. Servants surged forward, congratulating him for winning his mock battle with Gilliam while welcoming him home.

Despite his growing uneasiness, he forced himself to respond in kind. Graistan was so changed. He had not expected to feel like a stranger in his own home. And, it was her hand that showed in its every corner. He lingered a moment, waiting for Jordan, but the boy did not appear. No matter, it was a short walk to the women's quarters.

He went no farther than the doorway of the big room, as this domain was the only one within his pale in which he was not welcome. The chamber with its many chests and pallets was nearly empty save for two old women working at the looms on the far wall. "Where is my son?" he asked of one, but she only shrugged and shook her grizzled head.

"Where is his nurse?" He looked around him. Here, too, there had been a thorough scrubbing and the room's meager furnishings rearranged. This wife definitely knew the meaning of cleanliness.

"I don't know, lord," answered the eldest, dropping her shuttle for a moment. "We do not see much of her any longer since the new lady came."

"She's gone?" Rannulf snapped to attention. "Where is Jordan if his nurse is gone?"

"I do not know," the woman repeated nervously at his angry tone.

He clenched a fist. She had promised, she'd vowed before God, Himself, on their wedding day to accept his natural son. But, she had not promised to let the boy live alongside her. Rage mingled with a terrible fear. What had she done to his son? He whirled on his heel and strode back to the hall.

"I want my son," he bellowed, attracting the notice of every soul within the room.

"Rannulf," Gilliam called from the door as he entered. "What is wrong? Where is Jordan?"

"What has she done to him?" he roared.

"What do you mean," his wife retorted smartly as he stepped into the hall from behind his brother, "what have I done to him? I have done nothing save what should have been done from the beginning." She placed her hands on her hips in angry outrage.

He stared at her. Where had she sent him? "And you let her?" he demanded of his brother.

"Let her?" Gilliam looked back and forth between them, his face clouded in confusion.

"Papa!" Jordan cried out from the chapel entryway. "Papa, you are home." The boy dashed across the room and launched himself into his father's arms. "Did you bring me anything?"

"You see," she snapped. "At last he is well dressed, properly cared for, and receiving lessons as befits his station."

Rannulf hugged the boy close in relief. "Is that any way to greet your papa, by asking what I might or might not have brought you?" He held him out at arm's length. "Why I believe you've grown in my absence. Did your nurse have to make you a new gown?"

"Nay, 'twas not Alais," Jordan said, idly kicking his booted feet out at his father. "Lady Wren did. You know, Papa, she was not a dragon at all. She likes me." He smiled at his stepmother from over his father's arm. "She brought Brother Matthew here to teach me my letters, too, so I might grow up to be a lord like you. She says you will find me a tutor, so I may have a sword. Will you?"

He set the boy down. "I had not thought about it," he said. At his son's crestfallen look, he added, "But, I will consider it."

"Oh," Jordan responded, then hesitated a moment. "Did you bring me anything?"

"Go ask Temric if he can find it for you," his father replied, with a short laugh. The boy started to dash away.

But his wife held out her hand. "Jordan."

He instantly stopped and turned back to his father with a deep sigh. "Pardon, I forgot," he said, simply. "My thanks, Papa. And," he added with a grin, "I am glad you are home," and raced for the hall door.

Rannulf watched him go, his heart torn with jealousy. Jordan had always been his alone. He did not care to share the boy, especially not with his wife. He glared at her.

"How dare you think me capable of harming that child," she hissed. "And, it was insufferably rude of you to turn your back on the townsmen this day." She started to say more, but seemed to choke on her words.

"If the townsmen complain, I will apologize," he snapped. " 'Tis not on their behalf you rage. More likely that I tweaked your pride."

Her look spit fire at him, and her pale skin flushed. She whirled away and stormed from the hall.

Gilliam laughed.

"What is it you find so amusing, brother," he demanded harshly.

"The two of you," his brother said with a smile, then strode away without waiting for a response.

He clenched his fists in impotent rage. His house was changed, his son was taken, he was the butt of his brother's amusement. "May God piss on you all," he muttered, then commanded in a louder voice, "I want a bath in my chamber and bring me something to eat. And, butler, bring me a big ewer of wine."

"My lady has already ordered it for you, my lord," It was not the butler who answered, but his young assistant.

"Then," he ground out between clenched teeth, "I want ale, not wine."

Rowena raged blindly into the kitchen, grabbed a wooden spoon, and slammed it down on the cutting block. The head snapped off and flew across the room. She hit the block again with the remains of the spoon. The shaft snapped in two, and she hurled the pieces across the room.

"My lady," the cook cried out as she reached for a second spoon, "what have I done? Wait, stop, I need that."

Through the haze of her anger, she dimly heard his cries. It was still a full minute before she could release the utensil. "Pardon," she managed, through clenched teeth.

"Did you come to change the menu we'd planned for our lord's return?" The portly man nearly twice her size almost cringed before her. "There is yet time, if you wish."

She struggled mightily with her emotions and won. "Nay, 'tis not that. The meal will remain as we had planned it. Never mind me." With that she retreated from the cooking shed and made her way into her garden.

The small plot of land that was the lady's garden had been stolen from a corner of the courtyard and enclosed with a tall fence. When she'd first arrived, it had been like the rest of Graistan, neglected and disused, save for the kitchen herbs. Although it was still too wild for her tastes, it now showed the beginnings of order and form. She seated herself on the bench amid the thyme and pinks to stare blindly at the blooming fruit trees espaliered against the walls.

That insufferable, horrible, boorish, hateful man.

The dying sun left behind it a bloody sky. Shadows crept stealthily toward her, turning the rosemary into hulking, tormented forms. Each darkening moment brought her unrelentingly closer to sharing her bed with him. Nothing had changed; it would be no different than the first night. The memory of his rejection made her stomach clench.

"Are you here, Lady Wren? Oh, there you are. I could hardly see you." Jordan entered the garden and stood hopefully before her. "My papa has brought me a pony of my very own. Temric says I may ride him on the morrow. Cook says I must ask you before he can give me something for him."

She stirred herself from her bitter thoughts and smiled at her stepson. "How lucky you are to have such a generous papa." How could anyone, even that man, believe she could do this boy harm? "Tell Cook you may have what you wish, although I do not know what there is save a mealy apple or two."

"My thanks." He gave her a quick kiss on the cheek and hied back toward the cook shed.

She rose with a sigh and slowly made her way back to the hall. How could she be a dutiful wife to a man so hateful? And what next was she to expect from him? Likely he would destroy all she had built simply because he could.

Inside, servants gamed and chatted away their idle evening hours while the dogs danced and played around the room. It was all so unfair. Her rage flamed back to life.

Rowena drew a deep breath. Nay, this was wrong; anger was always unproductive. She must be calm and rational when next she saw him. More importantly, she had to be comfortable. But to rid herself of her finery meant she must retreat to their bedchamber; and she was not yet ready to once again confront him.

She hesitated. Wishing she could be free of her heavy garments only made them all the more uncomfortable. There was no choice but to change. Well, she had commanded that his bath be laid in the solar. There was no reason for him to be in their bedchamber.

She quietly climbed the stair, then peered cautiously into the room from the antechamber. It was empty. She glanced sadly about her. What if this was her last night here? How easily she'd become accustomed to the luxury and how deeply she would miss it. She slipped swiftly into the room.

"And you let her?" She froze as the words exploded into the silence around her. "Is there no one in this keep who could say nay to my wife?" He was speaking to someone in the solar. She turned to see that the door between the rooms was ajar.

"Who was I to stop her?" It was Alais's voice that answered. "She took Jordan from me. Had not the dear child begged on my behalf, she would have sent me from the keep. I am not allowed any freedom with him. I may not naysay anything she tells him. I am not a good influence on the boy, she says. Now, all I ever hear from his lips is 'the lady told me this,' 'the lady told me that.'" The nurse's voice grew louder as her complaint continued.

Rowena hurriedly removed her silver chain, placed it into its casket, and put the box aside as she listened. She should close the door, but to do so was to reveal her presence. Then, again, she'd be gone in a moment. She unpinned her wimple and released her hair from its tight roll, meaning to replait it once she was dressed.

"You say I should have stopped her? Who am I but a mere servant or so she told me. Do you think I am mistaken when I said she'd set me out? It was she who dismissed your butler and set his feet upon yon road without one pence to warm his pocket."

"She did what!"

His shocked tone surprised her, but then she remembered he had not witnessed the man's drunken incompetence. Surely, he would agree that a chance at life was better than a head without a body. She seated herself in a chair and slipped off her shoes and stockings.

"Aye, aye," the nurse continued, obviously enjoying her tale now that she understood she would bear no hurt for it. "She said he drank the best and served the rest, but who would know for sure if it weren't all spit, since we who serve drink only ale and beer?"

"But, the man's been here all his life. Where did he go?"

Rowena removed her fine gowns and folded them away with great care. Dressed only in her sheer linen chemise, she reached for her everyday dress that hung from the pole behind the bed.

"I know not. But, you should also know it was at her hands that Master Hugo had his strange fit and died. And she has Lady Maeve locked in a convent as well."

"She's done what with Maeve?" he choked out. "No more!" he cried. "Have someone find my wife and bring her to me."

A chair scraped, then footsteps neared the door. He was coming into the bedchamber! If he found her here, he would think she'd eavesdropped apurpose. She dropped her gown in panic. There was no time to dress and no escape without a dress. She slid onto the bed and took refuge in a fold of the bed curtains.

The door crashed shut into its frame. Her husband stalked into the room. He wore only a bedrobe, which lay open over his broad chest, and a pair of chausses, which clung damply to his hips and strong thighs. His dark hair lay in moist curls around his face. She eased farther into the shadows as she caught sight of his evil expression. He did not look to be in a mood to listen to any explanation she might give.

He grabbed his cup from the tray on the table

and lifted it to his lips. Finding it empty, he held the ewer upside down over the cup. Not a drop was left.

"Damn," he shouted and threw the ewer at the wall. It shattered against the embroidered hanging and fell in wet pieces against the carpeted floor.

She gasped.

More quickly than she could catch her breath, he was at the bedside, his hands on her arms. "You were listening by the door." His words were hard as flint.

Rowena struggled in his grasp. "I was not. Until you say otherwise this is still my chamber as well as yours. And you were certainly not trying to keep the conversation private." She ceased resisting and let him pull her off the bed. To her surprise he released her.

"Did you dismiss my butler?"

"I did. He was a drunkard who did more harm than good." She lifted her chin and met his stony gaze with an icy look. " 'Twas better that than reduce him to a pigherd."

"And his brother?"

"Is still your master falconer. I am not a fool," she ground out, crossing her arms before her. "I would not punish a family for the actions of one member."

"And what of my wardrober?" Lord Rannulf took a threatening step forward.

She refused to be intimidated. "His own guilt killed him. He raided the treasury for the Lady Maeve's sake."

Her husband caught his breath as if in pain, and whirled around to lean against the hearth wall, his back to her. "How much," he managed in a strangled voice.

"Four marks in coin. If jewels are missing, I do not know, for I am not familiar with what was there. Neither do I know what he gained from the sale of our stores," she said, sitting back onto the bed. "He said he stole for the love of the Lady Maeve and that she used the knowledge of his thievery to force him to take more still." A moment passed in silence. "I understand how you might be upset with me, my lord, if all you hear are the tales brought to you by one jealous servant. Do not listen solely to her, speak with your people. They are well content. I have tried to be a good wife to you."

He jerked around, his eyes hard. "A good wife?" he spat out. "I return to find you dressed in jewels when you tell me my keep is impoverished. I see you have spared no expense in glorifying this keep when the king demands yet another round of knights' fees from me. God's teeth! I had to pay double for the dubious privilege of wedding you."

Rowena leapt to her feet. "Dubious, indeed," she snapped. "I beg you to remember that my father will pay half that fee. These gowns were mine already, and the chain only borrowed from your treasury. Restoration of the keep cost you nothing, save for my hard labor and that of your servants. Our only expense has been for the supplies I bought to feed us because the storage bins were bare. Should we have starved?"

"But you are not content to simply beggar me," his voice overrode hers, "you must also trespass into my family. Do you leave no part of my life as mine alone?"

"You gave me your leave to become a part of your life the day after our wedding. I offered you my skills and my devotion to duty. In return, you said your servants were at my disposal. I have only done as you commanded."

"You have stolen my son from me." His words were hard.

Hers were strident in denial. "Stolen your son? How foolish, of course I have not. He is in the stable feeding the pony you brought him."

"And when did you decide that I was not properly caring for him?" he asked, his voice heavy with sarcasm. "Who knows better when a child is ready for book learning or swordplay, the child's father or a convent-raised chit who's barely even borne a man between her thighs much less a child?"

She glared at him. "I may not have borne a child, but I can recognize need when I see it. Were you aware that the Lady Maeve had convinced Alais that I meant to kill the child? That stupid cow would have kept him in a barren tower room with only a single meal each day in order to protect him from me. Or, perhaps I am mistaken in thinking it Maeve's order. Perhaps, that is how you intended him to be treated. If so, what kind of parent are you? I would not let the meanest scullery lad live like that in my keep."

She yelped in pain as he again grabbed her by the arms. This time his hands bruised her. "Vicious bitch," he breathed, his voice low and dangerous.

"Let me go," she demanded.

"Mayhap pain will reach you where reason cannot." His mouth twisted in a mean line. "This marriage of ours is a mistake of the worst sort. Well, no longer. I'll not share my life with a nasty shrew whose tongue is sharper than my sword. Say farewell to Graistan this night, for on the morrow I will see you returned to Benfield."

Rowena sneered. "On what grounds? You made

very certain our marriage was consummated. What of those sons you needed? You will hardly get sons from me if I am at Benfield."

"Aye, we are wed," he said coldly, "unfortunately and truly wed. I'll not contest that. As for sons, I have one. Take your pretentious airs and be the fine lady of Benfield, for I'll not have you here."

She stared. He meant it. He would take it all from her. Her heart exploded in panicked rage. "Your dirty son of a sow," she screamed as she kicked out at him. "I have nearly killed myself to bring this keep to its present state, battling hostile servants and a cruel woman without you at my side. It is not enough for you to force me into marriage, but you must belittle me before the entire town of Graistan. You say I have left no part of your life untouched. Well, what of mine? You took all my hopes and desires that day. You'll not steal this from me. I will not go!"

She threw herself backward. Beneath his crushing grip the fine linen of her sleeve tore, and she slipped one arm free. But, his hand on her other arm was an iron band. His face was black with rage. He raised his hand.

"No," she cried out and lurched back. If he struck her now, surely he would kill her. In hopeless desperation, she threw herself against him. If he could not reach her, he could not hit her. Her free arm clutched around his chest. He gasped in surprise and released her. Instantly, she wrapped her other arm around him.

Only then did she see her error. He grabbed her by the shoulders. How long before he pried her away? "Do not kill me, my lord," she cried against his chest.

His breathing was shallow, his heart raced. She

could feel its beat against her cheek. Mary, Mother of God, help me, she prayed. "Please," she whispered hoarsely, meaning to say more, but her voice broke; she was not accustomed to pleading.

He released her shoulders and set his hands against her waist. "Let go," he said, but the muscles of his chest were still tensed, as if to strike.

Instead, she resettled her grip, pressing herself even more tightly to him. "You will hit me" was all she whispered and cursed herself as a coward.

"Let go," he repeated, his words rumbling against her ear. "I am calm now. I will not hurt you."

A moment passed and, then, another. Still, she did not move.

He gently stroked her hair. "Let go." The palm of his hand cupped her cheek. Despite her resistance, he lifted her face up from his chest.

She kept her eyes shut and tensed for the blow that must surely follow. His fingers lay warm against her jaw. She bit her lip to stop its trembling. When he sighed, she opened her eyes just a little.

The madness had left his face, although anger remained. She saw it in the muscle that twitched along his jaw. His thumb moved slightly across her cheek. Then, his gray eyes clouded and the harsh contours of his face relaxed into something akin to acceptance.

Slowly, her arms loosened. She stepped back. Her legs trembled. "You tore my chemise," she said, her voice quiet, awed by the height of his rage.

"And lost my mind as well," he replied with a crooked grin.

She blinked, fighting sudden, unexpected tears. Her knees buckled, and she began to fall. He caught her to him. "I was afraid," she cried softly, her head cradled against his shoulder, her fingers soft against the hard contours of his chest. "I thought you would kill me."

His lips touched her forehead. "Never, never goad an angry man," he murmured, his mouth moving softly against her brow as he spoke. He leaned his head against hers.

For a long moment, they stood in silence. She knew the warm silkiness of his skin against her hand and the strength of his shoulder against her cheek. Beneath her palm she felt the steady beat of his heart.

His lips touched her cheek in a gentle kiss, then he released her and stepped back. She looked up, sorry he had moved and ended the moment. She memorized the arrogant line of his straight nose, the curve of his mouth. His cheekbones jutted high over the strong line of his jaw and chin. Dark auburn hair lay in fine curls against the strong column of his neck. Under her watchful gaze, his eyes darkened to blue and filled with an odd sadness that seemed to beg for her touch.

She raised a hand to the newly shorn hollow of his cheek. His skin was rough, yet soft beneath her palm. He shut his eyes and leaned into her caress. Her fingers traced the line of his mouth. When he kissed her fingertips, she caught her breath and would have withdrawn her hand had he not taken it in his, lacing his fingers between hers.

"Dear God in heaven, never have I been in such a rage," he breathed, slowly drawing her nearer. "You raise such passions in me." He touched his mouth to hers, his lips moving slightly in a soft kiss.

She clung to him and let the gentleness of his kiss wash over her. He wanted her. Surely, that meant he'd not send her away. Still, if she wished to secure her place at his side, she'd have to make him hers, just as she had made his home hers. Her mouth moved in response to his as her arms slipped around his neck. As she drew herself up against him, she gasped against the searing heat that filled her.

Her skin burned against his as she felt the strength of his chest against her breasts, felt his hard thighs touching hers. In dizzying response to these sensations, she forgot about walls and keeps, halls and servants. Instead, she caught her breath when his kiss deepened in defiance, as if he expected her denial. But she met his hunger with a very real need of her own.

His hand slipped inside the remnants of her gown and found her breast. He kissed her cheek, her neck, the base of her throat. Lost in the wonderful, terrible need that consumed her, Rowena ran her hands over the broad planes of his chest until she felt the soft linen of his chausses. He made a quiet sound of pleasure when her fingers played along the drawstring waist.

There was a tap at the door. "My lord," a servant called out, "we cannot find your lady. Shall we begin a search?"

He straightened. She stared up at him. Slowly, slowly, he smiled, his look fierce with desire. "Never mind," he said, his gaze trapping hers as he eased the torn gown off her shoulder. The garment fell into a pile around her ankles. She wore nothing beneath it. He drew a quick breath. "I have found her."

Deep in sleep, Rowena pulled at the bedclothes. They were caught somewhere near the end of the bed. It took a moment to open her eyes. She peered hopelessly toward the foot of the bed, but the darkness was nearly absolute, as they'd let the fire die and forgotten to light the night candle.

Her outstretched hand found her husband's shoulder. He shifted slightly at her touch. The memory of their bed play made her shiver. At the center of her being awoke a throbbing need that she knew only he could ease. She bit her lip and mentally recited a prayer of protection for her heart. Would this time be like the last? In the morning, would he once again be the cold, hard man he'd been after their wedding night? Oh, dear Lord, but he might still send her away. She clenched her eyes shut on that thought. Did he not realize that this was now her home, too?

Perhaps, as he understood and saw all she had done for him, he would like her better. Aye, if she guarded her tongue and did as he bid until he'd grown accustomed to her, he would come to accept her.

She crept from the bed and brought a burning splinter back from the solar and set it to the wick of the thick night candle. Even though it stood near the head of the bed, its meager flame was enough to show her the bedclothes bundled near the bottom of the mattress.

Its pale illumination touched her husband's face. She smiled. The resemblance between him and his son was so remarkable. It could not be so hard to care for the father when she already loved the son. Then, her smile faded. The very thought of losing Jordan broke her heart. Even if rejection and pain were the price she paid, her husband must never send her away. Graistan must be hers for all time. Resolved, she slid back into the tall bed forgetting to retrieve the bedclothes.

Her husband opened his eyes just a little later. "Why did you leave?" he murmured.

"I was cold and could not find the bedclothes in the dark," she whispered back, sliding down beside him.

"Impossible." He grinned slightly. "There is nothing cold about you."

"Do not tease me," she whispered in shy embarrassment. He only chuckled and put his arm beneath her to draw her near. When he nuzzled her ear, his warm breath set her skin to shivering. Her arms slipped around him when he set his lips to the spot behind her ear, and she eased downward until their hips met. His shaft moved in new life. She caught her breath as her body answered with its own desire. There was great pleasure in knowing she could wring this reaction from him.

"Who is the tease now," he said hoarsely against her ear. His free hand slipped into her hair to cradle her head and turn her face to his. Their lips briefly met, then he rolled back down against the mattress as if to escape her. But she did not release him. Instead, she came to rest on her side against him.

He sighed. She did not yet know him well enough to read his expression, yet he seemed troubled by something. He combed her hair with his fingers as though distracted. "Why did you lay with me? After I threatened you with violence, why—?" He seemed ready to ask more, but his whisper died into silence as his fingers descended the peak of her breast.

"I—" she started, barely breathing the word as his hand left her breast and his fingers drew curving lines against her stomach. "I—" She caught her breath as his hand slid lower still to find her soft woman's flesh between her thighs. "I, oh, I cannot think when you do that." She kissed his throat, needing to touch him somewhere to release the lovely pressure he awoke.

"That," he said with a smile, his fingers once again teasing her breast, "is answer enough." She shivered in response, then lay back in the mattress. It took only the slightest tug to convince him he should lay atop her. When she lifted her hips in invitation, he made her wait an exquisitely long time before he finally accepted.

Rannulf was awake long after his wife had dropped into contented slumber. She lay in the curve of his arm, her breathing even and peaceful, long strands of her hair falling across his chest. In all his life he had never once raised his hand in anger toward a woman, not even Isotte. Until this night he had not believed himself to be capable of such violence. But this spit of a girl had goaded him until he had near destroyed her in his rage.

Not only had she taunted him, her rage had met and matched his. As her anger, so her passion. He closed his eyes as his body reacted pleasurably to that thought. On the heels of pleasure came doubt.

If she were still the innocent she'd been on their wedding night, she should have cowered from him after he'd threatened her very life. Instead, she'd met him willingly, even wantonly, as though she truly desired him. Was this simply passionate innocence or something more calculating? If so, then for that purpose did she seek to use him? Could it be she was already with child and could now claim the babe his, but "born too soon"?

He closed his mind against these painful thoughts and eased his arm out from beneath her. Deep within him there was a longing to believe what his senses told him, that she desired him for no other reason than himself. Yet, the past had taught him he could so easily delude himself. How was he to know the truth? Rannulf rolled away and lay sleepless for hours.

# Chapter Ten

*R*OWENA sat bolt upright and pushed her tangled hair out of her face. Light flooded into the bed from the solar's open door. She glanced quickly about. The room was empty; he'd left her sleeping. Why? To secretly prepare for her departure?

With an anxious cry, she threw herself off the mattress, snatched on her robe, and hurried into the solar. Her personal items still lay where she'd left them. She dashed to the windows, only her clutching hands holding the garment closed over her nakedness.

The courtyard was bathed in the lazy warmth of midday. No baggage wains stood waiting to be filled with her belongings. No peasants and oxen milled about waiting to carry them away, nor was there a mounted escort ready to send her back to Benfield.

She released her breath in a long sigh, then squinted down at the crowd of stable hands clustered at the inner gate. They were peering out into the bailey. She looked beyond the inner walls to see what'd caught their interest. It was Jordan astride his new pony.

With a scream of delight even she could hear, he sent the small beast dashing full tilt across the bailey and through a flock of unwary geese. Feathers flew as servants scrambled to catch the fowl. At the far end of the yard was Gilliam, now doubled over in laughter, and beside him, Rannulf.

An odd sensation awoke at the sight of her husband's broad shouldered form. The sun burnished his dark hair with a coppery glow and gleamed golden on his soft gown. Although she tried from this distance, she could not make out his expression. As if sensing her interest, he looked up toward her windows. She gasped and stepped back, then wondered why she'd done so. Surely, he'd not seen her.

"Enough of this foolishness," she scolded herself and threw open the door to the women's quarters. "Ilsa?! Ilsa! Where are you?" Without waiting for an answer, she stalked back into the solar. At least the maid had thought to lay out a ewer of water and a fresh washcloth. She dampened the square and scrubbed her face.

"Here I am, lady," the old woman said, stepping spryly into the solar.

"Bring my clothing," she snapped as she tossed aside her robe. "Why did you leave me sleeping?"

"Lord Rannulf told me not to disturb you." Her maid held out her chemise.

"But, it is so late and I had much to do with the feast this afternoon. And"—Rowena hurriedly pulled the garment on over her head—"above all, I have missed mass." Following this, she donned the loose white undergown and slipped her feet into stockings and shoes.

"Well," Ilsa said with a nervous laugh, "what is one from seven? Besides, you look rested. Perhaps you should sleep late more often."

"You know what my wishes are. Why did you listen to him when I have commanded differently?"

"Oh, lady, but he is my lord. Will you worry me between you like two dogs with a meaty bone until I snap and am useless to you both?" The old woman twisted her hands into her lady's simple blue wool overgown.

Rowena opened her mouth to reply, only to shut it against the angry words waiting to tumble out. If she vented her fears and frustration over her marriage on those around her, she would soon destroy all the faith and confidence she'd so strived to build. "My apologies," she said after a moment, "I am not fit to be with this morning."

Ilsa helped her into her overgown and pulled the laces tight as Rowena knotted her belt about her waist. At last, she tied her key ring into place on the belt's long tongue. When she let it fall, the many keys jangled merrily at her knees.

"Sit, lady, and let me fix your hair."

"Today, I will do it for myself."

"But, it is my duty to—"

"Go." Her tone quickly sent the old woman back into the safety of the women's quarters. Rowena sat in the chair and tore the comb through her long tresses. It would have taken that woman a half an hour to do what she could do for herself in minutes.

Suddenly, the solar's door burst open. "Lady Wren, Lady Wren," Jordan screeched, "you should have seen me!" He was fair dancing with excitement. His hair stood straight up from his head, and his robe was smeared with mud. "You should have seen Scherewind. That is my pony, I have named him Scherewind for he is faster than any other horse."

"Oh, but I did," she interrupted. "Ooof," she gasped as he leapt into her lap. "Have a care with me, my heart. I am no burly man like your father or your uncles."

"Pardon," he said, in the same breath with, "You saw? Was I not the fastest man on horseback you have ever seen?" He waited expectantly for her nod and, when he received it, yelled in pleasure. "I knew I was."

She laughed. "I also believe we are now short a goose or two."

He had the grace to look sheepish. "Papa says I will learn to be more careful if I must help Cook pluck the one Scherewind killed. Do I have to?" he asked, his eyes wide with hope of reprieve.

"Jordan." The stern, hard word made both the child and his stepmother start in surprise. Lord Rannulf stood in the doorway, his fists clenched at his side and a dark expression on his face. "Why did you come here when I sent you to the kitchen?" His voice was not loud, but there was no mistaking his anger.

"But, Papa," the boy whined pitifully, "it will be so hard. Must I?" the boy pleaded to his stepmother. Instinctively, protectively, her arms tightened around his slim shoulders as he burrowed even deeper into her embrace.

"Put him down." It was no request. Her husband turned his hard gray gaze on her. "I'll not have you stepping between me and my son."

Rowena stiffened at the command in his tone, but knew he was right in what he ordered. Although she loosened her hold on the boy, she was not ready to free him. "Jordan, someday you will hold the lives of others in your hands," she said, turning her full attention to this child she loved. "If you do not learn to accept responsibility for your mistakes, how will they be able to give to you their loyalty?"

"But, I cannot do it," he cried. "I am only little."

"Cannot or will not?"

Rowena looked up at the sudden softness she heard in his voice. Rannulf now leaned casually in the doorway, his arms crossed over his chest. When he lifted a brow in response to her look, his mouth seemed almost to bend in a smile. "If you are man enough to ride the pony, you must be man enough for this. I will brook no further disobedience from you. Go. Do as you have been told. And," he continued, "it will be tomorrow that you eat the fruits of your carelessness. Today, it seems we feast. I understand there will even be mummers."

The child in her lap crowed in excitement. "Players! May I see them now?"

"You have something else to attend to," his father told him. "Off with you to the kitchen. I wish to speak with your stepmother."

The boy's look was beseeching as he slipped from her lap and started toward the door. "I will be more careful of Scherewind, I will, I vow it," he offered, still hopeful.

"I have no doubt you will," his father replied, deaf to the pleading in his son's voice.

Rowena said nothing, only bit her cheek to keep from smiling as the boy hung his head and walked from the room as if he were going to his death. How could father and son be so alike in look and yet so different in disposition? Where her husband was moody and unpredictable, his son was calm and happy. Had Rannulf been like Jordan once, long ago?

Her husband shut the door as he entered and turned to face his wife. "Cover your hair," he said brusquely, "my brothers will be here in a moment."

Her heart fell at his harsh tone. So, there was no

change between them. The softness she had seen was only for his son. She stood and pulled her hair over her shoulder, her fingers flying as she braided it. When she glanced up, he was watching her. Her face reddened at his intense look, and she turned away to tie the thong at her braid's end. Then she deftly fastened on the plain linen head scarf Ilsa had laid out for her.

"I saw you at your window not long ago. You were not yet dressed."

His statement startled her, and she whirled to face him. "You saw me?" she gasped out. If he had seen her, had others noticed her as well? Once again her cheeks burned.

His eyes were narrowed and hard once again. "I hope that is not your habit, for I will not tolerate it."

His patronizing tone reawakened her anger and chased away the shame. "Of course it is not my habit," she snapped. "I only wished to see if you were—" she caught herself before she added, removing my belongings. No need to borrow trouble.

"If I was what?" he snapped back. "Still within these walls?"

What was he talking about? Where else would he be? With a sigh of frustration, Rowena reined in her emotions. She had no wish to provoke him again. "It is nothing but a woman's foolishness," she said, with a small smile. Within her heart, she prayed she was right, that she's been foolish to believe he might send her away.

He watched her a moment longer, then the tension eased from him. With startling suddeness, he grinned. "So, you admit to an occasional foolishness, do you?"

His question took her aback, and she only stared

at him. When she said nothing, he laughed and seated himself in the chair she'd left. With his long legs stretched out before him, he looked only marginally more comfortable than Gilliam had been in the same chair.

"What you said to Jordan," he said a moment later, "it was good. I only told him that he had to do the chore. You have told him the why of it." His voice was almost choked, as though it cost him to say the words.

A compliment? "He is a good boy," she managed in her surprise.

"What is this name my son calls you?" He peered up at her, his expression neither hostile nor friendly.

"Oh"—she laughed self-consciously—"when I had first come to the convent one nun mangled my name so badly it came out 'Wren' and so it stayed these many years. It is silly, I suppose, but I am accusomted to it and it is easier for Jordan." Her voice trailed off into silence.

"Wren," he said softly a moment later, as though trying the feel of it on his tongue. "It seems a flippant name, and one that hardly suits you."

There was a tap at the door. "Come," they said in unison.

"Good day, my lady," said Gilliam as he entered and came to stand before the hearth. "Here is Temric, brother. Now, what was it you wished to discuss?" Temric silently followed his youngest noble sibling and took up his place beside his lord's chair.

"Aye," Lord Graistan responded, "I wish to know why the Lady Maeve was sent from my walls with no word to me of your intentions. She is my ward, and I am responsible for her. Unless you can show me good reason not to, I must bring her home."

Gilliam blanched. "Nay." His voice was weak.

"She is well cared for as a guest in the convent at Hazelbrook. Why can she not stay where she is?" Rowena asked with a sinking feeling. Maeve had been right. "My lord, do not bring her back. She has wreaked havoc in here."

Rannulf released an irritated and confused breath as his glance moved from one to the other. "Will one of you tell me what happened that caused you to send her there?"

His wife answered quickly. "We discovered it was on her behalf that Hugo raided your treasury."

"And you have your proof?" her husband asked softly.

"Hugo confessed," she started to say, but he waved that away.

"You are no priest. No doubt he sought to ease his own guilt by dragging an innocent down with him."

"If only you had seen his pain," she replied, "you could not say so. Besides, what would he have done with the coins if he'd not given them to her?"

"That is a different issue," he said more loudly. "I will accept that you felt her guilty of this theft, but that still leaves the question of why was there no letter asking for my permission to send her away from my walls."

She shrugged, but the gesture covered the truth. Each time she'd sat to write to him, her pen refused to form the words. Maeve had been so certain she'd be returned to Graistan. So, Rowena had delayed until it was too late. "We had received your message saying you'd soon be home, so we waited."

"Do not bring her back," his younger brother said quietly. "She only seeks to hurt those around her. She can do you no credit here."

"Surely you are mistaken," Rannulf said, his confusion and irritation growing more apparent. "She has lived here two years, and never have I witnessed any misbehavior. No doubt she has her faults, but so do we all. I cannot see that she has ever done any harm."

"Harm!" Rowena sputtered in outrage. "Ask your servants what she's done. Ask the assistant cook who lost a finger at Maeve's hand. Ask the mother of the girl over whose head boiling water was poured as punishment for clumsiness."

He shook his head in disbelief. "If this were true, if these things were happening beneath my own roof, why did they not come to me?"

She only shrugged helplessly. This was something she'd often wondered herself.

"Because, you were too caught up in your own grief to listen to your servants' complaints." Temric's words startled them all. His usually harsh voice was unexpectedly gentle. "You have let the past blind you here."

"How can you say I have ignored them? Have I not just spent my morning speaking with all my folk as I do after any absence? You make it seem as if I have mistaken an evil vixen for a helpless widow and have set her loose to torment my people."

His brother stood unswayed by the assault. "You have a wife now. There is no place for Maeve here. Do I need to explain to you why Maeve's people threw her from her home with only a few coins in exchange for her dower? Nay, I think you know as well as I, although you have long refused to see it."

"Do not bring her back here." Gilliam's face was twisted in pain. "Or, if you do, release me from my oath to you so I may seek my fortune elsewhere. You cannot ask me to be under the same roof with that woman."

"What?" Lord Graistan leapt to his feet in shocked surprise. "But you have only just returned home. Where will you go?"

"To King Richard in France. It will be one less knight's fee you must pay." His brother tried a jaunty smile and failed.

"I cannot believe this," Rannulf cried now in utter frustration. "My older brother lectures and my youngest brother threatens to leave home all because of one helpless woman. What is wrong with you two? By God, my wife is near believing the woman is a witch!"

He strode to the door and struck it with his fist. "So, to keep you happy, she must go," he ground out. "But what of me? Will any man trust me again if I break my word and send one so defenseless from my hall? So, tell me, what am I to do with her?"

Rowena gave a quick, sarcastic laugh. "I suppose you could find her a husband," she said.

Rannulf stared at her in astonishment for just an instant, then breathed, "Aye, and I know the man. Was not John of Ashby just telling me how he despaired of finding a wife he could afford? I will offer him Maeve."

"Wait," she protested, shocked that he had taken her seriously, "wait, I spoke only in jest. She's fit for no man to wed. Far better for her that she remains at the convent."

But he paid her no heed and spoke over her words. "Of course, how foolish of me. No doubt this is what she, herself, would desire. I can give her no dowry, but John will take her if I lower for her life's span the amounts of foods and goods he gives to Graistan. Aye, I'll also give him a bigger portion of the bridge tolls."

"Not the tolls," she cried out. "That is too much."

"It seems it is a small price to pay to rid you of her," he snapped back. "Are you so greedy?"

She stared at him and knew no word she uttered would change his course. "Nay, my lord, I have misspoken," she replied in defeat.

Temric's eyes narrowed in consideration. "But will Ashby agree? The woman is no prize." For this moment his usual guarded expression was gone. Rowena studied his face. His resemblance to his brothers lay in his strong, angular cheekbones and stubborn jawline.

"What say you?" Rannulf retorted. "She is a handsome woman with graceful manners."

The smaller man only shrugged. "If you say so. Then, shall I send a messenger to Ashby with your offer?"

"Aye, but, I'll have royal approval before I see this wedding done. No accursed fee this time." Lord Graistan smiled wryly. "Ready your fastest messenger to leave for Ashby this night. By mid-May I'll have his approval and have Oswald draw up their contract. By month's end, we'll have the crown's agreement as well. Mark my words, this one'll not be the morass mine was. We'll see it easily done."

Temric gave a short laugh. "Marked," he said.

Then, Rannulf's brow creased in consideration. "But, here is the perfect opportunity to introduce my wife to my vassals and castellans." When he looked up, his smile was broad and relieved. "Aye, we'll throw Ashby the finest wedding ceremony possible and invite them all. A rich celebration will ease the sting of having missed my wedding, such as it was."

Rowena was stunned. "But, my lord, we have barely enough to keep Graistan until the harvests are in. And, when we do have the harvest, we need everything to rebuild our own stores. Where am I to find food for guests?"

Her husband's grin slipped some. "You will do as you have done before. Buy what is needed."

"But we have so little," she started.

"If you desire to keep my accounts, you will find the resources," his voice overrode hers. "Graistan has never been tightfisted before, it will not start now."

She opened her mouth to argue him into understanding, but Temric intervened. "Perhaps it is best to save planning until Ashby has said 'yea' or 'nay.' Have you anything else for me? No? Then I am off. Good day, my lady." He bowed briefly in her direction and strode out, surprising the serving woman who had just tapped at the door.

"My lady, Cook would like to speak with you before you give the command to begin serving. Otherwise, all else is in readiness," she said, then exited.

"Good, for I am starved," cried Gilliam, as he leapt to his feet, his gaiety forced and his smile false. He hurried across the room and out of the door before anyone could stop him.

"Gilliam," his brother called out to no avail. "What is wrong with that boy?" he growled out as he came to his feet. "And what is wrong with you? Do you know no better than to contradict me before my family? If I say we eat on golden plates, we eat on golden plates, damn the expense."

"Best you find yourself an alchemist, then, my lord, for your golden plates will have to be made from lead."

"Damn your tongue," he bellowed. "Do not say me 'nay.' "

Rowena glared at him, opened her mouth to retort, then stopped. Anger had twisted his mouth into a thin line, and the muscle in his jaw was tense once again.

"You are right," she finally said in a quiet voice, "I should not have spoken so before your brothers. I beg your pardon. Being a wife is something very foreign to me, my lord, but I am trying to learn." She sent him a small, shy smile. "I not only admit to an occasional foolishness, but my mouth tends to be a might hasty as well."

Surprise drove the rage from his eyes. His shoulders relaxed and his fists opened. "Well," he said, "that is true enough."

"You need not agree so quickly," she shot back.

Her husband gave a short laugh. "You have my apologies. I think we must needs discuss this matter of my treasury. I need to know where the truth lies."

She fought a swift wave of possessiveness. Not his treasury, hers. She wanted no interference in her plans for Graistan. Then, she caught her breath. So, now where was the difference between herself and Hugo? "I am at your convenience, my lord."

"Since this feast of yours will keep us for the rest of the day, we will have to find another time."

She nodded in agreement. "Please, my lord, remember how hard everyone has worked to make this a day of rejoicing. They are proud of all they've accomplished in the past several months, and are looking forward to hearing kind words from you for their effort."

"You do not need to lecture me on my duties," he retorted. "I have been lord here for nearly a score of years and have learned a thing or two in that time."

She jumped in surprise at his sharpness. "I meant nothing by my words. I only meant . . ." she paused. What she'd meant to do was to remind him he would need to introduce her at the meal. To do so was to acknowledge and confirm her place as Graistan's chatelaine. But she could forgive him forgetting it, not so if he refused her. Better to wait and see. "Pay me no mind, my lord. If you will excuse me, I will meet you at the table." At his nod, she hurried from the room.

After assuring the cook everything was just as she'd desired, she returned to her chambers and donned a dark green overgown. Although simple and plain, it was a rich samite and a goodly step above her workaday dresses, sufficient for a family celebration. With a fine wimple and a necklet of garnet, which she wore at Ilsa's insistence, she was ready.

When she entered the hall, she looked about with a critical eye. The room appeared right festive beneath brightly glowing torches. Its freshly painted walls gleamed, seeming even whiter against the bright colors in the hangings and on the rafters. The many tables, all covered in white cloths, were hung with garlands woven from flowering branches and willow withes. Her every step brought with it the scent of sweet herbs. It was with pride that she made her way to the high table where her husband sat with Sir Gilliam at his left.

The young knight seemed recovered from his earlier depression and held out a filled wine cup. "Sister," he cried, spearing a smoked eel with his knife to hold it up for all to see, "you remembered! Thank you, my dear and most beloved lady." But the fool's grin on his face told her how he struggled still to hide his uneasiness.

So, when he reached out to catch her hand as she passed, she laughed and slapped his fingers away. "Do not be so silly," she said warmly, a gentle reminder to calm himself. She seated herself to the right of her husband and leaned forward to continue speaking to Gilliam. "You would not let me forget. For weeks you have told me how much you like smoked eels."

"How fortunate you are, brother, to have such a good and caring wife." Rannulf only glanced between the two of them and said nothing as the meal service began.

They dined on venison seethed in wines and herbs and lamb in a richly flavored sauce. With the season still so new, there was little in the way of fruits, but spring vegetables were offered in both soup and stews. As each new dish was presented for her husband's approval, she glanced surreptitiously at him to gauge his reaction. There was nothing for her to see. When he spoke to her, it was only to offer her morsels of food in a polite, but distant, manner.

It had nearly reached the hour for Vespers when the cook brought out the sugary sculpture that indicated the meal's end. He carried it slowly around the room for all to see. It was Graistan, represented in all its splendor, from green tinted icing as grass to tall walls colored white. The newly promoted butler, now the keep's highest-ranking servant since Hugo's death, stepped forward. It was he who made a pretty speech on behalf of all the castle folk welcoming their lord home once again and returning to his castle.

When her husband stood to respond, he was careful not to forget a single soul in recounting the changes he'd seen and expressed how grateful he was for their efforts on his behalf. Save her. Not once did he mention his lady. It was as though she did not exist. If any noticed it, no one commented upon it.

With the meal finished, the entertainment began. The hours passed, but Rowena could not hear or see, so deep was her depression. Pray God that he had only forgotten. To think he would hold her in so little regard.

"My lady?"

She started from her painful thoughts. The players were retiring. Would he do it now? Had he only waited? "Aye, my lord?"

"I slept poorly last night and am tired to the bone. I will retire now and wish you to attend me."

Disappointment ate at her heart, but she hid it behind a tight expression and nodded her agreement. He stood and held out his hand. When she laid hers upon his, his fingers, long and graceful, closed gently to trap her hand into the square strength of his palm. Despite her emotions, she could not repress her shiver of reaction to his touch. She glanced up at him.

He stared back, his eyes half-closed and his mouth bent in a small smile. His fingers moved ever so softly against hers. Her pulse leapt, her heart suddenly pounding.

"Good even, all," he called out, leading her away from the tables. She did not resist him. "I thank you for your welcome and bid you to stay and enjoy the entertainment."

Together they climbed the stairs and, a moment later, he had closed and latched their bedchamber door. The silence in the room was deafening after the noise of the hall. Somehow, this privacy made her hurt all the worse. It dulled her senses, and she could not react when he drew her into his arms nor respond when he kissed her. Yet, when he released her, she keenly felt his loss and wanted his arms around her again.

"So, that's to be the way of it, eh?" His gray eyes were cold and his look, hard. "You are too naive to know that one night will not convince me."

She turned away, confused as much by her erratic emotions as by his words. Her keys clattered loudly as she twisted her hands in her belt. The raucous noise reminded her she'd vowed to make him hers. Pushing him away would surely not help her in that end.

"Take those damn things off," he snapped, "and call a servant to bring up some wine." He threw himself down in a chair and sullenly studied the leaping flames on the hearth.

She did as she was told and used the waiting time to silently scold herself for her attitude. Thus, when the wine arrived, she had slipped out of her clothing and wore only her bedrobe. She filled his cup and came to stand behind his chair. "My lord?" She handed it to him from over his shoulder; he took it without a backward look.

There was something magnetic about standing so near him when he could not see her. The dark gold material of his gown stretched taut across his powerful back, almost binding against the curve of his upper arm. She laid her hands on his shoulders. He started slightly. Beneath his gown and shirt, his muscles were corded with tension.

Touching him made her fingers tingle. She studied the way his hair curled slightly against the collar of his gown. How odd that it should look so brown now, yet glow red in the light. Lost in her musing, she idly shaped one strand to lay around the curl of his ear, pressing it in place with a light touch.

He caught her hand in his and, with a swift tug, pulled her around the chair to sit in his lap.

"Is it yea or nay?" he asked, then raised a brow when he noticed she wore only her bedrobe.

Yea or nay? She stared at him in confusion, still trapped in the sensations of the prior moment.

"If you will not say, I will simply take it," he said, somewhat harshly, then bent his mouth to hers.

This time her body burst into lively response to his kiss. She laid her arms around his neck and pressed herself against him. Cradled in the strength of his embrace, it was easy to forget hurt and let the moment be all that was important.

Rannulf let his suspicions be washed away as desire surged through him. Once again, her reaction stunned him. When she'd refused him earlier, he assumed she'd left the bedchamber for refuge in the women's quarters where he could not go. In that moment, he'd been sure what waited for him. There would be weeks of coldness after which she would announce she was with child. Everyone would comment on how swiftly his seed had taken root. Some might even believe it.

Yet, she had stayed, even served him. When she touched him, chills of longing shot down his spine at her play. Whatever her reasons, her body offered him much pleasure, much pleasure indeed. He forgot to be cautious. Instead, he indulged himself in the incredible sensations she woke within him.

# Chapter Eleven

WHEN Rannulf arose early the next morning, his wife yet lay in a sound slumber. And so she should after their exertions of the past night. She curled beneath the bedclothes, her hair, black as a raven's wing, carelessly strewn over the bolsters. God's blood, but he wanted her again. He hastily dressed and slipped from their room.

It was still an hour before sunrise when he exited the keep with his foresters. In the gray light they rode through the silent woods, their passage waking rich scents from the moist, cool earth. Unwilling to break the deep stillness that lay all around them, he only nodded as they quietly pointed out the changes, be they restorations or removals, they'd made both in clearing and copse.

Then the sky lightened to golden pinks and pure blues. Dawn's wind rustled through brush and tree and the birds began to stir, first one, then another and another until the branches were alive with their songs. Rabbit and squirrel darted away from their passage through the feathery new growth. In the distance he heard the trumpet of a stag and a bull's challenging bellow.

A deep breath filled his lungs with the spicy air. It would be a good day to hunt. Aye, his kennel master had a new litter ready for blooding. He could spend the day sorting his tangled thoughts. That was just what he needed. His chore finished, he turned his steed back for Graistan. Aye and he'd take Gilliam with him.

Dogs belled at his return as the sentry called out a greeting. The ring of hammer on anvil in the smithy competed with the ring of steel to steel in the tilting yard where Temric drilled his men. The bailey was alive with the bleating of sheep and cackle and call of poultry. Maids and men chatted as they fed their charges, whether they be bovine, ovine, or fowl. A cock crowed from the inner wall and stable lads whistled and sang as they tended the horses and swept the stalls clean.

He dismounted and handed his reins to a groomsman, then commanded his huntsmen to prepare for the day. All that waited now was his companion.

The hall was awaft in the scent of the day's baking. As with yestermorn, all the tables were up and at the first hearth stood a huge iron pot in which a thick vegetable and grain potage bubbled. Set out on trays were fresh breads, cheeses, and hard-boiled eggs. He grimaced, sick to death of eggs, having eaten so many since the Easter tribute.

"Gilliam?" he called out, expecting to find his brother at the table.

"He's at mass, my lord," a servant informed him.

Rannulf nodded his thanks, somewhat surprised. Before the Crusade, once a week on Sunday had served his brother well enough. He seated himself at the high table and carefully studied the massive room as he waited. It was truly a pleasure to see it restored to what it had been under his stepmother's rule.

A serving woman handed him a cup of watered wine, and he took bread and cheese to break his

fast. He glanced toward the end of the room, then
looked again with a frown. There was no mistaking
where Gilliam's interest lay.

His wife and brother stood conversing just beyond
the chapel's entrance into the hall. Even in her plain
gown and simple headdress, his wife caught and
held his interest. She glowed with vibrant life. Ah,
but what pleasure he found at the touch of her lips
and in the gentle curve of her body. While she
seemed intent on whatever she was saying, his
brother only laughed. This obviously irritated her,
for when he offered her his arm, she shoved it away
and started up into the hall. When she caught his
gaze, her expression dimmed even further.

If she was so unhappy each time her eye met his,
why did she so freely offer herself to him? To what
purpose did she use him? He looked away, trapped
between doubt and desire. But, to recognize her manipulation was to be armed against its outcome. She
seated herself next to him. "Good morrow, my lord,"
she said flatly.

"So it seems," he said mirroring her blandness.
Then he turned toward the young knight. "Gilliam,
I am for hunting this morn. Will you come?"

"Hunting? Me? Just point the way, but not until
after we break our fast." His brother seated himself
and began to eat.

Rannulf watched in amazement as the boy finished several bowls of potage and a full loaf of bread
before starting on the cheese. "No wonder we are
impoverished," he chided. "You, alone, will eat me
into penury."

"At least he now uses manners." His wife
laughed. "I will never forget my first morning at
Graistan."

He watched as Gilliam blushed. "I had forgot

that," he said in shame. "What you must have thought."

She only shook her head and laughed. "I forgive you."

"What is this?" Rànnulf asked, a wave of jealousy sweeping over him at their private memories.

It was his wife who answered. "He sought to drive Lady Maeve from the table by eating like a peasant. He drank from the pitcher and spoke with his mouth so full that he spewed crumbs at me." She leaned forward to look past him at the young man, her blue eyes dancing in amusement. "There, I have paid you back for every one of those silly jests of yours."

"Augh!" the young knight clutched his chest, "I am mortally wounded."

Rannulf forced himself to smile at their banter. "What reason had you for driving Maeve from my table?"

His brother's grin slipped just a little. "I said all I will say about her yesterday."

"How can you be so sure? After all, you knew her only a little."

"I am sure." There was no amusement left in his face now.

"Are you certain there is no other reason?" He needed to say no more. Gilliam knew. He saw his own heart reflected in his brother's eyes.

"Nay," the boy breathed, vehemently shaking his head.

"Sweet Mary, but I am sorry I said anything," his wife sighed. "This is a subject best left to die."

He threw his hands up in submission. "I still cannot believe her capable of all you describe. Nevertheless, it is resolved and I will hear no more talk of you leaving Graistan, brother."

The young man stared at his hands, then raised his head. Pain, deep and intense, filled his eyes. "Why would you wish to keep me here? At best I am a poor steward. It seems I am the cause of only your trouble, never your good." He threw himself to his feet, but Rannulf caught him by the arm.

"That is not true. There have been times when you were my only good. Do not leave." Why had he spoken of the past? How could he have believed the wound would so easily heal in Gilliam when it had festered for so long within himself?

His brother only shook his head and averted his eyes. When he was finally released, he fairly ran from the room. Rannulf stared after him, not knowing how to mend the gap between them. He started with surprise when his wife lightly touched his arm.

"I doubt he will leave you," she said. "He dearly loves Graistan, but I believe he loves you more."

He turned toward her. "You are fond of my brother." There was no need to question what he knew to be true.

"I suppose I am," she said, her brow creased in consideration. "He has been a great help to me in these past months, although I at first despaired of understanding why you had made a steward of a man who could neither read nor write. Now I see it is his loyalty and his love you value. But, he's no clerk and would be far better suited to holding a keep of his own, even if only as your castellan."

"No doubt you would think so. A castellan travels less frequently than a steward." His voice was harsh.

She shot him a curious look, as if she could not understand why he'd said what he had. "Do you think me so close with a coin that I would begrudge the cost of a steward's travel?"

How easily she danced around the truth, never

denying she was attracted to his brother, only evading the issue. He could tolerate no more of this topic. He turned his attention back to his bread and cheese.

"I missed you at mass this morn, my lord. You left without telling me your intent. I asked the chaplain to delay the service, but you did not come. Will you attend on the morrow?"

"It is my business if I do or not," he said harshly. He could hardly bear to scrutinize his own soul much less let a churchman have a try at it. Her suddenly horrified expression almost made him laugh.

"You never attend mass?" she breathed in question.

"Did I attend mass at our wedding?"

"Aye." The answer was whispered, although she obviously found meager solace in the thought.

"Let me worry over my own soul," he said.

"My lord, we are ready as soon as you are." It was his chief huntsman.

"Good," Rannulf said with relief, glad to be freed of this conversation. "Find Sir Gilliam and say to him, I beg his pardon and dearly desire his company this day. If he resists, tell him I will tie him to his steed if need be."

"As you wish, my lord." The huntsman laughed and strode away as he came to his feet.

"My lord." His wife caught him by the sleeve. "Are you still set on a grand celebration for this wedding? We were to discuss it."

"Later. I am tired of plans and schemes and contracts. We will talk when I know whether Sir John accepts her or not."

"Please, I beg a moment with you. I swear that is all it will be." She came to her feet, her lower lip caught between her teeth, the very picture of consternation.

"As you wish," he replied, and led her to the hearth, away from the general bustle of the servants. "Speak, I am listening."

She stood uneasily before him. "I know you will probably not credit what I say, but my heart insists that I speak. It is wrong, this wedding of yours. She is not fit to be any man's wife—"

Rannulf abruptly raised his hand, and his words overrode hers. "If you intend another harangue against her, I will not listen. I have made my decision."

She stared up at him for a long moment, the worry in her eyes slowly dying away. "Aye, I see that you have," she finally said in reluctant acceptance. With a heavy sigh, she turned and picked up a stick. "Sir Gilliam says Ashby is only a wooden hall with a single village on its lands." As she spoke, she poked at the coals that lay upon the hearth floor.

"Now what is your point, woman? Stop that before you choke us with smoke."

She set the stick atop the burning logs. "Is this man you've chosen strong enough to control her? More importantly, what if she refuses to accept him as her husband? Can you control her?"

"She will accept him," he said in absolute confidence. "I am her guardian and may marry her as I see fit. John is a good man. She could do far worse."

"Lady Maeve is accustomed to a more luxurious way of life. Ashby will not support her needs." Her voice was even and unemotional.

"No doubt it is better than a convent," he retorted.

"So you would say. Would you grant me favor?"

He stared down at her. There was nothing in her

clear blue gaze or the soft set of her lips to indicate what sort of boon she wanted. Under his scrutiny she smiled a little. At last, he nodded.

"For the sake of your folk, my lord, please, do not release her from the convent until the very day she is to be wed. I know you do not believe what we tell you, but the servants are uneasy with her here."

He felt the tension drain from his shoulders as he relaxed into consideration. What was it he had feared she might ask? "I think it is all foolishness, but I cannot deny that others do not see it so. I will honor your request for that reason."

It was in obvious relief that she took his hand and briefly raised it to ther lips. "Thank you, my lord."

The shock of her touch ran through him like a sword's thrust reawakening his latent desire for her. How did she do that to him? He reached for her, meaning to draw her into his embrace when she spoke and destroyed the moment. "But what will you do about the coins she stole from you? How will you get them back from her?"

He froze. So, here was the point to her softness. She would not try to humble him by revealing to the world what a fool he'd been to so implicitly trust his wardrober. His pride would be destroyed so that she might gain some power over him. "You've no proof she was involved."

"How else can you account for her rich gowns and jewels? Unless it was you who supplied this poor widow her finery." There was something more than curiosity in her tone.

"Me? I needed buy her nothing, for she had plenty when she came."

"If you did not buy them, then who did? There can be no doubt that she bought them here. Several merchants actually came to ask after her when she no longer visited their establishments. If you will not believe me, ask them. And where, save Graistan's coffers, could she have acquired her riches?"

Rannulf stared down at her for a long moment, remembering the times he'd complimented Maeve on her attire. It had pleased him that she took such care with her appearance, for it reflected well on Graistan's prominence. Why had it never occurred to him to ask her where she'd come by her gowns? He'd just assumed she made them from the fabrics in his storerooms. As his doubts rose, his pride reared back and would not let him face them. To acknowledge the possibility of his wife's accusations was to render himself thrice a fool.

"What would you have me do? Tear the clothing off her back?" he asked stiffly. "When she is married, she will trouble you no longer."

"That is all?" she protested. "But, she has stolen from you."

"If I do not choose to call it stolen, it is not stolen," he returned angrily. Why could she not let it be? She was determined to prod and poke on what was rapidly becoming a very sore issue with him. "There is no more to be said."

She huffed in annoyance. "I cannot understand your attitude. You say to me that the king had demanded double the marriage fee for the honor"—her voice lingered sarcastically on the word—"of marrying me. That is two year's income. He also levied another scutage. And yet, as if to reward this woman for her many misdeeds, you shower her with a dowry and a costly wedding ceremony and forgive her her thefts."

Rannulf tried unsuccessfully to control his seething temper. Not only did she seek to humble him, she would do it before the whole hall. "Are you jealous?"

"Nay," she shot back, her word like the scrouge of a whip, "I am livid. What she has taken belongs to my children. I will not have their inheritance stolen."

"How touching," he said coldly. "Instead of harrying a defenseless widow, why not extend your concerns to conserving expensive spices used in unnecessary feasts. If this is your way of guarding my treasury, you'll not be long at my purse strings."

She stared at him, her slender jaw tight with rage, her eyes snapping blue. "For shame! That celebration was necessary, indeed, for the servants needed to honor you if only to remember who is their lord. Your neglect here is legendary. As for spices, we have none save pepper. All that was in our meal was the cook's skill and what herbs grow in our garden. It lightened your purse not one whit."

How dare she chide him as if he were a child. He grabbed her by the arms. "Lower your voice, madam, or better yet, shut your mouth."

She tore free of him, her breath coming in hasty gulps. "You great ass," she finally got out. He stepped back at the rage in her eyes. "I have worked my fingers to the bone turning this pigsty into a home for you, and you, you—oh!" With that she turned and ran to the stairs.

Rannulf stared after her, stunned into immobility. Then came anger. What right had that immoral little shrew to call him an ass?

"Rannulf," Gilliam called from across the room. "They cannot hold the dogs much longer."

With a foul word, he stormed for the door. Never had there been a more ill-fated combination of that woman and her tongue. While her curves tempted him, her every word sent him bristling to arms. In the courtyard, he leapt into his saddle.

Gilliam grinned at him. "Marital troubles, brother? What you need is a little blood to clear your thoughts." His grin only widened when his brother scowled. "Your loss is my gain. Now I am sure to have the better day. All those who did not lay their money on me are poorer already." He set heels to his mount and raced past the stable and out the gate. Despite himself, Rannulf laughed and threw himself into the mad race to catch his brother.

Rannulf sat before the fire in the solar. He was bored. Although the hour was late, the days of mid-June were long and the sun still hung above the horizon. There was nothing left to do this day. Temric and Gilliam were occupied in the stable, and Jordan was already abed despite the continuing brightness of the sky. He'd considered asking his wife to come bear him company, but quickly discarded the notion.

How simple it had been to adopt a pattern of avoiding her, for if they did not speak, they did not fight. What he'd meant to last only a few days, until his bruised pride had healed, swiftly became seven, then fourteen. After Ashby's agreement came, those two conflict-free weeks grew into nearly six, as he waited for Oswald to secure royal approval for the wedding through his master, the bishop of Hereford. By then, shunning his wife during the day to keep the peace had become a habit he was loath to end.

But their nights were different. Within the intimacy of the bed curtains, he saw no reason to resist his attraction for her. So he gathered her into his arms and made her body sing to his needs.

The door opened. He turned in anticipation only to sigh in disappointment as he nodded to his wife. Her eyes held such an odd mixture of tenseness and sadness, he was tempted into asking, "Is something amiss?"

She paused, then seemed to think the better of speaking and walked to the window instead. The graying light accentuated the hollows beneath her eyes. He knew better than any how troubled her sleep had been these last few nights.

"Was there something you wanted?" he prodded. There must have been some reason for her seeking him out. After all, she had quickly accepted their daily silence and even made certain their paths never crossed during their waking hours. It was obvious that she, too, found their carefully enforced truce a relief.

"Have you had any word?" she finally asked without looking at him.

"Nay. I will warn you when I do." He stared down at the flames.

She sighed raggedly and turned to him, almost grim in her movements. "Are you still set on this celebration? You said once that you wished to review the accounts to better understand your situation. If you will just look, you will not be so quick to berate me for crying lack when the planning begins."

He frowned. She seemed as dull and leaden as the gathering clouds. "Are you well?" he asked, finding in her face some small signs of illness.

Surprise flitted across her expression for a brief moment, then her eyes became lifeless once again. "I am well enough, my lord."

He shrugged. If she did not want to speak to him about it, he would ask no further. "You do not sound yourself."

"Myself?" she whispered, an almost sarcastic edge to the word, then hurried on. "So will you do it?"

He nodded and rose slowly to his feet. "It seems I have nothing else pressing, so let's have at it then."

The treasury was dark and damp, its thick walls trapping the cold within it. The lamp reeked, and the brazier's glowing coals only warmed the air that stood directly above it. His wife had laid out the records on the table, then retreated to sit in perfect stillness on a nearby chest while he studied the parchments.

As he scanned the pages, his heart fell. It was as she'd said. Hugo had made no attempt to hide what he'd done. But that amount was trifling when compared to the shortages in tribute from his holdings. While his wife believed Hugo had sold the supplies to further enrich himself, he saw something far more sinister.

He stared at her over the parchment's edge. "Did you not say you'd questioned my bailiffs as to what they'd sent to Graistan these past two years?"

"Aye, Gilliam collected all that information for me. As you can see, what Hugo has noted is far short of what they sent."

"What makes you certain that it was Hugo, not they, who shorted us. Is it possible they knew of his thefts and used his guilt to hide their own thievery?"

The question startled her, and she frowned. "I had not considered it in that way, my lord. But, such a conspiracy seems so unlikely."

Rannulf turned back to the parchments. Not if they'd been sure no one else would look. Was Temric right? Had he let the events of the past blind him to the present? If so, he'd jeopardized his very existence, and it was well past time he came to his senses.

"It seems it would be unwise of us to indulge in rich celebrations just now." He stood and pushed the stool beneath the desk. Somehow, it was relief not disappointment he felt at this. "I doubt if Ashby will mind. He's never been one for show anyway."

"Thank you, my lord," she murmured gratefully as she gathered the accounts and put them away in their casket. When she turned back, she smiled a little. "See, it is not so bad to have me at your purse strings. Truly, I hold Graistan's good in my heart."

He stared down at her. She was such a pretty thing. Why did she always wear those plain gowns and rough headcloths? She ought to dress in rich colors and soft materials as befitted her station. Not that her simple garb hid her beauty. But what had happened to the vibrant life that had once filled her blue eyes?

He ran a gentle finger along the curve of her smooth cheek, expecting to see that spark he now knew so well leap into existence within her gaze. Instead, she stepped back out of his immediate reach.

"I am grateful to you for doing this, my lord," her voice a throaty whisper, "but I must now be back to my chores." When she tried to turn, he caught her by the hands.

"Surely, there can be no more for you to do this day with the hour so late."

She tried to pull free of his grasp, but he refused to release her. "Really, my lord," she insisted, her voice growing just a little firmer as she continued, "I must go."

"What do we have servants for if you do all their

work? Did you not just say you carried Graistan's good in your heart? Am I not Graistan? I have nothing to do and would greatly enjoy your company."

"My company?" she shot back. Here was the glow he had missed. It came to life as her eyes narrowed and her mouth straightened into an angry line. "Do not make me laugh." Then she gasped, as if shocked by what she'd said. With a desperate tug, she tore her hands free only to cover her face with them. For a full moment, she stood there, seeming to fight some inner battle, then dropped her finger shield. The dullness was back. "As you wish my lord."

Desire died with the resurgence of anger. "Such a heavy burden you must bear," he started, but was interrupted by a rapid tapping at the door.

"My lady, my lady, are you there?"

With a muttered curse, he yanked open the door. "What is it?"

"My lord, I did not expect to find you here," the porter gasped out, his broad face flushed red. "There is a messenger for you with urgent news." Even as he spoke, a man strode swiftly across the room and knelt before Lord Graistan.

"My lord," he said, "I have come this very day at all speed from Oswald of Hereford to deliver this into your hands. He said you must read it immediately, and I am to wait for your response and instructions." The man set the folded and sealed parchment into the nobleman's hand.

"Good work," Rannulf said. "Go to the kitchen and see that they feed you well. Tom, this man's mount is to get an extra ration of oats in reward for his haste." Then, he turned and reentered the treasury to be nearer the lamp as he opened the message.

Here were all the agreements for Ashby's wedding, signed and sealed. This was hardly urgent. He frowned and set the parchments down. All that remained was a single, hastily scrawled note. He read it once, then read it again in disbelief.

"How can they dare," he growled, and read it again. "I have the wills, where is their proof?"

"What is it?" She came to stand at his side as if to peer into the note.

"Your father is dead," he blurted out as anger rose. "It appears that it happened nigh on a month ago. But, your fine lady mother did not see fit to tell us. Rather, she has gone in secret with your sister to your grandsire's overlord, the Bishop of Hereford, to claim your mother is your grandsire's only, legal heir."

His wife paled until he thought she would fall. "She swore it," she breathed out. "She swore she would disinherit me for usurping Philippa. No," she gasped, her voice cracking as she grabbed his hand. "My lord, my lord, you cannot let her take this from me."

Rannulf frowned at her. Was that all that ever concerned her? Lands and coins? Where was even a show of grief for her father? "Rest assured, I have never lost a hide of what was mine to another, and I will not now. It must please you that my cousin's message has now saved us the cost of a war, eh?" His words were sarcastic and hard.

His wife stared up at him, her blue eyes dark. "Fields and farms," she whispered, "duty and bitterness. I have honored the agreement we made at our wedding." With that, she tore open the door and was gone.

He glared after her, then sighed in resignation. Was he not the one who had, how had she put it? ". . . bought this piece of merchandise without fully

examining it before purchase." Now he was con-
demned to this farce of a marriage. Damn her anyway for always awakening the worst in him.

He stared at the note once again. There was
much to be considered before he answered Oswald's
message. Perversely, he hoped it would come to war
and let him vent some of his bile. He snuffed out
the lamp and covered the brazier before leaving the
room. At least it would be something to do.

# Chapter Twelve

ROWENA stood at her solar windows and stared out them without seeing. Her father was dead. How sad that he had died and she could feel nothing for him, not even relief at his passing. Then her heart lurched. What if her mother succeeded in making a pauper of her? What then would become of the fine Lady Graistan? She squeezed her eyes shut. With her wealth gone, he would soon find a convenient excuse, some previously undetected degree of relationship, and she would be lady no longer. What reason did he have to keep her? None.

She stumbled across the room to her prie-dieu and knelt before the tiny, candlelit altar. Her lips moved as she silently prayed, but there was no serenity for her to find this night. Suddenly, words welled up and spilled out of her. "Mary, Mother of God," she cried, "I do not want to lose him."

Lose him! She laughed at the irony of it. How could she lose what she'd never had? The arrogance of it stung her to the core. She'd set out to tie him to her so Graistan would be hers. Instead, he had humbled her as she had never dreamed possible. Warrior that he was, he'd breached her defenses and taken her as his own all the while holding himself aloof from her.

How could she have come to care for a man who'd ignored her, even shunned her, these last weeks? She sighed in sudden understanding. It had begun the day she'd arrived at Graistan, when the castle folk accepted her as their own and firmed when his son had become her heart. And what happened behind their closed bed curtains had finished it. He might hide behind the mask of hard and angry lord during the day, but beneath the cloak of darkest night in the silence of their bedchamber, he showed her his gentle tenderness. And after their loving was finished, when she met his gaze, his eyes were filled with a warmth meant only for her.

It had been easy to convince herself that in time he would accept her, even care for her, as the rest of Graistan had. But she had deceived herself and seen only what she chose to see. She was no more to him than a hide of land waiting to be plowed and made fruitful. When her usefulness was at an end, she would again be nothing to him. The pain in her heart grew until it became unbearable.

The door flew open without warning. She leapt to her feet, clutching her beads to her chest. It was her husband and his brothers. He managed the smallest glance at her. "Pour us all a cup of wine, will you, Rowena?" he asked blandly, then sat in one of the chairs.

Pain retreated into a steady, dull ache as she complied. Rannulf nodded in thanks as he took his cup from her. After she'd served the others she moved back to stand at the windows.

He sipped at his wine, then spoke. "Try as I might, I cannot find a cause for this ridiculous ploy. Oswald has both wills. They cannot truly expect the bishop to believe deathbed utterances to some illiterate priest as better than the man's acknowledged will. And this secrecy! When we challenge them they will look like cowardly fools."

"But do they even know of the wills or that Oswald is the bishop of Hereford's right hand?" Gilliam pointed out. "It is obvious they expected no challenge, only the granting of the inheritance to Lady Benfield." He shot Rowena a quick, reassuring smile. She had not the confidence to return it.

Her husband leaned back in his chair and frowned. "Well then, they have gambled all and lost it on the first roll of the dice. Their subterfuge can only make the bishop look more closely at everything else they've said." An easy silence sprang up in the room after his words.

Rowena studied him for that moment, the straight, stubborn line of his nose, the hard curve of his jaw and perfect arch of his brow. Oh, but even now she could remember the incredible sensations of their lovemaking. How could something so wondrous be a falsehood?

"Still," he finally said, "both wills are unusual, and I must submit them to scrutiny if I am to have what is mine. What if there is some flaw we have not considered? What is the worst that could befall us?"

"Although I cannot believe it is likely, Benfield's widow could get her father's lands despite the strictures against it in his will," Temric replied. "Then, what if she remarries? She is not so old she couldn't bear another child."

"She could not marry if I had wardship of her" was her husband's rapid response. "With Oswald's help it is quite possible I would get it. But what of Benfield's will? What if Bishop William decides the elder sister is legitimate as they are claiming? The court must then divide the estate evenly between the two daughters, ignoring all else." He made an irritated sound. "I should have known it all sounded too easy when Benfield first explained it to me."

"There is one other possibility you have not considered," Gilliam said. "What if Benfield's widow planned all along to have this settled by judicial combat? That would explain Lindhurst's presence. He might be her chosen champion."

Her husband's eyes widened in surprise. "Gilliam, where did you learn to think so deviously?" he asked with a laugh. "But if that were all there was, there'd be no problem. Although I doubt the bishop would allow such an unlawful event to occur."

Rowena's heart jumped at what she heard. Could it be true? "You would fight for me?" she blurted out, then wished she could call the words back for she knew she was mistaken.

"For you?" Rannulf responded harshly. "You, I have. It is your inheritance I want."

She did not have time to stifle her gasp of pain. With a hand pressed to her lips to stop any further evidence of the hurt he'd done, she whirled to face the window.

"Damn," he said, sounding almost as pained as she felt. "My pardon, that was badly said."

"Badly? It was more than that." Temric's voice was filled with anger.

"Have I not just apologized?" Rannulf snapped back. "Since you are so insulted, brother, I will do it again. Rowena," he called across the room to her. "I did not mean it as it sounded, my mind is elsewhere."

She nodded without turning, but Temric's surprising defense warmed her. Her husband might see her as nothing, but there were others who did not feel so. Should this not content her? Why wasn't it enough?

Behind her, Lord Graistan was speaking again. "Well then, everything now rests on our ability to turn this to our advantage. In February, I sent word to my lady's two castellans telling them of our marriage and the inheritance. I think it is time I sent emissaries from Graistan—"

She let the conversation eddy around her, her thoughts drifting away from the challenge to her father. He'd been determined to find his daughter a protector. Why could he not have been equally concerned for her happiness? Would that she'd never known of Graistan rather than to have her heart torn in two this way. Gilliam's words broke into her thoughts, and she once again turned back to face the room.

"But, if we are all in Hereford, your lady will be left here alone and unprotected," he was saying.

"Nay, she comes with me," her husband replied. "She is the rightful heir and must be appear to claim her inheritance."

"Then, who will be here?" The young knight frowned slightly as if considering options. "Temric's the nearest thing you have to a castellan for Graistan."

"Now, here's a thought," Rannulf stretched his long legs out toward the fire. "Arnult, the young knight who now tutors Jordan in arms, came well recommended to me by my foster brother. I've seen him practice at arms, and he does well enough. But, I know he's never turned his hand to manning a keep. Here is his chance to try, as well as mine to learn if he has the mettle for it before Michaelmas comes 'round and we move to Upwood. Besides, when this inheritance is settled, there may well be a place for him on her lands."

In that instant Rowena saw in Gilliam's face a naked longing, as if by the very wanting of it he would be given a keep of his own. Longing was followed by despair. She nearly gasped in understanding. He believed his brother would find a keep for a strange knight but would not do the same for his own blood.

"Rannulf, you seem to have overlooked something." Temric's harsh voice startled them all. "Now that you have all you need for this wedding of yours, what will you do about it? Who knows how long you'll be in settling the inheritance."

"I had forgotten." Rannulf peered over his shoulder at his elder brother. "I can hardly leave Maeve at the convent much longer. I suppose they could be married now, but the haste of it will sit badly with John." He stared into the fire for a few quiet breaths, then smiled. "I have it. To sweeten it for him, I will farm to him our village across the river from his keep and give him the hide of arable land to the south of his demesne. He's been after that bit for years.

"Temric, prepare a messenger to ride to Ashby this very night. The moon is yet full, and he will be halfway there before it sets. We'll have this wedding the day after tomorrow and all hell be damned if we do not."

Her startled cry brought all attention on her. "The day after tomorrow?! You cannot be serious. What of their banns?"

Her husband's glance was steely gray. "That is easily resolved to my benefit. The abbey in town is building again. Since I am his greatest patron, the abbot will be eager to grant me the right to wed them whenever I choose."

"But what sort of celebration can I provide in such a short time?"

"I put that into your very capable hands, my sweet. No doubt you will surprise us all with some miracle." There was no compliment in his voice.

She opened her mouth to argue, then realized that to do so would be both futile and a waste of time. Instead, she sped across the room. The door to the women's quarters fairly leapt from its leather hinges and crashed against the wall. "Ilsa, Margaret, rise, rise now I say," she cried out at the mass of sleeping women. "And, you, Emma and Anne."

"Rowena," her husband called irritably, "what are you about? 'Tis well past time to be abed. Let them be."

She whirled on him. "I have less than two days to concoct something that will not bring shame upon Gristan's name. You have given me permission to create a miracle. Now, do you get out of my way so I might do it, or will you serve the bride and groom potage and bread for their wedding feast?"

"As it appears you have no further need for me," Temric interjected before his brother could respond, "I will take my leave and get that man on his way." He bowed briefly toward her and withdrew as his youngest brother leapt to his feet.

"By your leave, Rannulf, I will be on my way to Upwood tomorrow. I received a message from Sir Jocelynn regarding the wall extension you requested he build. He wishes me to come and approve what's done to date. I'll be gone no more than three days."

Rowena did not wait for the solar door to close behind them. "Up, women, up," she exhorted, "we have work to do. My husband wishes to hold a wedding here day after tomorrow."

"What," Ilsa cried out, shoving her wiry gray hair from her eyes in sudden panic. "Do I wake the seamstresses? Are there gowns to make?"

"Are there?" She shot the question over her shoulder to her husband.

"Nay" was his clipped answer.

"I know the bride has need of nothing, but what of Ashby? Will the time be so short that he will not have a gown suitable for a wedding?"

Her husband opened his mouth to reply, then paused. "He will come without thinking of his appearance," he finally answered.

"Wake the seamstresses. What size is this Ashby?"

"He is near to my height, but bigger."

Ilsa scrambled to her feet and pulled on her overgown. "Bigger how?" she asked, her head still within the gown.

"In the belly," Lord Graistan replied.

"Use one of my husband's old gowns as a guide," Rowena broke in, "and make it much wider. Somewhere we will find a rich belt to make a present of, so the robe will fit the man. Anne, you must go wake Cook, for he likes you best." Anne had the grace to blush, for she had not known her lady was aware of their affair. "Tell him I will be down anon, but he must draw up a list of suggestions based on what we now have in store.

"Emma, I need you to ask the butler if we have any suitable wines in store. I know we do not, but let him tell you this. Let him ramble for a time, for only then will he remember which wine merchant can find him what he wants. I need you to listen for those names, as we must send a cart there first thing on the morrow. Margaret, you will prepare the nuptial chamber. The room in the north tower is big enough. My lord's bed should fit nicely into it."

"Not the tower chamber," her husband broke in. "They should use our chamber."

"As you wish. Then, Margaret, you must take down the bed in our chamber and set up my lord's in its place."

"That is ridiculous," Rannulf interrupted. "Leave it where it stands."

"Nay," she said vehemently and turned to him. Her back was stiff, her fists clenched at her sides. "She will not sleep in my bed."

"Woman," he warned. Bathed in only the low light from the fire and the few candles she kept about the room, his face looked no softer than that of a statue's. Only the hard gleam of his eyes betrayed that this was a man and not stone.

But she would not cede to him on this. Every discordant note between herself and her husband seemed to spring from Maeve, and what little happiness she had known so far in her marriage she had found in their bed. She'd give that woman no chance to poison her life any further.

Rowena's voice was no more than the sigh of a breeze when she spoke. "My lord, no one but you and I have shared that bed. It is precious to me."

Startled surprise showed in his face, then something akin to a smile briefly touched his lips. "Bah," he said, "why should I care what you do?" But his pleased tone belied his hard words. There was no time to consider the implications. As he strode out of the solar, she turned back to her maids.

"Margaret, use as many servants as you need, but see to it that my lord's bed is prepared within the hour so he has a place to lay his head this night."

"My lady," Margaret asked, "is it true this wedding is for Lady Maeve?"

"Aye," she replied, and ignored the twinge of guilt that followed. This was a mistake; she should not allow her husband to wed his vassal to that woman. She suddenly realized all her women stood in uneasy silence.

"Thank the Lord the moon will have waned in two days," Emma finally breathed, her words echoing everyone's thoughts. A witch's power was at its height with the full moon.

Rowena held up a cautioning hand. "I will grant that Maeve is a hateful woman, but I'll not have anyone name her witch. She has lived these past months within sight of God and survived. No witch could do that."

Somehow, in saying these words, she felt better about this match. God had seen the woman now, and he would have destroyed her had she been truly evil. "Besides, such a charge will hardly make her husband love her better, would it? The breath of such an allegation would do us far more harm than good. Instead, let us put our joy at her departure into our efforts for her wedding. Off with you all. With luck, we will all be abed before dawn, although I do not hold much hope of it."

As her maids scrambled to be at the tasks she'd given them, Rowena pushed aside all worries over her inheritance. For now it was more important to take Ilsa into the treasury to find cloth suitable for a groom's attire. At least there was something to do.

# Chapter Thirteen

"*J*OHN, well come to Graistan," called Lord Graistan from his stance beside the hearth. "No doubt you are soaked through to the bone. And Nicola! This is a surprise. I did not expect to see you."

Rowena leapt from her watching position at her solar door, straightened her gleaming red-brocade overgown, then started for the stairs. A big man dressed in muddy mail and a dripping surcoat and cloak strode across the hall to take his lord's hand in his own. Carrying a basket that made her follow more slowly was a tall, willowy girl in stained and sodden clothing.

"What, her?" Ashby's voice was gruff but without the steel to make it commanding. "Aye, she should have been married and gone years ago, but the damned boy died before the deed. Since then, I've not been able to convince her to accept another."

At the base of the stairs Rowena signaled for the warmed wine to be served to their guests before she started toward the hearth. Her husband glanced up, then looked again. She'd forgotten he'd not seen her yet this morning. His expression mellowed as she neared him.

She knew, for Ilsa had told her, how well she looked in this scarlet overgown with its golden embroidery. But, she'd had other reasons for choosing it. By wearing it over a plain white undergown with a single strand of amber beads as her only adornment, she attempted to reflect Graistan's prominence without overshadowing the bridal couple.

"And this," he said, taking her hand as he guided her to his side, "is the new Lady Graistan, Rowena, late of Benfield. My lady, this is my vassal at Ashby, John, and his daughter, Nicola."

She smiled up at her guests. The man was as massive in girth as in height with iron gray hair that stood out from his head in stiff curls. Of features he was unremarkable, but his merry brown eyes revealed a simple soul.

Beneath her cloak his daughter wore a dark green gown cut in the style of twenty years past. The hemline barely reached to mid-calf, as if it had been made for another much shorter than she, and was bunched about her waist with a carelessly yanked belt. At first glance, the girl seemed as plain as her father. However, she had a wealth of thick, brown hair that escaped her untidy braid in loose coils about her face. As she rose from a clumsy curtsy and met her lady's gaze, plainness was dimmed to insignificance by her striking hazel eyes filled with a far greater intelligence than was apparent in her sire.

"How pleased I am to meet you both," Rowena said with a smile as they were each handed a cup of warmed wine. "And, I must apologize for what surely seems a strange request to wed so quickly. Word of my father's death has only just arrived along with a challenge to my inheritance. We are very grateful for your agreement to all this haste."

Sir John drank deeply while his daughter sniffed at the steaming contents of her cup. When he had wiped his mouth with the back of his hand, he grinned. "No matter, my lady. I've been a widower so long, I daresay a wedding could not come quickly enough for me."

"You are kind, sir," she started to say, but the girl interrupted.

"Well, it is too swift for my tastes." Her voice was husky, and her words were tart with suspicion.

"Nicola," her father warned, but the young woman waved him off.

"Nay, Father, you have not even seen your bride. Who knows what sort of woman you might bring into my home?"

"Nicola," Lord Graistan retorted with a smile, "you know when your father remarries, his hall will no longer be yours but his wife's. But, then, you should have long ago found your own hearth and family. How old are you now?"

"She is nearly ten and seven," Ashby sighed, "and if you can make her bend to your will, my lord, you are a better man than I. No matter who I suggest or what terms I negotiate, she refuses to accept the man."

"No one forces me from my own home," she snapped back. "Ashby is all I want. Now leave off me."

Rowena straightened in shock at the girl's open and rude defiance, fully expecting her father to slap some respect into her. But her sire only stared shamefacedly down at the floor. She glanced at her husband. He gazed down at the girl, a single, raised eyebrow conveying both his disgust at her behavior and his struggle to remain polite.

When no one spoke, she leapt briskly into the void. "Now with all that said, the Lady Maeve should be here shortly, and there remains only two hours before it will be time to eat. My lord felt it would be best if you, Sir John, and your intended bride might first dine together, to see if both parties find the other to their liking. Then, by the grace of God, we will celebrate a weddding after that."

Sir John, still bright red in embarrassment, cleared his throat. "You are so kind, my lady. Please accept my apologies on behalf of my daughter. If only her mother had lived longer. I have failed to teach her any manners or womanly softness."

Nicola glanced at them all. "And glad I am of it."

"I can think of several ways to impart manners," Lord Graistan muttered, but his wife's voice over-rode his.

"Think no more of it," she said soothingly. "No doubt she is overwrought by the suddenness of all this. Sir John, we expected that this hasty date might leave you little time to prepare. I have taken the liberty of having clothing arranged for you. If you will deign to come with me now, I will make a bridegroom out of you."

He smiled his thanks and offered his arm. She laid her hand upon his, then looked beyond him to his unrepentant daughter. "Nicola, come along and let my maids find you something dry to wear."

After seeing the girl into Ilsa's capable hands with orders to offer her a bath and allow the girl to choose something suitable from Graistan's coffers, she escorted Sir John to her solar. As was customary for the lady of the hall, she assisted him in removing his armor and bathed him, then helped him don his new robes.

The gown was of pale gray trimmed about the cuffs and throat with a simple, embroidered pattern made rich by the use of copper silk. There was a darker gray cloak lined with fox; the rusty-colored pelt was Ashby's own, sent in tribute some years back. Rowena presented him with a fine, pliable leather belt studded with brass buttons. In Nichola's basket her maids discovered a thick gold chain and an ancient, ornate cloak pin meant to use as his adornments. For chausses he wore a gold pair of Gilliam's, their long length giving more room to his greater girth. As to shoes, there was nothing that fit him, so his boots were cleaned and buffed until they looked nearly new. At last, she pronounced the man fit to be wed. His sudden blush was charmingly boyish.

Waiting outside the door was his daughter, her hair straightened, but she still wore her awkward green garb, although it had been dried and brushed clean. "Why, Nicola, was there nothing to suit you?" Rowena asked, glancing at Ilsa. The old woman opened her eyes wide in frustration and shook her head.

The girl's jaw jutted out. "I want no borrowed riches. Ashby provides me everything I need or desire. This is my best. I'm sorry it not good enough to please your refined tastes."

Her father squeezed his eyes shut in mortification, angry color rushing into his leathery cheeks. "Nicola," he started.

"Never mind," Lady Graistan replied easily, "all that's important is that she is comfortable. Come downstairs. My nose tells me that our meal is ready and, I, for one, am starving."

As they descended into the hall, Maeve's silvery laugh rang out. Despite her best efforts, Rowena's heart quivered in trepidation when she saw the woman at Rannulf's side. She silently prayed that her husband was right and Maeve would not defy him.

She watched them as she and Sir John crossed the hall, for they made an attractive pair. Maeve's pearl-studded gown of pale lavender was a good complement to her husband's deep blue gown with golden embroidery at the throat and sleeves.

"Rowena, my sweet chick," the woman purred triumphantly, "how good it is to see you again." Her hair gleamed golden red from beneath the wisp of silk she wore as a wimple. The jeweled band that held it in place sparkled in the torchlight. "And, you, too, my lord, although I have told you that once already this day." She smiled up at him and clasped one arm about his waist. There was nothing sisterly in the curve of her body against his.

Rowena nearly stumbled when her husband drew the woman closer still and returned her smile with great warmth, too much warmth. It was a moment before she recognized her sudden surge of emotion as jealousy. Had she been wrong about them? Nay, surely Maeve would have gloated over it if he had bedded her. She carefully schooled her face to prevent anyone from finding the least evidence that she was affected by their behavior.

"My, is our little lady not stunning in that brocade." Maeve turned slightly to consider her lord's wife. "Here is a color that truly does her justice. But what is this I see? Such dark rings beneath her eyes. Brother, what had you done to this poor thing? But, then, she has this common habit of believing she must work her fingers to the bone. No doubt you could not stop her."

"Aye, that is so. I have not seen her in two days, so busy has she been." He still smiled down at his sister by marriage as he led her forward. "Maeve, here is why I asked you to dress in your finest for this day. I would like you to meet my vassal, John of Ashby. John, this is my ward, the Lady Maeve."

"Lord John." The fair woman gifted him with a brief but sultry smile as she bent her knee only a little in greeting, finding nothing whatsoever interesting in the older man.

The knight gaped. "You—you have all your teeth," he stuttered out.

"Mmm," she murmured, "how perceptive of you."

"John has made a generous offer for your hand in marriage," Rannulf said quickly, "and I have agreed. You take with you for your lifespan a part of the bridge tolls, as well as a hideage of land and the rights to the village across the river from Ashby." The volume of his voice grew to hide her sudden gasp. "Even if you cannot pass these holdings down to your heirs, it is far richer than what you took into your first marriage and will, hopefully, ease some of the hurt your relatives did to you when you lost your dower."

"Marriage," she said slowly, her eyes darting from her intended to her lord. "Why, brother, this is all so sudden." There was an ever-so-brief note of hurt in her voice. "I barely know what to say."

"Then say nothing," he replied graciously, yet with obvious relief at her calm reaction to the idea. "Now that I have remarried, there could be no place for you here. I sought only to make you lady in your own right."

"She must show she knows how to care for the keep first." Nicola's hard words startled them all. "There is much more to Ashby than embroidery and fine gowns."

Her father whirled on her, his fist held high. "Nicola, hold your tongue," he bellowed.

The girl whitened in shocked surprise, startled into instant quiet. "Papa," she cried in a small voice.

"Nay," he barked, "you have been impossibly rude." He turned back to Maeve. "My lady, please excuse my daughter. I have done a poor job raising her. What she needs can only be taught to her by a woman of quality. It would do her, nay, nay, it would do this old war-horse good if you would accept my offer for your hand in marriage."

She studied the man's earnest face, then glanced at the girl, who was yet ghostly pale from her chastisement. Her gaze became somewhat troubled as it slipped from her lord to her lady and back once again to her suitor. Then, her brow cleared as if she'd seen the answer to a particularly difficult problem. "Oh, you poor, sweet man. I can see how it has been so hard for you. And, she is nearly past marriageable age. So here is why you are in such a hurry to find a wife." She turned gracefully to the man and drew a deep breath. Lord John's gaze wandered down to the ripe curves of her breasts outlined beneath her tightly fitted gown.

"That his daughter is a hoyden is true enough," Rannulf answered for him, his grin now wide and easy. "But, it is not his hurry by my need that has brought us all here today. Months may pass before I will be free again to see this joining completed. My lady has just come into her inheritance, and her rights to it have been challenged."

"Challenged! How awful for you, Rowena," Maeve said and smiled more widely now, as if his words confirmed her conclusions of the previous moment. "When is this wedding to be?"

Rowena looked on in wonder at the woman's sudden, buoyant happiness. Could it be true that she had longed for a home and hearth of her own? However unlikely that seemed, here she was accepting this arranged marriage without the slightest complaint.

"Why, this very day, if you will have me," John replied, suddenly finding his voice.

"Aye, sister," Rannulf said. "Look about. We have decorated the hall in your honor. First we will dine, then, if you find you are agreed to it by the meal's end, you can be wedded. After that there will be musicians to entertain us throughout the evening. It will be a gay evening, indeed."

"But, where will we marry? Surely not here by your chaplain. He is stone-deaf. How will he know what we say? Oh, dear," she gasped prettily, "but what if Lord John and I are related?"

Lord Graistan only shook his head. "There is no impediment in your lineage to prevent this joining, and the abbot has graciously lent us his chaplain for the service." He pointed toward the robed priest already seated near the head of the lord's table. The man nodded to them all the while eagerly eyeing the door as he awaited the arrival of dinner.

"You have thought of everything," she cried to Rannulf, her happiness growing greater by the moment. "You are so kind to trouble yourself on my behalf." She turned her attention back to Lord Ashby. "My, what a big man you are," she said coyly, laying a slender hand on his arm. "Ashby must keep you well fed, my lord."

"Aye," he replied, now seeking to woo her by whatever means necessary, "that is does. Our forest supplies us game for every meal, and the furs it produces are of the highest quality. Ah, Lady Maeve, you will soon love Ashby as I do, for there is no place like it in all this realm."

Lord John couldn't take his eyes off his bride

throughout the rich meal. He doted on her every
word, sought for her the most tender morsels of
flesh and fish. He would not even let her lift her
own glass from the table.

On Maeve's part she often leaned toward him,
brushing her breasts against his arm as she commented on the various dishes and prettily thanked
him for his care of her. Her laugh rang out again
and again at even his most feeble attempt at a jest.
She seductively stroked the fur trim of his cloak,
marveling at the softness of the fox. A brief sweep
of her fingers against his cheek brought a boyish
color to his leathery skin, as she asked extremely
detailed questions about Ashby.

Rowena stared at Maeve and wondered at the
woman's growing ebullience. Could it be that the
stay in the convent had changed her? She fought
back a wave of uneasiness. Or was that just a selfish
rationalization for allowing this joining to go forward
without a word to Lord John about Maeve's past?
Was it not her duty to at least warn him that his
wife had been an adulteress and a thief? She
glanced across the two at her husband. He met her
look with a smug one of his own. Since he did not
believe it, she knew he'd never allow it.

Then, her gaze darted to Nicola. The tall girl sat
slumped in her seat, ignoring the food before her
despite the efforts of the chaplain to be polite. Her
expression was one of despair. Rowena laughed a
little. The girl was obviously unused to such harsh
treatment from her father. Not that she hadn't
heartily deserved it.

When the meal was done, Lord John fell to his
knees and begged that Lady Maeve accept his offer.
She did so with a warm, sweet laugh. The ceremony
at the chapel door before the watching eyes of all

of Graistan's folk was simple and direct as befitted a widow and a widower of little consequence. After an abbreviated mass, the musicians piped them back into the hall, then began to play in earnest.

The servants quickly cleared the room so the dancing could begin. In moments, the open area between the hearths was filled with folk, whirling and stamping to the tune. After a first dance with his bride, the bridegroom offered Rowena his hand. She smiled and accepted.

But instead of leading her into the dancing, he stepped aside a bit. "My lady, it is my daughter, damn her. She is such a stubborn mule of a girl." His words caught in his throat, and she saw the pain in his eyes. "I do not know what to do with her anymore. Everything I say, she contradicts; everything I do, she criticizes. I know she is hurt, but—Could you speak with her? You seem so kind and wise for one so young."

"When you flatter me that way, Lord John, how can I possibly refuse." She laughed. "I suppose it might be said I've had some experience dealing with women being so long at a convent. But where is she? I have not seen her since the ceremony ended."

"She is sulking behind yon wall hanging," Sir John said his voice low and shamed. "I fear she might become destructive if she broods over this long enough. She has that habit at home. Not that she's ever hurt anyone," he hastened to add at his lady's startled look. "Just broken pots and torn things and such." His voice died away. "Please?"

Rowena gave a quick laugh. As she had guessed, it was his daughter who had ruled the roost at Ashby until this day. No doubt Nicola was deeply stung. "I'll do what I can."

"Thank you," he replied warmly, then left her to

once again claim his bride. She made her way to the wall and pulled aside the embroidered material to slip into the darkened, narrow alcove behind it. Nicola leaned against one wall. Tears trickled down her face.

Rowena stood beside her in silence for a long moment before finally asking, "Is it so bad as that?"

The girl did not move. "Thief," she declared in a voice filled with trembling anger, "you have stolen my home from me."

"Selfish girl," Rowena retorted swiftly. "I did no such thing. Your father wished to wed and spoke to my husband about it months ago."

"Had it not been for you and your lord, he would have had no success finding a woman. We were all happy as we were. We needed no interference." Her shoulders shuddered as another sob shook her.

"Happy? Your father's eagerness hardly speaks of a contented man." From beyond the hanging, they heard the muted ring of Lord John's laugh. His daughter shook at the sound. "It was you, not he, who was happy with matters as they stood."

Nicola threw back her head in pain. "All I have ever wanted was Ashby. What if she bears him sons?"

Rowena sighed. "I doubt if she will, she is far older than she might appear." Although she dared not say it, she did not think Maeve would allow herself to undergo the rigors of childbirth. "It is possible your father hopes for sons, but I would guess he meant only to find companionship for himself in his later years."

"He has me," the girl cried out, her voice filled with childish hurt.

"But, who will replace you when you have married?"

"If only you had not interfered," she cried again, turning her face toward the wall, "then the possibility of my marriage would never have arisen. So, how long will it be before my stepmother rids herself of me? As your lord so aptly pointed out, my hall has become hers."

"What a spoiled child you are," the Lady Graistan snapped. "If you truly loved your father, you would dry your eyes and not begrudge him his happiness." The girl glanced at her in shame. "As to finding you a husband, I think it will not happen quickly. Our Maeve is not one who likes to dirty her hands in order to get her daily bread. If you serve as Ashby's chatelaine and do not challenge her, she will not bother herself with you."

"Could this be true," Nicola breathed in disbelief. "I was certain she would wrest it all away from me. And if she remains barren, Ashby will still be mine alone. Mine, to keep and hold."

Rowena stared at her in shock. "You cannot mean what I think you do. Without a husband?" She was stunned when the girl nodded. "You are mad."

"Am I?" Nicola countered. "I can do it. I know Ashby's folk and field better than anyone. And, when I was eight, I told my father I wished to be a knight. He thought it was quite a jest to let me train with his men."

"He let you train with his men? With a sword?" The Lady Graistan stared. "His daughter? What was he thinking?"

"Well, after a time he forbid it, but it was too late. I had learned what I needed and kept practicing where he could not see. There are many things he does not realize I know, and I can hold Ashby better than any man."

"I will allow that you believe that," Rowena replied, "but it changes nothing. Ashby is not yours to keep. It is my lord's, held by your family only in agreement with the lords of Graistan. If there are no sons, then you will have to marry or face challenge after challenge from your neighbors or some second son looking for a quick bit of land as his own. There would be nothing left of Ashby or its folk by the time you prove your point, Nicola," Rowena laid her hand on her girl's arm for emphasis: "Your life cannot stay as it has been, it must change. And, no matter how you fight it, it will happen."

She only pulled away and pressed her hands to her ears. "Nay, I will not hear you," she cried out. "Go away, go away and leave me be."

The Lady Graistan's voice was gentle as she continued. "Believe me when I say that I know how hard it is to be shoved suddenly into a new life. You are strong and will make of it something that is yours alone." She paused. "When you are ready, ask one of the servants for Ilsa. She will see you to your bed and help you if you need it. Good night, Nicola." With that, she stepped back into the hall and the merriment of the celebration.

"Ah, there you are," her husband said with a smile as he caught her arm and drew her to his side.

After so long a time of public avoidance, his open approach startled her. A moment later she understood. His face glowed with the warmth that could only be found in a cup. Drink, not desire, had driven away his usual reserve. When she said nothing, he lifted her from her feet and whirled her around in time to the music. She yelped in surprise. "My lord! You are squeezing the life out of me." He loosened his grip, but did not completely release her, and she slid down against him. Her eyes flew open wide. The drink had awakened more than just his humor.

"My God, but you are beautiful," he breathed. "My bed has been cold and lonely without you these last nights." The harsh lines of his face had softened, his gray eyes were filled with his desire for her. When he stroked her cheek, she bit her lip to keep from crying out as a rush of wanting filled her. God forgive her, she had missed him, too.

"Brother," said Maeve from just behind them, "come, have this dance with me."

Startled, Rowena stepped back, then watched in angry dismay as her husband set his cup on a table and offered Maeve his hands. With neither a word nor a glance to her, he stepped away. From over his shoulder Lady Maeve shot her a brief and triumphant glance.

Jealousy and pain exploded within her. Oh, she was beautiful to him, the way a copse was beautiful to a woodcutter. She was only good enough to share his bed and breed him sons.

"My lady?" Lord John offered her his hands. "Would you dance with me?"

"I would be honored," she replied with a smile she did not feel. Putting her small hand into his callused palm, she struggled to present the best face she could to her husband's castellan. To her surprise, she enjoyed herself. The man's size belied his agility, for he was a competent dancer, spry and light on his feet. And only when they were well into their third tune did he mention his daughter.

"So, it went well?"

"Aye, at least I believe so. Your daughter has some strange notions, but I think she is better reconciled to your marriage now. Do not expect her to attend your bedding, though."

There was a sudden light in the man's brown

eyes. "Excuse me, there is something I forgot to say to my lord."

He released her and left, mid-step, to stride across the room to Rannulf. She backed out of the way as the dancers broke apart around her then wove back into two lines, one all male, the other female.

"My lady," said a servant who appeared at her right. "Your lord says to tell you that the bride must be made ready. Also, you must be quick about preparing her. He does not think he will able to restrain the groom for longer than a quarter hour."

Rowena glanced around the room until she saw her husband. He was refilling his cup from the ewer at the far table. Why send a servant to tell her, why not tell her himself? Because she was not worthy of his notice. With a sour taste in her mouth, she announced to the room it was time for the bedding.

The bride bid a fond farewell to her husband and happily climbed the stairs. When she was led through the solar to the master's chamber, she cried, "Why, sister, you have given me your own room. I am honored."

While the priest blessed the bed, five of Graistan's most stout-hearted maids encircled the bride to remove her finery. "How kind your lord has been to do all this for me," she called from over their shoulders. "Surely, I can find some way to repay him for the care and effort he has made on my behalf this day."

Her voice seemed light and happy. "To think that if you had not banished me from Graistan, none of this would have happened." She continued speaking around the maids as she donned a sheer, silken robe to cover her nakedness. "John is such a simple man, I am sure I shall have no marital discord. We shall have a cozy, little hall with but two villages to provide for us. No doubt we will have many long, bucolic years between us."

Rowena frowned slightly in disbelief. These were all the things that should have enraged Maeve. Yet, she seemed completely content. "He was my lord husband's choice for you," she said tentatively.

"Oh, do not be so shy of accepting my compliments," the bride responded with a little laugh. "It may have been Rannulf's idea, but no doubt you rejoiced at the man, sister."

Just then, there was a knock at the door and the bridegroom called for the right to enter. The maids moved behind Lady Maeve while Rowena came to stand at her side. Instantly, the bride leaned toward her lady to harshly whisper, "My spies tell me how dearly you have already paid for crossing me. Your husband despises you and in his hate he has finally turned to me for comfort." There was triumph in her quiet voice.

"You lie," she shot back.

"Do I or has he only deluded you so well you cannot see the truth? Think on it. Ashby is so close, and John is such a fool. Nay, your husband is mine, my fine lady, and it is you who has driven him into my arms. He intends to be my lover and make a mockery of your marriage. It will humble you far better than any of the plots I had devised over these past months. Your downfall will be sweet, indeed."

"You lie," she retorted, this time with less surety as the door flew open and the bridegroom and Rannulf entered.

"You will see," Maeve hissed, then stepped forward, her sheer bedrobe falling open as she did so. "Come, husband," she fairly simpered, her expression without a hint of her previous emotion, "come to our bed this night."

Rowena put an end to the ceremony as quickly as she could without insulting John, then returned to the hall. The servants were still dancing. She looked for her husband, but he had disappeared. Where? To make arrangements for a tryst?

She stood stock-still amid the noise and confusion, torn asunder. Was it true? Lord John's name had come so quickly to her husband's lips. Lady Maeve believed it; this is why she had so happily agreed to wed. When a servant offered her a cup of wine, she took it and drank deeply to steady her nerves.

Her husband startled her when he spoke from behind her. "Did I not tell you she would do as I said?" His tone was patronizing, and he was obviously pleased with himself. Pleased because his arrangements had worked out so nicely?

Her insides turned to ice. "Oh, she has done it. At first I could not understand why she was so cheerful over it all, but now I know for she has told me why. You and she are to be lovers."

He stared down at her, his features freezing into a dark and dangerous expression. "What did she ever do to you that you should hate her so? You will hold that vicious tongue of yours, or I will publicly name you liar."

"Do not rush to spew denials, dear husband," Rowena's voice was even, but inwardly she reeled. "How foolish of me to expect it. You call me a liar, yet I have never lied to you. When she steals from you, you find her a husband and gift her with a substantial dowry." She continued with a calmness that belied the roiling hurt within her. "You were so determined to bring her back here, even when we'd told you what she'd done. It was only Gilliam's threat to leave that caused you to relent. And, I in my selfish desire to be rid of her, I did not think to question your swift turnabout."

"You dishonor me with your presence," he said, his words low and cold. "Leave me."

"Do I? That sounds strange coming from you. As for leaving, I have not finished with you yet." There was a desperate edge to her voice, and she fought to suppress it. It would not do for him to see how much his betrayal hurt her. "The least you could have done was to keep it private, but every soul, including poor John, saw the greeting that you gave her."

"No further, madam." His face was a bitter mask, his eyes as sharp and hard as the steel of his sword. "You'll not treat me so. Behave yourself or I will confine you with your women."

Rowena snarled quietly in barely controlled rage. "I am treating you only as well as you treat me," she hissed, "and if you do not like it, choke on it. But, I won't stand idly by while the two of you humiliate me before my servants. You had better reconsider, or you'll learn quickly enough where the power lies at Graistan. So it's common now to manage one's hall, is it? Well, if you like her moldly bread so well, I'll see to it that that is what you eat."

"Hold your tongue, woman," he said, his voice growing steadily in volume. "Quit your lunatic ravings and be gone with you." His final words were a thunderous roar that rang out over the hall. Everyone came to a sudden halt, the music dying away into a shrill shriek.

"Gladly," she hissed, unwilling to let the servants hear what transpired between them. "But it is I who am done with you. You want my inheritance, well go fetch it from my sister. As for locking me away, I will not give you the opportunity. From now on I will make my bed with my women, and you can find your pleasure with any whore you choose, except her."

She whirled and ran, not caring what direction she went, only wanting to be away from him. As she reached the screens that guarded the outer door, his cup crashed to the floor at her heels. "Go, then," he thundered. "I have had enough of you to last me a lifetime."

She ran outside and down the stairs. It was by instinct alone she found her way to her garden's gate. Here, she leaned against that door, her breath coming in huge, tearless sobs. "God forgive me," she cried out to herself, "but I hate him."

"God forgives you your lie and so do I."

# Chapter Fourteen

"*T*EMRIC!" she cried out, leaping away from him in fright.

"My pardon, I did not mean to startle you." He opened the gate. "Why not come sit for a moment and settle your senses. You seem overwrought," he added dryly.

Rowena laughed, but the sound was nearer a sob. She hurried within her garden's shielding walls to walk agitatedly up and down the sole path. Her brother by marriage leaned casually against a tree trunk. It was only the enclosing privacy of darkness that finally loosened her tongue. She let fly the harangue she'd so long suppressed.

"I have kept his home, seen to his table, denied him nothing, and what does he do? Not only does he treat me as if I were the least of his servants whose only value to him is in my inheritance, he plans to betray me with Maeve. What have I done that he should so deeply hate me? Why must it be with her?" Her voice broke in a breathless cry and she stopped, her hand pressed to her lips to still her pain.

"Betray you with Lady Maeve?" Temric's surprise filled the air around them. "What do you mean?"

She whirled, her heels scratching deep marks in the gravel path. "Maeve told me that my husband has arranged her marriage to Sir John so the two of them could be lovers."

"And you believed her?" he retorted. "After all she's done, you believed her? Surely, when you told this to Rannulf, he set you straight."

"Nay," she cried out in wild hurt, "he protected her. He threatened to name me a liar when I repeated what she'd said."

"Listen now and make no mistake on what you hear. Rannulf could no more do what you accuse than he could fly. Whether or not he will stray from his marriage vows, I cannot say, but my brother would die before he dishonored his man by laying with that man's wife." His voice was as deep and soft as the night around them. The very tone of it made his words unassailable truth.

"Am I to believe you when he, himself, would not deny it?" Yet, she held her breath waiting for his answer.

"What you believe is up to you. I can tell you what I know and let you make what use of it you will. I know Rannulf better than any man alive and I tell you now, he is not capable of what you accuse."

She paused as the rightness of what he said filled her. It was only then that she realized the enormity of what she'd done. Like the angel with the fiery sword who'd banished Adam and Eve from Paradise, her burning words had irrevocably driven her husband away from her. She sat on the bench as rage and hurt were replaced with despair. "How could I have been so blind to her trap? Sweet Mary. I have destroyed my marriage over her, just as she desired."

"Well, I do not doubt you shocked him with your accusations, but it does him no harm to find you can be driven to a jealous rage over him." He stated it so matter-of-factly, as if it were nothing at all.

"Not jealousy," she sighed, "but fear of humiliation drove me to accuse him. Oh, Temric, tell me something, anything, that can be done to ease this accursed match of ours. I cannot spend my life surrounded by so much hate. What is it about me? I need only speak two words to send him raging in anger. Whatever you suggest, I swear I will do it, although now I fear it may be too late."

"Accursed." He managed to make that single word ring with ironic amusement. "Now, there's an accurate description for this trap into which we shoved you. Your union will continue to be troubled until Rannulf can see himself free of his past. That I cannot change. But why did you cease to try?"

"Cease to try?" she cried out. "What is there left to do that I have not already done, all of it wrong. I have even accused him of adultery."

"That may be the only thing you've done right so far. Now, tell me what you have done save let him belittle you and treat you as if you did not exist? Three nights ago he spoke to you with unforgivable rudeness, and you let him do so unchallenged. I took you to be a different woman. Was I wrong?"

Rowena gave a harried sigh and hugged herself. "If I cannot have the man, I will not lose the hall," she breathed.

"Here's a particularly odd turn of logic. Do you think you secure yourself here by allowing him to treat you without the respect due to your position?"

She shook her head in frustration. "You are right, I do know better. But, Temric, his anger comes exploding out at me from deep inside him. Dear God, I could not live with the shame if he were to beat me before my own servants." Her last words were almost a sob.

"Nay, this is again something you need never fear from Rannulf."

"You might be right if it were anyone other than I at whom his anger is directed. When I should remain calm to soothe him, he says the one thing that drives away all my common sense and control. I find myself goading him, although I cannot explain why I do it. I thought if I were silent, he would come to care for me—so, I gritted my teeth and humbled myself—aye"—the word sprang from her in enraged anguish—"I have borne it all while it ate my stomach through to my spine. I do not know who I hate worse for it, him or myself."

"It has not been all silence." His calm, certain tone told her he knew they shared their bed as man and wife.

"Ilsa talks too much," she said darkly.

"I do not need old women to tell me what I can see in my brother's eyes."

"If that is what I must do to keep my home," her voice died away into the night.

"Now you are truly lying."

"Let me," she snapped back. "It does not hurt as much if I say it so."

There was a long, quiet moment broken only by the echo of music from the hall and the rustle of wild creatures moving within the garden. In that time, the moon lifted above the wall. Its pure light made silvery trace work from branch and bough.

Temric sighed, and she studied him. His harshness was gone or at least hidden for the soft illumination revealed only sadness. "I would have warned you, but I was loath to interfere in my brother's life. There'll be no peace for you here, at least not of the kind you knew at your convent. How you must regret what you have lost."

She hesitated to answer, for what she could not have from the church she'd found here. "Nay, I have no regrets." Then, suddenly, she straightened. "Do you say that my lord intends to send me back? Then you may tell him that I will fight him with every ounce of my strength. If I must stay locked in with my women for the remainder of my life, I'll not leave Graistan."

Temric's chuckle rumbled deep within his chest. "To the best of my knowledge, he has no such intentions. My brother needs your pride and your arrogance, not the quiet nothing you have shown him. If you had been a biddable child, he'd not have married you."

"You are wrong," she returned with firm certainty. "My father forced him to fulfill their contract. He accepted me only to avoid losing my inheritance."

"And I tell you, my brother went to Benfield that day to say he would not complete the deed despite the richness of your holdings. Do not forget that I was there as well and saw what you saw, but also what you did not see. Your father could never have forced Rannulf if my brother hadn't found something about you he could not refuse."

Rowena stared at him, as if she could pick the truth out from the white and black relief of his face. "Even if that is as you say," she replied quietly, "I fear your words have come too late to be of any help to me. I have held my anger too long and vented it too soon. I did not only accuse him of intending betrayal. I have also told him I want no more to do with him and have sworn to confine myself to the women's quarters."

To her utter astonishment, he laughed aloud. "Good work, my lady. First you show him your jealousy, then you remove yourself from his reach.

That'll tweak him right merrily. It looks as though you needed no help from me after all."

"How can you laugh," she said, a little irritated by his amusement. "You come to see why I stop trying, then laugh when I say I have not only quit fighting, but have also left the battlefield. You laugh when I have now lost all rights to the title 'Lady Graistan'?"

He only smiled. "You have lost nothing. Of your rights to this keep, you took those in one masterful stroke on your first night here and will hold them as your own until you choose to release them. You know that. It is my brother you want. Do not shake your head at me, for only a blind man could not see it. If you had no place for him in your heart, Maeve's words would not have given you a moment's pause."

Stung into silence by his statement, she watched him straighten as if to signal the end of their unexpected conversation. "There has been an ocean of heartbreak here that has trapped us all in its chains until we believed we'd never again be free. Yet in you come and sweep most of it clean, as if it was no more to do than lift a spilled cup and wipe away the slop. You have opened the door for him, now Rannaulf must free himself."

"What happened here? What plays between Rannulf and Gilliam, and how is it Maeve has such a hold over them?" she asked softly, but his upraised hand forestalled any further question.

"Ask your husband. If you are the woman I think you are, he will tell you."

"It is too late," she whispered to herself.

"Not yet," he answered easily.

"So you say," Rowena sighed. Despite his words, she found no reason to hope. "But, I thank you for your friendship. Oftimes, I feel so alone. Until I came to Graistan my solitariness never pained me. Here, where there are so many who love me and I should feel accepted, the hole in my heart seems greather than ever."

"You, lonely? I am surprised," he said, sounding genuinely so. "You know who you are."

"Know who I am? What do you mean?"

"I mean that you are noble by class."

"What was peerage to do with loneliness or identity?" she returned in quiet confusion. "A title did not spare me from being an unwanted daughter, rejected by my mother simply because I was my father's spawn and only desired by my father as a weapon to use against her. Who am I now but the Lady Graistan, except that Lord Graistan will not acknowledge that that is who I am." She plucked a pink and held the bloom to her nose. Its warm, rich scent eased the throbbing in her head. "Identity has nothing to do with being common or noble nor should you judge it so."

"My apologies. It is an unfortunate habit of mine, since I am both and neither." His smile gleamed lopsidedly in the moonlight.

Rowena leaned forward a little to brace her elbows on her knees. "But, Rannulf loves you so. I cannot believe he would deny you if you asked him for your acknowledgment as the son of his father."

"Oh, he would give it to me, all of it, Graistan included. But it is not his to grant. If my father—" His voice went so flat and hard, he had to turn his face away from her for a moment to escape the pain he'd revealed.

"You are the elder," she said in understanding. If not for his bastard birth, he would have been Lord Graistan.

The man's tenseness drained away, she saw it in the steady drop of his shoulders. When he again faced her, she read resolve in his shadowy outline. "Well, I have pried ham-handedly into your deepest secrets. It is only just that I should grant you the same courtesy. Aye, I am the older by only months. My mother was Rannulf's nurse, for his mother was sickly and died giving him birth. But, do not think I have ever coveted him his birthright, for I have not."

"You would not care so for him if you did." And in speaking these words, she knew Temric was right. It was no title or building she fought for, she ached for what these brothers shared, the thing that touched every soul within this keep and of which she'd had so little in her life. Their love for each other was like the mortar that held Graistan's walls stone to stone. It created an unbreakable bond that even Maeve, for all her trying, had been unable to destroy. And suddenly she knew it was only her husband who could fill the hole in her heart, no other. And this he would never grant her for she, herself, had dealt her chances a deathblow.

"We were raised together, trained together, and would have been knighted together, had our father lived or so Rannulf insists." Temric spoke on even as her despair deepened.

"And you were not knighted?" It was with great cost that she kept her voice unemotional.

"Nay. We were nigh on eighteen when he died, and Rannulf, being so close to his majority and forward for his age, took his spurs along with his inheritance."

"There was nothing for you?" It seemed odd that a man who so loved his bastard child to raise him in the hall with his heir would forget him in his will.

"Why should there have been? I was not his legitimate son." Try as mightily as he did, he could not hide how it had hurt him and how it hurt him still. The harshness in his voice was not meant for her, and she knew it. He sighed, then stepped away from the tree. Even if she had not seen it, she would have known his expression was once again closed and hard. "Now, mayhap, you might do me a good turn, my lady."

"If I can, I will." It would be her only chance to repay him for his friendship. There'd be no further confidences between them, not this night and most probably ever again. It was not his way.

"My mother is recently widowed and has asked me to come to her. She and my stepfather were wool merchants and makers of parchments, and my half brothers are yet too young to be of great help to her. She claims to need my company, but what she really wants is my strong back for some time to come." He paused here, as if thinking on his mother's situation.

"You must leave Rannulf," she said in slow understanding, "and he does not suffer his family leaving him with much grace."

"You have put the problem in a nutshell, my lady. But, go I must. There are two sides to my family, and I cannot be torn down the middle, even to please him. I have promised her to be there before Midsummer and that is now just weeks away. Mayhap you can make him understand."

"Well, I cannot imagine I will have the chance, but I will try," she said, then rose to her feet.

"That is all I ask," he said, his sudden smile so like his brother's. "Now, let me see you back to the hall. You really should not wander about unescorted in the dark. These men of mine are a rowdy crew when they've had a drink or two too many."

Rowena smiled wanly as he offered her his hand. "I was not thinking when I left, or I would never have come this way, but you know that."

"So I do." He led her out of the garden and to the base of the outer stairs. "Now, go quickly. I will watch until you are safe within."

From his chair near the hearth, pushed well to the side and out of the way of the celebrants, Rannulf watched his wife reenter the hall. She wasted no time in crossing the room and nearly ran up the stairs. It was as if she could not wait to reach the women's quarters to be free from his grasp.

There was no cause for her to hurry. He wanted nothing more to do with her. He drained his cup, wishing he could as easily wash away his now bitter regrets. This marriage was an error of the gravest sort, and her wealth was his only compensation he'd ever gain from this union. Once he'd settled her inheritance, she could take up residence at Upwood and be out of his life.

Hours passed. The servants ended their amusements and pulled out pallets and benches to find their peace in sleep. Yet, he lingered on, unwilling to retire to the tower chamber that had been prepared for two and would now be occupied by one.

The summer night had begun its swift descent into dawn, and there was naught but embers on the hearth when Temric entered the room. Rannulf watched as his brother crossed the hall, stepping carefully over snoring bodies.

"What do you want," he asked sourly when he came near enough.

"So you've not been able to drink yourself into forgetfulness after all."

Lord Graistan made a sound that was only half laugh. "Unfortunately not, although I can no longer feel my feet. There's nothing strong enough to stop the ache in my head. Are you so solidly in her camp that you've come to taunt me?"

"Do not put me in the middle of your silly spat," his brother said mildly.

Rannulf made a low, angry noise. "Not so silly. She accused me of planning to betray John with Maeve."

"Did she? I didn't know she cared enough to worry over whom you bedded. I thought the two of you didn't speak."

He gave his brother a sharp look. "I doubt she was jealous over me. She has only two concerns—her pride and her coins. Anyway, I am sick to death of her vicious tongue. See what price I again pay for my foolish desire to own a pretty thing? I should have learned my lesson from the last time when it ended in disaster."

Temric stared down at him for a long moment, then shook his head almost sadly. "You cannot compare her to Isotte. They are cut from different cloths. Open your eyes, Rannulf. Will you destroy a fine wife in order to prove yourself cursed?"

Lord Graistan jerked as if the words had physically impacted with him. He opened his mouth to protest, but before he could speak, Temric continued. "I came to give you this, not to discuss your marital problems. Oswald's man tapped at the postern only moments ago." He dropped the leather scrip into his brother's lap.

Rannulf dug into the packet and found the message, then squinted in the low light to make out the words. "Oswald," he said and laughed, "you devious fox." He glanced up at Temric. "Our cousin has whispered reminders into the bishop's ear of how wondrous the hunting is in our chase. The bishop, being extraordinarily fond of the sport, can be convinced to bide awhile here before he completes his return to Hereford. It will then be convenient for him to take this time to determine if the wills should be set aside and the inheritance reconsidered. I doubt it can hurt our cause if the hunting is as good as promised." He grinned widely. "I am to meet them where the river crosses the north road on the morrow to make a formal invitation.

"In the meanwhile, Graistan must be readied." He briefly studied the message once again. "The bishop presently travels with two knights, for whom only one must be provided with a bedchamber, besides Oswald and his master, of course. There are some twenty others, all of lesser consequence, servants or soldiers."

He came to his feet already eager to be gone. "Bear this message to my wife for me when she rises. She is to tear the purse strings from the purse and not to stint in the slightest thing. If we haven't enough in coin, she is to borrow what she needs. Tell her the bishop eats but once a day, but that meal must be rich with delicate sweets and soups to accompany his fish and fowl. And he requires wines of the finest quality."

"You will have to move your present guests from your chamber to accommodate the bishop," Temric reminded.

"John will understand." Rannulf waved that concern away, then stepped around the hearth to lay a hand on a man's shoulder. "Ulric, wake up. I need you to creep quietly into my chamber and retrieve my armor and my best surcoat. Take care you do not wake the newlyweds."

The man rubbed his face as he rose and straightened his shirt and hose. "Aye, my lord," he muttered, and stumbled toward the stairs.

"Temric, I'll take ten men with me. See that they are dressed in their best and their horses well fitted out. But it must be quick, as I wish to ride as soon as I am armed."

"They will be ready before you are," said his brother as he walked away.

Rannulf was still studying the message when his servant returned with his clothing and armor. He was followed by Maeve, who was swathed in a blanket, her golden red hair tumbling over her shoulders in long waves.

"My lord, what is amiss that you must dress so swiftly in the middle of the night," she cried in a low voice while touching his arm with gentle concern.

"Maeve! Did this churl awaken you? My apologies to you and John, as well. I had not expected to need access to your chamber tonight." He spoke more gently than was his custom. It was as if his tone could wash away the stain of his wife's accusations, even though Maeve knew nothing about them. He waited, still smiling, expecting her to immediately excuse herself and return to her husband.

"Your armor? Is there an attack? Oh, my lord, my heart stops at the thought of you in danger." She stepped nearer now and gazed up at him. Her face was all gentle curves and beautiful hollows, her eyes warm with her concern. She laid her hand upon his upper arm, her fingers stretching upward toward his shoulder.

Rannulf shifted uneasily at her touch. When she did not withdraw her hand, he took her fingers in his and stepped back. "Nay, no attack. I must meet the Bishop of Hereford this morn regarding my wife's inheritance. You should have no concern for me, Maeve. Brothers"—he gave emphasis to the word as he let her hand slip from his grasp—"you must forsake when you cleave unto your husband. Now, go back to your bed and think no more of it. If John asks, I should return before the sun sets tonight."

She sighed softly, baring one arm to lift her hair over her shoulder. The blanket sagged open to reveal the curve of her breast. "You are right, but I am so newly married, surely I can be excused. I must unlearn my habit of worrying over you."

Now he frowned sharply. "Cover yourself, madam. Dear God, this is your wedding night. What sort of man is John to let you come down like that? Go back to bed."

She laughed, low and husky, and did not pull the blanket back up over her shoulder. "You may drop your pretense now. Really, all this concern over my husband. And a meeting with a bishop? At this hour? Such a story. If you are worried over your man carrying tales, you need not. I will make very certain he keeps his mouth shut. Oh, my poor heart, until he woke me, I despaired of finding a moment alone with you."

She stepped forward, exposing one long, slim leg. The firelight glimmered on her bare thigh. "Your greeting yesterday was balm to my soul. If you had not held me next to your heart when you proposed this ridiculous marriage, I would not have known what you intended."

"Intended? I intended nothing, and my greeting was no more than a greeting," he started, but his voice caught as he remembered his wife's pointed remarks about the same event. He'd only meant to sweeten the news of so sudden a wedding. Where had he erred?"

"Nothing more?" she insinuated, her voice like the sensuous rasp of silk against skin. "You drew me into your embrace and held me as you had never held me before, and now you would say it was nothing? Do not lie to yourself, Rannulf. It is me you desire. I know how unhappy you are in this marriage of yours. Look, here I am beside you. I can ease your pain. Let me love you as you deserve to be loved. And don't fret over John, for I can manage him. He is very simple."

"No."

Hard and cold, the word hung so heavily in the air between them that even the smoke could not rise. Instead, it curled and circled around them until it filled the space between them. She made no movement except to tighten her fingers into the blanket.

He stared at her, truly seeing her for the first time, and what he found in her eyes made him look away in sickened shame. Why had he been so determined not to recognize her for what she was?

When he finally spoke, his voice was taut with pain and revulsion. "How could you believe this of me?" He rubbed a hand against his brow, then turned to face her once again. "How? You have lived beneath my roof for years, and never have I touched you or given you any sign that I desired you. What did I do that gave you cause to believe me capable of dishonoring a loyal man who has done me no harm? Tell me now, so I may be sure to never do it again."

He watched her face, but her expression did not change. Neither did she move to draw the blanket closer, and there was something obscene in the way that simple wool sheet draped about her to reveal her breast. He reached out to yank the edge of it over her shoulder until she was decently covered once again. "Sweet Jesu, this is your wedding night. To do a man so on this night of all nights, it would stain my soul forever."

"How very righteous of you," Maeve purred dangerously. "But this must be a new side of you. You could hardly have been so righteous when you left my sister to die. How grateful you must have been when she breathed her last. After all, it solved the problem of what to do with the bastard she carried. Tell me, my lord, did you ask for whom she cried as her lifeblood ebbed away? Or could you not bear to hear that she'd cried for Gilliam and cursed you for separating them."

Rannulf closed his eyes as his stomach rolled. He tried desperately to shove the memory away, but Maeve's words were like daggers ripping away all his carefully constructed barriers. The scene exploded to life in his memory, every detail clear and fresh as if it had happened yesterday, not five years ago.

Isotte, only just past her fifteenth birthday and pregnant with the child he had not fathered, had miscarried. The midwife did what she could, but she could not stop the bleeding. Blood had soaked the mattress and dampened the bedclothes; even his own clothing had been filled with it.

"Aye," he said softly, as an odd sense of peace flowed over him. He opened his eyes as the scene faded gently away without any of the horror it had once held for him. In its wake came sadness, but it was a sadness without pain. "Aye, she cried, but it was for your mother, child that she was. Poor thing had only me and the priest to bear her company. At the end she clung to me. All I could do was hold her until she was gone. And when we laid her to rest, it was I who cried for her.

"But, I doubt that was what you hoped to gain with your ploy. Have you anything left to use against me or is your arsenal now spent?"

Maeve only shrugged casually. "Call it a desperate attempt to hurt you for rejecting me, if you like, a parting blow. Now, I'll give you a warning. You are a cuckolded fool, not once, but twice. Is this the same as the last time, or do you know what's afoot at Graistan? I'm told you are never far from Gilliam's side these days, my lord."

She stared at him to see what effect her words had had. Rannulf only looked down at her, his face expressionless, his eyes hard and cold. She sighed. "Ah, well, see what you want to see."

She turned toward the fire and held her hands out to catch what remained of the departing warmth. "But really, Rannulf, if you had to see me wed, why choose such an oaf? Did you see how he smeared grease on my sleeve? Now I am to be a farm wife, with geese and goats forever at my heels." The sudden sharp edge to her voice hinted at real despair, but it disappeared as she continued. "How rustic. He is worse than my first husband."

"Dear God, what have I done," he whispered in horror. "I refused to believe them. Rowena warned me. I said she hated you and saw the worst for her own reasons. John is a good man who deserves better than you," he bit out. "Well, it is done and there's no hope of undoing it. I, myself, saw to that. But I can still warn him. Perhaps he can beat some goodness into your soul."

"Too late," she said with a tiny laugh and a confident lift of her brow. "My power over him is complete. He is smitten and will not hear you." She tilted her head until the firelight revealed her at her most beautiful. A soft smile turned her lips upward ever so slightly, and her eyes sparkled. "Challenge me, and I will see you destroyed in your man's eyes." Then she made him a mock bow and turned on her heel to start back toward the stairs.

"Ulric, escort her," Lord Graistan commanded. "Make certain she returns to her husband's bed. Wake two fellows and tell them they are to stand by either door to assure that she stays there until her husband rises. When you've done so, come help me dress. And all of you who have listened here this night, if one word of this incident is repeated to anyone before I have spoken with Sir John, your heads will be the forfeit."

The man nodded his assent and hurried after her. When he returned, his lord already wore the padded woolen chausses and shirt that served as buffer between his skin and mail. After they had pulled and shrugged the mail shirt in place, they paused for a breath.

"I have been a fool," Rannulf said to himself, not expecting a response from his servant.

"Aye, my lord," said Ulric, "so you were. But, then you regained your senses and wed your lady, may God preserve you both." The man turned to lift the metal stockings and missed the marked reaction the nobleman had to his comment.

# Chapter Fifteen

OWENA waited impatiently for her guests to descend. They were already an hour late, an hour she could have better spent on preparations for the bishop's arrival. Instead, she'd had to dress in honor of the newly wedded couple. Now, they lingered upstairs while she could do nothing save pace here in front of the tables set for the midday meal and dwell on the horror of the previous evening's events.

Not that she hadn't done enough of that last night on an uncomfortable cot in a drafty corner of the women's quarters. Dawn's light had found her still blaming herself for so stupidly falling into such an obvious and waiting snare. Despite Temric's insistence that there was yet hope, she could see no escape from this morass.

"Well, good morrow, Rowena, dear," called Maeve from the balcony fronting the second floor. She wore a sleek silk undergown of pale peach with an overgown of darker orange embroidered in gold, and her hair had been carefully plaited with bright ribbons. Rowena's eyes narrowed. No doubt it had been these vain primpings that were the source of their delay.

"Perhaps you should say afternoon, love," John corrected. "We have slept most of the day away."

Her husband was a marked contrast to his wife, for he wore his stained and rumpled wedding attire and looked as though he'd barely run a comb through his hair.

His new bride leaned close to him and blushed prettily as she agreed with the throaty comment, "So we have."

Lady Graistan schooled her features into calm, and stepped forward to greet them as they descended the stairs and entered the hall. "I hope you found all to your liking in your chamber."

"I did," murmured John to his wife, "did you?"

His bride returned his look with a quick smile, "What do you think, my love?" Then she turned toward her lady and cried, "Oh, but you look as though you haven't slept a wink all night, you poor dear." The barest hint of gloating suggested she knew full well what havoc she'd wrought.

"It was all the excitement," Rowena said as she shrugged away the comment, then girded herself to accept without reaction all the subtle, nasty barbs that would surely follow. To her surprise, the fair woman did not pursue the matter.

"My, what a stunning gown. I don't believe I've ever seen it before. That shade of blue is just the color of your eyes, and those black and silver brilliants on the trim!"

Only at great cost did the Lady Graistan stay still while the woman fingered the tiny, shining stones and beads. How she wished she could strike out and hurt as she had been hurt. But what purpose would it serve? It would not change what had happened nor would it endear Graistan to Lord John.

She could not even give Maeve all the blame when it had been her own, stupid jealousy that had placed her so securely in the trap. Imagine, jealousy over a man who wanted naught to do with her. Her heart lurched again.

Lady Ashby turned to her husband with a husky sigh. "Oh, John, do you think I might one day have such a gown?" Then she seemed to catch herself. "Oh, what am I saying. I'm sure it was horribly expensive, and I most certainly do not need another gown."

"If it pleases you love, you may have three and damn the cost," John replied, his own eyes alight with pleasure.

"Oh, sweetheart, you are so good to me," she breathed, and leaned full against him to touch her lips to his cheek.

His sun-darkneed skin reddened in pleasure. He pulled her into the curve of his arm as he spoke to Rowena. "Have you seen Nicola this morn, my lady?"

"Aye, she was up early and is now in town with my people. Will you come to the table so we may begin serving?" She indicated the two chairs at the high table set there especially for her guests before she continued speaking. "She said there were some items she needed to purchase for your stores. I expect her back within the hour."

"Ah, yes, she'd mentioned she would do so." He led his wife around the corner of the table as he asked, "Is Lord Graistan about? With all these carts going in and out, you'd think he was preparing for a siege."

"Nay, nothing like that." She didn't wait for them to reach their seats before she signaled that the servants from the kitchen were to set their trays on the table at the same time that the butler filled cups and the water bearer brought around his basin and towels. Usually, these events occurred in solemn and careful order to give the meal its proper formality.

John pulled the heavy chair out for his wife. Lady Maeve managed to make the act of sitting down a single, sinuous movement, then turned star-bright eyes up to her husband. "Thank you, my lord," she breathed.

"My pleasure, wife." He grinned again, as though he was no more than a score instead of two score and ten. Then, he turned to his lady. "So, what's afoot here?"

Rowena sat beside him on a bench. "Late last evening, my lord received word that the Bishop of Hereford is coming here to decide upon my inheritance. My husband has gone to escort his party to Graistan."

John intently watched the butler fill his cup as he listened to her speak. With a motion to the man, he indicated the servant should linger while he drank deeply, then refill the cup before moving on. "Ah," he breathed in enjoyment. "Graistan serves a fine wine, my lady. Poor Rannulf. To host a bishop is an expensive proposition. Such esteemed guests are quite beyond Ashby's means and, thanks be to God, we will never have to bear that burden."

"Oh, my," Maeve breathed as if awed, "a bishop, here. Well, I am surely glad this responsibility did not fall upon my shoulders. You are so competent, while whatever I try seems to fall half done from my fingers."

John gently patted his wife's hand. "Now, now, love, you must not berate yourself so. And you need never worry over such details if it does not please you. What are servants for if not to care for you?"

"I do not know," she said, as if the thought had never occurred to her before this day.

Rowena turned gratefully away to hold her hands above the washbasin as a servant poured water over them. Her movement hid her disgust. After she'd used the towel, she bid the man to move on to John. It would have been better for all concerned if the woman had been confined to the convent for her life. She would twist the poor man into knots, only to toss him away when he no longer served her purposes.

"Here, love, will you have some of this dish? It looks like fowl with"—he stuck his finger into the sauce, then into his mouth—"with a sweet onion sauce," he announced to his wife. "Very good, too, my lady."

"My lord," Maeve reprimanded sweetly, "you must wash your hands first. See, here is the man with the water for you right behind us."

"Oh, so he is. I'm afraid we've forgotten to maintain such courtly formality at Ashby. With just my daughter and I and so few visitors, well, we have let it slide. Mayhap, you will retrain us country oafs, love." He laughed as he washed his hands. After that, he filled their trenchers from the trays in front of him. With his spoon, still held high and oozing sauce, he turned toward his lady. "You realize that such a judgment could take weeks, especially if the hunting stays good. To have a house full so long, well—would it be better for Rannulf if we were to leave?"

"Have a care," Maeve said, with just a shade of hardness to her voice, "the spoon is dripping."

"Pardon, love," he said absently, and thrust his utensil into the foodstuff. He wiped his fingers on his robe front as Rowena answered.

"My lord left no word regarding the length of the visit, but he did say that you were to continue here as long as you like and join the hunting if it pleases you."

"John," his wife cried out, a shade too quickly, "we couldn't." When they both turned to look at her, she hurried on. "There will be so many people here and so little privacy." Her voice was husky with intimation as she curved herself against her husband's shoulder.

Once again, Ashby's face flamed. "I think you are right, my love. We would just be in the way here, what with all the dignitaries. But, we must stay until Rannulf returns to give him our thanks and bid him farewell."

"Of course. To do otherwise would be rude," Maeve replied, then smiled brightly at him. "I suppose if it is only one night that we must spend apart, it is not so bad. Here, love." She had his cup refilled for him. "There will be a lifetime of nights for us."

"Aye, a lifetime," he said, with a sigh, then dedicated himself to eating. As with the night before, he doted on his wife until she exclaimed she was sated and could eat no more.

Rowena grew increasingly more heartsick as she watched. It was so wrong. Maeve did not deserve a man as kind as this one. There was no pretense in his affection for his wife. His every look and touch spoke volumes. She turned away to hide her own despair. Oh, to be cared for in that way, to be treated as something prized and of unreckoned value.

"Sister, is it not a glorious day," Maeve said, bringing Rowena's attention back to them. "It is such a relief to see the sun after so much rain.

Traveling yesterday was horrid. You should have seen the mess it made of my cloak."

Her husband smiled in commiseration. "It was miserable. It was fortunate for us that Ashby lies so nearby, or we'd have drowned before we arrived. I hope the weather holds through tomorrow for our journey home."

"Do you think it will not?" his wife asked so quickly, the question was almost sharp. She stuttered in her attempt to soften it with her following words. "I—I only mean that the convent—where I have resided these last months—is but a few minutes ride from Graistantown. My new home is so much farther. If it were to rain"—she paused here and caught her breath as in sudden thought—"but, no, pay me no heed. If I must, I will. We must wait here for Rannulf's return. But I know I could not tolerate to spend two nights away from the privacy of our own bed, so we will have to leave on the morrow, rain or no." She clasped his hand in hers.

Her husband gazed down at her for a long moment, then turned to face his hostess. "Do you think Lord Rannulf would be insulted if we were to depart this day?"

"Nay, love," she protested sweetly, "we have decided that we must stay. Do not risk damaging your overlord's love for you by acceding to my silly whims."

"Dear heart, the more I think on it, the more I see the sense in taking advantage of a fine day for our traveling. Truly, we will just be in the way here, and Rannulf has more important matters with which to concern himself." He looked back to Rowena. "We will abide by your verdict, my lady. Should we go or stay?"

Lady Graistan glanced to the fair woman at his side. That Maeve wanted to leave as soon as possible was obvious. Why she wanted to go was beyond guessing. Could it be she had some spurned lover with the bishop's party that she did not wish to meet again? But it was for selfish reasons alone that Rowena finally spoke.

"I know my husband will regret not having bid you farewell himself, but he will understand your need to have the privacy of your own home. Depart, if you wish."

"Do you want to go?" John tucked his wife's hand beneath his arm and gazed down at her.

"I want only to be with you." She smiled gratefully up at him. "Take me home, husband."

"With pleasure, wife." He stood and helped her to her feet. "Please excuse us, my lady, but we must prepare to depart. Will you send to town for my daughter?"

"As you wish, Lord John," she said as they walked away. They had disappeared up the stairs before Ilsa left her seat at the servant's table to join her lady.

"Now, why do you think she wants to be gone so quickly?"

"Do not question the gift, Ilsa," Rowena replied. "Still, it is strange." She stood and started toward the butlery. "Well, if we are to ponder over it, it must be later rather than sooner. I hope they hurry and leave. The sooner they are gone, the sooner I can get out of this gown and into my workaday gown. Have you finished the upper chambers?"

"Aye. We have only to prepare your room once the happy couple have departed. Shall I leave the bed where it stands or do you want yours returned to its place?"

"Nay, leave all as it is." It was still her bed, and

she'd keep it stored as long as she desired. "Allen," she called across the room, "have these tables cleared and put away, but make certain our best service is ready should the bishop wish to dine this evening."

"Aye, my lady."

But, she did not hear him, for she had already exited through the back of the hall and into the butler's domain to see how he progressed.

With so little to pack and Maeve's cart still loaded from the previous day, it took less than an hour for Ashby's party to prepare. Nicola had no more walked into the gate when her father called to his men to mount up. As he assisted his bride into the saddle of her palfrey, Sir John said, "I hope you'll not change your mind and find yourself distressed at missing the chance to bid your lord farewell. We could yet stay another day to make a proper good-bye."

"A woman must forsake her family and cleave unto her husband," his wife said, "and, besides, I have so much to learn. Just think, there is grain to be winnowed, butter to be churned, and bread to be baked. I shall be busy every moment of the day. Perhaps I shall be so overworked, I will have nothing left at the end of the day for you, you poor dear thing."

"Never," he retorted with a besotted smile. "Nicola will see to it that you are never overburdened. You are so frail and delicate, you must have a care you do not become ill."

His daughter sent her lady a brief and telling glance, but said nothing as the sentry's call rang out over their words.

"But, who is this coming," the new Lady Ashby said, with a swift glance at the gate. Something akin to panic appeared ever so briefly in those pale eyes. Once again Rowena wondered what she could possibly fear from the bishop's arrival.

But it was Gilliam who rode through the gate. Lady Maeve seemed to relax in relief, but her words were filled with disappointment. "And, I had hoped it was Rannulf so we might bid him farewell after all."

The young man glanced around the group gathered in the courtyard as he drew his mount to a halt and slid from the saddle. He turned rudely away from any contact with them and strode directly toward the hall door. "My lady, I will speak to you inside after they have gone," he called back over his shoulder.

"Why, I was wondering where you were hiding," Lady Ashby called out, her tone perfectly reasonable. "Will you not come congratulate me on my marriage?"

He stopped in his tracks, then slowly turned toward her, ripping his gloves from his hands. "You have my heartfelt congratulations," he said coldly.

"Oh, what a sweet child you are," she cried in seeming innocence of his hostility. "But it is customary to kiss the bride, is it not?"

"Not for me," he retorted, his deep voice reverberating off the thick walls.

Rowena saw Sir John's brows draw down as he recognized the insult to his wife. He started forward, toward the center of the courtyard, his stance aggressive and tense.

She hurried to Gilliam. "Bite your tongue," she whispered. "Go and wish them both well. It will not kill you to do so." In a much louder voice she continued, "Has your visit to Sir Jocelynn gone so ill that you come home all frowns and bad temper?"

He looked down at her, sighed, and took the hint. "Aye, it was not at all what I expected." To her, he whispered a swift aside, "It was short by an hour." Then he strode across the yard to meet Ashby. "I apologize for my rudeness, Lord John. It's only fortunate for me that my journey home did not go just a little longer or I would have missed the opportunity to wish you well. And your—lovely lady, too." He stumbled over the compliment, his teeth gritted in a smile.

"Why, Gilliam," John said, with a hearty laugh. "I hardly knew you, though I should have realized who you were. Not many a man looks down on me save you and your brother. I swear you're taller now than when last I saw you before you left for the Holy Lands. My bailiff tells me you are your brother's steward and came to call at Ashby while I was at Nottingham with Lord Graistan."

"Aye, Lord John, so I did at my lady's request. She was seeking to familiarize herself with Graistan's holdings and dues. That's a beautiful corner of the world you have there." His voice revealed a wistful longing and she remembered how sure he'd seemed that his brother would never grant him his own keep.

"Ah, so it is," John graciously agreed, now completely mollified.

"Did you realize you've got a soft corner on your south wall? I noticed it, but did not recognize what I saw until after I'd left that day."

"Nay," Ashby said in surprise and interest. "Well, we've had trouble there before. Moisture from the river seeps into the walls and rots the mortar. Once noted, easily repaired. Do you remember my daughter, Nicola?" He pointed to the tall girl who still stood beside her mount. "Oh, how foolish of me. Of course you must have spoken with her when you were at our hall."

"But, I did not. She was out when I arrived, and I could not stay the night. The bailiff said she was with a woman in the village who was giving birth." He studied Nicola for a long moment, then smiled a little more naturally. "But, I vaguely remember something—dear God, I think I was twelve and she seven when last we met. If I remember rightly, I was royally perturbed because she followed me everywhere for the duration of our visit. Grown a little since then, girl," he said to her. "Lord, you could almost look me in the eye. I am much more amenable to being followed these days," he teased with a friendly glint in his bright blue eyes.

Nicola graced him with a narrow-eyed smile, but said nothing as she mounted her horse without the aid of a groom. Then, she leaned down, meaning to left her basket, but Gilliam grabbed it up before she could reach it.

"What are you doing," she demanded. "It is mine, give it to me."

"Glad to be able to serve," he said with a laugh and set it into its net at the back of her saddle.

"Did I look as if I needed your assistance?" she snapped back. "If I had wanted help, I would have asked."

"My lady, your courtly manner will make me swoon," he replied, his grin now wicked with amusement. He turned to her father. "My, she is a pretty thing, but is she always so outspoken?"

"Always," Ashby sighed. "Now, hold your tongue, daughter, before you insult Lord Graistan's brother as deeply as you have insulted Lord Graistan."

"Nicola, have a care" came Maeve's warning, "he'll play the part of gallant, for he is quite a swain. There's more than one girl here who's borne a fair-haired babe by him." She smiled at them both, deftly maneuvering herself back into the center of attention. "Oh, John, I think we must hurry along. I see clouds building."

"As you command, my lady," he said with a smile. "Thank you again for your hospitality, Lady Rowena. When your lord returns, give him our grateful thanks and wish him well on his endeavor." He mounted up and signaled the party to start forward. "Farewell," he called back.

"Aye, farewell, dear sister," Maeve called. "Do not forget me. Be assured that I will never forget you or all you and your lord have done for me." She rode out through the gate. Nicola and the rest of Ashby's men followed.

"Good riddance," Gilliam breathed as they watched them exit the gate. "She'll trouble us no longer."

"Oh, Gilliam," Rowena said, her voice almost a cry. "It is so wrong. She'll use John and make a mockery of her vows to him. Would that I could take back the words I spoke the day I suggested it."

He unlaced his mail hood and pushed it off his head. "There is more than worry for Lord John in your voice. What has happened here in my absence?"

"It is nothing." When he would have insisted, she shook her head and held up a hand to still him. "I have more important things to tell you. The Bishop of Hereford is on his way here this very day. He intends to resolve my inheritance while he enjoys our forest."

Gilliam lifted a brow. "Oswald has been busy. I suppose this means my chamber has been confiscated? I thought as much," he responded to her nod. "Then, I'll take myself down to the garrison. When is the bishop to arrive?"

"Before sunset is all the message your brother left for me, which could mean two hours from now or eight with it so near midsummer."

He nodded, then studied her for a long moment. She shifted uncomfortably and tried to smile, not realizing how badly it failed.

"Poor Rowena," he said softly, "you look so sad. How you must wish he never wed you. It sits poorly on my soul when I see him treat you as he has."

"It is not so bad as that," she protested quickly, trying to hide her pain with words. "You mistake sadness for exhaustion. Last night I saw no more than an hour's rest for tossing and turning in an unfamiliar bed."

Gilliam grinned. "You are a poor trader in falsehoods, my lady. Well, if you need a friendly ear who'll listen to your troubles and spread no tales after, I am willing."

"Thank you," she said, with a more natural smile. "Know that I value your friendship, and it does make me feel welcome here." Why was it not enough for her that her husband's kin and her servants had such care for her? "Now, if you hurry from your mail, you may yet find the remainder of our meal in the kitchen. There was lamb seethed in rosemary sauce," she said with a teasing tone, knowing it was one of his favorite dishes.

Gilliam's face mellowed in anticipation. "Say no more. I am on my way. My man can unarm me there while I eat."

"And I'm off to remove my woman's armor." She

plucked at the sleeve of her elaborate overgown. "Maeve is gone, and the bishop has yet to arrive, and I am dying of heat." She smiled wryly. The young knight shouted with laughter and hurried to the kitchen as she returned to the hall and her preparations.

# Chapter Sixteen

RANNULF rode hard up to Graistan's outer gate, shouting to the sentry almost before he'd slowed his mount. "Tell me, has Ashby left yet?"

"Aye, my lord," the man called back. "A good four hours past."

"Damn." He slid from the saddle and led his tired mount through the portal. Gone she might be, but Maeve was mistaken if she believed herself free of him. Handing his reins to a groom, he started across the bailey.

If his confrontation with Maeve had been postponed, the same was not true for his wife. At the very least she was due an apology, if she'd accept it. He could only hope he'd not yet done what Temric suggested and destroyed all hope of peace with her.

In his short absence, the bailey had already been transformed. The western end of the green expanse was now sectioned off into fenced yards. In some of these makeshift pens stood his wealth of horseflesh, others contained animals destined for their meals; there were cattle, swine, and sheep for the nonclerics and servants.

For those who had tied their souls to the church, there would be fish, everything from carp to pike to eels. He wagered that the fish merchants were already stocking Graistan's fish pond, which lay near the river.

But his wife would have bought more than this for their important guest. There would also be plaice, haddock, and shellfish, among others. And, birds, multitudes of birds. No doubt, John Fowler and his sons were hard at work capturing the larks, blackbirds, and thrushes that would be baked within swans and peacocks. These creatures would supplement the more mundane daily fare of doves, geese, and chickens.

Laid out to dry on the fresh grass were newly washed linens, bedding, and toweling. Blankets aired on the wooden rails that marked the practice lists. The laundresses still carried their filled baskets down to the outer gate and beyond their walls to the river.

When he reached inner gate, three servants rushed past him without giving him the slightest glance, so intent were they on their own business. The courtyard was thronged with folk and carts, all crowded around the stairs as casks of wine and other foodstuffs were carried up into the keep. As busy as it was in the yard, the hall would be worse. His people were trying to find space for half again as many visitors as there were residents. No doubt whole storerooms were being repacked, rooms emptied and refilled, to achieve it.

Caught in a sudden, silly fear, he stepped back from the entryway. Now was hardly the time to seek her out. It was more than a quick word he wished to give her. There were things he needed to explain, things that she, more than anyone, deserved to know. It would have to wait—if she would hear him at all. His past behavior certainly did not warrant her present attention.

"My lord," called the pantler, stirring Rannulf from his thoughts. "What are you doing here? I've just come from town, and I saw no sign of the bishop's party. Can he truly have come already?" There was a note of panic in his voice.

"Nay, I have returned early. The bishop delays his arrival for a time. Carry that message to your lady, will you, since I'm loath to brave the hall just now. Tell her not to fret over this change, but she should come to me when she is free. I'll be with Temric in the garrison. Be sure to tell her that."

"So I will. Shall I send your man to you?"

"Nay, do not bother. I'll find what I need from my brother."

"As you say, my lord." The pantler nodded, anxious to be at his work. His lord gestured a sign of release, and the man sped on his way.

Rannulf entered the keep through the postern gate, nodding to the man who guarded this tiny entrance, and crossed through the chapel to the garrison room that lay beside the hall and beneath his own bedchamber. It was wonderfully cool and dark inside, especially after an hour's hard ride in metal beneath the warm sun. He pushed off his cap of knitted steel with a sigh of relief and removed his woolen underhood.

Why had it not occurred to him until after midday that Maeve might seek an early departure to prevent her new husband from speaking with his lord? Had he not been so incredibly tired, he would have immediately realized it was the only safe course open to her. Yet how had she managed it? Left on his own, Ashby would never have gone without first gaining his lord's release. It most certainly was not customary for a guest to leave before personally thanking his host either. But gone they were.

He stepped into the crowded room. "Rannulf," Temric said in surprise, "what are you doing here? I heard no party ride in."

"For good reason. It is only I who have arrived. Temric, I am tired to death and practically fried beneath this metal. Help me out, will you?" He slipped off his surcoat and dropped it to the floor.

"Here"—his brother kicked several short stools out of the way and pushed back a stack of pallets— "kneel here. You there, put away your dice and fetch your lord a bucket of water and a cloth so he might wash. You, Walter, bring your lord some wine and a clean cup, and be quick about it."

"But see that it's well watered," Lord Graistan amended, then knelt at his brother's feet. Temric slowly and painstakingly removed the unwieldy long-skirted mail shirt. Once free of that, Rannulf stripped himself of his metal chausses, then swiftly shed his protective underclothing. "How did Gilliam tolerate it in the Holy Lands?" he breathed in relief as cool air flowed over his overheated skin. "I'll take that cup now."

The soldier handed him a cup and pitcher of wine as Temric spoke. "He says Richard was wise enough to march them only in the cooler morning hours. Still, there were those who dropped with the heat. I suppose Gilliam was too young and foolish to believe he could die that way, so he was spared." His rough voice was filled with a fond amusement. "Big man, small brain, I always say."

"Only because you are not as tall as we," Rannulf retorted with a laugh.

"So, what of the bishop?"

He answered with a twisted smile. "It is not only on my behalf that he comes. He's irritable and travel weary, having gone cross the country and back again

on Hubert Walter's business. He thinks to once
again drag me into service for the crown. It seems
the archbishop's found new duties for England's
knighthood."

"Uncompensated, of course," Temric said wryly.

"Of course," he replied, drinking deeply from his
cup, then refilling it to drink again. "At any rate,
Oswald was a little overeager. William always meant
to delay his arrival here until my dear mother and
brother by marriage could join him. He said, and in
all fairness I must agree with him, that to call them
to come while he is my guest is to suggest his decision will be biased in my favor.

"In the end it was quite a dance of etiquette we
played, each of us outdoing the other in politeness.
We finally agreed that I should leave Graistan with
my lady, while he resides here and awaits her relations. With Gilliam to play host and hunt master in
our fertile chase and a richly stocked larder, my
interests will yet be well served."

"And where do you go?"

"First, to Upwood where my lady will stay, then
on to Ashby, to warn John against his wife." Temric's eyebrows shot up in surprise, but he said nothing, only pushed forward the bucket and cloth so
his brother could make use of it.

While Rannulf washed away the grime and sweat,
he spoke. "When I sent Ulric to retrieve my armor
from my chamber last night, he returned with
Maeve on his heels. She came wrapped only in a
blanket and her hair to offer himself to me."

His disgust at her proposal had only deepened the
more he thought on it. Her actions had struck a
deep blow to his pride. It was not only Maeve who
had thought him capable of such dishonor, so had

his wife. Did others see this as well? He waited for his brother's reaction.

"Then, she was disappointed." The easiness of Temric's voice along with the calm surety of his words were as balm to a burn and urged him forward with his tale.

"Quite. When she realized I would not bend to her seduction, she strove to hurt me by revealing she knew a part of the story of Isotte's death. But she did not know it all and had assumed the worst. It is my guess she'd hoped to gain some hold over me by revealing her knowledge of it." He paused. "Dear God, it was the evil way she used her words that chilled me. That's when I vowed I'd tell her husband of her actions when I returned today. Now, it seems she's run to ground at Ashby, and I will have to meet her there."

"You were warned," Temric said evenly, "and not only by your own folk. Did you really never question why her first husband's people set her aside and took her dower after his death?"

Rannulf frowned a little. "But, you know that is not so uncommon, especially when there are no children from the marriage. Gilliam and my wife made her sound so mad. How could I credit their tale when I had never seen anything like it from her and had lived with her so much longer? Now I have tied poor John to her for his life. If I leave it as it is, it will stain my soul. I wonder if she believes herself free of my intent to warn John?"

His brother shook his head. "Nay, she's too canny for that. And, be warned. She's seen to it that John's already well smitten with her. It's no good crossing the love struck."

Rannulf shrugged off his brother's words. "John is my most loyal vassal. Nothing she can do will change that. I know your robes are too short for me, but lend me a shirt, will you?" he asked, drying his face and torso on a bit of rough toweling. "I need a bite to eat after which I intend to find a quiet corner here and sleep."

"Help yourself," said Temric as he threw open his chest.

"Good thing your robes do not fit," Lord Graistan mused, "brown, brown, or brown, so many choices."

His elder brother cuffed him on the shoulder. "Beggars cannot be choosers," he said, then laughed. "You may claim exhaustion, but it's been a long while since you were last in so light a mood."

Rannulf once again donned his heavy chausses, then took one of Temric's shirts from the neat stack within the coffer. "If that's true, then I welcome it."

"So, you're finally ready to speak with your wife," Temric offered blandly.

He shrugged into the loose-fitting linen shirt, not surprised at the remark. There were times when his elder brother knew him better than he knew himself. "God willing, it can still be done. I think it is time to mend the gap I put between us," he said as he rolled up the too-short sleeves.

"Come to your senses, have you?" His brother handed him his boots.

"Thought you'd be pleased," Rannulf offered back, mimicking his brother's short style of speech, then ducked when he would have cuffed him again. He laughed as he hurriedly closed the door behind him and left for the kitchen.

Two hours after Ashby's departure, Rowena crossed the courtyard on her way to the stables. These were to have been cleared of all save the very finest beasts and the stalls were to be spread with fresh straw. It was here that the bishop's grooms and cart drivers would find their beds along with the stable lads and grooms who usually slept among the beasts. In a freshly cleaned stable with the weather so mild, it was likely they would find more comfort than those within the hall.

Gilliam met her halfway. "We can house mayhap ten men at the back of the place, depending on how many of the better mounts you wish to stable here. How many you can cram in above with our folk, well, who knows." He eyed her change of attire. "You certainly look more at ease, but far less like the lady of the manor."

Rowena smiled briefly and touched the sleeveless overgown that protected her loose-fitting, homespun gown of gray. "Ilsa would prefer I never dressed like this, but for what I wish to do today, anything else is too fine."

Suddenly, her stomach lurched. She clutched her midsection in surprise and pain. The pain instantly faded away, but it left her so sick, she wondered if she'd find the garderobe in time. She blinked hard; his face swam wildly before her. With a coarse word that made him laugh with surprise, she closed her eyes and swayed.

"Rowena!" he cried, and grabbed her arm. She tilted forward and leaned against him when her knees would have given way. Blackness tunneled in on her vision, and only his powerful arms around her kept her standing. "What is this"—she heard his voice as if from a far distance—"are you ill?"

For the briefest of instants, there was nothing but velvety blackness. Light was the first to return, but she still could not see. Sound came next, but the noises she heard were muffled and oddly distorted. She became aware of the softness of his gown beneath her cheek and his arms around her. While she knew she should move away, there was nothing she could do. No sinew or bone would obey her command.

As she drew a deep, steadying breath, she felt her vision settle back into its appropriate perspective, and her stomach calmed. Slowly, she pushed away from her brother by marriage and took a trembling step back. "My apologies, Gilliam. I do not know what happened."

From behind her came her husband's harsh voice. "Happened? Everyone in this yard can see what happened."

Rowena's eyes widened in shock as she whirled to face her husband. He stood directly behind her clad only in shirt and hose. This was not possible If he were here, where was the bishop? There was no sign of the dignitary's arrival. "What are you doing here?" she blurted out.

"I seem to have surprised you both," he snapped back.

Gilliam's hard cold words silenced her awakening rebuttal. "So everyone can see what has happened, can they, Rannulf?" His eyes were narrowed as he glared at his brother.

She gasped. She'd never even dreamed the young man capable of such harshness. "You may let go," she said to him as she pushed away. "I can stand now," she added rather loudly. "The spell has passed."

"Are you sure?" he asked, his voice gentle for her, yet its very gentleness was meant as a barb for his brother. She stared up at him in horror. He was making it worse on purpose. Stepping anxiously away, she turned to face her husband, but he had eyes for no one except his younger brother.

"Have you no more sense than to stand here before every soul in the keep with your arms about my wife?"

She yelped in startled surprise at Gilliam's sudden growl of anger. "What right have you to chastise me? I have done nothing wrong here." His words were like steel, slashing dangerously into the air between the two men. "Is this your kindness? Am I ever to be your scapegoat? Well, I'll not join you in this living hell of your making, brother," he spat the word out. "I did my penance on the stony soil of the Holy Lands. You saw to that."

"You stupid pup," Rannulf said grimly, but the sting was gone from his voice. "I made you no insult, only wished to point out how improper it looked." He spread his hands out before him in a gesture of peace.

"And I will call you liar," his youngest brother ground out. Rowena gasped as she looked at him. Had she thought him overly young once? There was nothing of the boy left now, only the look of an experienced and battle-trained knight. "Think hard before you answer too quickly."

Now, her husband's eyes narrowed. "How do you dare?" he asked coldly.

"Think hard before you answer," the young knight repeated. "Or, if you wish, meet me on yon field and say it to me with your sword." He paused, as if waiting for his brother to accept the challenge, then continued. "It is time we parted ways, brother, and gladly so." With that, he turned on his heel and stalked out of the gate.

"My God," Rannulf breathed as he stared after him, "what have I done?" His head lowered for a moment as if in pain, then he turned on her, his eyes blazing in rage. "What in God's name were you doing? Why did you fall into his arms that way? Or is this your revenge on me, to make such a show in front of me and all my folk?"

Rowena cried out, wishing she could cover her ears and stop his words before they reached her heart. "My lord, how could I have done so? I did not even know you had returned."

"Now, that puts an even more heinous look to the whole matter, does it not?" His sarcasm cut to the bone.

"Stop it," she snapped back. "Why ask me for an explanation if you only intend to twist what I say into something else? I took a sudden illness and nearly fainted. He caught me as I fell."

"Try again. That lie is tired after being used by so many women. It insults me when you think I would believe it."

Again his words struck out at her. Suddenly, she realized he sought to ease his own pain by hurting her. Her fingers curled into her palms. Anger too great to contain boiled up within her. With a scream of utter frustration, she hit him squarely in the chest with both fists.

"You idiot, you fool," she shrieked, "see what you want to see, then. It is not Gilliam who is your scapegoat, it is I." She tore off her overgown and threw it at him. "Here, take this. It is the badge of my ladyship at this place. Have it back. I am quit of you and Graistan." She swung her foot and knew it met his shin in bruising impact.

He yelped and leapt on one foot, but she was too enraged to enjoy her handiwork. "You treat your pigherds better than you treat me," she screamed as she turned. Dust flew from her heels as she ran from the courtyard, down through the bailey to the postern gate.

"My lady, stop," cried the man who watched the portal. He spread himself across the gate in an attempt to prevent her departure. "Oh, stop, please. Do not leave without an escort."

"Move, churl," she snapped, her voice low and furious. He leapt aside and she stomped through the stone arch, then stormed off along the narrow winding path that led down to the river.

"But where do you go?" he called after her as the washerwomen all straightened from their pounding and rinsing to look up at her and the keep.

"Away," she shouted back, her voice echoing angrily against Graistan's high walls. "Tell that stupid son of a worm I married that I am going away."

# Chapter Seventeen

ROWENA knew nothing but the red heat of her rage as she strode angrily along the river, which followed the town walls to the road at the foregate. Nor did anyone give her a second glance as she passed. Dressed in only her plain gown with a simple headcloth to cover her hair, she looked no more remarkable than any other modest townswoman out about her daily business.

But once she'd stepped away from the protective walls, common sense returned. There was no haven for her here. She stared ahaead on the dusty road. Fields and forest, orchard and village made a peaceful patchwork from the surrounding countryside. But these were his holdings, his lands. She needed a sanctuary beyond his reach.

To the east lay the convent where she'd confined Maeve. They would take her in, but her heart would break if she were so close to Graistan and could not return. Would Jordan cry when he found she'd left without even a word in farewell? She breathed a ragged sigh, but now there was no going back.

From within the town walls came the sound of screaming along with splintering wood. The sudden commotion woke her from her twisted thoughts. Hoofbeats thundered and people shouted. She did not need to look to know who it was. She grabbed up her skirts and leapt from the road and raced across a field toward the forest beyond with its concealing trees and brush.

A glance behind showed her a single rider erupting through the gateway, sending carts and cursing townsfolk sliding into the ditch at either side. Rage put wings on her feet. Yet by the time she dashed between the first trees, she could almost feel his horse's hot breath on her back.

"Leave me alone," she yelled, cutting suddenly to the right. Here the trees were close, and a horse could only walk. She ducked beneath a low hanging branch, seeking growth that was denser still. Twigs and thorns raked her skin and tore off her headcloth. Too slow!

She flung herself out of the other side of the thicket. He stood there waiting for her. With a cry, she struck out wildly. There was a satisfying depression of flesh beneath her hand. When he grabbed for her, she whirled away, sprinting through the trees.

"Rowena, this is insane," he called to her as he chased her. "It is useless, I have you."

She screamed in wordless rage, but knew that he was right. Her foot caught on a root. Her palms scraped against the tree's sharp back as she tried to catch herself. His arms closed about her waist, and they fell together. When she would have scrambled away, he dragged her back. She twisted around to strike out at him, and he grabbed her arms. Suddenly, she lay on her back, her arms pinned at her side, while he sat atop her thighs.

"Let me go," she cried out, struggling hopelessly from beneath him.

"You little fool," he growled. "What were you

thinking to leave my walls? How long do you think you would live without my sword to see you safe?"

"Better a swift death than the torture of life with you," she shrieked, writhing beneath him in an effort to overbalance him and win free.

"Best you stop that," he said, his voice so full of sudden amusement it shocked her into stillness. She stared up at him. His gray eyes were warm with his awakening desire. Laughter softened the lines of his mouth and awoke strong creases in his lean cheeks. Here was the handsome man who had so charmed her on their wedding night. "I have never hunted a woman before. I found it—exhilarating."

Her stung pride made her cry out. "You are laughing at me." With every ounce of her strength she sought to throw him off.

He laughed again. "Aye, but at myself as well." He loosed her arms. When she struck out at him, he caught her hands as if she were no more trouble to him than a fly. Then, holding both of her hands in one of his, he ran his free fingers through his hair in a distracted gesture. "You may as well cease, I will not let you go."

She yelled out her frustration, damning her womanhood, damning him. There had never been any escape from him or from their marriage. Whether she lived in his keep, a convent, or a hovel, she belonged to him. Her anger died against this realization, and she caught her breath in a choking gasp. The same aching pain that stabbed at her side tore her heart to bits. "Aye, you have me. I concede. But you only need me until you have my inheritance safe in hand. If I vow to help you obtain my lands, will you promise to let me live elsewhere?"

His smile died, and his eyes saddened. "Sweet Jesu, to hear my own words thrown back at me,"

e whispered. "I have treated you so badly, I do not
eserve to be forgiven. Tell me I will not lose you,
o."

Her eyes widened in disbelief at his words. "Lose
e?" she angrily spat out. "You cannot lose me. As
u, yourself have said, you own me."

"Too late," he breathed to himself. "Nay, it is
raistan that holds your heart. I have no claim on
u, and now I have driven you from the only thing
at binds you to me." He released her and eased
way to sit beside her. Pain radiated from him.
Temric is right, I have been determined to prove
yself cursed. I have destroyed my home, my
rother, and, now, you. Even Temric is leaving.
here is no one left. I am alone."

She lay still, finding no sense in his sudden
hange. Above this tiny glade the canopy of fresh,
reen leaves rustled against a sky of crystal blue.
he gentle breeze brought her the scent from a
earby clutch of lilies. Beneath her head, the moss
as springy and soft. Golden sunlight trickled
rough the branches to find the auburn in his hair
nd gild the strong planes of his face. He gazed
ff into the woods, his expression all harsh lines of
eartbreak.

Suddenly she knew if she were to walk away, he
ould not pursue her any farther. So why did she
ot rise and leave? Her eyes clenched shut against
he truth she kept trying to escape. It was not pres-
ge or power or any keep she wanted, it was him.

She rolled to her side and pushed her tangled
air back to better study him. "How can I believe
ou after what you said to me, to Gilliam?"

He jerked as if startled by her voice. When he
urned to look at her, he seemed surprised to see
he was still there. It was a moment before he

spoke. "When I saw you in his arms, I wanted t
kill him. You are mine, and I could only see tha
he was holding you. The words fell unconsidere
from my lips." He stared down at his clenched fist
in his lap. "Then, when I realized what I'd done t
him, I struck out at you as a way to ease my ow
pain. Mea culpa," he breathed.

Against all her better judgment, her heart leap
at what he'd said. Jealousy? Over her? She reache
out and touched his hand. His fingers opened t
enclose hers in his. "Your apology is accepted," sh
whispered, hardly daring to believe and half con
vinced she'd just see his scorn again.

He studied her for a long moment, then seeme
content with what he saw, for the corner of hi
mouth quirked upward. The bitterness she'd com
to know so well seemed to melt away with this mo
tion. "We are a couple of strange ones, eh? Yo
have scandalized my folk by attacking me befor
them all, while my ride through town has done th
same. No doubt it will cost me a pretty penny, al
though I cannot say I regret riding down the courve
sier. What a pompous ass. A few bruises could d
him nothing but good." There was the oddest glim
mer in his eyes, something between laughter an
tears.

Rowena stared at him. "You rode him down?" sh
breathed. "But he sits as headman on the counci
this year." Of all the town's guildsmen, this one wa
the most powerful as well as the most arrogant. H
would, indeed, make a complaint and cry loudl
about all the hurts done to him.

Her husband tried to stifle his grin. "He leapt int
the fishmonger's trough to avoid me."

"Poor man," she tried to say, but her inner visior
of the scene drove her pity away. Laughter gurgle

out of her. Then, suddenly, unexpectedly, a terrible, terrified sob broke free. She covered her face with her free hand in a desperate attempt at control, but it did not stop the next gasp, or the sob after that.

"Rowena," he murmured, his voice filled with sorrow as he drew her into the circle of his arms and held her close. She cradled her face against the curve of his shoulder as tears flooded from her. His fingers caressed the back of her neck, their pressure soft against her nape.

Tears flowed from her, ripping away the locks she'd placed on all the hurts that had ever been done her. She cried for the forlorn child she'd once been, for the loss of her far-flung goals and ambitions, for the pain of his rejection, and for the new sense of belonging she'd discovered at Graistan but did not yet know how to accept.

"I'm so sorry." He softly murmured it again and again against her cheek. At last, drained and empty, she caught her breath in a hiccuping gasp. "Hush, sweet. Hush. Be still. I will not let you go."

She heard his voice, heard his kindness, and felt his gentleness. And then, she knew. Here, in this wild place and away from the source of all that was wrong between them, they would begin again.

Her fingers burned with the heat of his skin through the thin material of his shirt. She slid her hand upward along the strong column of his throat. The soft curls of his hair lay within her reach. A shiver wracked her as she combed its silkiness with trembling fingers. Then she caressed the hard outline of his shoulder and upper arm.

He shuddered just a little, his voice dying away until only the lively quiet of the woods remained. She pressed her ear to his chest and heard the steady thud of his heart. His fingers curled beneath

her chin and lifted her face until his lips touched
hers. Her breath caught at the quiet sweetness of
his kiss.

But this was not what she needed. It was his
passion for her she craved; she coveted his demanding need to fill the newly borne emptiness
within her. Her mouth melded to his, teasing, taunting until she felt him shake against her onslaught.

His fingers raked through her hair to cradle her
head while he took her mouth with his. A deep sigh
escaped her as she slid her hands beneath his shirt
to caress his chest. Her fingers found the waist
string on his chausses and loosened the knot, then
slipped inside.

He groaned and tore away from their kiss to lean
back as her hand closed about his shaft. His heat
seared her, bringing throbbing life to her womb.
With a muttered word, he ripped off his shirt and
eased his chausses over his hips. They, and his
boots, flew behind him. She laughed at his eagerness, the sound sultry with her own rising need. But
her amusement died into awe as he knelt before
her, every inch of him revealed to her in the soft
summer's light.

Mary, Mother of God, but he is beautiful, she
thought. The wide sweep of his forehead, the arrogant line of his nose, his mouth curved in a smile.
His eyes burned with his desire for her, their gray
lights intense and hot despite the cool color. She
laid her hands on the broad stretch of his shoulders
as she studied the solid curves and planes of his
torso. At last, her gaze caressed the proof of his
need for her, and she touched the tip of his shaft
with a finger.

"Love me, Wren," he asked, his voice heavy with

more than physical need. "I have been cold and dead these past years until you came. Love me."

She caught her breath at his invitation, at the use of her private name. It shivered through her, promising much for the future. With a smile, she stood and pulled her loose gown off over her head. Beneath it she wore only a thin, linen chemise. When she would have shrugged free of that as well, he shook his head. "Let me."

Slowly, he lifted the sheer garment, kissing each newly revealed inch of skin from her knees to her inner thighs until he reached her nether lips. When he touched his mouth to that most intimate part of her, she could tolerate no more. Her legs shook, and she sank to kneel on the ground.

He tossed away her undergown and cradled her breasts in his hands while his mouth met hers. When his fingers teased her nipples into hard points, she drew his face down to them. His mouth against her sensitive flesh made her cry out in longing.

It felt so different here. True, before today his touch had made her shiver and shake, and his kisses had teased her body into readiness for him. But then she'd only been focused on seducing him into caring for her. Now a different goal had been awakened.

His caresses reminded her of their wedding night and the odd longing she had known for that greater something from their lovemaking. She gasped in sudden excitement. A new, delicious tension sprang to life within her. It made her need to touch the very part of him she so desired.

He caught her hand. "Nay," he breathed gruffly, "touch me and I swear I will explode. Sweet Jesu,

I want you, but this time, I seek only to pleasure you."

But her own needs made his words almost unintelligible. She knew only that he urged her to lay back, that he kissed her breasts, her stomach, then finally her womanhood, until she hoarsely demanded that he enter her and grabbed him by the arms as if to force him. He laughed and acceded to her command. But even this simple act became sweet torture as he eased into her with such deliberate slowness that she finally thrust upward to sheathe all of him within her. His deep groan at her unexpected motion made her smile.

He moved with agonizingly slow movements, teasing himself as well as her. With his every motion that impossible tension grew. It made her writhe beneath him as she sought relief from it while praying it would never end. Her legs clasped him hard to her, her arms bound him. His thrusts grew faster, harder. She raised her hips then cried out when her tension exploded away and burst into waves of pleasure. They washed over her, each one more exquisite than the last. She buried her face in the curve of his neck, her hands clutching, grasping against the incredible sensations. His movements quickened, and he begged her to let him have his own fulfillment.

Incapable of answer, his passion carried her along to greater and still greater enjoyment, until she felt she would die if it did not end. Then, with a final, searing flood of heat that rippled and surged over her, her husband groaned in his own pleasure.

She could not move. She closed her eyes and sank into the soft completeness of it. When he lowered himself to lay upon her, she savored the touch of his skin on hers, his fingers in her hair. She gloried in his weight atop her. His arms closed around her and he rolled to his side, pulling her against him. "My God," he breathed in ebbing passion, "I will never let you leave me."

She lay content beyond expression in his arms, her head pillowed against his shoulder. Sensations blurred, and she drifted into sleep.

She awoke to the chirping of birds, the bark of a vixen to her young, the scurrying of mice around them. With a sigh, she stretched just a little while still in the circle of his embrace. Deep within her lay the warm memory of their passion and her fulfillment. She cherished it and made it precious. Oh, but dear God, the very movement of her skin against his was an almost painful pleasure.

He stirred, but his breathing remained even and untroubled. She looked up into the lacy boughs above them. The sky was stained rose and gold with sunset. "The bishop!" she cried out frantically, trying to lift his arm from her while rising at the same time.

His embrace tightened, and he dragged her back down beside him, then he sighed and opened one eye. "The bishop does not come today," he murmured. "Weren't you told? I sent the pantler with the message when I arrived. You are warm." He closed his eye, kissed the top of her head, and tucked her back into the curve of his shoulder.

She relaxed against him in relief. "Nay, I heard nothing. I suppose he did not find me in time." It felt so right to lay next to him like this. There was such wonder in the pleasure he had given her. She greedily wanted to experience it again, but not here. "They will be closing the gates soon. Should we not go back before they begin searching for us?"

"They already have," he whispered back without

opening his eyes. "Do not stiffen so, it was only Temric and when he found my clothes, he looked no farther." His mouth had quirked up into a smile at her reaction. At last, he opened his eyes and studied her.

She gently touched his cheek, awed by the warmth and acceptance she found in his look, then she sighed with worry. "You are so changed. How can this be and all so suddenly? I am so afraid, Rannulf. Tell me that when we leave here, this will not have been a lie." Her heart caught at the very thought of how his rejection would hurt her now.

He briefly closed his eyes against the depth of pain he'd caused her. "I have a tale to tell you, but it is very difficult for me. Will you dress, then come sit with me so I can say it?"

She nodded and rose quickly to gather up her shift and gown, then hand him his shirt and chausses. When once again properly clothed, she sat down next to him ready to listen. But he was not content with that. He drew her to him until she rested with her back to his chest, protected in his embrace. His gaze aimed out away from them, his focus far outside this tiny glade of theirs.

"Six years ago I wed Isotte DelaCroix. She was a beautiful girl, but much petted as the family's youngest daughter. She had little dowry, having gained what she did have through the auspices of a bachelor uncle. I had been a widower for two years and, although I could have wed a woman with more wealth, I found myself wishing to be the master of such a beautiful creature. Unfortunately, she was only fourteen when we married, and found my thirty years to be enormously old and me quite frightening. When it came time for our bedding, she cried and pleaded with me to spare her. So I did so."

Rowena looked at him in confused curiosity. She opened her mouth to ask, but thought the better of interrupting. Nevertheless, he caught her motion and glanced aside at her, then smiled. "You are too naive. There are many ways to bloody sheets to the satisfaction of worried and overprotective mothers.

"I took her to Graistan, her virginity intact. Once home again, other matters held my attention. I do not know if you recall that our family yet claims a keep in Normandy? Aye, my father's younger brother holds it, but he has no surviving children and is now quite old. It will come to me when he is gone. It was for him that I left England, to serve in his stead whilst our Henry fought his war against his son, our present king. I did not leave again until the old king's death in June that year.

"When I arrived home, I discovered that Gilliam was here. He'd returned to recover from an illness so grave, his foster father had not expected him to live. But live he had. I suppose it could only be expected that these two so close in age should seek each other out in their mutual loneliness and boredom. There was no one here to see that they were kept apart. Friendship became love, and love became loving. If only I had not left her alone," he sighed, then fell silent.

She lay back into the hollow of his shoulder and watched him for a moment. He tried to smile, but couldn't. He rested his cheek against her hair before continuing. "I truly thought I had forgiven all. I cannot blame Gilliam for being sixteen and hot-blooded. Nor can Isotte be charged for being what her family had made her, a spoiled child who had never before denied what she desired, save when they married her to me. But, God help me, he took what was mine; she gave him what she would not give me." His voice broke as he tried to continue.

She lay her hand on his clenched one and when he opened his fist, she twined her fingers between his. Suddenly, many things were making sense. There remained only the question of why he had sent her to Graistan knowing that she and Gilliam would be there alone. Had he meant to test his brother and his new wife? Or had it been a test of his own forgiveness and trust?

"There is worse to come," he said and continued. "He had got her with child. I had been gone too long and home too little to claim it was mine." He shot her a grimly amused look. "There has never been a child twelve month's in coming. By this time, Richard had been crowned and was calling knights to his crusade. I convinced Gilliam's foster father to join them so my brother would be gone for the babe's birth. As for Isotte, I kept her confined and out of the reach of her family, thinking that once the child was born and enough time had passed, no one would care as long as I accepted him.

"But, she hadn't the intelligence to see what she'd done was wrong and hated me for sending Gilliam away. It was obvious she would never be a wife to me, not that I wanted her any more. When she became ill, I dismissed her complaints as a spoiled child's manipulation. She begged to see her mother. I would not allow it. I could not tolerate the truth of their actions coming to light.

"Then, she began to bleed. We called the midwife, but there was nothing to be done. It was late in the pregnancy, and we hoped the babe might live." He shrugged uneasily. "Something went wrong. She died. Gilliam's son died, both sacrificed to my pride."

She slipped her arms around him and held him tightly. He sighed, then lifted her face to kiss her cheek. "My guilt over her death has driven me to do a number of things I now have cause to regret. You were right."

Her eyes widened in surprise. "About what?"

"Maeve." He paused for a brief instant. "I think I brought her here to absolve myself of her sister's death. To find my own peace, I had to blind myself to what she was and what she did. This I managed quite successfully until you arrived. But you, you forced, nay demanded, that I acknowledge a truth that I just as stubbornly refused to see. No doubt I would have destroyed us both over her had she, herself, not confronted me. Last night, when I received Oswald's message, I sent my man into our chamber—"

Her heart clung to his naming his chamber theirs.

"—to retrieve my armor. When he returned, Maeve followed him. She made me a proposition I found most foul, the same one that you had earlier suggested and for which you had been named liar. Although I sent her back to their room, I told her I intended to speak with John about her when I returned with the bishop."

Rowena blinked. "So that is why she was in such a hurry to leave us today. She almost twisted Sir John into knots before he finally conceived the idea as his own."

It was Rannulf's turn for surprise. "Then she was not so sure of him as she let on. Good. There is yet time." His cryptic comment was punctuated with a nod of satisfaction. "We must absent ourselves from Graistan for a week or two until the bishop calls us back after your relations arrive. I had intended to send you to your dower properties while I went elsewhere. But, perhaps, if you do not mind, I will ride with you to Upwood before going on."

A single shaft of happiness shot through her at this. "I would be honored." She stared, then frowned slightly. "You do not intend to go to Ashby, do you?"

"I have no choice," he sighed. "Last night, I vowed to warn John against her. I cannot allow her to come between me and my man."

"Before she left, she said she would never forget what we had done for her. It sounded like a threat, although I dared not warrant it as such then."

"Empty words, promising what she cannot deliver." When she would have said more, he pressed a finger to her lips. "Nay, do not say it. I have vowed to go. Only death can prevent me from doing what I have vowed." Then, Rannulf grinned broadly. "John may be love struck, but she has yet to get her claws into him. Think no more on it. Come, my sweet, let's go home."

# Chapter Eighteen

**R**ANNULF whistled to his horse, who whickered in friendly greeting from just beyond the trees. And why not, when the beast had just spent a gentle summer's afternoon cropping meadow grasses with no bridle, saddle, or hobble to restrain it. Rannulf vaulted onto its back and pulled his wife up to sit in front of him.

The lanes within town were quiet as dusk gathered to lay velvet shadows against the massive walls of his home. With heel and knee, he guided his mount through Graistan's gate and to a halt in the bailey. Here, the sheep murmured and settled for the night. A cock crowed in irritation as his hens shifted on their roosts.

There was no need within him to speak, so he said nothing as he slid to the ground, then turned to help his wife descend. She came lightly into his arms, and he found himself loath to free her from his embrace. When she laid her head on his chest and sighed, he closed his eyes against the mingling of hurt and hope that awakened within him. By God, it was right to have settled their differences, but why had he needed to destroy his brother in order to accept what she gave him?

From out of the darkness came a stable boy with a lead to take his horse. The child's movement dis-

turbed his wife. When she stepped back, he let her
go.

"Rannulf," she said, her voice low, almost shy,
"how are we to go in without being seen?"

He looked down at her, somewhat surprised at
the question. "Why would we wish to do that?"

"Well"—she twisted her hand into a fold of her
skirt, a now familiar gesture that indicated she was
nervous—"my dress is stained and torn, and my hair
is uncovered and unbound, and well, I—" she hesitated, then continued even more quietly—"Well, I
hit you in front of them and called you names. I
had a right to my anger, but I should have kept it
private, between us. Instead, I have diminished you
in their eyes with my behavior."

What an interesting contrast she was. She could
be as young and foolish as Jordan, only to act as
priggish as an old grand dame in the next moment.
He reached out and cupped her face in his palm,
then touched his lips to hers. Her mouth clung to
his, soft and pliant. When he would have drawn
back, her arms went around him until she leaned
full against him. His flesh tingled as she moved to
stand on her toes, sliding her body upward along
his, and his desire for her once again burst into life.

It was he who tore away, he who drew the shuddering and unsteady breath. She had all but driven
away his common sense. In another moment he
would have been willing to take her again, right here
in this open place and damn the consequences.

She looked up at him, the gentle curves of her
face touched with both confusion and concern at
his sudden retreat. Before this day, he'd had no
complaint over their lovemaking, for she had more
than fulfilled his needs. But this afternoon all that
had changed. By giving herself freely to him, hold-

ing nothing back, even reaching out to touch him, he learned that everything that had come before was inadequate.

He started, astounded by sudden realization. The flame of wantonness that drew him ever to her as a moth to a candle, it was all for him, only for him. When he had awakened her passions on their wedding night, she had cleaved solely to him. There had never been another for her nor would there ever be. Had she known this when she gave him her body?

"You are mine," he whispered, overwhelmed by exultation and torn by fear.

"Aye, but I do not think I mind it so very much as I did this morn," she replied with a soft smile, mistaking his meaning. An easiness crept over him with her words, and he smiled in return.

From behind them came a polite cough. They turned in unison. It was the pantler, but his gaze was focused up into the darkened sky filled with newly borne stars. "My pardon, your lordship, my lady, for my interruption, but I did not wish you to think me derelict in my duty. My lord, I would have carried your message to your lady, but I did not find her until just now. May I assume she has been apprised of the bishop's late arrival?"

"You may," Rannulf returned with equal formality, stifling his desire to laugh.

"Ah, well, then I need say no more," the man continued, still keeping his eyes averted. "I am glad to see you both safely returned." He seemed to choke a little on his final words, then turned briskly and strode back to the inner courtyard. No doubt he would carry the news of their arrival to the whole hall.

He turned to glance down at his wife. She stared

after the man, her forehead creased in concern. It was not she who had done him any harm here at Graistan. There wasn't a soul within these walls who hadn't known him for the whole of his life or he, theirs. Nothing she did or said would change that bond. It was she who was the stranger here, the outsider. His silences and now his open accusations of adultery had threatened her carefully carved-out position.

Well, what he had so steadily undermined, he could now completely secure. "Do not worry so," he said, and started toward the inner gate. With his hand holding hers, she had no choice but to follow.

They were up the stairs and almost past the door screens before she realized he intended to walk through the very center of the hall. "Wait, my lord, stop," she protested, trying to hold back, but she slowed him not a whit. "Please, Rannulf, wait," she tried again, but they were already well within, and it was too late.

He strode to the spot between the two hearths where everyone would have a clear view of them. "Good evening to you all," he said with a broad grin. Although he had not let her go, his wife slipped as far behind him as she could in an attempt to hide. He drew her forward, holding her at his side with an arm about her waist. "This night, I do something that I should have done in May. I must now present to you my wife, the Lady Rowena of Graistan."

In the instant of stunned silence that followed his words, he looked down at Rowena, who stared in sublime embarrassment at the hearth. Her hair, so incredibly dark and thick, fell free about her, tangled with leaves and a few, tiny star-bright flowers. The rag she dared call a dress bore a multitude of tears, and was grass-stained and muddy. Her brow was smudged with dirt, yet she had never looked more beautiful to him. He lifted her face and kissed her.

At first she remained unresponsive, but by now he knew she could not long resist him. His mouth moved against hers, teasing from her the reaction he desired. She sighed, her arms creeping around him as her mouth opened to his.

The room exploded into laughs as his people stomped their feet and cheered. "Like father, like son, eh, Lord Graistan?" someone yelled. "Aye," another retorted, "although I think he's slower to learn than his father."

"Nay," a woman shot back. "Lord or no, you'll not give a man credit for what a woman has wrought. 'Twas Ermina who captured Lord Henry, not the other way 'round, just as our lady now holds Rannulf. A woman only runs when she knows she will be chased, isn't that right?" A chorus of female voices rose to agree with her.

His wife laughed and tore away from his embrace. She looked up at him, her wondrous blue eyes sparkling in joy, and her face filled with such happiness he could not help but to smile in return. "Thank you, my lord," she whispered, then closed her eyes and buried her head against his shoulder.

Rannulf wrapped an arm around her to hold her close as he addressed his folk. "For those who may not yet know, on the morrow the bishop will take up residence here at Graistan until my wife's relatives arrive. My lady and I will retire to Upwood until we are called to return by the bishop. In reward for all your hard work and effort this day, I suggest you share a round of beer and ale, and drink a toast to us. Since we are both tired and hungry, we will not be joining you, but drink to us nonetheless."

As he led his wife up the stairs, they were followed by a cheer as well as a few, explicit comments. "Hungry, mayhap," one man called out, "but it's not food they crave."

"And tired it is that they say they are? Do you believe that, goodman?"

Rannulf sat bolt upright, startled awake by the soft creak of the door's leather hinges as it opened. "Who is there," he whispered hoarsely.

"Papa," Jordan called quietly, his young voice trembling with tears. "Papa, I have had a dream."

The instantaneous drain of tension from his muscles made him sigh. He thrust open the bed curtains and peered out past the puddle of light from the night candle and into the darkness beyond it. "Come here, then," he said.

His son hurried across the room and crawled up into the tall bed. He curled onto his father's lap and looked up. The flickering candlelight made his tears gleam like jewels. Rannulf drew him closer into the curve of his arm and kissed his head. "Now, what is this dream of yours? Can you tell me?"

Jordan drew a shuddering breath. "You made her go away even when I cried that she should stay. Then, you were angry at me, and you made me go away, too. I was so sad I cried and cried."

"And who was it I made leave?"

"Lady Wren, Papa," he said around a short sob. "Did you really make her go as Alais said you would?"

How easily and deeply this woman had wound herself into his family. It was as though everyone save himself had been eagerly waiting to welcome her. He now doubted if he could ever have succeeded in sending her away.

To his son, he shook his head. "Of course not. She is my wife and, as such, she lives with us. See, here she is, lying beside me just where she is supposed to be." How odd to say the words to his son only to feel the rightness of them within himself. He reached over to gently stroke her cheek. "Wren, wake up a moment. Jordan is here. He had has a dream and is worried over you."

She stirred sleepily, then pushed the hair from her face. As she moved, it stirred the warm scent of their lovemaking from the sheets. "Jordan," she said, her voice still husky from her own dreams, "my heart. I am here and well." She yawned, stretched, then sat up. "See?"

"You didn't leave." He squirmed free of his father's embrace to wrap his arms around her neck. For a moment she hugged him tight, then kissed his cheek.

"Of course not. Where would I go? Graistan is my home, just as it is yours." She rocked him gently in her embrace for a few moments until his head drooped sleepily against her shoulder. "Sweetling, you must go back to your own bed in case Alais should awaken and find you missing, then go about screeching that you've been kidnapped again. That would be horrid, wouldn't it?"

"Aye," he murmured, "she was so loud, she woke us all up."

Rannulf lifted the boy from his wife's arms and set him onto the floor. "Are you content or will your sleep be troubled still?"

"Nay. It was a baby's dream. I won't be scared of it again. Good night, Papa."

"Sleep well." He watched his son trot from the room.

"Thank the Lord," Rowena breathed from beside

him. "He will not go back for me, and he is awful to sleep with. He tosses and turns and kicks."

"So he does," he agreed quietly, while a quick stab of jealousy thrust through him. But it died almost as swiftly as it was born. He could not deny Jordan his "Lady Wren" when the boy had no mother. The girl who'd birthed him had left her son with her lord, more than content with his promise to raise the child as a recognized son.

He leaned over to kiss his wife and felt within him the still glowing embers of their passion for each other. But she drew away with a contented sigh, slid back down beneath the bedclothes, and into her dreams.

Perhaps it was her convent upbringing that had taught her to fall so quickly and deeply into sleep in order to squeeze as much rest as possible between night services. Whatever it was, he had not the knack of it.

He settled back against the bed wall, his thoughts drifting to the past evening. When they'd entered their bedchamber, she'd been angered to discover someone had dismantled the bed John and Maeve had used and returned their own bed to its rightful place. It had taken more than a little talking to convince her that there was time enough on the morrow to speak with her maids over this supposed act of insubordination.

He, on the other hand, had understood completely the meaning behind her bed's return along with the can of water warming on the hearth for washing, the tray of foods on the table, and the ewer of wine with two cups beside it. This was Ilsa's handiwork. She, better than anyone else, understood what had happened between her lord and lady this day, for she had been his stepmother's loving slave.

But then, so had he. Ermina had taken him into her heart as her son almost from the moment of her arrival at Graistan. Even after she bore her own children, the love that lay between them had not changed.

So, Ilsa felt that he and his wife were not so different from his father and his stepmother, did she? He smiled against the memory of his parents' many arguments, some of which were legendary among Graistan's servants. Lord, but they had been a fiery pair. Yet Ermina had always known just how to sweeten her sting and, God's teeth, how his father had loved her. When she'd died, he had gone with her, although he lived on another three years after her death.

When he remembered his father's pain, the years of loneliness after his wife's passing, he frowned. To love a woman so deeply was perhaps not such a good thing. Women died too easily. He knew that well enough, having lost mother, stepmother, and two wives already. Then, he shrugged away the thought.

There was no reason to believe he would care for his wife the way his father had loved his stepmother. That was a rare thing indeed. More likely, their marriage would become a sort of partnership; she in command of her own sphere and he in his, both equal in their own right while respecting the other's abilities and sharing their children. Although he did not deny his attraction and desire for her, desire was not love.

His wife shifted slightly. He looked down at her and could not resist touching her hair. It was sleek and soft against his fingers. Tonight, when she'd

stood combing it before the fire, light had gleamed
through the thin shift she wore to boldly outline the
lush curves and tight lines of her body. As she
moved, the material would now and again stretch
taut against her breasts until he could clearly see
the outline of her nipples. He'd been so deeply engrossed in watching her, he'd forgotten what he'd
been doing until she'd reached to take washcloth
and water can from him to bathe herself.

But he had not relinquished them. Instead, he
had washed her, taking care to wet every morsel of
her skin. When he had finished with the cloth, he
had done it again, this time with his mouth until
she cried out in full realization of her pleasure. Nor
had he ceased his ministrations until she once again
cried out while he had found his own enjoyment
within her. Desire was most certainly enough.

He sighed, his thoughts then drifting inevitably
back to Gilliam. Rannulf had been fourteen and a
squire well on his way to earning his spurs when
his youngest brother was born. All had seemed well
at first. His father had written full of pride that,
even at his age, he had been able to sire yet another
son. Then something had gone wrong. The moment
of his foster father telling him the news remained
forever fixed in his mind. It had been so hard to
imagine Ermina dead.

He supposed he could have hated the baby for
her death, but instead he'd done as he was certain
his stepmother would have hoped. He'd vowed to
care for her son as she had cared for him. Yet, all
his intentions had come to naught, and now he had
destroyed what remained of his relationship with
Gilliam by a jealous accusation that he'd known to
be untrue the moment the words left his mouth.

"Too late," he said in pained regret. "I hope you will forgive me, Ermina, and know that I did try."

"Lie beside me, my heart," his wife murmured, speaking to Jordan from deep in her sleep. "It is only a dream and will all be gone in the morning."

Rannulf loosed a short, bittersweet laugh, then did as she bid. Once he'd gathered her into his arms, he drifted slowly into an easy and dreamless state.

# Chapter Nineteen

"So, Rannulf, have you decided which you prefer? Will you lie abed with only sticks and twigs for a mattress or in this decadent bower you've created for yourself?"

Temric's rough voice jolted Rowena from her sleep, and she sat straight up. Only her hair covered her nakedness and the bed curtain lay wide open. She could as clearly see the man who casually leaned in the open doorway as he could her.

With a gasp she clutched the bedclothes to her chest. He only smiled. "Then again, if she were my wife, I suppose I would not reject out of hand any place for trysting."

Rannulf sat up and stretched, untroubled by his brother's sudden appearance in his private chamber. "You wouldn't know a tryst if it hit you. My brother, the monk. Pardon, Wren," he said to her, "Jordan left the door open last night, and I forgot to close the curtains after he left. So, what brings you here this morn?" This he asked of his brother.

"I only came to tell you before some other did it. Gilliam's gone."

"Damn." He rubbed his face with his hands, his palms rasping over his beard's growth. "He gives me no chance to make amends. Do you know where?"

"To his brother."

"Well," Lord Graistan muttered, "I'd already planned to go to Upwood, it is not so far from there to—"

"Rannulf, let him be. It has done you both a world of good to lance this boil of yours. Now you must give him time to sort out his own thoughts." Temric's easy posture belied his commanding words.

Rowena stared at the two of them. "His brother?"

Her husband shot her a quick glance. "There are gaps in your knowledge of the FitzHenrys, I see. He has a full brother, Geoffrey, our younger half brother by my father and my stepmother, Ermina."

"Oh, aye, Ermina," she said quietly, recognizing the name. Why, when she knew so much about the lands and keeps that made up Graistan's holdings, had she never learned more about the family who held the title? Well, at least she now understood why Gilliam had no inheritance. Rannulf had received his father and mother's lands, while by right this Geoffrey had his mother's holdings.

Her husband was speaking to his brother. "It goes against my nature to let him leave without resolving this trouble I made between us. Dear God, in what regard can he now hold me?" He sighed helplessly. "Temric, I told you yesterday I intended for Gilliam to play host while the bishop resides here. Since I cannot retract my invitation, I need someone here I can trust."

His brother straightened and tensed. "Do not ask me, Rannulf. It would be an insult to the bishop to put one of my ilk into your chair."

"Your ilk?" Rannulf snapped back. "You are my brother. Oswald knows that."

"Enough. I will not do it," Temric said harshly. "What of young Arnult, Jordon's tutor? You were

ready to make him your castellan had we gone to
Hereford."

"He's young and inexperienced. How will he know
what to say or do?"

"I have always found him polite and well-spoken.
He comes from a good family and is well trained.
You said so yourself. You need only tell him what
he must do, and he will serve you well. Besides, I
will soon be gone."

"You would leave me now, after Gilliam has run?
You cannot. Damn it, what is it Alwyna has offered
you that I have not?" Rannulf's words were almost
a cry. "I would give you a keep and make you lord
of your own lands, yet you spurn me to become
what? A wool merchant."

Rowena's heart lurched. She had vowed to help
Temric, and now was the time for it. But doing so
meant she must test the limitations of her husband's
new fondness for her. Fear of losing what she had
only just gained made her hold back in the hopes
her words would not be needed.

"I am making no choices between you." Temric
put a hand to his head as if in pain. "I told you in
January that I would be gone by Midsummer."

There was no choice, she must do it. She lay her
hand on her husband's arm and was grateful when
he did not pull away. "My lord, Temric is but one
man, he cannot be in two places at the same time.
If he has promised, he must honor that promise and
you would not respect him if he did anything else.
Besides, you have had him for years; it is she who
needs him now."

He said nothing, but took her hand in his. She
drew courage from his movement and twined her
fingers between his. When she continued, it was in
a voice no more than a whisper. "It may be a sorry

consolation to you, but I will be with you. You will not be left alone."

She gazed down at their joined hands. His fingers were long and tapered, his palm large. Her small hand was dwarfed when his closed around it. There was both fear and need in his hold, but slowly, slowly, he relaxed, and she knew he'd found in her the strength he needed to face his loss.

"You are right," he breathed, his words so low she barely heard him. "I have tried to hold them here as mine when they are not mine to keep. But if they must leave us, why must it be all at once?"

Rowena tensed, overwhelmed by his need, for he would quickly put her in their place. Even as he held her hand, she felt him fold around her to draw her within him and never let her go. She wanted to cry, to run again. He would crush her, bury her, until she lost herself within him and was no more. How could anyone bear such closeness?

Then fear flowed swiftly away in acceptance and understanding. She loved him; with all her soul she loved him. Whatever he needed, she would give and find her own pleasure in doing it. And, unlike his brothers, she would never leave him. This place, every stone and soul within it, was a part of her.

He raised her hand to his lips and touched a brief kiss against her fingers. "Temric, if you will not take my place, will you stand beside Arnult for as long as you can to see he makes no misstep?"

"That I will do for you." His brother's voice was deep and soft. When she looked at him, Temric met her gaze, his eyes warm with gratitude.

"My thanks," Rannulf replied with a small smile, then continued in a firmer voice. "Now, out of my room and stop eyeing my wife."

Temric offered him a jaunty salute and a wide

grin. "I do admit to being envious." With that he turned and strode out of the solar. Her husband only laughed as he freed his hand from hers to throw back the bedclothes and sit on the bed's edge. "Well, at least I've laid the matter out in the open between the boy and me, as Temric has said."

She smoothed his pillow and watched the eddies and hollows her fingers made in the feather-filled cushion. "Why do you and Temric always speak of him as if he were yet a child, not a man full grown? He is older than I, and you do not see me as a child, do you?"

Her husband laughed. "Nay, that I most certainly do not." Then, he sobered and turned on the bed to face her. "But, you are right. He is a man full grown, and I have forgot that more times than I care to admit. I suppose it is because I have been his father since he was three. It is hard to recognize when your child is a child no longer."

"I think this makes more trouble between the two of you than anything that happened in the past. You know he wants a keep of his own," she said softly.

"He has never spoken of it to me."

"How could he with what lies between you? And, if he had, would you have granted it to him?"

"I cannot say," he hedged, and once again she heard in his voice his desire to keep his family with him.

"Why must you hold them so tightly?"

"Aye, what good has it done? They are either gone or going," he retorted harshly.

She only laughed. "Nay, my lord. You cannot keep them away. Gilliam will return when he can speak his mind to you as an equal, and Temric, well, he will stay away only as long as it best serves his mother." When he shot her a skeptical look, she shook her head and smiled. "Oh, he's no merchant, you know that. He only goes because she needs him now."

"Sorry consolation, indeed," he said, his gray eyes so warm it took her breath away. When he reached for her, she came easily into his embrace and savored the subdued heat of his kiss. But when he would have made it more than that, she pulled away.

"I cannot," she breathed, already regretting her movement, for that magnificent excitment was once again building within her. "If we are to leave for Upwood this day, there is yet so much I must do that all will be ready for the bishop's arrival. Oh, Lord, I cannot dream of how we will afford all this on top of the fine you must pay for marrying me. God knows what you'll have to give the bishop as gifts during his stay."

"You worry too much. Graistan has always had sufficient means, and it always will."

"Easily said, especially by you," she retorted, sliding off the bed and pulling on her bedrobe, "who's let his treasury be emptied while he wasn't looking."

"Rowena," he warned, but she only laughed.

"I know, I know. If you say we eat on golden plates, we do. But, in that case it is I who must be your alchemist. It is fortunate you have me, my lord, or you'd soon be as poor as a villein's widow." With that she jerked the robe belt tight about her waist.

He laughed. "You give up too easily. We could have fought, then——" he let the word hang suggestively between them.

She smiled, but whirled away when he reached for her. "Ilsa," she called as she danced out of his grasp and into the solar.

"There was time," he said, sounding both amused

and disappointed. "Wren?" When she looked back, he was leaning in the doorway to the solar, his eyes warm as he watched her. She took a step toward him. He held out his hand and smiled, creating those creases in his cheeks she found so attractive. In another moment she would have been lost, but Ilsa's entry into the solar from the women's quarters drew his attention. "Good morrow, old woman."

The servant appreciatively eyed the naked length of him with the boldness granted to women of her advanced years, then gave a gapped, long-toothed grin. "Pea brain. Some men haven't the sense the Lord God gave a fish. It's right time you straightened yourself out. My lord." She belatedly added the honorific.

Her husband seemed neither perturbed nor put out by her harsh words. "Consider me properly chastised," he said with a laugh, then retreated into the bedchamber and shut the door behind him.

Ilsa turned on her mistress with a fiery gleam in her eye. "And you!" she spat out. "I expected you to know better. Now pay close heed as you are not always wont to do. For the next several months you are not to run or lift anything or strain yourself in any way. It is bad enough that you must travel, but running from the keep in your condition! Jesus, Mary, and Joseph!"

"You are daft, Ilsa. What are you talking about?" her lady snapped. "What condition?"

"Come now, girl, you count far better than I ever have and, at my best reckonings, it has been nigh on two months since you last had your woman's flux."

"What?" Rowena cried out, rapidly figuring the days for herself. "Nay, it is not possible. I've had no signs, there's been no illness. You are mistaken."

But, it was true. She'd not had her flux since her husband had returned home in May, and she was never late.

"Not possible? With you as regular as the moon?" retorted Ilsa, echoing her mistress's thoughts. "You are with child. As for signs, for these last weeks you have been overly tired and hollow-eyed. And, yesterday, did you or did you not faint?"

"Faint?" Rowena questioned. "It was only a dizzy spell caused by overwork and tiredness." Still, her hand crept to the curve of her abdomen. Was it possible? Could it be she bore a child, hers and Rannulf's? Suddenly, she wanted nothing more than for this to be true. It would be something shared and special created between them. "I am with child," she breathed, then smiled broadly. "I am with child," she repeated in awe.

"Aye, aye, now do not go softheaded on me. A woman's first often sets on less securely than the ones that follow, and I'll not have you endangering a potential heir. And you having to dash off to Upwood to please a bishop. Hmmph!"

"Upwood?" Rowena said stupidly, still trapped in the wonder of her discovery. Then, she caught her breath. She was going to Upwood, but Rannulf was going on to Ashby. Her hand tightened on her abdomen as a terrible sense of foreboding washed over her. Perhaps he wouldn't go if he knew she bore his child.

"Oh, have you forgotten that already? Good God, but I've got enough to do in packing your gowns without having to fasten your head back to your neck as well. Go sit in yon chair, and I'll be back in a moment with a little something to straighten your thoughts." She hurried from the room.

But Rowena did not do as she was bid. Instead,

she returned to her bedchamber to find Rannulf sitting in a chair while his man shaved him. Although his expression remained impassive, his eyes smiled at her.

"Rannulf, do you still intend to go on to Ashby?" she asked bluntly.

He caught Ulric's hand and tilted his head to the side to better see her. "Aye." Although it was only one word, there was no mistaking his determination to make this trip. Nothing she said would alter it.

Rowena sighed in resignation. "My lord, exactly what is it you intend to do when you arrive at Ashby. You can hardly snatch her back from John. They are now man and wife. And if he is as smitten as he appeared, will he even hear what you say?"

"Well, if he cannot hear me, I will ask him to swear to me again, saying that I had intended to do that this day. After all, the additional properties the marriage brought him makes the reiteration of his vows necessary. Once he has spoken those words, his vow will certainly protect our relationship until he can hear my explanation. It would serve us well to warn him to have a care with his treasury, though."

"Nay, you need have no worries on that score. I would guess that Nicola holds those keys, and Maeve will have much ado to wrench them free from her grasp." She gave a small laugh, remembering the tall girl's odd words.

He smiled at her, and she smiled back. For a long moment, they watched each other. It rose within Rowena to tell him of the child that now nestled beneath her heart. She felt words fill her throat, but her mouth wouldn't open to free them.

It was too soon for this. Everything had changed too swiftly. Last week she had yet been the shunned wife and, yesterday, had even tried to run from this place she loved so. As much as she wanted to, she was not yet ready to trust his change. Besides, he might deem it necessary to hold himself aloof from her in order not to endanger the babe, thus cheating her of the affection she craved from him. Nay, it was far better that she hold her news tight, a secret to reveal once she was sure the babe was well rooted within her womb.

"Was there something else you wished to say?" he finally asked.

"Nay, I think not," she said slowly.

"Hmmm, as you wish. I would leave before noon today. Can you be ready by then?"

She frowned and rapidly calculated which tasks could be completed without supervision. "Aye, that is possible. But only if I can leave Ilsa here to see to what I have not finished." If she was to keep her pregnancy a secret, it was better to leave behind all those who knew. Knowing Ilsa, that would be all her women.

"That is your choice." He touched his lips to her fingers, then released her hand. She gave his a swift smile and returned to the solar, firmly shutting the bedchamber door behind her.

"Oh, there you are," said the old woman, standing in the center of the room bearing a cup. "Here, drink this."

"Nay, Ilsa. I've too much to do to muddle my head with wine just now. My lord would leave before noon."

"Noon," the maid retorted. "That is barely enough time to pack for us, much less see to the other matters."

"There will be very little to pack. I am going alone. I will take only one white undergown and two overgowns, the blue and the green. Pack no chains or circlets, for I will not wear them. Upwood is a rustic place, and I have no need of finery there."

The old woman stopped, mouth agape to stare at her. "What? But who will see to you?"

"Surely there are servants at this manor. Ilsa, I need you here to see that all goes as planned."

A sudden light of understanding glowed to life in Ilsa's dull, old eyes. "You've not told him, have you?" She jerked her head toward the bedchamber.

"Nay, the time is not yet right. I will wait until I know that the babe is secure within my womb."

The old woman's eyes narrowed. "If you do not tell him, I will."

"Tell him and I swear I will banish you to your daughter's house in town, and you'll never see the babe," Rowena threatened.

"You would not dare," she breathed, then cried out, "but, my lady, you need me now more than ever."

"Aye, that I do," she said, regretting the pain she was causing, "but only if I know you will keep your mouth closed when I tell you to do so."

Ilsa bowed her head in defeat, her desire to see this child's coming too important to jeopardize, even for what was sure to be her lord's favor. "As you wish, my lady. I will stay."

She laid her hand on the old woman's arm. "Be content in knowing that if I cannot have you at my side, I will have no one else."

Although the maid only sniffed, there was a certain aura of pleasure about her motions. "Aye, my lady. Now, what would you have me do?"

"Ah, there you are. Will you be ready to leave soon?" Rannulf called up to her from the hearth

where he stood next to Arnult. The young knight
still frowned in concentration, as if he memorizing
the instructions he'd been given.

"I am ready now," she returned as she descended
to the hall. Margaret followed her down, bearing
her single basket.

Are you sure you do not wish to take some of your
maids with you?" He glanced at Ilsa, who rolled her
eyes in frustration. "I do not mind slowing our pace
to accommodate a wain."

"Really, it is not necessary," she said. "Do I look
helpless? Is Upwood bereft of servants? I cannot
imagine that we are staying more than two weeks.
I think I shall survive it if I must dress myself or
comb my own hair for that time."

He gave her a broad grin, then turned back to his
temporary castellan. "Have you any further questions? Nay? Then we are off."

# Chapter Twenty

ROWENA let the warm, late June day lull her into lazy satisfaction. It was fine traveling weather. Newly sheared sheep grazed in the meadows, bright dots against the consistent green of the hillsides. Wheat and barley stood tall in the fields, bending slightly in a playful breeze. The moist, tilled earth exuded a rich scent that spoke to her of her own fertility. How different this was from her first trip with her husband. Then everything had been cold and barren. Nay, not barren, asleep.

She turned slightly in her saddle to better see Rannulf. He was deep in conversation with Temric, who rode to his right. His brother had chosen to accompany them for the first hour until he had to turn north and meet the bishop's party. Both men wore animated expressions as they discussed the politics of a country whose king found his subjects boorish and barbaric, and would not stay to govern them.

She studied the two of them. Now that Temric was more familiar to her, his carefully trimmed beard and darker coloring no longer hid their resemblance. When he smiled in response to a comment of Rannulf's, she wondered which of their ancestors had gifted to all his descendents this distinctive grin.

Her husband had long since removed his helmet and pushed back his mail hood. The afternoon sun teased vibrant auburn tints from his hair. His face had swiftly bronzed since summer's onset, and the darker color accentuated his pale eyes. Quick expressions played, one after the other, across the strong planes and hollows of his face. The simple joy of being wanted by him slowly crept over her and made her smile.

"What are you smiling at?" he asked, startling her.

"You," she said with a little shrug.

"Does my old and ugly face amuse you?" Despite his harsh words, she heard the pleasure her attention gave him.

"You are neither old nor ugly," she responded before she caught herself. "My lord," she protested, "you are trying to trap me into complimenting you."

"Did I not warn you that I am quite vain?" He laughed.

"Enormously so." Temric snorted the remark in a fond tolerance born from years of closeness.

"Can I help it, I like hearing compliments?" Rannulf replied, sounding for all the world like Jordan when the child was sorely aggrieved.

After Temric had left them, her husband indicated they should ride ahead of the remaining troop, as though he desired a bit of privacy. But when she drew abreast of him, he rode on in silence. With patient curiosity, she resettled herself in the saddle only to find he was closely watching her. "My lord?"

"I wanted to speak with you over Gilliam," he said, "but I am having trouble marshaling my thoughts. Mayhap you will have some idea, where I have none." His voice died away in pain.

She studied him for a brief moment, then sighed.

What he wished to hear, she would not tell him. "He is your steward, and the harvest will soon be upon us. You have no choice but to replace him." When he turned and opened his mouth as if to protest, she held up a gloved hand to forestall him. "Do not say it, for you know as well as I, our state is too critical to go without him for long. Besides, he is no steward. Let us hire a man with the learning necessary to do what must be done."

Rannulf stared down at his hands on the reins. "You are right," he said after a long moment, "but will he not think that I have cut him from my life and no longer want him?"

"Not if you grant him what he needs: a keep of his own."

"Would that I could," he said softly. "Mayhap, there will be something on your lands that is suitable for him." At his words an easy quietness fell between them, and they rode on together.

The road was busy this day with the pack trains and wagons of itinerant merchants making their way westward, bound for the next great fair. For as far as the eye could see, only one man was coming eastward. Although the horse he led behind him seemed a fine enough beast, he walked hurriedly along, looking both purposeful and harried. When he caught sight of the device on Lord Rannulf's shield, he leapt to the center of the road and waved.

"My Lord Graistan," he called out several times, until he was sure he'd been heard, and the lord of Graistan would stop for him. Only then, did he show the nobleman proper reverence. "My lord, I was on route to Graistan this very day to deliver you this message from my Lord Ashby. My horse has lamed himself, the stupid dolt, but here you are before me, and I will not be late at all." He reached into his leather purse and pulled out a carefully folded bit of parchment.

As her husband took the thing, Rowena recognized Ashby's seal at its edge. She tensed. This could be naught but bad news no matter what it said. He skimmed the message, his frown growing as he read.

"Will you tell me?" Rowena asked after a moment.

"It is only politely worded phrases to thank me once again for the wedding and the bride. The one who wrote this, for it is certainly not John's priest whose hand I know, does not even apologize for leaving without gaining my approval or bidding me farewell." He fingered the wax disk that marked it as having originated at Ashby. "My God, it means he's already given her access to his seal. I never believed she could move so swiftly." When he looked up, his growing concern was evident in the tenseness of his jaw. He handed her the scrap, and she swiftly read it.

"Nor does she think you are free to move," she retorted. "The last she knew, we expected the bishop's arrival at any moment. Aye, these words are written to provoke you into a deep, cutting worry made all the worse because your visitor traps you at Graistan. Still, it is obvious that she intends to cause what damage she can between you and John."

Her husband turned to her, his eyes now alight with burning rage. "How her heart will quail when we come tapping on Ashby's gate this evening."

"This evening? We? If that is your plan now, we had better send a messenger to Sir John warning of our arrival." Even as she spoke, she knew how he would answer.

"I see no reason for it. I have called at Ashby

before without such formalities. Besides, it would spoil the surprise for Maeve." His sudden grin was rakish.

"Are you certain that is wise? Such a surprise might do you more harm than good. I think I'd sooner corner a wild boar than her."

"And, you," he said, touching her cheek ever so briefly, "are giving that woman more credit than is worthy of her. What harm could she possibly do us? I should be insulted that you think me such a puling infant that a woman might be a threat to us." He was not insulted; rather he seemed flattered by her concern.

"Rannulf," she started, but he interrupted her.

"Nay, do not argue. It was I who let the snake into the garden when I ignored those wiser than I and married the two of them. There, in your hand, is proof that I cannot afford to let matters remain as they are for even another day." In his expression, she saw concern for his man and their longstanding relationship. Whether he admitted it or not, he worried that Lady Maeve might have already brought some discord between them. She studied him for a silent moment as their men caught up and drew their mounts to a halt behind them. At last, she sighed her reluctant approval. "We go to Ashby," she said.

He gave a brief, hard nod. "Good," he said, and turned to glance back at his men. "You, Watt, you know Upwood well enough. Tell Sir Jocelynn that we will be delayed a day or two." The man nodded and spurred his horse off ahead of them.

Rannulf turned to Ashby's messenger. "If you wish to proceed on to Graistan, there will be food and shelter for you there as well as aid for your horse. We'll not wait for you, if you intended to return to Ashby."

"I'll go on to Graistan, then, my lord," he called. But, the nobleman had already set spurs to his bay and called the troop forward. In no more than a moment's time, they'd left the man by himself on the roadbed.

They kept their pace swift until well after Compline. When they were but a few miles from Ashby, they slowed to rest their mounts, a fact no doubt appreciated by those they passed. It did not take many days without rain to dry mud into a choking dust.

With Midsummer now so near, the sun would not find its bed for hours yet. The long days gave the advantage to those industrious enough to work harder for themselves than for their masters. To the travelers on the road, it meant they could make those extra, few miles before darkness finally fell.

Rowena glanced up at Rannulf. He was concentrating on the road ahead. She followed his look to see two wains, one of which appeared to be missing a wheel. "What is it?"

He gave a short laugh. "Huh, I think I know the man." He set heels to his bay's sides. "Wren, you stay with the others. Walter, come with me."

Rowena watched him hold up his hand in greeting as those around the carts sheathed their swords. In a few moments, she and the rest of the men were near enough to hear. "My son warned me that the wheelwright had cheated me." There was no mistaking Graistan's most prominent cloth merchant's thin and reedy voice nor his bright garments. "Look at me, now, stuck here with my goods spilling out onto the ground. I was late beginning my journey, and the fair starts tomorrow." He held fisted hands to his brow in frustration.

"Have you sent to Eilington for a wheelwright? It lies just beyond that hill."

"Aye, my lord, but my man's been gone the better part of an hour now. I cannot afford to send another in case of thieves."

Lord Rannulf straightened. "Walter, go to Eilington to let the bailiff know what's afoot out here. Whilst you're there, look about for Peter's man and see to finding someone with the skill to mend this wain. If there is none, then perhaps the villagers might lend a wain if he lets them hold his as collateral. You, you, and you"—he pointed out the men he wanted—"bide your time here until Walter's return with either craftsman or cart. After your errand's done, you can rejoin us at Ashby."

"Thank you, my lord," the merchant said as his shoulders drooped in relief.

"What is good for my merchants is good for me, eh, Peter?" He smiled. "I want you to be able to afford the rent I charge you. I'm told you've enlarged that warehouse of yours, the one along the river."

The man's answering smile was not quite so broad, then he laughed. "You have me there, my lord," he replied.

"Good journey to you," Rannulf called as he turned his horse back along the road.

"And you, too, my lord. My lady." The man nodded to her as she passed.

Walter and his men had yet to rejoin them, when they climbed the final rise before reaching their destination. Below, ringed by a single line of stone wall, lay Ashby. To the north was the forest of oak and ash, from whence came its name, while to the south stood a village of a good seventy homes. Beyond the cottages lay the crazy patchwork pattern of their fields.

Fronted with ditches on two sides and defended by the river on the others, Ashby's walls encircled a surprisingly large bailey with orchard, mill, ovens, and garden all within it. In the very center sat a square, stone tower with manor house attached. Unlike the wattled dwellings in the village, this great house was built of timber on a stone foundation and was much bigger by length and girth than the cottages; but it still bore only a thatched roof. Its massive wooden doors were banded with iron and half shielded by a porch at the top of the stairs. At the eastern end of the building was a short ell that spoke of a private chamber.

With the serene lushness of summer gathered around it, Ashby was, as Gilliam had said, a beautiful place. The river glistened in the sun against emerald banks dotted with willows and wildflowers. The breeze made fields of gold and green ripple and wave. Sheep and geese grazed on the common lands. Whitewashed cottages stood out against their green gardens and the dark stone of the protective walls.

As they rode to the bridge that would take them across the river and onto Sir John's holdings, the locals caught sight of them. Those in the fields stopped their work to look, while those within town came rushing to their doors to see the strangers. Several ran for the castle, no doubt to warn their lord of this unexpected arrival.

A quiver of doubt shot through her. They really should have sent word to John that they were coming. It was rude to appear unannounced. She glanced at her husband. He wore an easy expression as he surveyed this place, and his confidence reassured her.

When the toll collector at the stone bridge that spanned the river recognized the name he was given, his eyes opened wide. With a hand, he motioned to his boy to dash into the keep with the news. "My lord, please, pass by," he offered, but did not immediately move out of their way.

At last, Rannulf leaned down slightly. "Do you need something else?" His harsh question made the man jump aside.

"Nay, nay." He laughed wanly. "Please pass by."

The path leading to Ashby's entrance turned directly off the road. The drawbridge, a long tongue of wood fastened by chain through the wall and attached to winches on the inside, was lowered over the water-filled ditch as it should be on a working day. But within the bailey, there was complete silence. No man stood on the walls; no servant walked from barn to house. Not even a dog sat enjoying the evening's sun on its back. The stable windows were shut and barred. Beneath its shielding porch, the hall door looked to be shut as well.

She glanced at Rannulf. His expression was now grim. When he returned her look, she could see the disbelief in his gaze. "We leave," he said harshly, and roweled his big bay around. Too late, the winches groaned in the gatehouse as the bridge lifted. They would not reach it in time.

"Dog," Sir John bellowed out as he threw the hall door open. Her husband lifted his shield in ingrained reaction even before the bowmen on the tower's roof stood and loosed their missiles. Rannulf leaned over to cover her as best he could. Although bolts bounced harmlessly from the long piece of metal, the surprise attack took five of their men, and her little mare screamed in pain.

Ashby's lord raced down the stairs, bared sword

in hand. He wore his mail shirt hastily pulled atop his clothing. "Raper of women, killer of children! Die, like the dog you are."

Excited by the sudden fray and the smell of blood from her mount, Rannulf's bay struck out, crashing his gigantic hoof into the smaller horse's flank. Rowena leapt free as her crippled mare fell. She rolled away from the flailing hooves and scrambled to her feet to watch in horror.

"You used her," John raged, his blade rebounding off Rannulf's shield.

"You are mad," his lord shouted back. Men leapt away from him and his dangerous mount, two already cut and bleeding. "I never touched her."

Hands dragged Rowena back from the fighting. She had not the sense to resist her captor or even to turn to look at who it was. Incapable of sound or motion, she stood frozen in terror.

"Liar," Ashby roared, once again throwing himself at his lord. He managed to land a blow against the mounted man's thigh. Blood stained Rannulf's steel chausses. "Drag them down," he called to his men. "I will show you how I treat filth such as you."

One of their men screamed as he took a bolt in the neck. The attackers surrounded the smaller mounts of Graistan's soldiery. Rowena watched as Ashby's men dragged two more from their horses; she watched their few fall beneath flashing blades. She could not breathe. If they unhorsed Rannulf, he would die.

Again, his bay rose, striking out at those who surrounded him. It trampled one while Rannulf used his sword just as effectively. A man lost an arm, another his head. John threw himself forward, intent on pulling his lord down. Rannulf beat him back.

"Stop, Papa," Nicola screamed from behind Rowena. Her female voice could not thread its way between the cursing, shouting men. The clash of swords and cries of the wounded muffled any chance of that.

Taken in surprise, most of their men now lay dead or wounded. Their blood mingled with those few of Ashby's forces who'd fallen with them. Another volley of bolts flew. Sir John's men had the last of them from their horses. Now, only Lord Graistan on his massive steed remained.

"He is mine," John bellowed, and rushed forward, intent on killing the horse if he could not reach the man. Time slowed. The bay thrust forward in attack. Ashby's sword drove deep into its neck. As the beast jerked away from the pain, the heavy man was pulled upward, vulnerable for that instant. Rannulf leaned forward and swung his sword down in a great arc. He caught his vassal at the midsection with the full length of the blade's honed edge. The powerful blow lifted the man, snapping ribs and cutting through his mail.

Still screaming in pain, the horse rose again. Its movement freed Ashby from its master's blade. The wounded man dropped to the ground. But the archers above had seen their opportunity. Rannulf arched in pain when the bolts impacted with his shoulder, even though they could not penetrate his closely woven metal shirt. Unbalanced by the blows, he reeled in his saddle as his horse leapt forward, still striking out as its life ebbed. Then he fell to the bloody earth as the bay dropped to its knees beside him.

The sudden silence was awesome.

"Papa," Nicola screamed again, her hysterical cry

now echoing eerily off the walls around them. She tore around Rowena to race to her father's side.

Rowena did not waste her breath in words as she sped across the space to Rannulf. He lay on his side, blood washing his face from where his head had hit the ground. With a trembling hand, she touched his throat and felt his heartbeat against her fingers. She turned him slightly to touch her mouth to his and felt his breath against her skin. He lived. Never had she known a greater relief.

"There are four more coming." Lady Ashby's voice carried from the hall porch to ring about the bailey. Rowena watched the fair woman in her pale and pretty gowns descend the hall stairs and come to stand over her new husband. "Fool," she continued in a low voice. "It was punishment, not murder, I sought. Now you've left me no choice but to finish what you started." She was completely unaffected by the carnage around her.

Rowena turned back to Rannulf. If her husband was to continue living, she'd have to keep this bitch from his throat. Since his method of warfare had failed, she would try it her way, for she was armed with weapons against which the woman had no defense. She leapt to her feet and pushed her way through the crowd of men who surrounded the fallen Lord Ashby.

Nicola was murmuring in a low and soothing tone to her father as she pulled up the tails of his mail shirt. "There, do not fret," she said as he groaned in pain when she moved him. "Hush, Papa, it is not as bad as it feels," she lied. "It is lucky you are so fat, or you'd have been sliced in twain. He's broken your ribs here, and this gash is deep, but you will heal."

But John had eyes only for his wife. "I know you

bid me to stay my hand, but I could not bear to look upon him knowing what he'd done to you." His voice was a thready whisper.

Rowena's words startled them all. "And what had he done to her, Lord John? Tell me, for I dearly wish to know."

"One of you take her away and finish her," Lady Maeve snapped out.

"Nay," John countermanded, shaking his head at the men who laid hands on her. "I have saved you, too. You do not know what he has done, for he's hidden his true nature from us all," he said to his lady. "He raped and used my wife, and when she bore him children, he murdered them. He took"— he paused a long moment to catch his breath, then started again on a different tack—"he beat her and abused her."

"Would you like to hear a different version of this tale she's spun for you?" Rowena focused her entire attention on the only man who could now save her husband's life. "I would tell you of the men she's used, how she robbed our treasury—"

"Foul lies! And I thought only to protect you," Maeve cried in sweet outrage to her lady. "Why do you listen to her, love? I see now how she will betray me when I have only thought of her as my sister. Make her stop."

"Nay, I would hear what she has to say." John closed his eyes and swallowed, then slowly refocused his attention on Rowena.

"But, not now," his wife went on, her voice soothing and warm as she knelt down, staining her gown and hands with her husband's blood. "You are so hurt, I fear for your life. We will take you inside, and you can listen to her later." She pressed her lips to his forehead.

John ignored her. Instead, he asked of Rowena, "He does not abuse you?"

"Nay," she said, and also knelt beside him. "But, you should not have to ask me that. You know him. Your wife has used you; she has twisted your affection for her to make you her weapon of revenge against Rannulf for some slight he did her. Can you not see how her tales have inflamed in you this unnatural hatred for your lord? See? She has no response to me."

"My lord," Maeve protested, but Rowena spoke on, her commanding voice overriding the other woman's words, finally forcing her into silence.

"Know I say the truth when I tell you he did not rape her. It was he who locked his doors to keep her from crawling into his bed. She bore him no babe. But even if she had, you must only think on Jordan to see the truth here. Would a man who so loves a serving wench's get, kill any other babe of his?"

Now she took his hand. "He loves you, John. He came today to see that all was well with you. When you left so suddenly from Graistan, he feared he had slighted you in some way." If they lived, she would confess and do her penance for the lies she told. "How could you let this woman pollute your vows to him? You have betrayed him without even giving him the chance to speak in his own defense."

John stared up at her, his brown eyes glazed in pain. Now that his rage was spent, she saw him mentally recoil in the horror of what he'd done. Slowly, his understanding grew. Maeve saw it as well.

The fair woman cried out in very real concern. "She lies; she would do anything to save him, for without him she will lose Graistan."

"John," Rowena went on in her final thrust at Maeve, "he trusted you, just as his father before him trusted you. Aye, you have betrayed him, but he lives still. It is not too late. Spare us, and I vow on my soul that your daughter will not be stained by what has happened here today."

"Nay," the woman cried, as she watched her husband slip from her control.

"Nicola," he breathed, his gaze moving slowly to the girl who bound his bleeding back and side with strips torn from his gown.

His daughter lay a hand against her father's leathery cheek. "You were wrong to attack him, Papa, without hearing what he would say to Maeve's charges. Even she tried to stop you. Sometimes, that temper of yours"—her voice trembled—"oh, but Papa, if you must die, I will die with you. You need do nothing to save me," she said, her healing hands once again busy at their task.

He returned his attention to Rowena. "There is a thread from St. George's cloak within my hilt. Swear it to me, now."

She laid her hand on his bloodied sword. "I swear it will be so."

"Richard," he called, then coughed at the effort it cost him. When his man leaned down to hear him, he continued. "At all cost Lord and Lady Graistan are to be preserved. They must not die. Swear to me that you will see this done."

"I vow it, my lord," the man said.

"Fool!" Maeve screeched, leaping to her feet. "You stupid fool. Four more of them come. If you had killed them all, there would have been none to bear witness to what has happened here today." But, it was too late. John had slipped into unconsciousness. "Fool," she said again, her face twisted in rage.

"Damn you, you will not destroy me." She whirled on Richard.

"Do as I say or the might of Graistan will come crashing down on this place. Kill those four who come; kill all who remain alive of this party. When they are all dead, we will bury them in the forest and claim they never arrived."

Richard gave her a scornful stare. "How many witnesses must we also kill to still their mouths? Nay, you cannot hide what happened here today."

"Do as I say! I am your lady," she screamed.

"I do not serve you," he retorted. "My oath is with my lord, and what he commands will be done."

"Nay," she screeched, pressing still fingers against her temples. "Nay, I will not die for this man's stupidity." Then she caught herself. Rowena watched as her expression calmed and her body curved into her most feminine posture. "Aye, Richard, you are right, you cannot break your word. But think of this. If those men out there were dead, no one would carry back word of what has happened here. It may buy us only three days, but that could be time enough for your lord to regain his wits. When he is stronger, he will be able to resolve this matter with no further bloodshed. But . . ." She leaned forward just a little. Richard stood stonily beneath her assault. "But if they warn Graistan, Gilliam will be here tomorrow, and we will all die, your lord as well as you, when you could have saved us all."

He studied his new lady for a long moment. "All that I do from now on, I do to serve my lord the best I can. Just now your words make sense, so I am listening. But you take warning. I can only die once and, if I must, it will not be for your ends."

"I do not care if you do it for the devil himself, as long as you do it," she purred sweetly. "Only make sure you see all four dead, even if you have to chase them all the way to Graistan's gate."

Walter's anxious voice floated over the wall to them. "My lord, what goes forward in there? Call to us so we know all is well with you. Why are we being kept out?"

Rowena threw back her head and screamed at the top of her lungs. "Run to Gilliam, Walter, to Gilliam." But she knew even as she voiced the words, he had not heard her. There was a sudden pain that melted away into darkness.

# Chapter Twenty-one

**R**OWENA groaned; her head throbbed. She squinted her eyes against the pain, but that only made it worse. Beneath her face was a hard and dusty wooden floor. With another, muffled groan, she pushed up just far enough to look around her. "Rannulf?" It was so dim, she could barely see.

"Rannulf?" she cried again in the start of panic. There, there he was, across this small room, stretched full-length and facedown on the floor. She rose to her knees, but her vision swam so viciously, she nearly fell again. It was another long moment before she attempted to rise any farther. This time, her senses held true.

"Oh, my sweet love," she sighed as she came to kneel beside him. Her fingers sought for, then found, his pulse. She closed her eyes in a brief prayer of thanksgiving, then touched the torn skin on his brow. Her husband jerked in reaction.

"Quietly, my heart," she said, gently stroking his hair as she looked around her. They were confined in an empty chamber with a wooden door and four walls of stone. This could be no other place than the upper room of the stone tower.

He shifted slightly, then murmured, "Wren, you are still alive." There was great relief in his voice. "Are you hurt?"

"Nay." Her hand raised in reaction to his question, and she briefly touched the bruised spot on her head where she'd been hit. It hardly seemed worth mentioning against the gravity of their present situation.

"Where are we?"

"It is a stone room. I think it is the tower."

"Are we locked in?"

"I do not know," she said in surprise. It had not occurred to her to try the door. Even if it had been open, she would not have left him. She rose and crossed the room in a few short steps. The door had no handle; only the insertion of a key would free the latch. "Aye, we are locked in."

"Damn," he groaned quietly, and rolled cautiously to his side. She returned to sit beside him and pillow his head against her thigh. "I remember nothing after striking John. You must tell me everything that has happened since then."

Rowena sighed before starting. "John had believed Maeve's tales of rape and abuse. That poor, simple man was no match for her cunning words and sweet lies. It was only when I made him think about it that he saw how he'd been used in her revenge against you. Once he understood, he made his master-at-arms swear to preserve our lives."

"And that is why I lie, mailed but swordless, my wounds untreated, in a locked storeroom with no pallet between me and the bare floor?" He managed sarcasm despite his pain.

"I do not know why we are here," she cried out in frustration. "Truly, he made his man swear that we would be held safe. Rannulf, we should have sent word. Our unexpected arrival caused John to impulsively strike out at the man his wife claimed was a monster. Even Maeve had not planned murder and tried to stop his attack. She'd meant to hurt you by destroying John's loyalty. Now her mischief has exploded in her face, and she knows full well that it will cost her. If she must die, she will try to take us with her when she goes." Her sudden laugh was bitter and short. "Mary, Mother of God, I thought she would choke on her rage when John's man refused to finish us."

"What of Walter?" he asked quickly, grasping for the only hope left.

"Well," she hesitated, remembering her futile cry, "I think they have been killed. This man of John's would delay news of their treachery in the belief that his lord might recover enough in the next days to settle the matter with you. He thinks they have less than a week's time before we are missed by Graistan and Gilliam. If only it was true! What will Sir Jocelynn do when we do not appear in a few days?"

"Nothing, but wait. He has no cause to suspect that we've fallen foul here at Ashby. Nor will any at Graistan miss us." Rannulf groaned quietly. "If Walter has died, I fear we will as well, for I cannot believe John will survive. Now, what of the wound in my shoulder? I cannot bear to reach around to touch it."

"You have no wounds there. Your thigh yet seeps, and your head is cut." She gently touched her fingers to his shoulder. "I hope you did not break anything in your fall."

He struggled to sit up and gasped with the effort. "Help me remove my mail. If we are to die here, I will do it in what little comfort I can purchase."

A key turned in the lock. Rowena, caught holding

Rannulf's weight as she levered him into a sitting position, could only stare in surprise.

Nicola stepped swiftly and silently inside. The tall girl turned quickly to shut and lock the door behind her. By the light of the tiny lamp on Nicola's tray, Rowena could see the medicinal supplies upon it as well as the bucket that hung from her arm.

Rannulf tried to turn himself to see, but could not. "Who is there," he whispered harshly, incapable of any louder noise.

"It is Nicola, my love," Rowena replied. "She's come to help."

"Do not be so sure," the girl replied, her tone filled with accusation. "Richard said you should be locked in here to keep you safe from Lady Maeve. He meant that I should feed and care for you, but he has not ordered it. I know that Maeve wishes you to die, and I have led her to believe that I will not help the man who has laid my father at death's door. Now, I have come to you so you can give me a reason for doing otherwise."

"Rannulf was injured because your father betrayed him and attacked us," Lady Graistan replied, unable to comprehend that this girl would come only to taunt them. Surely, she would not protect the woman who had led her father to his injuries. "He would have dragged my lord down and killed him. My husband was only defending imself."

"True, my father did wrong, but what of Lord Graistan. He knows how my father's temper can get the better of him. Why, then, would he wed him to this evil woman whose words so goaded a good and loyal knight until he hated his lord and exploded in rage when the man appears unannounced at his gate?"

"My fault," Rannulf whispered. "I would not believe—"

"You do not know how she twisted him. I heard her lies, I saw him believe them while not one word I spoke reached past his new affection for her to settle in his ears."

"Please," Rowena said, staring in disbelief as the girl still held herself aloof, "you must help us."

Nicola continued, her words now trembling with tears. "Are you any better, Lady Graistan? You dared to barter with my life. Aye, I know what you did. By promising to save me, you have used my father's love for me to gain what you wanted. But now it is my turn to do the trading. I will treat your husband's injuries and thwart my stepmother's plans for your death, but only if you will not hold Papa accountable for the evil you, yourselves, have laid upon him. If you wish to live, Lord Graistan will swear to me to spare my father."

Her lady nodded for Lord Graistan. "He swears," she said.

"I cannot give what he has already forfeited," Rannulf said drawing himself up, his words halting as he gasped in the effort. Where worry and concern could not move him, outraged honor could. "He has attacked me, meaning to do me mortal hurt. His life is no longer his, but mine."

"You hold your tongue," Rowena snapped at him, her voice grim and hard. "It was your stubbornness that led to this ill-fated wedding. It was again your stubbornness that brought us here without a word to smooth our path. Now, would you doom us to death so you can say for pride's sake that his life was yours? Well, I will not let our child die because you are too stubborn to see beyond your honor."

There was a moment of quiet following her words, then he managed a huff of amusement. "I was wondering. Nicola, she is right. It is I who brought this all upon myself. If it is in my power to do it, I will hold him safe for you."

The girl's sigh was so deep, her tray rattled with the force of it. "Thank you," she said. Two quick steps and she had crossed the room to kneel beside them. "Can he sit by himself? No? Too bad, for that will make it harder for us to remove his mail." She put her bucket to one side, and set the tray and lamp down beside them.

"Lord Graistan we will have to move your arms. If your shoulder is broken, well, there is no help for it. You must bear the pain."

"I will think of it as penance for my idiocy."

"Do not laugh," Rowena cried, "I cannot bear for you to laugh over this." As Nicola steadied him, she lifted the mail skirt out from beneath his hips.

"Prepare yourself." The girl paid them no heed as she grabbed the back of the shirt. "Hold him upright for me," she commanded her lady. "Do not let him fall while I work it off."

Rowena did as she was told and watched the girl who had raged over her father's wedding do this task with the same authority and confidence that the Lady Graistan knew in her household management. And her efficiency made short work of it, where his wife's fear of hurting him might have cost Rannulf much pain. Once he wore only his coarse chausses, he sat, rather leaned heavily against his lady, while Nicola picked bits of metal from his leg wound and the myriad spots of broken skin on his back where the bolts had crushed the mail through his undergarments. At last, the girl eased back on her heels.

"You are fortunate. Nothing is broken, and there is no sign of deeper injury. You will be purple with bruising for days, both on your head and your back." She rinsed his thigh once again, completely unaffected by the blood that continued to ooze. "I feel like a traitor. My father is hurt far worse."

"Nicola," Rannulf said with a sigh, "I pray he recovers, for we have much to speak about, he and I."

There was a tap at the door. "Lady Nicola?" It was whispered through the keyhole.

"I come." The tall girl rose swiftly to her feet, unlocked and opened the door. Two servants entered, one bearing a pallet and a pot, the other bedding and a sloshing pitcher. They did little more than drop their burdens and retreat. Nicola shut and locked the door quietly after them.

"If Lady Maeve thinks we do nothing, she will not bother herself further with you. After I sew your leg wound, I must be gone. You will have to make up your own bed, my lady." There was the barest hint of scorn in her voice, as if she felt the job was beyond the Lady Graistan's capabilities.

Rannulf's laugh was quickly caught back in pain. "She can do it," he persisted hoarsely. "She can even comb her own hair and dress herself."

"Oh, love, do not laugh," Rowena admonished him again. "There is nothing funny here."

His hand closed around hers. "My sweet, it is laugh or cry, and I prefer to laugh. Besides, our situation has remarkably improved in these last moments." Then he closed his eyes against the stab of Nicola's needle. "Stop," he said, "my head is spinning. If I fall against her, I might hurt her and that babe she bears. First, give me some of that drink, for I am parched with thirst, then let me lie down."

While Nicola helped him hold the pitcher of watered wine to his mouth, Rowena leapt up and laid out the pallet, swiftly putting the bedclothes in place. Between them, they laid him back on this mattress. Then she held her husband's hand and gently stroked his hair while the girl went swiftly to her needlework. Somewhere in the midst of it, Rannulf drifted into a place where pain could not reach.

When Rannulf finally knew he'd returned to the living world, Nicola was no longer in the room. His wife sat beside him, and, although he'd not yet opened his eyes, he knew she cried. As well she might, for his folly had put them in a place where they might as easily die as live. It was his own shame that kept him from speaking to her.

Then, suddenly, she lifted his hand to her lips and pressed a trembling kiss against his fingers. "I cannot bear to think that you might die," she whispered. "Please, do not die."

He sighed and tightened his hand around hers. "Do not cry, sweet," he muttered. "I will not die." There was no hope of that. Besides, it would be too easy an escape from this morass.

The knowledge that he was once again conscious only seemed to make her tears fall faster. "Oh, Rannulf, I am so afraid. I have only had you such a short time, and there is so much more left in my life. Do not leave me, I love you."

Her words made his breath catch in his chest in hopeful disbelief, then he sighed and released the air in the impossibility of it.

"You speak those words because you are

frightened. And, as welcome as they might be to my ears, I think you are mistaken," he managed, stopping between words to catch his breath in effort. "Until only days ago, I have been a less than ideal husband, and now I have nearly cost you your life. What reason could you have for loving me? There has not even been time enough for you to even come to know me, much less come to love me."

Yet, even as he spoke, there grew within him a desperate need to hear her repeat the words. He prayed that she'd meant them and that her reasons for loving him would convince him of their truth.

His wife rubbed her free hand against the tears that stained her face, and drew a shattering breath. "But, I have known you for months, since February."

"Hardly. I have been gone most of that time." He loosened his grip on her hand only to twine his fingers between hers.

"Aye, you were gone, but your son was not, nor was your brother nor your people. Your kindnesses to them was in their eyes when they thought on you, and I heard your gentleness when they told their stories of you. Every time I looked at Jordan, I saw you. Aye, you were angry, and for that you have explained and apologized. Then, in our bed"—her suddenly hushed voice was shy as she continued—"you did not hurt or take, you made me love you." Her words died away into silence.

Rannulf closed his eyes against the enormity of his contentment. She loved him; it was true. He needed to touch her, to hold her close. At his tug on her hand, she slipped down to lie beside him. When he reached out and turned her face to his, their lips met in a gentle union. With her kiss, he

felt his life begin anew, even in this dark and
terrible place. He murmured in wonder, "You love
me and you will never leave me, for Graistan holds
your heart as it does mine." Then the urge for sleep
overtook him, and he drifted peacefully into its
healing embrace.

Morning's light brightened the room just a little
as a tiny slice of sunlight entered through the
narrow, east-facing window. Rowena opened her
eyes slowly, knowing a new queasiness. Although it
was not enough to make her empty her stomach,
it was uncomfortable. She'd had nothing like it at
yesterday's dawn. Was it because she now knew she
was with child and expected sickness, or was it only
because she'd eaten nothing last even? At any rate,
it passed quickly, leaving only an odd heaviness in
her womb.

She rolled toward Rannulf; he still slept. A brief
touch to his brow said he had no fever. Arising,
she took her beads from her purse and recited her
prayers, adding grateful words of thanks for their
continued survival. With that familiar ritual
completed, she stripped off her filthy gowns and
wimple, and tossed them into a corner. Dressed
only in her shift, she went to stand at the tiny slit
in the stone walls.

Ashby's bailey stretched, green and fragrant,
down to the river. She could hear the water rippling
and gurgling along its banks while it tumbled and
glittered in the newly reborn sun. From a willow's
crown, a lark threw it's song high into a cool and
cloudless morning sky. Men whistled and sang in
the distance. A sheep bawled, so did a child. The
fresh breeze brought the smell of baking bread. How

could something so horrible have happened in such a peaceful place?

Heartsick, she turned away from the view. In her purse she found her comb and went to sit, tailor fashion, on the edge of the mattress. Last night she had ignored her hair, and now she would pay the price. She loosened the long braid and began to slowly work the comb through her tangles. When her hair was once again smooth and straight, she drew it over her shoulder to plait it.

"Leave it," Rannulf said hoarsely, startling her. "I like it loose around you."

She turned swiftly to face him, her hair flowing around her in soft waves as she moved. "I did not know you were awake. How do you fare this morn, my lord? Have you any pain?"

"Aye, but you can ease it if you will help me rise so I can use that pot."

Rowena made an irritated sound at his flippant manner, but did as he bid her. "Good Lord, but you are heavy," she said, as he leaned on her after rising from his knees to his feet.

"It has never seemed to bother you before," he quipped. "Hold a moment, my head is spinning again. If I fall, let me drop. I would not hurt you or that babe of ours."

"I will not," she declared, resetting her arm around his waist.

He shielded his eyes with his hand for a moment, then took a breath. "It is better now. Let go, I would make the few steps it will take me by myself." When she clung, he said, "Wren, do not hold me. I am useless to us now. If we are to ever win free of this prison, I must speed my healing. To do that, I must get my feet back under me, and right quickly, too."

He managed the short distance, but he had to brace himself against the wall. When he'd finished and turned, she gasped, for his face was white with his effort. "Damn it, I am too stiff to retie this string. Do it for me, will you?" He leaned against the wall while she once again knotted the waist string of his stockings. This time, he did not complain when she held him for the few steps back. But when they reached the pallet, he balked.

"Nay, I will not lie. It causes me too much pain. Push it up against the wall and let me sit. You can wad the blankets up behind me to aid me." When she hesitated, he snapped, "I can stand for as long as it will take you to move the pallet."

"As you wish, my lord," she retorted sarcastically, but did as he requested. She placed the mattress near the window so he would have the sun to warm him for as long as it shone into the room. After she had propped him up to her own satisfaction, she handed him the pitcher and he finished what remained in it. Slowly, his color returned.

"You look better now. How is it with your head?" She took the emptied container and stood back a step to set it near the door.

"Well enough." The words were short and harsh. He was staring out the window at the sky above. "Why did you not tell me you were with child?"

"I did not wish to raise your hopes, my lord," she said quietly. "Ilsa says a woman's first often sits less securely than those that follow." She could not bring herself to tell him the rest of the truth, that she would die of a broken heart if he valued her only for the child she bore.

"You put my child and yourself into danger

because you believe you might lose it?" His words were so hard, almost cold.

"Nay," she retorted, anger at his stupidity leaping to life in her heart, "you put *my* child into danger because you were hell-bent on coming here and would not listen when I tried to tell you what might happen. And it is a good thing that I came. If not for me, you would be lying dead next to that damn horse you love so well."

"Ah, Roland," he said sadly and sighed, still not looking at her.

"What, no word of thanks to me? I have saved your life, but all you can think of is that animal?" Her voice rose just a little. He had room in his heart for a beast of burden, but none for her. Why had she spoken to him of her love? No doubt, he would use it against her someday. She turned her back to him. "Would you have liked it better if you'd died and left me a widow with a child who would never know his father?"

" 'Tis not the men in my family who die young," he retorted harshly. "If you'd not been with me, my concentration would have been intact. As it was, I was half out of my mind in worry over you. Dear God, I thought Roland had killed you when your mare fell." He paused to catch his breath, as if his intense speech was costing him dearly. When he continued, his voice was filled with pain. "If I had known you were breeding, I would have insisted you stay at Graistan. All women are weak, but breeding women are the worst. I should know. I've lost my mother, my stepmother, and two wives to some stage of childbearing."

Rowena turned slowly to stare at him, but he refused to look at her. "You are worried for me?" she said in growing wonder.

He shot her a short, irritable glance. "Well, of course I am. I am injured to the point that I cannot protect you while we sit trapped in this godforsaken room with no food yet this morn despite that girl's promise. And only after I've practically killed you with my foolishness do I discover that you are with child. You should have told me." Once again his gaze was focused out the window.

"Nay, that is not it." Her words came from her in amazement. "You are terrified that this babe will be the death of me." He slowly turned his head, and when he met her gaze, she was awed by what was in his eyes. He could not bear that she might die. His love for her radiated from him.

What a fool she'd been not to realize that he might, too, have come to care for her as she had for him. It was not for possession's sake or to keep her inheritance that he'd chased her down. It had been to apologize and bring her home as an honored wife. While she had gloried in his attention yesterday, for it fed her love for him, she had not seen that with his every word and touch, he had made her one with him and given her his soul.

"I am precious to you, and you cannot bear to think of losing me," she whispered before she realized that she hoped to tease words of love out of him.

"Wren," he said softly, "do not badger me this morn. I am hurt in both body and spirit. A man I thought I knew has been turned against me, and I myself helped it to happen. I am sick with fear for you. You are right, I do not wish to lose you when I have barely had a chance to know you. Now, come sit beside me and let me put my arm around you. I need to feel you close, for I have a sudden loneliness."

"As you wish, my love," she said gently, burying her joy. She slipped down beside him to join him in the sunlight.

The room had once again dimmed before Nicola finally appeared. "My pardon for being so late," she breathed as she darted in the door. She bore a basket with breads, cheeses, and slices of meat pie. There was a pot of rich broth for Rannulf and a pitcher of small beer. On her arm hung a bucket of fresh water for washing. Behind her stood a servant bearing the basket of personal items that had been packed for Lord and Lady Graistan. The man swiftly shoved it into the room, then left.

Nicola locked the door and went quickly to her patient to check her handiwork of yesterday. She seemed satisfied with what she saw. "Maeve is gnashing her teeth in rage, for they've not yet found your four men. I heard Richard say, they'd ridden all the routes to Graistan, and there'd been no sign of their passing. He says they are hiding in the village or, mayhap, in Eilington." Her hands flew as she rewrapped bandages.

"How fares your sire?" her husband asked.

The girl sighed. "He is no worse nor had he awakened yet, but when I whispered to him that you wished to talk with him, he seemed to rest easier. Now I must go. I doubt if I can come again before the morrow." She slipped out and locked the door behind her.

"Here," Rowena said, handing him his broth. She watched as he made short work of it.

"Now I'll have bread as well," he said.

"You should have no more than broth," she replied, suddenly remembering a lesson long ago learned from the convent's infirmaress. "It is not good for injured folk to eat too heavily."

"Piss on it, I am hungry. You hand me a roll, or I will get one myself." There was laughter in his voice, and his expression was suddenly much lighter. "And when I am done, I will want to wash and dress in something clean. Best you use the water first, for I will leave it bloody."

She handed him his bread, then turned with great hunger to the basket. All of a sudden it seemed the child within her made her hollow with its need. She ate well. If the foods were simple, all was fresh and savory with herbs and onions. When she was finished, she washed, then helped him.

Afterward they dressed, he in fresh chausses and a clean shirt, she in a linen undergown, dyed light blue. There was no need within their prison cell for more formal attire and the weather was warm enough to allow it.

"This is much better," he said in relief. "I hate the feeling of dried blood on my skin."

"Gilliam says you hate feeling dirty at all. I think he finds your insistence on cleanliness oppressive." She tossed the reddened cloth into the bucket and pushed it away from them.

"He would," Rannulf said, then suddenly laughed. "So, Walter has eluded them, has he? I had not thought him capable of so much independent thought. My hope for the future grows with every passing moment." He yawned and smiled once more. "I think I will rest awhile."

She helped him to lie down, then tossed the blankets over him. "Rannulf?"

"Hmm?" He peered up at her, his brows raised in question.

"If—nay, when, for I will not say 'if'—when we are done with this ordeal and the judgment on my inheritance is settled, may we please have a more normal life? I am tired of all these doings. I think more has happened to me since I married you than in the whole rest of my life."

He laughed and settled down against the sheets. "It would be my pleasure to provide you with nothing but my dull company in an uneventful life. I can see it now. Year after boring year will pass. Now, let me sleep."

# Chapter Twenty-two

*R*OWENA awoke on the fourth full day of their captivity with a steady, dull ache in the small of her back. She stretched against it, then once again fought the turning of her stomach. As much as she wanted this child, she was already deadly tired of being sick. To make matters worse, what had once been an occasional sharp pain in her womb was now a far too frequent visitor.

After a few minutes everything eased into a more normal queasiness, and she turned toward Rannulf. He still slept and lay with his back to her. Although his skin was still purpled with bruising, the marks were rapidly fading to a pale yellow-green.

She arose to do as she had done the other mornings. But once her prayers were said, her hair combed, and she'd washed and dressed, there was nothing left save to stare outside and wonder how much more confinement she could tolerate.

The view was as quiet and peaceful as it had been the other mornings. If she put her hand through the window slit as far as it would go, she could just feel the fresh breeze against her skin. It would be another fine day while she was trapped inside.

Slowly, as the minutes passed, all her aches and pains, even the queasiness, disappeared. There was an odd finality in the feeling that followed, as though it would never plague her again. She breathed a grateful sigh.

Behind her, she heard Rannulf rise. "How do you fare today, my sweet?" he asked as he began his morning ritual.

"Much better," she replied, turning to greet him with a swift smile, then immediately turning back to the narrow window. She dared not watch. He was so prickly about her help, yet she could not bear to see him struggle. Never mind that it took him twenty minutes to do what she could have done for him in just moments. What else did they have, but time?

At last, he came to stand behind her. "Has that pain returned? You look pale this morn." He kissed the top of her head, then her brow when she looked up at him.

"Nay. In fact, I feel better than I have for days. I think it is only the confinement that weighs on me. I am bored." She leaned back against him.

"You could come back to bed, and we could sleep again," he said. "Unless you prefer to drive yourself mad with ennui." His arm came around her. She shivered when his fingers splayed to gently rest against the curve of her breast.

"Sleep, indeed." She laughed, not at all displeased by his interest. But she stepped slightly forward to dissuade him from continuing. It would serve him right for all the times he'd snapped at her these last days. When he pushed aside her braid and kissed the nape of her neck, she ignored him the best she could. "I know full well what you mean, and it is not sleep." There was a sudden tremble in her voice.

"It will help to pass the time," he suggested, his

voice warm with desire. When his mouth touched her ear, her eyes closed, and she drew a deep breath against the thrill of pleasure that shot through her. She leaned her head back, resting it against his shoulder, exposing more of her neck to him.

"You are not strong enough yet," she murmured.

"Yesterday, I was not strong enough. Today, I am." His fingers slid ever so slightly upward to cup her breast. Her breath caught in her chest.

"I would not have you hurt yourself by laying atop me." Despite her words, she made no move to pull away.

This made him laugh in deep amusement against her throat. "And I thought it inconvenient to wed a virgin." She let him turn her slightly so he could once again kiss her nape. Then he continued speaking. "I can see I have neglected your education when there is so much left to teach you. The very thought of what you do not know sends chills down my spine."

"Pay them no heed, it is only your wounds healing," she sighed, but he was already leading her back to their pallet.

"Now, you must pay strict attention if you are to master this art," he said, his gray eyes warm and filled with both desire and laughter.

Screams and shouts shattered the morning's peace. Animals bellowed and cried. The world outside their makeshift prison exploded in sudden activity. Footsteps rushed past their door and upward to the roof above them. Rannulf whirled back to the window.

"What is it," she cried, as the horrible screaming and shouting continued.

"I think the village is afire," he said. "Smoke is billowing out across the river."

"Afire?" she breathed in new terror. These simple places with their flimsy walls and reed roofing burned with the utmost ease. She looked at him. "And what if the fire spreads here?" she breathed. "The hall is wood and will not offer any resistance to flame."

"Aye, but our prison is stone, not wood," he said, but she was not placated.

"Aye, so it is. All the worse for us. The fire will draw up through here like a chimney. And we are locked in." Her hand touched her growing womb. "Poor child. We have not given you much chance, have we?"

Rannulf drew her close. "Hush, sweetling. You worry over what has yet to happen. This building is protected by water and stone. No fire can leap so far."

They listened, straining their ears for some clue as to what was happening. Minutes passed. Slowly the noise from the inhabitants quieted even if the smoke continued to billow. Rannulf frowned. "They do not seem to have tried to fight it at all," he said.

"John of Ashby!" The deep, bass voice was clearly audible even though it seemed to come from beyond the outer walls. "Give me my brother, or I vow I will do more than burn your village. Only God can save you if you've harmed a hair on his head."

"Gilliam," Rannulf breathed in wonder. He turned to her as his brother chanted out a string of obscene promises of what would happen to Lord Ashby if his captives were not freed. Her husband's eyes were alight with amazement and joy. "It is Gilliam. He has fired the village. My God, he has set siege."

"Walter must have heard me after all," she replied in pleased satisfaction. "I was so sure he hadn't."

"Heard you?" His brows drew down in his confusion. "What do you mean?"

She shrugged. "I was so positive my voice was not loud enough to carry over the walls, I saw no point in mentioning it to you. Once the attack was finished and John had commanded that we live, Walter came calling at the gate wondering what was afoot within. Maeve had told John's man he was to follow our remaining four all the way to Graistan to finish them. So I shouted that Walter should go to Gilliam. Maeve did not know that your brother was no longer at Graistan." She touched a finger to her temple as she frowned in consideration. "Mayhap he did not hear me and simply thought of it himself."

"My clever girl," he said, then he threw his head back and his laugh rang out, wild and free. "And he came for me." With his arms wrapped around his wife, he lifted her feet from the floor and whirled her around in his joy. "He came. My brother is out there, and he has come to free me."

"Rannulf," she cried, "let me go before you hurt one of us."

"Never, I would rather die than let you go," he said, although he ceased to turn in a circle. Instead, he caught her face in his hand and leaned to kiss her. His mouth touched her cheek, her nose, her brow, then her lips. His kiss deepened until this simple meeting of their mouths became a wild mating. She was dizzy with his need, his joy. She clung to him, her hands joining behind his neck so she could pull herself closer still.

He cupped her head in his palm, his fingers burying into the wealth of her hair. His mouth raked across hers, slashing and demanding her response. She melted against him. It did not matter that he was hurt or that Nicola might throw open the door at any moment. It only mattered that she wanted him, that her love for him made her feel whole and complete.

It was he who tore away, catching his breath in great gasps. "It is truly for me. You only do that for me. Oh God, Wren, you will not die, I will not allow it. You are mine and only mine." This time, when he kissed her, it was with a tenderness that shot through her heart. "And you have given back to me my brother," he breathed against her lips.

But she no longer cared that there were men outside the walls or that the village burned. Pressing herself against him, she trapped his mouth with hers. When he pulled away, she cried out in disappointment. But as she opened her eyes to look at him, she caught her breath.

Never had she seen his eyes so soft, not for Jordan or his brothers. Even as she studied him, he lifted her beyond them in his heart and made her more dear to him than they would ever be. He folded her within his being, binding her with chains to make her his prisoner for all his life. And that was good.

"I love you," she breathed. She touched his cheek with gentle fingers, again overwhelmed by the feeling that filled her. He leaned against her caress, his eyes closing. Her fingers moved to the fine strands of hair along his cheek. She pushed them back, curling them around the curve of his ear. He sighed and once again opened his eyes. Now, their gray depths were filled with the unmistakable lights of his passion for her.

"Besieging is a slow and tedious process. We have

nothing but time to waste," he murmured as he
once again placed his mouth on hers. Her need was
a fire that consumed her. And when he finally let
it consume him, he saw to it that he was not hurt
in the slightest.

Rannulf leaned back against the wall and watched
his wife again try to peer out the window. She wore
only her undergown, and that thin bit of material
clung to the pretty curve of her back. His desire for
her awoke anew, completely oblivious to its previous
satisfaction. Never had a woman excited him more
than she did, nor made him more content. He smiled,
feeling for all the world like some lovesick pup.

Oh, she had her faults. She was independent,
even self-contained, and to a greater extent than
he'd ever thought he could accept. But, somehow,
that seemed to make her all the more dear to him;
it made her the woman he loved.

Loved. Within him still lay a core of resistance
to the very thought of this. Despite himself, he remembered his father's pain and how his father's
mourning had hurt his sons. Surely, there was a
way to have one without the other. He shook his
head in confusion and put the puzzle back in a corner of his mind. It would wait until they were home
again. With his brother at the gates, it was only a
matter of time before they were free.

"Wren, come sit down. It will be days before anything happens. Gilliam has only arrived two hours
ago. Even if his equipment is here, rather than trail-
ing far behind him, he's not yet had time to have it
constructed and in place."

Suddenly, there was the oddest series of sounds.
His brows shot up with his surprise, then he dismissed the thought as ridiculous. It could not be.

Then a single explosion of sound reverberated through the bailey and echoed into their tiny chamber. His wife leapt back from the window in fright. "What was that?" she gasped.

"And, then, I could be wrong," he said in amazement. But Geoffrey's holdings were much farther from Ashby than was Graistan. To have brought the ballista here so quickly, and have it already working, meant they'd marched through at least one night, more likely two. But what in God's name was Gilliam doing using such a machine against a wall? With its ability to shoot missiles great distances, it was better suited to raining terror down on the stronghold within, rather than at the walls themselves.

"What is it?" she cried again, holding her hands over her ears as a second explosion of sound echoed around them.

"A ballista. From the sound of it, Gilliam is firing at the south wall. If he's firing at the wall, I wonder if he's using bolts or stones?" he asked in quiet preoccupation. But why that wall when it was one of the two protected by water? And what if the engine did work to soften this strong, defensive line? Gilliam would be days doing it, and he'd still need to get men across the moat to finish the job.

Now, that would be a very tricky business, indeed. A wooden bridge could span the distance, but Ashby's men would hardly sit idly by while miners took down their walls. Nay, fire, boiling water, and other missiles would rain down on both men and bridge while they picked their way through. It seemed a hare-brained scheme at best. Then, again, who was he to judge? It had been his own hare-brained thinking that had trapped them here in the first place.

"I do not like it," she said, coming to sit beside him. He put his arm around her. There were three more explosions and, then, silence.

Above them, he heard footsteps. One man called down, reporting that there appeared to be no damage yet. Another answered from the bailey floor. Again, no damage was reported.

When the silence continued, Rowena pushed away from him, but just a little bit. "Why do they not surrender and give us to Gilliam?"

"Were I in this Richard's place, I would do as he is doing, simply sit quiet and still behind the walls. I would offer no resistance, but neither would I give over. Nicola said her father opened his eyes yesterday and spoke a few words. No doubt, his man knows this and thinks he will soon hand the whole problem to his lord."

"But if Ashby's man were to give us to Gilliam, would it not be the same?"

"It is not, and he will not do it. That is a decision belonging to his lord. He has only been ordered to preserve us and so he shall, even if he must keep his lady at bay to do it. That is good for us, but not so for Gilliam. I doubt he knows what has become of us. I've not heard one word of response uttered by Ashby's men, despite Gilliam's constant callings and shoutings. It seems that this Richard stands fast to the man who holds his oath, wagering that John will live, the walls will stand, and he'll not be held responsible for what has happened."

There was another reverberating explosion. She cried out again, clutching him tightly and burying her face against his chest. "I do not like that sound."

"Ah, my sweet, it is the sound of freedom." He laughed. Four times in an hour's passing, the ballista sent its missile against the wall. But when it finally ended, there was no man atop the keep, so he heard no call. Instead, there was shouting from the south corner of the bailey.

He listened carefully, gathering from the sounds of the voices, more than anything else, that Gilliam had put some sort of bridge in place. No doubt, his brother meant to cross the water and check on his handiwork. Ashby's men would be on the wall above, if not attacking the besiegers, at least keeping their eyes on them.

His wife looked up at him, and he caught his breath at her magnificence. Her hair color was so rich and such a contrast to her creamy skin and dark blue eyes. He stroked her cheek with a gentle finger, then pulled her closer still. She lay her head against his chest, and her trust in him spoke to his soul.

But what if this babe of theirs killed her? The very thought of her death, of the great rending absence she would leave behind, not just in him but in his family and folk as well, made him cold.

Then, again, what if the babe did not take her? It might well be he faced a full and happy life with her. She was so much younger than he, it was more likely he would precede her into death. He would leave her a wealthy widow who would all too quickly be remarried.

That thought rankled. Better that she went first, for he could not bear the idea that another man might hold her. Would she burst to life with desire for her next husband as she did for him? That he should think this way made him laugh.

"What is so amusing?" she asked. "Do I smell burning again?"

He paused to test the air. "Aye, and it is closer

now." Then, he grimaced. "I think Gilliam has put a bridge across the moat to see what damage he has wrought. Ashby's men are not sitting so still as I expected they would. They must have succeeded in setting it afire." The smell of smoke grew steadily stronger.

"Oh, sweet Mary," she whispered. "Poor Gilliam."

"Now, who was the one who told me he was no boy to be fretted after," he chided, no longer threatened by her affection for his brother and recognizing friendship for what it was.

"So," she said briskly, visibly forcing her thoughts away from what went ahead outside, "what was it that made you laugh?"

He smiled, still amused by his ridiculous thoughts. "I was thinking it would be better if you died first, for I would surely be a vengeful ghost who would haunt you if you were to remarry."

"Rannulf," she cried, pushing away from him. "That is morbid. Do not think like that."

He only laughed, enjoying his own foolishness. "Nay, not morbid, I am only imagining. Ah, I have the solution for it. We shall both live forever, then neither one of us will have to be alone." When she only stared at him in perplexity, he continued, "Play this game with me. Let me say that it is so. Would you live with me forever?"

She studied his face for a long moment and whatever she saw made her happy. Her eyes brightened, and she smiled softly. "Aye, my love, I would live with you for all time," she replied.

It was only then that he realized what he'd said and why she'd smiled so. There was no escaping it, no holding back. Even his own tongue betrayed him. This love of theirs was right and good, the way it was supposed to be between a man and his wife.

"Many women do not die in childbirth," she said, gently touching her fingers to his lips. He kissed her fingertips. "My mother did not, nor did Temric's. Nor did Queen Eleanor, and she had many children. She is strong and healthy despite her age."

"You are right," he replied, catching her hand and placing a kiss into her palm. "But I would still rather have you with me than trade you for the sake of a legitimate heir."

"But I want our child," she cried softly. "It is my gift to you, proof of my love for you."

"And what proof would you ask of me? Jewels, clothing, lands?" His tone was teasing but not so his heart.

Her eyes were soft and warm. "There is nothing more I want from you that you have not already given me."

She would not make him say it; she would not demand from him the final proof of his feelings for her. If he spoke them, it would be because he had chosen to do so. Would he? He drew a deep breath as his last fears shredded and disappeared. "Wren," he started, the words forming, then falling away to form again.

Suddenly, the door flew wide to crash against the wall. Nicola stood in the doorway, her hair in disarray and dirty charcoal streaks across her face. "Maeve has set the house afire and run. Your brother has breached our walls and is storming across the bailey killing everyone he sees. Even his own men cannot stop him. Hurry, he has sworn to kill my father. Here"—she handed him his sword—

"now, come and make good on your vow. You must protect Papa." Then she was gone.

Rannulf leapt to his feet, dragging Rowena up with him. "There is not time for you to dress," he said brusquely, jamming his feet into his shoes, then struggling into his shirt. "Damn, I am stuck, help me. And she left me no shield."

His wife dropped her gown and whirled to help him with his shirt. "You are still too sore to use one if she had. Now, go. The fire is getting closer. I can smell it."

He went quickly down the stairs ahead of her, sword at the ready. First, he would see his wife safe, then lend Ashby what help he could. But by the time they'd left the stairs and entered the hall, the room was already thick with smoke and with the screams and shouts of the folk trapped within it. Flames leapt in the roof above them, nibbling at the rafters. The fire rumbled in the thatching as it consumed the dry reeds; its ravenous hunger would barely leave them time enough to save themselves.

Servants were massed in panic at the backs of Ashby's men. These soldiers had opened the barred door to escape the burning building only to meet Gilliam's forces. Steel flashed and flew as those inside sought to break out, while those outside fought to hold them within.

There was no escape for them in that direction. Across the room a small group of serving men were hewing themselves a new doorway. Suddenly they broke through. The chunk of severed wall dropped to the bailey far below them.

The building drew a roaring breath, its death rattle, as air rushed into it. Fire exploded through the thatch, sending down bits of burning reed to set alight the rushes on the floor. In that brief instant, flames appeared in a dozen places along the walls.

He took two steps toward the new exit, but Ashby's folk turned, enmasse, and surged toward it, blocking their route. Flames appeared above the hall door and licked their way down with incredible speed. The portal became a ring of fire, driving Ashby's soldiery back inside. Those still outside the door retreated. Save one.

Taller than all the rest, he entered the room with his sword flashing about him. He chopped his way into the panicking crowd. "Gilliam," Rannulf called to him. The young knight did not hear him, so intent on murder was he. He swung his blade with grim efficiency, felling one man, then another, then a woman, oblivious to the danger around him.

"Wren, nay," he bellowed. She had stepped away and instantly froze at his scream. A whole section of flaming roof dropped to the floor before her feet. Now they could not reach either the door or the open wall.

"Come," he said, and grabbed her by the arm to limp as quickly across the room as he could. He went left along the tower wall to where the master's chamber lay. Within that room was a window. It would be quite a leap, but better broken bones than death. And there would be just time enough to make use of it.

The smoke grew denser as they crossed the hall. Another area of reeds fell away, and he saw that flames were well progressed into eating away the rafters. There was a peculiar squealing sound, and the wall near the door crumbled. Above him a huge timber groaned in agony.

If the roof fell in on them, they would have no chance at all. His breath seared in his lungs and made him cough. Suddenly Nicola appeared out of the smoke. She was dragging a coil of rope with her. Then there was Gilliam, almost within hand's reach and nearly on the girl's heels. He tried to call out, but could only cough.

The smoke swirled again, and his brother was gone around the corner. He stumbled after them, still holding his wife firmly by the arm. Here, in the ell, there was neither fire nor smoke, but it would be only moments before it reached them.

The clash of steel to steel brought him to sharp attention. "Stay behind me," he barked hoarsely to Rowena. She coughed her answer. He pushed open the half-closed door in time to see John, swathed in bandages and barely able to stand, much less to firmly close his hand around his sword hilt, fall to Gilliam's blade.

"Traitor," his brother ground out, his words colder than ice, "you've died like the scum you are."

"Nay," Nicola screeched, and launched herself at her father, but not to kneel beside him in mourning. She grabbed the man's sword and threw herself in bold attack against the big knight. His brother's sword was already drawn back for a killing blow.

"Gilliam," Rannulf shouted in warning, "do not hurt her."

"Murderer," Nicola screamed, as his brother whirled in disbelief to face him.

"Drop that sword, girl," Rannulf snapped, his own blade flicking out. But, instead of sending the weapon flying from her fingers as he had expected, she met his movement with a well-honed turn that nearly cracked his wrist. "What—" he cried out more in surprise than pain.

"You are alive," Gilliam bellowed in joy.

"Behind you!" he yelled as the tall girl swung the long and well-balanced weapon with a precision he could not comprehend. "Disarm her and hurry with it, or we will all die."

The young knight turned with incredible speed and met his attacker's blade. Although he pushed her back, she thrust out again, displaying skill and considerable training in her smooth movements.

"Wren, get that rope," he commanded, as his brother gave an unholy roar of laughter and met the girl's blade once again.

His wife dashed across the room and grabbed up the rope. Gilliam gave his sword a careless twist to tap the tip of it against his opponent's ungloved wrist. She screamed in pain and rage, but loosed one hand in reaction. Another small movement of his hand, and her father's blade flew across the room.

"Here goes the roof," Rannulf shouted above the ever growing thunder of the fire. By the time he'd taken the few steps to the window, smoke was billowing down at them. To Gilliam he said, "I want the girl," to his wife, "tie it to both handles. That way if it comes after us, it will be too wide to pass through the window. Quickly now, or we will all be roasted alive."

His brother's mailed hand snapped shut about Nicola's arm as he glanced above him and saw the smoldering ceiling. The girl writhed and screamed against his hold, but it did not affect him in the slightest. There was a low creaking, tearing sound from the hall as yet another section of roof collapsed. Again, that rafter groaned.

"Nay," Rannulf commanded Rowena, "loop it to the left through the other handle and then back again. If it makes the rope too short, we will drop."

"Murderer," Nicola raged against Gilliam's hold, her free hand scratching and clawing at his mailed glove. When she realized the futility of it, she dropped to the floor, making herself a dead weight. "Nay, I will not leave. Let me die with him. Murderer! He could barely rise and yet you killed him. Oh, Papa," she cried, her free hand clutching at her father's fingers. "Let me stay."

Rannulf yelled back at his brother as he tossed the now fastened rope out the window. "Do not let her go, Gilliam."

"You are fortunate, traitor's daughter," his brother said, grabbing the tall girl up by the waist. She kicked and writhed, but he only threw her over his shoulder. Her fists beat against his steel-clad back.

"Go," he said to his wife, who stood atop the trunk. He opened his mouth to reassure her, but she only nodded and slipped down the rope with amazing agility. Above him the roof exploded in flame. A burning bit floated down to rest atop the tangled bedclothes. They smoldered just an instant, then a tongue of flame appeared. "Go," he said to Gilliam. "Do not argue, you must bear her as you do it."

His brother shot him a broad grin. "I can manage, old man, now that I know you are alive." And he was gone.

Rannulf felt the blood trickle from his thigh where he'd torn his wound afresh. He grabbed up the rope, threw his sword to the ground below, then turned to lower himself out the window. He had only dropped beneath its sill when there was a massive explosion. Great, blazing daggers of flame shot out of the window and through the low-hanging roof. He was thrown away from the building. Rather than hit the wall, he released the rope and dropped to the soft turf below. Stars blinked into life before his eyes at the impact.

"Jesus God," he heard Gilliam say. "What was that?" When he turned his head to look, he saw that the concussion from the explosion had knocked his brother back and sent Nicola sprawling next to him. The girl lay facedown sobbing into the grass.

"Rannulf," his wife cried, scrambling over to him. "Sweet Mary, you are bleeding again."

"Aye, but I still live, and nothing has been broken, although I will now have bruises atop my bruises," he gasped out. "Let me lay here just a moment and catch my breath. Where did you learn to climb like that?"

She shot him a look both shamed and proud in the same instant. "When I was young and still at Benfield, I enjoyed climbing trees. I especially liked hanging upside down from the branches."

He laughed out loud. "With your gown hanging down over your face as well?"

"Nay, it does not do that if you wad it up and stuff it between your knees." Her grin was smug.

"Wren, I cannot even envision you doing something so frivolous," he said, his laughter making him cough up all the smoke he'd taken in. He grabbed her to him, holding her atop him in an embrace that was amusement, love, thanksgiving, and joy in one. "By all that is holy, I am glad I lived long enough to discover that about you."

"So, things have changed since I left Graistan, have they?" Gilliam looked down at him with a broad grin on his face, his helmet now tucked under his arm. Then he suddenly looked away, raised his hand, and gave a piercing whistle. "We are here and well," he called in response to the question. "Is all in hand? Good."

Rannulf freed his wife, who came lithely to her feet. He held out his hand to his youngest brother. "Help this old man up, will you?" His sibling easily lifted him to his feet, only to be lightly cuffed in return. "What in God's name were you doing running full tilt into a burning building? If you'd wanted to kill them, you only had to wait outside and they would have come to you."

"I was not thinking well. I was sure you were dead," the young knight said, his voice hardly more than a whisper. "And without having heard me tell you how sorry I was for what I'd said." He put his hands on the shoulders of the only father he remembered, as if he wished to embrace him but feared to do so.

Rannulf had no such hesitation. He stepped forward and threw his arms around the bigger man. "Stop," Gilliam cried, his voice thick with emotion, "my mail will cut you to ribbons, and you are already hurt."

"It is nothing," he said, stepping back. "What little healing remains will go quite quickly now that I am free. And now that I once again have you at my side. You will stay?"

"You would want me back?" It was a hushed and disbelieving question.

"Temric said it was good we'd lanced the boil between us, and he was right," he said. "You came for me when I had no cause to expect it."

Gilliam's eyes clouded with emotion, but he could only shrug as though it were nothing. In his embarrassment, he turned to his sister by marriage. "My lady," he said, smiling at her. "It is a pleasure to find you yet in one piece."

"I am so glad you came," she said.

Gilliam managed a quick bow. "Shall we retire to the south wall, my lady? My tent is across the moat. Rannulf, what would you have me do with her? Do you want her bound or guarded?" A jerk of his head indicated Nicola, who yet cried her heart out at his feet.

Suddenly Rannulf's heart went out to her. For all her odd ways, the tall girl looked like just what she was: a child who had just seen her father killed and her home destroyed in a very bloody fashion. He knelt at her side.

"You promised," she managed to gasp out, "you swore."

"Nicola, I am so sorry," he said, stroking her hair, "I was too late to stop my brother, but mayhap that was for the best. Your father was already dead. I killed him with that blow. No matter your skill, in time, it would have taken him."

"Nay," the little girl in her cried out, but he hushed her and went on.

"You would wish it to be otherwise, but it is not. Gilliam ended quickly what you would have prolonged. And, even if my brother had not done it, the fire would most surely have."

Again she denied his words, jerking back from him as if to be free of his comforting touch and soothing words. "Nay, I could have lowered him out the window."

He drew the girl up to a sitting position until Nicola leaned her head against his broad shoulder, tears now trickling down her face, although she no longer sobbed. "Child, he weighed more than twenty stone. You could not have done it, nor would he have allowed it. He would have commanded you leave him. He had lived his life, while yours is just beginning." Nicola's eyes closed again and, although her tears still fell, she was much calmer. "Hush, and be easy," he said, stroking her hair. "You are not alone. I am vowed to care for you and so I shall." When he tried to draw her to her feet, she resisted. "Stay here until you are ready. We will not leave without you."

"You do this for a traitor's daughter?" Gilliam held his comment until his brother had moved away from the girl.

"You will be good to her, boy, for she has saved our lives. If I had been a moment earlier, we'd have saved John's as well." He lifted a hand to forestall the complaint he saw in his brother's sudden wild and angry look. "It is a long story. Let her lie here and grieve. Where will she go? Now come." He gathered his wife close, and together they walked with Gilliam toward the wall. "Gilliam, tell me, how did you get in so quickly?"

His brother's response was matter-of-fact. "When I was here in March at your lady's behest, I noticed the mortar in that corner of the south wall had gone soft with moisture. I told—him about it as he left Graistan after his wedding. When Walter came to me with his tale, I knew he'd not had time to fix it." He grinned, his handsome face twisted in grim satisfaction.

"I used the ballista to drive a hole right through the already soft foundation, and a whole section came tumbling down. After that I lay a bit of planking across the moat, and we walked right in."

Rannulf stared at the young man in amazement. "God's blood. You will tell me what you've seen in all my other keeps, will you not? This was far too simple for you. We'd better have something stronger here when it is rebuilt."

His wife suddenly gasped and released him to hold herself tightly. "Sweet Mary, I think I will be sick," she breathed. "I need to sit." She was white with her pain.

Rannulf leaned down and grabbed her up in his arms. "Put me down," she gasped out, "you are hurting yourself."

"Nay, not in the slightest," he said. With his wife in his arms, he stepped through the breached wall and outside to freedom once again.

# Chapter Twenty-three

"*Y*OU must put me down," Rowena insisted as they crossed the moat. "I am hurting you."

"I will not and you are not. Gilliam's tent is only there"—he indicated with a nod of his head the mess of wains and beasts of burden, armed men and servants that massed at the forest's edge—"just across this bit."

With no further argument, she wrapped her arms more tightly about his neck. She doubted she could have walked even that short a distance. The dull ache of this morn was gone, replaced by a far worse twist of pain that set her teeth on edge and made her want to cry with the hurt it caused her.

When he turned slightly, she gasped, but not in pain. Behind him, and in her line of sight, lay the crumbling ruin of the south wall. Framed in the breach was the still burning manor house. Roofless now, and with only ashes for walls, the supports were still engulfed in flame. One of the massive cross beams had fallen, piercing the floor to enter the grain storage bins that lay below the hall. Fire, fed by the burning stores, shot up its long length.

Smoke also poured from the top of the tower. If Nicola had not released them—she caught her breath and could not even complete the thought.

All too many others had not been as fortunate as they. Around the foundation of the house lay the house servants and men who lived there.

The carnage had spilled out of the bailey and into the moat. Her husband now picked his way through the bodies of the men who had fallen in the battle to hold the wall. Some were Gilliam's, but most of them wore Ashby's armor. She recognized Richard floating in the muddy, reddened water.

Once again Rannulf turned, and she saw the village. What, five days ago, had been so lovely and serene was now a charred ruin. Not one house still stood; dogs and fowl sifted through the wreckage for whatever they would find. But there were still sheep grazing in their meadow, and the cattle—were in the barley field!

"Rannulf," she cried, tensing in his hold, "send someone to chase those cows from that field. That is our crop they are eating."

Her husband laughed. "Only you would think of barley when we've just battled for our lives and barely won by a hand's breadth.

"We will need every bit of what is ours this coming winter," she retorted tartly. "This place is fertile and well managed, and it could supply much of what we need now that it no longer has as many to support. I hope he's not killed them all or who will get the harvest in?"

Rannulf only shook his head and turned so they could both face the village. "He's not killed the peasant folk. Look, look closely. Show me a body lying there." Rowena looked. Unlike the bailey and the moat, there were no bloody, crumpled forms within the remains of the cottages. "He knows better than to cut his nose off to spite his face. If I'd been dead, this would have been part of his inheritance, right, my boy?"

Gilliam only grimaced as they walked past the giant crossbow that was the ballista and the pile of stones that would have been its missiles. "I do not wish to talk about it." He stopped at a large tree beneath which stood his tent.

Her husband kicked out Gilliam's camp stool for her and set her on it. "Would you rather lie?"

She shook her head. "Nay, I am better now," she lied. "Do you think we can leave for Upwood yet? I would be at some friendly place as soon as possible."

"Are you fit to ride?" His eyes darkened in concern.

"I see no difference between sitting here and riding," she replied. "The sooner we are there, the better I will feel." When he still hesitantly eyed her, she added, "Please?"

"If you are certain, love," he said with a nod. "Gilliam, can you spare some men and a few horses to see us to Upwood? We must bide there until the bishop calls us back to Graistan."

"Aye," his brother replied, and turned to a passing man. "Alfred, I want you and ten more men to escort my brother and his wife to Upwood. See to it there are suitable mounts for them."

Rowena sighed and laid her hand against her abdomen, as if her touch could ease the awful tension in her womb. Beneath her breath, so Rannulf would not hear, she murmured, "Hold tight, little one. It will not be long now." Surely, she could bear the pain for just a little longer.

Rannulf had not heard. Instead, he had turned to his brother to ask, "Where did you get the stones?"

Gilliam glanced back at the ballista. "Those?

There's a new quarry nearby. Perhaps, he was getting ready to build once again."

"My Sir Gilliam," called a man, coming toward the young knight. He stopped in startled surprise. "Lord Graistan, we thought you were dead!"

"Nay, not yet." Her husband laughed. "Love, this is my brother Geoffrey's ballista engineer, Alain. It is he who is responsible for that hole of Gilliam's. It is good work you've done here, man."

"Aye, when Sir Gilliam told my lord that he needed no more than my little toy"—he waved fondly at his siege engine—"I must admit that my lord had his doubts. But here we are and so it is. My lord," he said to Gilliam, "I've already sent word to Lord Geoffrey that he need do no more in your regard."

"Alain." Three men were coming near, two of them holding a writhing woman dressed in filthy homespun between them. "Look, what we found. These men have had a bit of sport with her, thinking she was one of the house servants before they realized the English with which she cursed them was so odd."

Rowena stiffened, for there was only one whom it could be. She watched from around her husband as Maeve was dragged nearer. The woman's fair hair was wet and tangled with mud. Her face was bruised, her lip cut and still bleeding. The coarse material of her gown had easily torn when the men had taken her.

"Maeve." Gilliam uttered her name in a single cold breath.

At the sound of his voice, the noblewoman stood still between her captors. "Ah, the beardless boy," she spat out as she slowly raised her head. "How did you like the taste of my revenge, eh?" Then she gasped in shock as she saw Lord Graistan standing beside his brother. "Rannulf," she breathed in horror, "but you were locked in. He could not have been quick enough to have freed you."

"Aye, you have failed," he said, calmly but with the same ice in his voice that his brother had revealed. "We are both here." He moved back to stand beside the stool and lay his hand upon Rowena's shoulder. "You have done your worst, and it was still inadequate."

The fair woman's broken and bleeding face twisted in a mask of sudden understanding and rage. "Nay, damn that stupid little bitch. She swore."

"A lie for a liar," her lady threw back. "After the many times that you have used others, I am surprised you did not see it when she used you." Suddenly, she was glad she now faced this woman. It was good that Gilliam's men had brought her here. Eventually, after all was said and done, she would have worried if they'd not found her.

The woman snarled, then turned her colorless eyes on Rannulf. "So, you are not dead. But have you yet opened your eyes? Poor Rannulf, not the virile lover that your brother is. If you did not have Jordan, I might think you incapable. Isotte carried your brother's brat. Whose get will this wife bear since you do not sleep with her?"

"Nay," Gilliam bellowed in pain and rage, grabbing at his sword hilt to draw it and finish what remained of the lady before him.

"Rannulf," Rowena cried out, "do not let him."

Her husband's hand shot out to stop his brother's sword arm. "Hold."

"Let me still her mouth," his brother pleaded. "She will spew foul lies no longer."

Lord Graistan turned to Rowena. "Why do you bid him to stop? She has forfeited her life this day with her actions. No soft wish or gentle plea of yours will save her neck."

"Aye, Maeve has forfeited," she agreed, "if not for us, then for the deaths of Ashby's folk that now lay upon her soul. But she has the right to confess her sins and be absolved before being sent to face her Maker."

"Spare me your prattle," Maeve sneered out.

But Rowena continued speaking. "More importantly, she had asked a question, and she shall have her answer before she dies. I would not have it sit on your brother's soul that he struck out in fear of the past when there is no longer cause for it." The pain that had abated some now grew marginally worse and made her shift uneasily on her stool.

Rannulf stared at her for a long moment, then slowly, he smiled. "You are right. Gilliam, hand me your sword. I would not want you tempted to leap out."

"Nay," his youngest brother said, almost crying in his pain, "nay, you must not listen. Do not let her speak."

"Gilliam."

As the knight reluctantly lay his weapon into his brother's hands, Rowena watched Maeve's eyes glitter with satisfaction. So, the woman still dreamed she had some hold over them, that she could use their past to control them. But it was a dream soon to be shattered.

"Now," Rannulf said, slightly juggling the sword in his hand as if unconsciously taking its measure, "this foul bitch has asked a question that I will answer for her. She wishes to know whose child my wife bears." Maeve threw her head back in startled disbelief as this news caught her unawares. "That's right, bitch. The child is mine."

"Nay, I do not believe you." The fair woman let the words fly in desperation. "It is a lie. This woman is all hard words and commands. She has done naught, but defy you and challenge your rights at Graistan. She does not even understand how to be your lady. The stupid twit dresses like a servant and behaves like some merchant's wife." The despair in her voice sounded almost true. For a moment Rowena knew a sort of pity for this woman. Was it possible that Maeve had loved Rannulf, at least to the best of her twisted heart's ability?

But her husband only smiled grimly. "You offered me a sweet face and pretty poses, and your attitude promised much. But even deep within my mourning, I believe I sensed your rottenness, for I could not bear your touch." Maeve stiffened at this pronouncement, her eyes flying wide. But Lord Rannulf was not finished yet.

"Would that I could blame you for this havoc you have wrought, but it lays only upon my shoulders. I needed you to ease my guilt and let you run amok among my own people and now, here, again at Ashby. It is time I put an end to this foul mummery of yours. As is my right, I pronounce on you a sentence of death for your crimes. You, there"—he pointed to the third man who stood a little aside from the lady—"run into the church and fetch the priest. Once he is done with her, she will be executed."

"Kill me, then," Maeve said, slumping as though in hopeless despair. She fairly leaned against one man's shoulder as a minute passed. It was this calm of hers that made her captors less vigilant against her sudden surge forward.

She tore free from their grasp. "But, I will take her with me," she screeched out. Her face was alight with hate as she threw herself at her lady. Rowena had no time to scream. She was shoved brutally from the flimsy stool, Maeve's hands around her throat. "Graistan was mine," the woman screamed.

Gasping for breath, she pushed at her attacker even as Rannulf roared above them. Maeve's enraged expression flattened in surprise. Then she was lifted by the back of her gown. Rowena's husband tossed the woman aside as if she were no more than a child's doll. He whirled after her as she fell, Gilliam's sword flashing in the air as it followed her descent. It embedded into her flesh with deadly ferocity.

Rowena lay on the ground, dizzy with pain and stunned by her fall. The new, horrible cramp within her ended suddenly with an explosion of warmth between her thighs. Rannulf was beside her, lifting her, crying out when he felt the wetness of her skirt against his arm. Blackness circled in on her. If she were to die, he needed to hear it from her one more time. "Rannulf," she gasped out, leaning her head against his chest, "I love you."

She sighed.

She had hovered just beneath wakefulness for a long while, but the effort to awaken took more strength than she could muster. There was something warm beneath her palm. She moved her fingers just a little. The warmth closed in, enfolding her entire hand. Somehow, this made it possible to open her eyes.

Above her there was only a dark and smoky roof. She frowned. That was wrong. Where was her bed, the wooden ceiling, the hangings? Slowly, for it took all the energy she had, she turned her head.

"Rannulf," she breathed. More was impossible.

His face was hollow with worry, his eyes so soft and gray, but filled with pain. Then, he slowly smiled, his free hand reaching out to stroke her cheek. When he spoke, it was to answer the questions in her eyes. "You are in the midwife's house at Eilington. It is loss of blood that makes you weak, but you are young and strong and will soon be well."

She frowned. Within her gaped an emptiness where once there had been life. Even as she willed it to be otherwise, tears filled her eyes.

"Aye, my love, the babe is gone. Ah, do not mourn so. Let me keep you to myself for a little longer."

She drew a deep breath and closed her eyes. He had called her his love. Her fingers tightened around his. "Home," she murmured.

"When you are stronger." There was a jostling beside her, then she was lifted into his arms. He sat on the pallet and cradled her to him as he rocked her gently in his embrace. Against his broad chest, with her head tucked into the curve of his neck, she felt the steady beat of his heart, as if it were her own.

"I thought I'd lost you," he breathed. "I thought you would die before you heard me tell you what I hold in my heart for you. Ah, Wren, I love you so. Without you, I would be nothing but an empty shell, the way you found me. That you could nearly die without hearing me say these simple words—I cannot believe I was so careless with your love for me."

But they were not simple words at all; they were like a magician's spell, creating a wholeness between them that made them one. This new sense closed over her to heal the aching rend left by the babe's departure. It reached further to touch what remained of the solitariness that had always lain at the core of her being. Loneliness fell away in shivering splinters to be replaced with warm contentment.

She lay easy in his arms for some time. Mayhap she slept, for when she stirred again, she felt refreshed and stronger. "Rannulf, am I your one, true love?" It was the question she had asked him on their wedding day, although then the words had been hard and twisted with sarcasm.

There was the low rumbling of muted amusement in his chest. He, too, remembered that day and her words. When she raised her head, it was to look upon the charming, handsome man who had so intrigued and worried her.

Bitterness and anger were forever banished, and he would hide no more behind them. "Aye, Wren, you are my one, true love. Am I yours?"

"Aye, love, you are." She lay her head against his shoulder once again.

"I love you," he murmured again, as if enjoying the feel of the words on his tongue.

Rowena smiled against the fullness in her heart. Had her father known? He had done far better for his daughter than he could ever have imagined. Aye, he'd planned that she should have a proud home and a grand life. But had he known he was also giving her a husband to love, one who loved her more than life itself?

# Historical Note

When I was in college, studying archaeology, I had absolutely no interest in the dull and boring Middle Ages. I mean, what did those folks do except sing plainsong and hack each other to pieces for honor's sake? When this story arrived and insisted it could only be written in 1194, I decided I had to learn more. My research revealed a highly sophisticated society whose complicated social behaviors developed in spite of, or perhaps because of, their primitive technology. I hope I've succeeded in letting my characters reflect the respect I have for this remarkable era.

A few notes for the purists: Ashby appeared before I knew there was a royal fortress by the same name. Since I was already accustomed to the name, it remained as it was. Graistan keep was originally modeled after a beautiful Castle Rising in East Anglia. And Rannulf is spelled as it is because that is how he spells it. I had nothing to say in the matter.

If you enjoyed WINTER'S
HEAT, you'll love Denise
Domning's next medieval
romance,

**SUMMER'S STORM**

Coming from Topaz in the Fall
of 1994.

Turn the page for a special
advance preview of
SUMMER'S STORM by
Denise Domning.

Philippa of Lindhurst dropped her basket on the grass and drew a deep breath against the weight of wet linen it contained. Her lungs filled with the spicy sweetness of summer's advent. Would that she could prolong these remaining moments, but Lindhurst's ugly gate stood wide and waiting.

She closed her eyes against the sight. Air, warmed by a midday sun hanging in a rare cloudless sky, danced against her skin. Lark and thrush wove a merry harmony against the distant bellow of oxen and men from the manor fields. Insects, like monks, sang their droning plainsong, forever caught on one note. She smiled in simple joy.

"Hie, hie, you stupid cow!" hissed Margaret of Lindhurst. Her blow landed squarely between Philippa's shoulder blades.

Philippa hunched her shoulders in pain and seeming meekness as her mother-by-marriage pushed past her on the narrow, grassy track. Cow, was it? Which of them looked the more bovine?

A thrill of defiance raced through her. She hefted the basket back onto her hip, then lowered her head until her face was safely hidden behind the fall of her headcloth. To mock and escape unscathed was the only weapon Philippa had against Lord Roger and his mother.

She shambled after Margaret, mimicking the old woman's waddling stride. The damp hem of her shapeless gown beat a quiet rhythm against her ankles until her wooden shoe collided with the walking stick. When she looked up, her face was utter blankness.

"Do you dare?" Margaret's watery blue eyes narrowed in rage. Hatred laid deep creases in her sagging face and flared in the knife-thin line of her nose. Even the stiff spikes of hair escaping from her head covering quivered with her outrage.

"What is it?" Philippa cried out in feigned distress. Adding a pitiful sob for good measure, she once again stared at her shoes. 'I beg you, tell me what I have done!"

"Barren imbecile." Roger's dam made the words a curse. "Why did my precious lad want only Benfield's spawn, a useless bitch with golden hair and airs too fine for her station? You were not worth the coins I paid for you." She drew a raging breath and continued, her voice low and dangerous. "I'll find a way to keep your inheritance and still rid my son of you. Mark me now, I'll see you finished."

"Aye, Mother, I am useless." And proud she was of it. Triumph coursed through Philippa when no blow followed her words. She'd won. But when Margaret remained silent, she peered cautiously up from her demure pose.

The old woman had turned away to stare across the treed expanse which lay between the forest and Lindhurst's defensive ditch. "Who dares to come trespassing here?" she demanded to no one in particular.

Roger guarded his worldly goods and his cloying privacy with the same iron fist. He was helped by the fact that Lindhurst lay so far from any roadway it was beyond even the most wayward of travelers. Any itinerant merchant bold enough to tap at their door was driven sternly from the gate with a warning never to return. Today, the quiet rolling field echoed with the indistinct sound of a man's voice, the creaking groan of a wagon, and the muffled thud of hooves against hard-packed earth.

The need to see who it was rushed through Philippa, but nothing drove either her husband or his dam to a greater viciousness than when a man looked upon her. She carefully eased her basket to the ground, then slipped with tiny, noiseless steps to stand behind Margaret. Concealed from the woman's line of sight, she raised her head to gape in awe at the first visitors in all her twelve years there.

At the lead was a young black-haired man of obvious consequence. Astride a spirited palfrey whose trappings and saddle cloth were shot with gleaming metal threads, his riding gown was vibrant blue, his stockings bright scarlet. A deep green hood and a cloak the color of an autumn oak, clasped with a golden pin, completed his attire.

Four men-at-arms followed this cockscomb, each sporting a vest of boiled leather sewn with steel links and a metal cap upon his head. They wore their swords buckled fast to their sides, while bows and bolts were strapped to their backs. If their mounts weren't the quality of their master's steed, the beasts were still a better quality than those in Lindhurst's stables.

Lurching and skittering along behind them came a silly little cart drawn by sturdy ponies. Too small for hauling crops or any other goods Philippa could imagine, it bore a brightly painted frame covered with greased and painted sheeting to shade the wagon's load.

At the rear, and maintaining an aloof distance from the rest, rode a single knight atop a massive steed. Beneath a sleeveless and unembellished surcoat, the knitted steel of his mail shirt and chausses clung to a powerful frame. His shield was also unmarked, but he needed no advertisement of his courage. Something in his solitary air, and the long sword belted at his hip, warned of his prowess.

She watched him lift off his helmet and set it atop his pommel, then loosen the ties on his mail hood. It slid back to his nape, revealing brown hair streaked with sunlight. Like the narrow beard which outlined his mobile mouth, his hair was neatly trimmed. His nose was strong and slightly crooked, the little flaw adding character to an otherwise handsome face. Dark, even brows slashed above his eyes . . . Philippa caught her breath in surprise.

Amber eyes alive with golden lights watched her. Even as his lips began the upward quirk of a smile, she snapped her attention to her toes. Idiot! she chastised herself. What if Margaret had noticed? Philippa would pay in bruises for her absentminded curiosity. Her desperate need to stare at the travelers was not worth the cost. Philippa studied her shoes and listened.

Temric Alwynason, master-of-arms at Graistan keep, laughed. Or rather he permitted himself a warm breath of amusement that passed for laughter. The little minx had stared boldly enough until she'd caught herself.

Although he found her interest mildly flattering, he had no taste for village lasses. Too bad, for he'd taken the impression that she was a pretty thing

despite her clumsy homespun gown and an aged
companion with a sour expression. No wonder the
lass was shy if that was her mistress.

"Temric!" Oswald of Hereford turned in his borrowed saddle to call back to him. "Join me. I'll go
the rest of the way afoot so I can speak with these
women, and your English is better than mine." The
cleric dismounted and waited, reins firmly in hand
against his fretful steed.

Temric nodded in response and urged his raw-
boned gelding ahead to dismount near Oswald. A
lift of his hand told his men and the cart driver to
stay where they were. There was nothing for him to
say. But the bishop's servant abhorred even a moment's silence. "Tell me," he said generally, "what
did you think of that tale Lindhurst told us the other
night?"

Temric afforded the smaller man only a brief and
emotionless glance before starting toward the mossy
walls that encircled Lord Roger's manor house. The
cleric matched him stride for stride. Oswald knew
as well as any man alive in 1194 that bastards like
himself and Philippa of Lindhurst had no right to
opinions on their betters. His jaw tensed in mild
irritation. Other noble families were content to ig-
nore their bastard brats, but not his. They had
pushed and pried to make him what he could not
be. Not that his common kinsmen were any better.

When Temric's silence remained unbroken, his
half cousin changed the subject and prattled on undaunted. "Bah, so rustic a place hardly justifies Lord
Roger's insufferable arrogance. Look, you"—he
pointed at the tongue of wood spanning the ditch
that fronted the walls—"a single man at his door
and none atop his walls? I'll wager our petty, prideful little lordling uses the same thatch for roof and

mud and manure for walls as do his peasants." He halted before the two women and shifted flawlessly into the language of England's peasantry. "Good day, goodwives. We've come seeking Lady Lindhurst. Do you know of her?"

The elder one straightened slightly, her hooded eyes and sharp nose casting a sly expression on her wrinkled face. "I am Margaret of Lindhurst," she said in her native French, "lady of this place. By whose leave do you come trespassing on my lands?" She made no attempt to straighten her patched gown or push straggling hairs back beneath her headcloth.

"Well met, indeed, my lady," Oswald replied smoothly, as if meeting ragged noblewomen wandering unescorted about fields was commmonplace for him. When he bowed low before her, Temric fought back the urge to grin. Like his clothing and his ceaseless chatter, the young man's courtly manners made an innocent mockery of the bishop he served.

"I am Oswald, clerk to Bishop William of Hereford. My lord sends us here to fetch your son's wife, the Lady Philippa. My lord requires her attendance in the matter your son brought before him."

The maid behind Margaret of Lindhurst abruptly straightened. Her gaze skimmed over Oswald, then flew across him as well. Temric sensed more than saw the confusion, mingled with fear and hope, that filled her expression. As swiftly as her reaction had started, it had ended. She once again lowered her head and regained her demure posture.

"How unfortunate for you that you've ridden so far only to turn around and ride back," snorted Lady Margaret. "My daughter by marriage cannot leave these walls save in my son's company or by his word.

When he last spoke to me, he said nothing of needing his wife."

"Do you refuse us?" Oswald stiffened, his dark brows drawn down over snapping black eyes. "Do not dare. My lord was very displeased when your son appeared without her against his specific command to the contrary. I'll not leave this place without her."

Lady Margaret touched the working end of her stick midway up the young man's chest, torn grass and chalky dirt staining his expensive gown. "Since when has a churchman ever required a woman's presence to decide any issue? If you truly represent Bishop William, return to your lord and say he must split her inheritance in twain and give us our half." She pushed gently, forcing the bishop's youngest administrator to step back.

Oswald slapped the crutch aside and thrust out his hand. Sunlight caught the bishop's heavy ring which he wore atop his glove. "Madam, here is your assurance that what I say is truth. My lord has commanded it and you must fetch her for me."

The old woman lifted her brows and sneered. "Fine clothing, pretty glass, and a nimble tongue, that is all you are. If Bishop William wants her, he can come hold his court here, instead of letting Lord Graistan curry his favor."

She pivoted on her walking stick, only to come face-to-face with the young woman behind her. "I forgot you. Stupid chit, have you learned nothing of proper behavior in all these years? You should not be standing here before these men. Go," she snapped.

When the girl hesitated, she waved her furiously toward the walls as if gesture alone would spur movement. "Go, begone with you," she snarled.

"Nay." A single word, given barely enough sound to be heard.

"What? What did you say?" Lady Margaret's shock died into a soundless gaping.

Sudden respect rose in Temric.

As if the act of speaking cost her dearly, the lass cleared her throat several times. Her voice grew in strength as she continued. "I would not know what a bishop wants from one so insignificant as I."

Temric started in surprise, then frowned in disbelief. Surely this meek mouse could not be the haughty lady who demanded she be declared legitimate despite her father's will! He glanced at Oswald. The cleric was stunned into immobility. Two steps took Temric to the young woman's side. "Lady Lindhurst?"

"Hey, hey!" Lord Roger's mother cried out in sudden anxiety. "Your man is too close. Call him back." She tottered forward as if to thrust him away from her son's wife.

"Leave him be," Oswald snapped, finding his tongue even as Temric turned a hard stare on the old woman. "He'll do her no harm."

Margaret made a frantic noise deep within her chest. Temric turned his back on her and spoke to the maid. He kept his voice low and mild for fear of frightening her. "Are you Lady Philippa, wife to Roger?"

"Aye, I am she." She looked up to meet his gaze, and Temric caught his breath at her beauty. Eyes, both green and blue in one glorious instant, shimmered like jewels against her creamy skin. Golden hair the color of ripe wheat escaped her rough wimple, straggling charmingly along soft cheeks. As different as she was from his lady's ebony and ivory coloring, there was a resemblance. He found it in the lilt of her brows and her wide cheekbones, along the gentle curve of her jaw and her smile. Where was the arrogance and pride that had filled her missive to the bishop? This woman was not capable of such emotions.

"My lady, can you tell to me your sister's given name so I might know it is truly you?" He waited to see her hatred. Surely that is what she felt toward the sister who had stripped away her identity.

"Rowena. My only sister's name is Rowena." Joy touched her lips and flushed in her cheeks. "Do you know my sister?" Her words begged for news of a beloved sibling.

There could be no further doubt. Here before Temric stood the woman he sought. She, like no other woman he knew, was his equal, bastard born but nobly raised. But where was her anger and hurt? Why this radiant happiness when her life had been destroyed by the revelation of her bastard birth?

Unnerved by her reaction, he turned away and said to Oswald, "We have found Sir Roger's wife."

"Nay," the dowager cried in frustration, limping agitatedly forward. "She is not my son's wife, she's just the village whore who pants after him. Would Lord Roger dress his wife thus? That creature is only a lying slut." She stared at the cleric, then glared at Temric. "You are mistaken."

"I am not," Temric replied mildly. "She has the look of her sister."

"Nay," the elder lady insisted. Her voice rose in raging frustration as she turned on the girl. "Nay, your foolish tongue will not cheat me of my rightful compensation for being saddled with a barren imbecile." Margaret of Lindhurst's mouth twisted in a vicious snarl. She raised her walking stick, and before either man understood her intent, she'd struck her daughter by marriage a mighty blow across the back. Lady Philippa fell without a sound and made no move to rise. Again, Margaret lifted her club.

Rage exploded in Temric. His hand dropped to his sword hilt, then snapped out to wrench the crutch from the old woman's hands. It spun from his fingers to land a dozen yards from its owner. "You have done enough damage for one day," he ground out. "I think I will take what I've come for and be on my way." He scooped Lady Philippa up into his arms.

"Do you dare to touch another man's wife so?" the hag trumpeted. "Lecher! Defiler! I'll see you flayed for your audacity."

"You may bring your complaints to my brother, Lord Graistan," Temric said, astounded that his tone was so calm. Every fiber in his being roared against the abuse he'd witnessed.

"Graistan! That thief!" Margaret screeched, then hobbled toward the manor's gate, crying all the while, "Come, come. I am attacked and Graistan's men kidnap your lord's wife. To arms, to arms!" Men raced from the gates at her call.

"Mount up," Temric ordered Oswald. "William and Alaric, protect our cart and driver as best you can. You two"—he nodded to the others—"are with me."

He glanced at the woman in his arms to see if she was conscious. She was. No tears filled her eyes, nor did she gasp in pain at what had to have been a bruising blow. Instead she stared up at him, her eyes filled with disbelief and a glimmer of hope. "You would take me with you? Away from Lindhurst?"

"Aye." Temric knew he should have handed her up to Oswald, but he found he could not release her. "Can you sit?" At her nod, he set her on his own saddle and mounted up behind her. With the old woman rallying men at arms behind him, Temric pulled another man's wife close into the protection of his body and spurred his horse into a gallop.

Philippa leaned her head against the knight's strong shoulder. She reveled in the tightness of his arm around her waist and the heat where her hip pressed against his thighs. The horse beneath her broke into a gallop.

Rushing air heady with freedom tore at her head-cloth and curled sweetly around her neck. They raced past the village church, then past the cottages and huts facing the track. Dogs darted foolishly toward the flying hooves, while the more intelligent chickens and geese scattered into the neat rows of peas, beans, onions, and herbs tucked close to each home.

She stiffened in a sudden flash of rage. Her back screamed in protest, the already bruising flesh throbbing in complaint. This day would mean her death. Her mind recoiled against the unfairness of her fate when she was only twenty and two. Then anger seeped away. She'd brought this on herself. She'd not only defied Mother Margaret, but she had allowed this man to take her from Lindhurst. Roger's pride could not bear it, and she would pay the price with her life.

She sighed in resignation. Aye, she'd pay, but only after Roger found her. Until that moment arrived she'd enjoy every instant without regret.

The churchman shouted, "Hold tight to her, Temric! They are after us."

"Then we shall play fox to their hounds," Temric replied, his mellow voice grim in determination. "You two go more slowly and toward Benfield.

Here." A swift yank tore Philippa's headcloth from her head before she had a chance to gasp or resist. "Drop this as you ride and do what you can to convince them you have her. Return to Graistan when you can."

A sudden change of direction sent Philippa sliding. She instinctively wound her arms around the knight's waist to steady her sideways seat on the saddle.

His quick laugh was rich with kind amusement. "Good. Hold me tight, for I've not risked all to lose you now."

No, she'd take no regrets to her grave. Philippa closed her eyes and turned her face to the wind.

# BUY TWO TOPAZ BOOKS AND GET ONE FREE ROMANCE NOVEL!

With just two purchases of Topaz books, you'll be able to receive one romance novel free from the list below. Just send us two proofs of purchase* along with the coupon below, and the romance of your choice will be on its way to you! (subject to availability/**offer good only in the United States, its territories and Canada**)

Check title you wish to receive: